HOLLOWAY

ALSO BY ELANA K. ARNOLD

Damsel

Red Hood

What Girls Are Made Of

Infandous

The Blood Years

HOLLOWAY

Elana K. Arnold

CLARION BOOKS
An Imprint of HarperCollins*Publishers*

HarperCollins Children's Books,
a division of HarperCollins Publishers,
195 Broadway, New York, NY 10007

HarperCollins Publishers, Macken House,
39/40 Mayor Street Upper, Dublin 1, D01 C9W8, Ireland

Clarion Books is an imprint of HarperCollins Publishers.

Holloway

harpercollins.com

Library of Congress Control Number: 2025946094
ISBN 978-0-06-299088-4

Typography by Jenna Stempel-Lobell
26 27 28 29 30 LBC 5 4 3 2 1
First Edition

For Max and Davis—my home, my greatest treasure,
my every delight.

Il y a assurément un autre monde, mais il est dans celui-ci.

—PAUL ÉLUARD

Our insanity is not that we see people who aren't there.
It's that we ignore the ones who are.

—ANDREA GIBSON

HOLLOWAY

1

From shortly before my sixth birthday until I was nearly eight years old, I did not speak. For over two years, not a single word.

It began in kindergarten, on Halloween. I remember because there was a festival on the blacktop where we played at recess. I loved the blacktop. It was painted with a web of yellow lines—some curved, others straight—that indicated the boundaries of various games. Here was in, there was out. Here, safe. There, not safe. If you understood the language of these stripes and half-moons then you could play the games, when it was time to play.

But when it wasn't time to play, or when something else was happening, like the Halloween festival, the lines lost their meaning. They made no sense anymore, and that frightened me. That meaning could disappear even when the yellow patterns and lines did not.

During the festival, everyone ignored the lines. Booths for games were set up right on top of them. There was a station for cotton candy, the air around it a cloud of sweetness that smelled pink. The pink smell made me think of my mother, whom I called Gillian. A little quirk in our family of three—my mother, my grandmother, and myself—that I called the adults by their names rather than by kinship terms. Like cotton candy, Gillian always smelled sweet, and also pink was her favorite color.

I was dressed as a butterfly. My grandmother—Big Nora, we called her, to distinguish her from Little Nora, or just Nora, which was me—had made the wings for my costume out of two silk scarves, one red, one yellow. They were fastened with safety pins to the back of my favorite long-sleeved T-shirt—the one I wanted to wear every day because it was so soft—and with stretchy hair bands to my wrists. When I moved my arms, the scarves fluttered just like wings. "As pretty as a butterfly and as busy as a bee," Gillian had said that morning as I fluttered around the kitchen of our apartment, and she and Big Nora both smiled.

From the cotton candy booth, I could see the numbers drawn in a wide, imperfect circle beneath the basketball hoop. This was for a game they called Cakewalk. We were to line up, and music would be played—"The Monster Mash"—and we would move counterclockwise in a circle around the circuit of numbers. When the music cut off, we were all to stop right where we were, and then a number would be drawn, and the winner would get a cake.

I didn't like "The Monster Mash" or the chalk numbers scrawled on the blacktop. I didn't like the crowded booths or the big kids in their costumes. I did like my costume and the pink smell near the cotton candy. And I did want to win the cake.

We moved in a circle—30, 29, 28—the chalk beginning to smudge as we went. The song was fast, and people were loud. A bigger kid behind me in a Snoopy costume stepped on the back of my shoe and I almost fell down.

When the music stopped, kids jostled and pushed to stand on a number. I was squarely atop the number ten—I remember that because when the volunteer mom felt around in a glass fishbowl and withdrew a scrap of paper, unfolded it, and called out a number, that was the number she called.

She waved me over to a long table where cakes were displayed and told me to pick one. I wanted a cake but I didn't know there would be more than one to choose from; there were too many and I couldn't decide, and my eyes filled with tears. It was too much, all of it already, and that's when I saw my mother crossing the blacktop.

Usually, Big Nora picked me up from school; on the days that Gillian did, it was almost always from aftercare, when it was dark. But here she was, even though the sun was right above me in the slate autumn sky. It was such a relief to see her. It softened the pressure that was building inside me as I stood on the blacktop, unable to choose. So I left the cake table and ran to her, my butterfly wings spread wide.

"Too many cakes," I said, and those were the last words I spoke for a long time.

Ten years have passed since I regained my voice. It was Gillian who helped me find it.

Now, the last day of August, 2021, I'm on the Métro, bleary-eyed and jetlagged, cutting beneath Paris. My brain understands that I'm in a different time zone, but my body doesn't, not yet. Yesterday, back home in California—where I used to live—I boarded a plane at six in the evening; when we landed, the flight attendant informed us that it was two in the afternoon. The magnitude of the disorientation that results from moving one's body at an unnatural speed across space and time cannot be overstated.

My brain knows that I can't fall asleep because that would mean

I'll miss my stop, but my body insists that I close my eyes. I lean my head against the wall of the Métro train. It's hard and cold and most likely not particularly clean, but what a relief to rest. When I close my eyes, there's Gillian, smiling at me. The warm weight of her hand upon my head.

Then comes a bark of a cough, and quick as a reflex, I press the metal piece of my mask across the bridge of my nose. The cougher is a police officer, white, in his sixties, I'd guess, wearing all the regular parts of a police officer's uniform—the jacket, the pants, the boots, and the cap, the "bonnet de police," a funny name, for Americans, for whom bonnets are associated with characters like Little Bo-Peep, charming little feckless girls—plus a mask, black to match the cap. Is the mask part of the uniform now, or is he required to provide his own?

This is the sort of thing that interests me—or that used to interest me, I should say. Before the virus and the shutdown, I might have asked him about it. Of course, back when I would have been interested, when I might have asked . . . back then, no one was wearing masks.

He's seen me staring, which I hadn't meant to do, but which happens when I get lost in detail. He raises a gloved hand—in greeting, to apologize for coughing, I don't know which. Latex gloves, black.

The virus can't be transmitted through nonporous objects, the way the flu can. That's one of the things we've learned. Just over a year and a half ago, when the virus was new, before we knew all the things we know now, television doctors demonstrated how to spray down groceries, how to use antibacterial wipes on hard surfaces, how to properly wash our hands, singing the ABC song as they lathered and scrubbed. Gillian and I sat side by side on the couch, clutching each other's hands as we watched the television doctor demonstrate handwashing best practices as if we were a whole country of preschoolers. It was ridiculous, but I was comforted. The doctor was describing the rules of the virus, just as the lines on the blacktop described the rules of the games. If we followed the rules, we would be safe. If we broke them, not safe.

I want to tell the officer that he doesn't need the gloves. That the important thing is the mask, and the vaccine. But words are hard for me again, for many reasons. It's not that I don't speak French—I do, and fairly well. Language has long been a special interest—along with art, philosophy, and animals of all kinds. I also speak passable Italian and German, some Hebrew, and English, of course. Big Nora spoke French to me when I was young, and occasionally Gillian would try, though my knowledge of the language surpassed hers years ago. It's funny—funny-strange, not funny-haha—that language is something that interests me so deeply, considering the times when language seems not at all interested in *me*.

Anyway, no one over here particularly wants to hear an American voice speaking any language, especially one telling others what to do, or what they should or shouldn't be concerned about. We've lost quite a bit of credibility over the past few years.

The officer's attention drifts as he scans the Métro car. For something to do as well as out of habit, I find the hand sanitizer in the pocket of my windbreaker. It's cold and I hate the smell of it, the slime of it too as I rub it between my fingers.

Over the intercom, a man's voice announces the stop as we pull into a station. The doors clang open, then closed. Another train on the tracks across from us, a high whine as it pulls away in the opposite direction.

We roll forward, too—it's funny, that their forward is that way, and our forward is this, and for a second it feels like we're going backward, not forward at all. I hold up my hands and watch them vibrate. I try to force them to go still but I can't make them stop. Control is an illusion, it turns out.

I place my hands on my thighs and try to focus on things that calm me—like the sound of the train's metal wheels, rolling along the iron rails. It's satisfying, the texture of the sound. Again, I close my eyes and lean my cheek against the window. The glass is cool and hard, I tell myself first in English, then in French, for practice.

The tracks are hard and made of iron. Les rails sont durs et en acier. I am safe, I am safe. Je suis en sécurité, je suis en sécurité.

It calms me to tell myself these things. Some of them are facts, and others are not. But it soothes me to say them, the way I used to be soothed by others.

There is no one left to soothe me anymore.

Everyone needs a way to soothe themselves.

Some ways are socially acceptable, and people might not even notice you're doing them: tapping a foot, for example, or drumming your fingers against your knee. Many young women twirl a strand of hair around their index finger, twirl and twirl the way soft-serve yogurt twirls out of the machine.

Some of the ways I soothe myself freak other people out, so I've learned not to do them anymore. When I was little—five, six, seven years old—when I was overwhelmed, I'd do things like spin, or hit my own legs, or pinch the soft flesh on the inside of my arm. I couldn't help myself, and so Gillian had to. My mother worked as a midwife's assistant, and later, as a midwife, but her main job, especially back then, was taking care of me. If we were at the grocery store, for example, there were about a dozen things that could set me off, things that back then I thought drove everyone crazy, but I guess were really just triggers for me. The sound the florescent lights made, for one, that piercing high whine. The way the grocery cart's small rubber wheels stuck sometimes and rubbed the linoleum. I couldn't stand that. The stink of the old man in the milk section. The baby screaming in its cart over by the bread—the sound, yes, but also the way its face pursed up, the wetness of its jutting lower lip, the threat of drool. The sudden temperature drop in the frozen aisle. The hint of rot somewhere in the produce section, maybe the broccoli, the deep underneath layer. My silvery reflection, distorted in the security mirror, high up in the back corner of the store. My favorite cereal, missing—discontinued, the clerk told us, raising his shoulders so casually, like the death of Honey Nibs was nothing to him, nothing at all.

And who had to deal with my reactions—me plugging my nose and gagging when our cart lingered near the old man and the broccoli bin, the way I tried to yank away and dart out the door when the baby's wail reached that annoying pitch, my meltdown at the terrible news about the Honey Nibs? My mom. There was no one else to watch me, so she had to take me along with her on errands like this—"We're a team of two, dearheart"—so she'd do her best to take me early in the morning, when the store was mostly empty and things were mostly fresh, or sometimes late in the evening, when things calmed down. Trying to make a game of it, she'd ask me to point out the most interesting boxes and labels, or she'd name the shapes we saw among the fruit—apple orbs and banana crescents and look there, in the sample section, the slivers of kiwi slices, each with a starburst pattern at its center.

And if there was something that bothered me, she would always remind me to breathe. That was Gillian's preferred self-soothe—breathing. Not autonomic breathing, the kind that your body does without your needing to be aware; rather, breathing on purpose. What she called "mindful breathing," or "breathwork." After Big Nora died, Gillian and I spent lots of time together practicing our breathing. It was one of the many ways she helped me to understand myself, and the world, and my place in it.

She learned the value of breath through her work with birthing mothers. And then, during the lockdown, she led video conferences for groups of people who needed to learn new self-soothing techniques to deal with all the changes, all their new fears and anxieties. Watching the video conference room populate as people joined her meeting astonished me. All the people she was helping—hundreds of them, every day, sometimes multiple sessions per day. My mother had been helping me to deal with light and noise and the stress of life for years, but I'd never really noticed that she wasn't just special to me; she was *special,* period. In the comment section that flew by throughout each session, people called her a force for good. A healer. A modern sage. And she was.

Gillian began each session with the same words: "Life begins with our first breath and ends with our last. And in between, we breathe, and breathe, and breathe. But how often do we do it *intentionally?*"

Then she led the group through a series of exercises—intermittent breath retention (breathe in through your nose for the count of four, hold your breath for the count of seven, blow out through your mouth for the count of eight); box breathing (done in a 4–4–4–4 count, visualizing the first inhale rising up, holding the breath as a second line travels at a right angle away from the peak, the third line descending in a line parallel with the first as you exhale, and the fourth line closing the box, forming a perfect square, as your lungs rest, empty); channel purifying (in through one nostril, out through the other); Hasyayoga (performed standing, with the left hand on the left hip, the right hand crossing the body to meet it, plastering a smile on your face and beginning a series of "ho, ho, hos" and "ha, ha, has" while moving about the arms, like a deranged Santa Claus). The variations seemed endless.

Gillian had already taught me these exercises. All of them were considered normal, acceptable self-soothing techniques. No one would bat an eye if, when overwhelmed, I took a moment for a few deep breaths, if I counted the rise and fall of my breaths with my thumb touching each fingertip in turn. She was right; people did seem less agitated when I focused on breathing than when I did the other things that helped me to feel calm.

Truthfully, even though it was helpful to focus on breathing, deep down I didn't really like it. I didn't enjoy the reminder that I'm a body that breathes and will one day stop. But I was proud of my mother for helping so many people feel even a little bit calmer during such a deeply unsettling time. I understood why so many people attended her classes, why they felt compelled to think so much about breath and breathing. After all, we were living—or trying to live—with an illness that stole the breath of thousands of people, every day. And at the same time we were being warned again and again how dangerous the breath of an infected person could be. Breathe, don't breathe, catch your breath, lose your breath, hold your breath, take your last breath.

The word—breath, breath, breath—haunting. I went to sleep with it—breath, breath, breath—I woke with it, gasping—*breath.* This was unpleasant, but it wasn't new. From the first moment Gillian had me practice with her, whenever I was made aware of the fact that my body was breathing, I've been struck with the fear that, now aware of it, I have to *stay* aware, as if awareness of the knowledge rendered breathing no longer automatic. I counted breaths for minutes or hours until eventually something distracted me, allowing me to forget to remember to breathe. Breath, death. Breathe, leave.

In those young years when I was without a voice, sometimes I woke in the middle of the night to the awareness of my breath—*breathe!*—and the certainty that I was the only remaining living person in the entire world. My mother must be dead, just on the other side of my bedroom wall. I'd steel myself to go to her, to confirm my worst fear. Before getting out of bed, I pictured the whole affair of it as clear and vivid as a memory—getting up, toes sinking into brown carpet, pushing open my door, turning her doorknob, and going to her bed. Bracing myself to hold my hand above her mouth, and to feel nothing. No breath.

When I finally worked up the nerve—sometimes minutes later, sometimes, hours—*oh,* the relief. The damp warmth of her breath against my trembling palm. Seeing her face, beloved to me, slack in sleep, not death.

Once, she woke with a start to find me there, my hand above her mouth, and she screamed.

Another time I found in her bed not one breathing body, but two—my mother's, naked and tangled with a man's, also naked, his pale white chest beneath a forest of black hair rising and falling in tandem with her breasts, squished against his side. That would be the last time I would check for her breath.

For about ten years, anyway.

I like the sound of the metal wheels rolling on the iron tracks, but when the train brakes to pull into the station, I do not like that sound. It's sharp and high, and it pierces me. I hold my breath until it stops, and then three more seconds for good measure.

We've arrived at my stop—Pigalle.

My pack is on the seat next to me, but when I grab it, it's stuck somehow, it won't budge.

"The strap is trapped under the glurb," says the policeman, waving his latex hand at the seat. He doesn't say "glurb," of course, but I don't know the meaning of the word he does say. It doesn't even sound like "glurb," but it makes that amount of sense to me. It's amazing how many words a language contains, how many tiny holes there can be in one's understanding, holes you don't even know are there until you fall into them.

The strap, it turns out, is caught on a hinge, easy enough to resolve now that I've found the problem.

The platform is dreary and tube-like. Its walls and arched ceiling are plastered—appropriately—in subway tiles, the first time I've seen them not as a kitchen backsplash or in a bathroom remodel on one of the renovation shows Gillian liked to watch, but in their intended environment, which pleases me. The near wall is punctuated with advertisements, each encased in a cerulean frame. I heft my pack onto my shoulders, climb the dingy stairs, and emerge.

The street is radiant in late-afternoon light. It's the last day of August, not as warm as it would be back home, but warm enough. Cars go by, and people, too, taking care to give one another space, but it's not crowded; streets everywhere are thinned. I share this corner only with a small family—two mothers and their children, one a toddler, the other an infant. The mothers peer together into the screen of a phone, one of them cradling the infant in a sling. The toddler, who holds the other woman's hand, is looking at me. On her mask are mice—Mickey and Minnie Mouse. American mice. I crinkle my eyes so she'll know I'm smiling.

When they leave, I turn to orient myself on the street. My shoulders are already starting to ache, I'm hungry, and I'm so lonely I could cry. But, I tell myself, you've gotten yourself here, all the way here. You're so close to doing what you came here to do.

And what will happen after that?

Well, I tell me, you still have $5,232, whatever that translates to in euros. The weather forecast is temperate for the next five days. For that long, at least, you have a place to stay. And don't forget about the reservation at the Louvre. All of that is good. Yes, there are bad things, too, but what do I expect? "Life isn't always an ice-cream sundae, Little Nora," I whisper into my mask, surprising myself. It's strange to make words again, stranger still to make Gillian's. That was something she used to say to me when my temper got out of hand, and I'd dissolve into tears or tantrums. The words in my mouth are bitter but also sweet.

Many words don't sound like what they mean. Also, there are words that mean one thing but have been twisted to convince people of something else, the opposite, even, of the word's true meaning. I've seen that happen many times over the past few years. But this word—"*bittersweet*"—it's the exact right word for the sensation in my mouth. I close my eyes and let the sensation fill me. The sweetness of Gillian's expression is good, but the bitterness is not good, so I won't say it again. That settled, I find the two parts of my pack's hip belt. Bouncing the weight of the pack higher, I click the buckle into place. I like the light resistance as the two halves prepare to join. I like the click they make, coming together. I'll focus on that, instead. The way the buckle feels and sounds. The glint of late-afternoon sunlight on an ochre rooftop, just there.

I won't think just now about why I've disembarked here, or what I came to Paris to do, or how, before I leave, my backpack will be four and a half pounds lighter.

2

My pack is heavy, but almost everything in it is essential. I've chosen very carefully the things I've brought, and the things I've left behind. There wasn't much to begin with; Gillian was a deep believer in "spring cleaning," whatever the season. She was a woman who, for better or worse, had learned early on how to let things go.

Most of her clothes, and mine, I took to the women's shelter. The furniture, the few knickknacks, all the books, and most of the artwork went to Goodwill—not the mattresses or the bedding, they weren't accepting any of that sort of thing anymore, because of the virus, they said, which made no sense to me but wasn't worth arguing about. It turns out one is entitled to three "bulk item pickups" each year as part of trash and sanitation service; I'd learned on the city website that I could have up to ten large trash bags collected, along with a number of "undisposables," such as the mattresses.

It hadn't been a little thing, the emptying of the apartment, even one as relatively spartan as ours. The cleaning supplies under the kitchen sink, for instance; what to do with those? They couldn't be donated because they'd been opened and partially used. But, what a waste to throw them away.

I'd knocked on Mrs. Kwon's door, the next apartment over. She peered through the peephole, called, "Hang on a second, hon," and returned to open the door a moment later, masked.

It was then I found how difficult speech had become. I managed—"Cleaning supplies. Do you want them?" But each word was barbed, a burr in my thick throat.

Mrs. Kwon's face, even in the mask, was a tragedy of compassion. I had to look away. "No thank you, hon," she said. Then—"I'm so sorry for your loss."

I nodded; more words hadn't been possible. The cleaning supplies went into one of the ten black bags. So did all of Gillian's socks, and underwear, and bras, and most of mine. So did her makeup and hair products, so did my sketchbooks and artist studies and half-finished reproductions, none of which I'd worked on or even glanced at in months. So did all my paints and pencils, school assignments, and even a stack of progress reports from elementary school, which I read through, one by one, before slipping them into the bags.

Nora is still having difficulties making appropriate friendships. She mimics the other children but does not yet engage with them in meaningful ways.

Nora does very well in her individual work but lacks the skills to partner with her classmates.

Nora seems adept at focusing deeply on that which interests her but fails to complete assignments that "are stupid," as she says. We have dialogued on several occasions about using appropriate language.

True, true, true. Trash, trash, trash.

My baby photos—how small I was! My own gray-green eyes, staring out of a baby's fat face. So solemn, as if baby me was already trying to decode the world. There were class pictures, too. Second grade, when I'd returned to school, a slash of wavy brown bangs across a serious brow. Third grade, the year I'd wear only stripes, a choice that didn't help me make friends. Fourth grade, and fifth—the same outfit in both, a creamy sweater made of some soft synthetic fur. And in each picture, from second grade through sixth, I'm holding my stuffed chicken, which Gillian had named Feather. I insisted on carrying it with me everywhere, for years, I loved it so. In the second-grade picture, Feather is a fat white puffball with a proud red comb; by the fifth-grade photo, she's more flat than fat, and her white has dulled to a sad shade of gray.

Feather had been a gift from Gillian, a surprise on the first day of second grade—"Don't you think chickens are just the cutest, dearheart? And did you know they're related to *dinosaurs*?"—and from that day, she'd been my favorite comfort object and near-constant companion. Until seventh grade, when Gillian insisted that it was time to start leaving her home. "For your own good, dearheart."

A few things, like documents that were once important, I took to our bank. For $136, I rented a ten-inch-by-ten-inch safe deposit box. Into it went all our identification documents—Big Nora's long-expired driver's license, and Gillian's; Gillian's birth certificate, and mine; all three of our social security cards; Gillian's expired passport, which I found tucked in the back of her sock drawer. Issued in March 2004, three months after I was born.

I look (looked? I'm still here, but they are gone) more like my grandmother than my mother. Like Big Nora's, my hair tangles and disobeys, and though I knew hers to be silver and gray with just shimmers of brown, she swore that when she was young, it was the same brown as mine. Gillian was a honey blonde, both in her passport photo and in the years since, through a combination of nature and artifice. Her eyes are (were) a true green; mine and Big Nora's, hazel. In the passport photo, Gillian's mouth is serious. That makes sense, as what she is planning to do is a serious thing. I keep thinking of this long-ago version of Gillian in the present tense, even though she's gone—every version of her, gone.

Holding her passport, I flipped to the document page. Only one stamp, blue, but it was blurred, illegible.

Gillian's Miata, I'd hoped to sell, but it wouldn't pass smog, and, I learned, in California a car that won't pass smog can't be sold. I donated it instead, to the public radio station, which was Gillian's favorite news source. Or, it had been, before the lockdown.

After paying for the cremation ($750), the balance on Gillian's one credit card ($3,447.83), the final month of the apartment's rent ($2,400), and purchasing the bamboo cylinder, I was left with just under $7,000. Then, the fees for my own passport ($130 application fee, $35 acceptance fee, plus $60 to have it expedited); the one-way ticket to Paris, economy class ($634); and a studio apartment in the Montmartre district for five nights, chosen for its corner location and its two walls of windows ($536).

After that, the apartment was empty. Almost. I left the Seurat poster on the fridge; someone would take it down, throw it away . . . but it wouldn't be me.

The only thing left to decide about was the Painting.

* * *

There were lots of things about being a mother—and about being my mother, in particular—that Gillian had to work really hard at. I know that. She'd had me so young, after all—not quite twenty when I was born—and perhaps she felt she wasn't a natural mother, the way Big Nora was. The things that seemed so easy for my grandmother, I can see now that my mother had to fight to learn: how to control her temper; how to modulate her voice into a tone I could receive; all sorts of things.

There's a word for what's wrong with me—autism—but my mother refused to use it. Labels don't do anything except put people in boxes, she said, over and over again. I knew she was right, even as secretly I thought that a box sounded like a wonderful place to be. Small. Knowable. Safe.

After Big Nora died, everything fell to Gillian—paying bills, keeping up the apartment, cooking and cleaning, taking care of me. I know it was too much for her sometimes, and she wasn't perfect—she could lose her temper just like anyone. But she never lost her faith. She tried, every day, to help me be a person in the world. Sometimes, the stress seemed like it would break her—being a single parent of an autistic child, trying to manage everything on her own, and the world around us seeming to grow darker, more complicated, more stressful and tense year after year. All the shootings across the country, wave after wave of violence. Those people in Michigan who were poisoned by their own water. And then the election in 2016, when I was in seventh grade. All those enormous tumultuous movements, like the shifting of tectonic plates, and our own home, too, where I could be an earthquake, myself.

It didn't make things easier, all the ways that I wasn't like other children. Things my classmates seemed to find perfectly acceptable—the interminable flicker of florescent lights; sounds like a popped balloon or the painful whine of an audio system malfunctioning; anything sticky or slimy, like the bright green stuff the other kids liked to play with; clothing that was too tight, or too loose; the metallic taste of cutlery—for me, each was a private torture.

And I know it bothered Gillian, the comments from strangers: the man at the post office, when I melted down because they were out of the stamps with dogs on them—"Quite the little princess, huh?" The mechanic, when we went to pick up the Miata and the scorched-grease smell burned my sinuses, making me pinch my nose and cry—"Your mommy must have the patience of a saint." The lady in line at the grocery store, when Gillian gave me a second stick of gum after the first lost its flavor and I needed *something* to distract me: "There's a kid who knows how to get what she wants."

No wonder Gillian would get frayed, sometimes.

But when it came to art, everything was different. It was a place where the two of us could meet. No worrying, the way we both worried when we were out in public—me, about the overwhelm; her, about the world's reactions. And art was a place where I could be still. I could disappear into a painting.

The first painting I fell in love with—in my head I call it the Painting—was a strange little thing that Gillian had framed and hung in the hallway of our apartment, on the wall between the bedroom doors. Often, I'd pull a kitchen chair down the hallway and climb atop it to get a closer look. The Painting was small and odd and off-kilter.

In the foreground, the interior of a spartan room—a closed door, a bed, shoes beneath a chair—and then a wide bright window, a field, beyond. The texture of wheat, golden. Odd things, out of place: orbs and curves, lines and angles, abstract shapes floating balloon-like in a silver sky. A lemon in the place of the sun. In the field: an egg, a dress, mushrooms, a ring of trees. The mouth of a dog, smiling. Light, shadows. Farthest, a curve of water, flowing. All of it bordered by a braided cord. The Painting seemed to be trying to speak to me . . . if only I could understand its language.

Recognizing my interest in art, and my talent for it, Gillian started bringing home reproductions of great artworks—mostly posters, a few prints—and she hung them all over the apartment. Whenever she could get away from her work for a day, she'd take me to a museum. And we spent lots of Saturday mornings in the beat-up Miata, driving to yard sales and thrift stores, searching for coffee-table books full of art; over the years we collected a great heavy stack of them.

The only thing I liked better than looking at art was making it myself. I loved every medium—pencils or pens, markers or crayons, an old set of chalk pastels we got at a yard sale.

Until Gillian bought me my first set of paints—a flat turquoise metal box of forty-eight watercolor squares, four rows of twelve squares each, Chinese White in the top left corner, Deepest Black in the bottom right, three brushes set into divots just their size—then, all I wanted to do was paint, or study paintings. And though my mother and I could sometimes be at cross purposes, like all mothers and daughters, I suppose, we had a shared language in discussing art, and artists.

"Art is something that makes us human," Gillian liked to say. "It separates us from the animals. And did you know, dearheart, that the earliest artists were *women*? They used menstrual blood as paint. There's the divine feminine for you, right?"

I looked it up once. There's no evidence the cave painters used menstrual blood. But I didn't tell Gillian; it made her happy to believe in the myth. Now, though, I wish I had.

In the books Gillian and I collected, art was *alive*, but in a way entirely unlike the crowded, noisy world. Monet, Manet, van Gogh, Picasso. Vermeer, Matisse, Cézanne, Klimt. Velázquez, Goya, Titian, Chagall. Morisot. Rembrandt, Rubens, Munch. Dalí. Gauguin. O'Keeffe, Kahlo, Kusama. Seurat, my mother's favorite.

Soft-bodied nudes, skin pink and pale. A bare-breasted Madonna in a red cap. A suit and hat, without a man within. A man, without a suit. Beautiful children with neatly brushed hair and neatly folded hands. Angry cherubs wielding spears. Girls at a piano. Stretchy flesh spreading like broken uncooked eggs. Flattened, angular women, breasts as triangular and pointed as their elbows. Fearsome shapes. Peaked and wavy paint. Amoeba-like curved figures—no straight lines—splattered with polka dots. A cacophony of color, a riot of texture, a whole world, but *quiet*.

The older I got, the more I began to appreciate the work of the surrealists and those who came after, the abstract expressionists. Max Ernst's *The Barbarians*—those enormous birdlike monsters, that gorgeous blue-green sky. Leonora Carrington's *Self-Portrait*: such odd perspective, with the rocking horse behind the figure's head; another horse, galloping outside the window; the hyena with its knowing eyes; and the way the woman sits, legs spread. Bridget Bate Tichenor's

Untitled—two eggs, with human eyes—masked—and human hands—gesturing, folded. Helen Frankenthaler's *Round Trip*—soak-stained, bizarre, two figures, grasping hands, falling from the sky.

I'm not sure why I was so drawn to the surrealists and the abstract expressionists. It was just . . . when I looked at their work, I felt uncomfortable . . . but in a good way. Their paintings seemed to tell a truth, a truth that most people couldn't see. The way they married what was above the surface, and what was beneath. Their acknowledgment that just because something wasn't realistic, that didn't mean it wasn't *real*.

Gillian preferred artworks that were traditionally beautiful, more straightforward. Her favorites were almost always works by impressionists and post-impressionists, especially portraits and large-scale scenes with an eye toward detail.

I saw the value of these works, too; really, all paintings were interesting to me, all of them had something to teach. And the best way to learn from them, I decided, was to reproduce them.

When I was eleven, I completed my first really successful reproduction. Monet's *Impression, Sunrise*. I used acrylics rather than oils, and it wasn't perfect, not by any measure; the ratio of sea to sky was off, anyone could tell that, and I hadn't gotten the shade of the fishing boat in the foreground exactly right. Still, I'd done quite a good job with the sun, both the shape of it and its reflection on the water. I gave it to Gillian on her birthday—her thirtieth.

The way her face lit up when she unwrapped it—an explosion of astonishment and pride. "You made this? All by yourself? For *me*?" And then she burst into tears.

That's when I learned how good it felt, to make *her* feel good. So I spent more time working on the sort of art my mother most loved, and I got really, really good at it.

When I painted something original, I almost always ended up slicing together elements of realism and impressionism and surrealism and abstract expressionism, too. When I showed these efforts to Gillian, she would tilt her head and squint like she was trying to make sense of what I'd painted, but couldn't. She observed them, of course—but she didn't *see* them. Not really.

And I liked being seen by my mother. So I got better and better at reproductions, especially those that were "beautiful," in her opinion.

But the Painting in the hallway never lost its pull on me. I returned to it again and again, wondering. I asked her about it once. It wasn't a reproduction like the prints she brought home; it was an original, I could tell. She told me she'd gotten it on the trip she'd taken when she was young. That was all she'd say. She must have loved it once, though, right? To have bothered bringing it home? And that felt hopeful to me, the idea that the person my mother once was—when she was younger, before she was worn down by the stress of everything, me most of all—wasn't all that different, in her tastes, at least, from me. Maybe there was a moment, long ago, when her taste in art overlapped perfectly with mine. Maybe time is funny like that. And maybe—this was a secret thought, something I kept deep inside and rarely even allowed myself to think in words—maybe if my mom had been that person once, maybe she could be, again.

It's all gone now. My books. My art. My hope. My mother, too.

* * *

I put off deciding about the Painting as long as I could, but the date of my departure arrived, and I couldn't avoid it any longer. I took it down from its hook in the hallway and carried it into the kitchen where the best light was, leaned it against the wall under the window, and sat across from it for a long time. I ran the pad of my finger across the thicker lines of the golden wheat, the curves and lines, wondering, as I did every time I touched them, how the artist managed that thickness, why he'd chosen to compose the Painting as he had, and what his name had been. I wondered other things, too, things I'd never get the answer to, now. In the end, I left it in the hallway between Mrs. Kwon's apartment and ours, hoping.

It turns out you can't really choose what you throw away, not really. There are many things I'd love to forget, but they persist.

And there are other things, things and people, I desperately wish I could have held on to.

Here's a question: Are we made real by being known and loved? Without others to affirm it—*I love you, I see you, I know who you are*—do we exist at all? Or are we like the falling tree in the woods, mouth open in a scream that makes no sound, for there is no ear to receive it?

There are things we get to choose. Many more things—most things—we have no control over. I chose to come here to Paris alone, but I didn't choose the why of the aloneness; I could only move forward in the reality of it. I took myself to the pharmacy, waited my turn, and allowed the pharmacist to stick a needle in the flesh of my upper arm; twenty-one days later, I returned for the second dose. I purchased the ticket from San Diego to Paris. I sent the apartment keys to the management company, certified mail. I packed my backpack—five pairs of underwear; five pairs of socks; a pair of black leggings; a pair of brown corduroys; three short-sleeved T-shirts, two long; a wool sweater; a knit cap; a windbreaker; my toiletries. A charging cord for my phone; my wallet. And, of course, the bamboo cylinder. I dressed in jeans and a hoodie, a thermal underneath, double-tied my boots. I called a car and waited on the curb, my pack at my side. I rode to the airport, masked and with the window rolled down. I navigated security, showing my brand-new passport and my vaccine card. I stepped into an airplane for the first time in my life. I didn't sleep the entire flight; I felt I couldn't, as if it was my consciousness and nothing more that held the plane aloft.

I keep telling myself the story of my journey. Repeating it, perhaps, in an effort to make it less true, to transform it from fact to fiction. But that isn't how truth works, as much as one might wish it so. Things that have happened cannot un-happen. Choices that have been made cannot be un-made. Meteorites that have fallen from the sky cannot un-fall. All we can do is make another choice: keep moving forward, or stop.

3

The Montmartre district is on the top of a small hill. To reach it, I have to climb a long flight of stairs. My pack is heavy and my feet ache, but there's nothing to do but climb. Even in my exhaustion, the charm of this place isn't lost. Beyond the massive, imposing cathedral of Sacré-Cœur are cobbled streets, uneven and speckled like a pony's coat. Redbrick walls, pink and yellow stucco buildings, peaked roofs and turned gables and arched doorways in greens and blues and black. Tiny old windows at all different heights. Clutches of tourists gawking—some masked, many not—and locals, maneuvering around them. It's not as crowded here as it must have been before everything that's happened, but there's a feeling in the air, a sort of shimmer. Like everyone has agreed to try it out again, this shared human experience of being together with strangers.

Street artists, some with charcoal, others with paint, many with umbrellas open to shade their work, signs announcing their prices. A man with an accordion. Most startling—two beautiful young men, kissing deeply in the shade of a tree. Like a relic, this closeness, this passion, this trust.

I'm lost and lost and lost until I turn the same corner for maybe the third time and I'm in front of the building from the website. I scroll through my messages and find the series of codes, use the first to unlock the front door, then go up six flights of stairs—it said the apartment was on the fifth floor, but I guess here they count the ground floor as zero instead of one, so there's an extra flight before I reach the level I'm looking for—punch in another code. Up a hallway, to the end, a third door. A third code.

Out of an abundance of caution (a phrase I'm so tired of), I hold my breath as I cross the apartment's one room to a bank of windows along two walls, the feature that drew me to select this place over more convenient options. Lungs burning, I fumble with the first window latch, finally figure it out and push open the window and breathe, air-starved. The curtains puff and dance. The kitchenette is to the left of the door, not much more than a sink, a hot plate, a microwave, and a half-sized fridge; the bed is across from the bank of windows; and behind a heavy brown curtain is the bathroom, just a toilet and a tiny shower stall, no sink.

It's damp, cold. Evening now. When the rest of the windows are open, I pull off the mask and unstrap my backpack. Ah. Back at the windowsill, I wait for fresh air to circulate.

This place costs too much; I should have stayed in a hostel. But even vaccinated, I don't want to risk shared space. And, even if there were no virus, I don't like to be that close to people.

I've only got five nights in this apartment, and I don't really have a plan for what will come after. But I can think about that later. Five days from now. After I've done the thing I've come to Paris to do.

The bed is made up in white sheets, with four good pillows and a white duvet. All of it smells like bleach. I unlace my boots and pull off my jeans, use the toilet and wash my hands in the kitchenette's little sink. But that's all I can do before I fall into bed, pull the duvet over my head, and disappear.

I sleep for fourteen hours and awake groggy and unmoored. Lost in a white cloud that turns out to be the duvet, I surface and blink into gray morning light. I left the windows open, and now I wear the duvet like a cape as I go to close them. Plug in the electric kettle, pour boiling water over a bag of mint tea I find in a cabinet, hunch over the steaming mug until I come fully awake. Technically, my beverage is tisane, not tea. True tea, whether white, green, or black, is made from the leaves of the *Camellia sinensis* plant; tisanes are anything else: infusions of flowers or herbs, fruits or spices. But I've learned it's easier to just call it tea. Most people aren't so interested in the subtleties of language, and many find hearing about them annoying.

Now I'm on the street. I've left nearly everything I own up those six flights. I've got my phone, bank card, vaccination card, and passport tucked in the interior pocket of my windbreaker. There's a fresh mask in my front pocket, and I pull my knit cap down over my ears; the day will get warmer, but it's early still. I've decided I'm just going to walk. Tomorrow, I have a reservation slot to visit the Louvre, but the city itself is art—layers of history and architecture, style and substance, both. Paris has well over two hundred museums, most of them open again since the mass implementation of vaccines. It's a dream for anyone who loves art to be in this city.

I don't need to wear the mask outside, but soon I put it on anyway. It's been a long time since I've been among people like this; I'm not worried about getting sick, but I don't like people looking at my face. (*Don't do that with your mouth, Nora, people won't know what to think.*) I've never been good at knowing when I'm supposed to smile and when it's not expected or welcome. Maybe I'll always wear a mask, from now on. It's nice in here.

Still, I thrill at others' uncovered faces. I study the curves and lines that compose each one: this triangle nose, that block chin, those apple-round cheeks. The endless variety of mouths, both their expressions and their shapes. A bowed lip. A flat line. A thick artistic red mouth stretched open around white teeth and moving quickly as its owner talks. The colors of uncovered faces, beautiful too, every shade from milk (a newborn glimpsed just as her mother pulls forward the canopy of her carriage) to nearly jet (the smooth brow of a stylish man, lighting a cigarette on the corner).

Each bare face is a gift, a sip of water when you can't remember the last time you drank. I'm here for the city but the Parisians are the city as much as the architecture, and soon I give in to the pleasure of people-watching. And over and over again, I turn, reach for my mother's sleeve, ready to point it out to her—the artful shadow there, where the tree slices that little girl's face almost violently, see? The surprising pairing of textures in that person's outfit—the rough tweed of the coat, the river of silk beneath. But of course, she's not here. Is it irony that she's not here, that I finally am, but without her? People use the word "irony" much too freely, applying it to things that are just coincidences or bad luck. In my mind, in both English and French, "irony" is heavy and cold and lead gray. Because the word "iron" is in it. "Iron-y." Like an iron. When I told Gillian this, she laughed. "But irons are hot," she said.

"That's the whole point of them." I'd said that irons aren't hot by nature; they're cold. They *become* hot, but that's always a temporary state.

"Every state is temporary, dearheart" is what she said to me.

I haven't eaten in nearly a full day, haven't wanted to, but the walking wakes my appetite, and I stop for food multiple times as I wander. Shapes here, too—triangle crêpes, rounds of cheese, a cone of hazelnuts. Later, a doll-sized cylinder of espresso.

I make my way to the sights one must see. The Eiffel Tower, visible from nearly everywhere in the city. The Arc de Triomphe, in the middle of a busy street. Notre-Dame, a mess of scaffolding built up around the burned carcass, swarming with workers. Impossible, isn't it, that they'll ever be able to restore it? More churches, and castles, and over there, the façade of the Louvre.

At first, I take pictures on my phone. Then I realize—who would I show them to?

In the early weeks of the pandemic, all I wanted to do was paint. I had to log in to school, of course, but it was easy enough to set up my laptop and mostly ignore it. Finally, at last, there were nearly no constraints on my time. I could lose myself in my work, in my own head. Lose myself in color and texture and shape. I painted as morning light turned to afternoon, as shadows shifted across the kitchen table, as day became evening, and lamplight replaced the sun. Behind me in the living room, Gillian breathed. *Breathe like a lion, breathe like a bear,* she rested flat on her back in corpse pose, knees splayed and palms up. Behind her droned the news: how to wash your produce, how to cleanse delivery bags and packages, how to disinfect your light switches, your keyboard, your doorknobs. How to distance. How to be alone.

The purpose of art is to find and reveal the connections that undergird the world. Art is a way to say the name of something. Art is a pattern of lines and arches, of stripes and half-moons. Art is a language, and for a language to function, the words must have corollaries in reality. "Chair" *means* something. So does a painting.

By the time I was in middle school, artwork—framed prints and posters, as well as my best reproductions—hung all over the house. Gillian's very favorite piece was the poster that she kept pinned to our refrigerator with four black magnets. *A Sunday on La Grande Jatte,* Seurat's most famous work. It was the only artwork she kept in the kitchen; everything else she hung in the living room, the hallway, the two bedrooms. But the kitchen, with its good light and the modest table, was where I liked to paint—and that was where she and I spent most of our together time. That was where she put the Seurat. And every morning, she poured her coffee and stood with the steaming mug in one hand, the other wrapped around her waist, staring at the image.

"One day," she would say—not every morning, but from time to time—"one day, when things aren't so hard, we'll go there together, Nora. To France. And we'll see for ourselves what Seurat and the rest of them saw, hmm, when they painted things like this. What do you say to that?"

I would look, and wonder: Can we ever see what another sees?

At various times throughout my life, different figures in the Seurat poster captured my interest. At first, it was the leashed monkey and the unleashed dog beside it that entranced me. Also, the lady sitting on the shore, turned entirely away from us; we can only see the back of her head, the near-perfect circle of her white cap encircled by a red crown of fabric that drapes all the way down her back to the grass. There's the young mother at the center of the canvas who walks toward us, also shaded by a parasol, whose daughter, the one who regards the viewer, holds on to her skirt. That's the pair my mother liked best; "You and me," she'd say, tapping them with her nail.

Gillian would look from the poster to me, and she would touch my hair with her soft hand. I have always liked to be pet. Long, slow strokes across the tangles of my hair, or a series of squeezes, down my arms. Firm pressure—no tickling. I like the reminder of where I can find the edges of me. As long as Gillian touched me in this way, I would stand perfectly still. Always her hand moved away before I was ready.

The next morning, I'm back at the Louvre, waiting my turn to go inside. The glass pyramid is aggressively modern, set in the courtyard of the vast stone palace. When the architects were tasked with creating a new entrance for the museum, it was scandalous. Someone called it a scar on the face of Paris. But I like it. It's the contrast I like, and also the harmony. Because a pyramid, as modern as this glass one may read, is ancient. Contrast and harmony, ancient and modern. Quite the feat, really.

The entry line snakes along a tall palace wall. Most everyone respects social distancing, little groups clustering together with their own people but leaving space from other groups. It makes it more obvious this way, who's with a group, and who's alone; if everyone had formed a regular line, the borders between us would blur, but this way, herded up and distanced, the lone visitor stands out.

One of the things Gillian always tried to impress upon me was how important it is to find a group and be part of it. *Humans are herd animals, Nora. We aren't meant to be alone.*

I know she was right, but I've always been okay with solitude. Even now, in this line, I don't mind it. Not very much, anyway.

I've got my vaccination card in case I'll need to show it to get inside. When the vaccine had finally been released, it had been scarce. We were asked to allow vulnerable people to get it first, but even so, newscasters reported that appointments were filling up as quickly as they were made available, and lines of people waited outside pharmacies each night, hoping for leftover doses. But by the time I finally got the shot, it was no hassle at all. A cold wipe of alcohol on my upper arm; a quick stab, a brief burning sensation, a Band-Aid. The day after the second shot, the call came that Gillian's remains were ready to be picked up. It would've been sooner, they apologized, but it was a busy time.

No one asks for my vaccination card, just my ticket. I have it pulled up on my phone; it's scanned with a beep; and I'm inside.

I spend the morning going from one room to another, one floor to another, up and down wide sets of marble stairs. Each room has a guard or two. They're all wearing the same basic uniform of black and white, and all the guards are masked, but behind the masks and under the clothes they're all different—genders and races and shapes and ages, so many ways to be a person.

I want to be moved by the Louvre; I expected to be. I limit myself to the fine art—I'd be lost in the Louvre for a month, if I let myself visit each exhibit—and again and again, I head toward a painting I've waited all my life to see in person—but the crowd in front of *Mona Lisa,* even now, is too thick to navigate. A screaming child in the Richelieu wing makes the room where Vermeer's *The Lacemaker* is displayed uninhabitable; a layer of perfume as viscous and dense as skunk spray clouds the Renaissance collection. Too much, too much, too much. By noon my throat is tight and my mask smothers, and I have to leave. As soon as I'm outside, I pull the mask beneath my chin and gulp cold air.

Breathe. Leave.

Wiping tears from my face, I walk as fast as I can away from the museum.

It was a mistake to go to the Louvre first; it's the world's largest museum, it's enormous, of course it was too much for me. So the next day, I try the Orsay. It's smaller. Not *small,* but smaller.

They have some Seurat. One, called *Trees, winter,* I stand in front of for a long time. It's sort of a desperate little painting. Mostly it's a gray-blue sky, slashes of rust for leaves in the wind. The bones of a bare tree. I check the plaque and learn Seurat painted it in 1883, a year before he began work on my mother's favorite painting. What a year that must have been—whatever transpired between 1883, when he finished this, and 1884, when he began *A Sunday on La Grande Jatte*. The two are different in so many ways. This one is small, and dark, and bare. The other is enormous. I've never seen it in person—it's in Chicago, it fills a whole wall. And of course it's full of people, full of life. Springtime, or summer. Leisure, and light.

This one—*Trees, winter*—is about the end of things.

Every painting has a way in. If Gillian were with me, she'd lean her head against mine and ask, "Where is it, dearheart?" Then she'd wait as long as it took for me to find it—the thing that invites. Here, I see it right away. It's the tree—not just its shape, but its placement, to the right of center and leaning left. Its trunk and main branch go this direction—left—even though the canopy of smaller branches largely moves to the right. It's like all these smaller branches and twigs counterbalance the tree's heavy main artery. The tree tries to go backward, if you read the painting from left to right. But it insists on moving ahead, in spite of itself.

If I were reproducing this, I'd sketch the tree, first thing. Then the main horizontal layers of the work: the uneven line of the ground—a cheery green grass, in opposition to the barrenness elsewhere—and that pewter sky, those rust dashes all across giving the painting its movement. You can imagine the wind current that scatters them. I could do a good job with this painting.

Just as there's no one to take pictures for, there is no one to explain this to. Even so, maybe I would stay and stare all afternoon, but a large American family invades. A rambling herd of them—three little kids; a teenager; two beleaguered parents. Only the teen is wearing a mask. The rest of them are talking loudly and the grown-ups keep passing snacks to the little ones to get them to behave—chips and apple slices and pretzel sticks. No food is permitted, and I can tell they know this because of the sneaky way they wait for the gallery attendant to look the other way before reaching into the bottom of the stroller for another round of treats. I try to arrange my face to let them know that I see what they're doing and don't approve, but either my mask obscures my expression, or they just don't care. Then the father sneezes loudly into his open palm. That's all I can take. On my way out, the teenager shakes his head. "Jesus, Dad."

Everywhere I go in Paris, the same dichotomy: those who are still taking every precaution, wearing a mask even when they're in a park, completely separated from anyone by an expanse of open lawn, and those who seem committed to acting as if the pandemic is well and truly behind us now, ancient history—going into shops and markets barefaced and belligerent, ignoring the hand sanitizer stations outside of restaurants—grabbing their freedom with both hands.

My own brain vacillates, too. It wants to recalibrate to normal, but it isn't sure, anymore, what normal is. When I'm in the Monet exhibit at the Musée de l'Orangerie, blissfully quiet because of its well-enforced "silent observation"—Monet himself stipulated that this was how his *Water Lilies* should be experienced—I'm so immersed that for one beautiful afternoon I forget that there was ever a pandemic or a shut-down at all.

When I'm in my room in the Montmartre district, alone with the cylinder of my mother's ashes, it feels like a shanda—a disgrace—that I've let myself forget, even for an afternoon, even for a moment—what's brought me here. *One day, we'll go there together, Nora . . . What do you say to that?*

What *is* there to say, to that?

4

The First World War was radically different from any war Earth had ever seen.

Machine guns, tanks, poison gas, aircrafts, submarines—all these innovations, mass-produced in factories for the first time, made warfare more deadly in ways that defy calculation. In the beginning, the soldiers didn't even have language to comprehend what they were witnessing, experiencing. I read that they'd pop up from the trenches—just for a moment, to get a look at the battlefield—only to have their heads exploded. They thought that if they were to be shot at, they'd be able to dodge incoming bullets in time. To us, today, it seems ridiculous—after all, think of the kids in school hallways, the Black churchgoers and queer nightclubbers whose bodies were torn apart in what they thought were their safest places, how we're trained now to expect the absolute worst, anywhere, at any time—but those men had no idea what was about to hit them. And when the war was over, many of the soldiers who weren't killed—tens of thousands of them—were so disfigured that when they showed their faces in public, children screamed and ladies fainted.

It was artists who helped them. In London, there was an organization within the government called the Masks for Facial Disfigurement

Department. In Paris, there was an American sculptor, Anna Coleman, who led the movement to craft realistic masks for the gueules cassées, as they called them—the broken faces. They weren't comfortable, the masks. They weren't the men's *real* faces—not everything can be fixed, after all. But they allowed the men to mingle in society. They let them fit in, more or less.

I'm not saying that as an autistic child, I was the same as a disfigured soldier from the First World War. But I'm not saying I was entirely different, either. When I had a meltdown in the park, or when I got excited and pulled my arms in tight to my sides and flapped my hands, when I struck my own forehead with my palm to drown out loud sounds or bright lights, other children looked at me with fear or disgust or embarrassment on my behalf, and grown-ups were often even worse.

The things Gillian taught me to do—to keep a rubber band in my pocket so I could fidget with it out of sight; to focus on box breathing if I felt my panic getting out of hand; to hold eye contact for the count of five even if it made the inside of my skin painful—these things were masks, too. "Masking"—that's what it's called when an autistic person learns techniques to hide their natural behaviors behind a façade of socially acceptable ones in order to fit in. To seem "normal."

Like the tin masks the soldiers wore, it isn't comfortable. It isn't natural. But who wants to make children scream and ladies faint?

Gillian wasn't a perfect mother. I'd never say she was. But I can hold two ideas in my head at the same time—she wasn't perfect; and also, for at least most of my life, she loved me in the best way she knew how. The skills she so appreciated in me, that enabled me to reproduce the artwork of the masters, were ones I could employ to mimic the behaviors of other people. And, just like when I managed a tricky reproduction, when I managed to find "a way in," Gillian was so pleased and happy that it made it almost okay—how uncomfortable the mask could be.

As my days in Paris dwindle, I visit smaller and smaller museums—the Marmottan, the Dalí, the Dubuffet. In between museums, I walk the streets, visiting parks and waterways and fountains. I look in every face and around every corner. Am I looking for my mother? Maybe.

The day before I have to check out of the room, I go to a funny little place, the Museum of the Counterfeit. It's in a town house a twenty-minute walk from the Arc de Triomphe. The first strange thing is that to get inside, one must ring a doorbell. Inside are six rooms. Herringbone floors and wood-trimmed glass cases, arched tall windows to let in light. Other cases, set into walls. Each display pairs a real item and its counterfeit. Some are what you'd expect—high-end purses and expensive sneakers and marble statuettes—but others surprise in their banality. Ballpoint pens, the type you get fifty in a pack. Boxes of cigarettes. And more kinds of medication than I would have guessed. One of the educational placards describes how counterfeit medications are a big problem in impoverished countries, where people are desperate for cures the rest of us can get in a corner pharmacy.

Some of the knockoffs are laughably poor; others are remarkably close to the things they seek to imitate. Little red and green discs indicate which are fakes and which are originals, and I look at each one, imagining which sets of discs could be switched without anyone noticing.

"And over here," says a voice in French, "are some things I'll bet wouldn't fool any of you."

It's a tour guide, a person of indeterminate gender, maybe twenty-five years old. They're walking with a group of middle schoolers and lead them to a case on the far wall. It's full of gaming equipment—consoles, headsets, games in boxes—and the kids rush to it, laughing and pointing and bumping into each other like overgrown puppies, a comfortable pack.

There's one kid who stands alone. He's wearing a mask like everyone else and is dressed similarly, too—jeans and sneakers, a sweatshirt with a kangaroo pocket—so maybe some people wouldn't notice right away the ways that he's different. But I've spent years seeing these differences in others, and being reminded of my own, enough to guess that this boy is autistic. It's there in the way he holds his head, tilted just a little to the left, and the soft bounce he does on the balls of his feet. The way he listens to the tour guide without looking at them. Some people might think he's ignoring what's being said, but I follow his eyes to the object the guide is pointing to.

When it's time to move on and the wave of kids flows into the next room, he lags behind, lost in his study of what is most interesting to him. I'm standing beside him now, curious to see what he sees.

It's a handheld gaming device, maybe twenty or thirty years old, and on it, in red block print: GAME CHILD.

He and I admire it together. I feel his enjoyment of the object, even though we don't speak. Not everything needs to be said out loud.

"Henry?" It's his teacher, circling back. "Come, we're moving on." She's kind but firm, and he obeys though it's clear he'd rather stay at this display, that it will have been the best part of his day. I watch him reluctantly return to his classmates, the wistful look over his shoulder, back to the gaming device. I know just how he feels.

When the virus began to spread, some people were very upset. Well—of course people were very upset about the sickness, spreading. What I mean to say is that when people first started to get sick and we were told not to go to school anymore and that we'd be doing our classes online for the foreseeable future, some of my classmates were upset. I was not upset.

I've never liked school, conceptually. It's always struck me as strange—the idea that just because a person is a minor, they have to submit their body and mind, five days a week from eight o'clock in the morning until three o'clock in the afternoon, to a system that forces them to perform tasks entirely dictated by that system, and then conscripts even more of their time into homework that must be completed or else the person—called a "student"—will be forced to remain in the school building for detention, after the release bell. It doesn't matter if the work that's required could be completed in one hour instead of eight—regardless of how long the work takes, every minor-aged child between the ages of five and a half and eighteen is obliged in this way, unless their guardian has opted them out through some loophole. And for all this time the "student" will not be monetarily compensated.

Once, in the third grade, I likened the school system to enslavement. My teacher that year, Ms. Gardner, a Black woman, was kind in her explanation about how my comparison ignored certain key aspects of both systems. She went on to explain why my comment could be considered offensive to a person whose ancestors had literally been enslaved not that long ago, and, further, the way in which my analogy cast her in the role of either enslaver or overseer, neither of which sat kindly with her. I understood her points and didn't mention my theory again. I did say that enslaved ancestors were something we had in common, as my own people—the Jews—had been enslaved by the Romans, though that occurred quite a long while before American whites enslaved Black people. She agreed that man's inhumanity to man was a long and troubled story but asked if we could please get back to the lesson at hand, which was long division.

All of this is to say that though many of my high school classmates were disturbed by being told to stay home from school, I was not. I had my paints and my corner in the kitchen where the good light was, and now I had access to that light during the day's best hours seven days a week instead of just two. I had a bathroom I could use whenever I needed it, without alerting the teacher and my classmates to my body's functions. I could turn off the camera on my laptop and watch the teacher without the sensation of *being* watched, which was a welcome change.

There was a lot of talk from other students about all the things we were missing as time went by without a return to school—hanging out by the lockers and dating and prom and graduation. Many of our virtual class sessions dissolved into disorganized complaining, the teachers doing their best to listen and empathize. It was true that we would be missing these things. But, I tried to explain once (only once), what about all the things we missed when we *were* in school? All the things we had missed over the last many years of conscripted education—both the experiences we might have had during those lost hours, and also the educations we might have crafted if we'd had the freedom to dig deeply into the things that interested us rather than going through the motions of learning the same rote lessons from textbooks that had been designed by special-interest groups and Texas politicians? I had both unmuted myself and turned on my camera to deliver this impassioned call to reason; this was the first time I'd voluntarily done such a thing. It was also the last.

My classmates were not the only ones upset about the disturbance in the school schedule. Gillian was, as well. "It's not normal to hole up like this, dearheart. It's not good for you, especially after how far you've come. How *well* you've been doing." She wasn't referring to my artistic skills, or my academic skills. It was my atrophying social skills that concerned her. And I hated to disappoint my mother. I hate to disappoint *anyone*, but most especially, her.

When Henry is gone, I have the room to myself once more, and I wander from case to case for a while. One placard describes the building we're inside, itself a reproduction—its façade is a nineteenth-century replica of a seventeenth-century palace. Layers upon layers upon layers. Even the word—"façade"—it's double, too. It means the face of a building, but it also means something pretty on the outside, meant to conceal the rougher truth beneath. The way Gillian taught me to model my mannerisms on her own, to cover up what came naturally to me with gestures and practices to make me, if not more like other people, at least less obviously different.

Real, fake. Face, façade.

It's an art, imitation. It can be harder than making something all your own.

Across the room are two paintings, twins. Their luster marks them as oil, a vibrancy that's particular to this paint. The richness of the black, most of all. I go across the room to get closer to the girl in the painting. A dog sits at her side, her hand on its head. The girl wears a white dress, a white hat tied beneath her chin with lace. She looks at the viewer; the dog cranes its long head up toward its mistress. If it weren't for the green dot and the red, I wouldn't be able to tell the original from the reproduction.

"Sometimes I wonder if the curators even know which is genuine."

It's the tour guide, standing now beside me. I can't tell if they're joking, so I nod.

"This your first visit to our museum?"

I nod again. "My first visit to Paris."

"Oh? Welcome, then."

I say thank you, and then we stand there together with the paintings. The longer I'm there, the more differences I spot; the one on the right has a clarity to the finest lines that's not quite represented in the one on the left. I point to it, and I don't have to say anything.

"Good eye," says the tour guide. "It's funny, though, isn't it, that the more precise version is the fake? Makes you wonder."

It does.

"It reminds me of Lascaux," they continue. "The cave paintings—south of here? Are you familiar with them? They're incredible. Ancient paintings, some of the earliest that have ever been found, discovered about eighty years ago. But after just a few years of people traipsing through, they had to shut the caves to the public. It was people's breath, you know, toxic. It was ruining the art."

Toxic breath—that is something I *do* know about.

"What's most incredible to me is what they've done since. They can't let people into the original cave, but they've reproduced it in a museum nearby. The shape of the cave—the slope of the walls, the dip of the cavern floor—and the paintings too, of course, even the etchings. What a thing to see. More impressive than the original."

I try to imagine such a thing, but I don't know where to begin. The tour guide tells me that along with the reproduced cave, there's a whole exhibition about how the caves were found, the history behind them. "It's called the International Center for Cave Art," they say.

Ancient paintings, the work of our ancestors. One of the things that makes us human—that's what Gillian used to say about art. And these were created by some of the first.

An ache. She would have loved to have visited the caves. And now she never will.

5

I've been in Paris now for five days, during which I grew attached to my Montmartre room: the view, the curtains, the bed. But none of it was mine, of course, and so I had to leave. Before I went, I washed and dried each cup and saucer; I stripped the linens from the bed and piled them along with the towels and washcloths in a basket left for that purpose. I loaded my backpack with all my earthly possessions. When I finally shut the door behind me, I stood in the hallway for a long time. Then I made myself go down the many flights of stairs and out onto the street. I've put this off as long as possible, but now it's Sunday on la Grande Jatte, and I'm here to spread my mother's ashes.

This is how I imagined it when we stood together before the Seurat poster on our refrigerator, my mother's hand atop my head: To get to the island, we would have to take a boat. Upon arriving we would find a fine blue sky, a grassy knoll populated by a collection of beautiful and stylish people taking in the sun, the crystalline river. Trees bowing gently to offer shade, the mainland visible across the cut of lilac water. I knew better than to expect a monkey, but still, I hoped.

As it turns out, no boat is necessary. The "island" is no such thing, connected as it is to the mainland by an easy footpath. The sky changes quickly here; it's gunmetal now, the sun disappeared behind a cloud. I go down a dirty stairwell, through an open gate, down more steps, and now I'm there, alone.

This can't be the same place as Seurat's painting. That park was green, leafy, expansive. This is a spit of paved land, a walkway with some benches, a dog park. A short green fence, knee-high, separates where I stand from the grassy knoll. Behind me are electric lamp-posts. A green-gated children's area with climbing structures and sand. A network of footpaths, arcs and lines that remind me of my childhood blacktop. Seurat didn't misrepresent the park by leaving these things out; when he painted his picture, they didn't exist. Bit by bit, the park of the painting has been traded out for the park I'm standing in. There's the Seine, at least, though the water isn't blue and shining, as I imagined it would be. It's murkier, which is appropriate.

Slowly, I go down the path until I come to a plaque, printed with an image of Seurat's painting and a short description. As wrong as it feels, this really is the place.

I try to see through Seurat's eyes, blurring out the newly constructed fences, the modern play structures. Where might a lady stand, wearing a jaunty hat and shading herself with a parasol? There, maybe? Beside her on the grass could perch a little monkey, just by the hem of her bustled skirt, collared and controlled by a golden chain. It's a bright day in the painting, glimpses of blue sky with soft white clouds. A warm day, warmer than today—in the painting, some of the men and children have bare arms. Seurat's painting is set midday, and so the source of light comes from the west, shadows falling eastward across many of the figures. The entire foreground is shadowed, in fact, except for a triangle of light in the bottom left corner of the canvas. The midground and background are brighter, but they're speckled in shadow, too, thrown by the foliage, the parasols, the hats. "Speckled" is the perfect word for the painting; the whole thing is speckled, rendered in a network of over two hundred thousand individual dots. "Pointillism," the technique is called. If you stand very close, all you can see is dots, and the painting loses meaning. Step back, and back again, and then—there. The impression appears.

"*Again,* dearheart?" My mother's hand on my head. I'm seven years old, nine years old, ten. Once, I tell Gillian that I feel like the monkey at the end of the chain. Her response—"You're not an animal, Nora." I don't explain to her that actually, yes, I *am* an animal; we are *all* animals.

I like to stand right up against the poster. It's midway up the refrigerator door, positioned so that when I stand like this, my nose touches the face of the little girl at the center, the only figure who's looking at the artist. Then I take measured steps back, tiny steps, as tiny as I can make them. I'm trying to find where it happens—when the image transforms from discrete dots into a story. *Where* it happens, *when* it happens . . . the same thing: the moment I perceive the difference, and the distance from the painting that causes it to shift. Eleven years old, twelve, thirteen . . . we inch the poster up the refrigerator's door again and again so the girl in the center remains in the same place, Gillian pleased each time—"Look how tall you're getting!"—until at last, when I'm close to sixteen and exactly my mother's height, we stop.

One speaks about a painting or a poem or a story in the present tense. It's always happening. It never ceases to happen. Well—if the painting is damaged or destroyed, I suppose then you'd talk about it in the past tense. I suppose that's a way for a painting to die.

Would Gillian be disappointed in this park, where I've brought her remains? In *me*, for everything I'd done to get here, and this, the result?

She'd do her best to hide it, I know she would. "You're trying so hard, I can see how hard you try." Her hands squeezing up and down my arms to calm me after I've failed, yet again, to control my body, to control my volume, to control my emotions. "Deep breath in—slowly, slower—now hold it—and let it out. There you go. It's okay, baby. We'll try again. We'll try again tomorrow."

I unbuckle my pack and set it down. It's a relief, the unburdening. But I'm not ready to open it.

After everyone started to get sick and I no longer had to leave the apartment, I had all the time in the world to study the poster. The monkey, of course; the lady and her daughter. The fisherwoman, the way her hat slants downward, her gaze, too. The straight clean line of her rod. The man in the foreground, with the triangle of sunlight just beneath his knee, bare-armed and smoking a pipe. A girl just upriver of the fisherwoman; her skirt with its bustle forms a quarter circle, a right angle attached to a neat arc. The rowers pulling their oars so earnestly through the water; the trumpeter playing his tune in the middle of it all. Circles and lines, dots and arcs.

But during those months, especially as time went on and things became more desperate, it was the lone man who drew my eye again and again. The way he holds his hand to his chin. One knee is bent—here, another triangle of grass, through the bend—his other leg stretched along the ground. He's wearing a black suit, a white shirt, a black top hat. His back is against a tree. He's not sad. He, I am certain, is death.

It's time for me to get on with things. I don't have all day; I need to figure out what I'm doing next, where I'll sleep tonight. There are a few cheap places across the river, I'll head over there in a little while. I'll find a place for the night—

And then what? Tomorrow? And the tomorrow after that, all the tomorrows left to come?

Back home, I spent my last weeks getting rid of things great and small. The only item I purchased beyond the things I needed to travel was the bamboo cylinder I'm pulling now from my backpack. You can buy anything online. It arrived in nondescript brown cardboard, just like anything else would—a new set of paintbrushes, a tube of cookies, a flashlight. It's fourteen inches tall, four inches in diameter.

I'm sitting, now, on this ugly spit of land, my mother's ashes cradled in my arms. A jogger—a woman—has to veer off the path to get around me, looks over her shoulder but doesn't stop.

There are so many ways to lose a person. Already I've lost my mother three times. The first time I don't often think about, and I barely remember those years—I was so young, and Big Nora took such wonderful care of me. The second time was slower, and I didn't really notice that I was losing her; it happened bit by bit, until it was too late. The third time was violent, sudden. Breath, then death.

And now I'm about to lose her again. *Here,* in this depressing nothing of a place.

"Are you all right?" It's the jogger, who has circled back to check on me.

I swipe tears from my face. "I'm not supposed to be here," I tell her. My body is humming like a hive of bees, and my French is loose, imprecise. "I thought this was the place, but I was wrong."

"Do you need—help? To find the right place?"

"No." I sniff hard, swipe my eyes with the back of my hand. I don't know where the right place is, but I know with certainty that this is not where I'll lose my mother for the final time. I set the cylinder into my backpack, cinch tight the straps. "I'll find it."

The jogger seems unsure about leaving me here, but at last she nods. "Take care," she says, and picks up her run again.

From an outsider's perspective, it would be easy to judge Gillian, to call her a bad mother for what she did. I mean, mothers aren't supposed to abandon their children. But the thing is, she was only nineteen when I was born. *I* can't imagine being a mother right now, or anytime soon (or maybe ever)—she must have been so overwhelmed. Whatever life she'd been planning probably screeched to a halt when she got pregnant. She could have gotten an abortion; obviously she didn't, and I suppose I'm glad I exist. But then, if she'd had an abortion, I never would have existed to wonder over the phenomenology of existence, or gladness.

I was so little when she left—just four months old—that it wasn't like I could even miss her. And it wasn't as if I was well and truly *abandoned*; I had Big Nora. Because I was so young, I don't have many memories of the years that Gillian was gone, mostly just scraps, images, sounds, feelings. But the things I do remember are lovely. Big Nora took wonderful care of me.

One thing I remember is that she would tell me about my mother all the time. As if any minute, for nearly four years, she expected Gillian to walk back through the apartment door.

* * *

It's funny—not funny *haha*—to consider that there's no one in the entire world I need to inform about my change in plans. No family, no neighbors from the apartment building. No teachers, or friends. If anyone cared to trace my thread, they could look at the charges to my debit card—the airline ticket, the apartment rental, the various museum tickets; there's no one, though, who would think to do this. No single person who knew what my plan was, coming to Paris, or what it is now, after leaving la Grande Jatte without spreading my mother's remains. No one who would care if I book a return ticket to the States in five days, or five years, or ever. I'm not expected; I'm not missed. I do wonder—is this, functionally, any different than death? This absolute aloneness?

Yes. It is. It is different. Because I still have a purpose. I still have a debt. I need to find a place—the *right* place—to spread Gillian's remains. I owe her more, so much more, but this is what I can give her.

After that . . . well.

Instead of heading from Seurat's park to a cheap hotel, I navigate to a sporting goods store. I wander the aisles, antiseptically bright under florescent lights, and make my choices. Just under six hundred euros purchases a tent, a pad, a sleeping bag, a can of pepper spray, and a larger backpack to hold it all. A place to stay, for as many days, weeks, months as I'd like, for only a little more than the money I spent on the Montmartre apartment.

Then I go to the train station and look at the board. There's a train leaving soon for Bordeaux, but it's another big city, not as big as Paris but still overwhelming. I choose one headed for Orléans, instead. An hour and a half later, I'm there.

A river city with a connection to Joan of Arc, Orléans is beautiful, its city center crowned by an enormous cathedral. A ten-minute walk takes me to the Bourgogne quarter, the merchants' district. Renaissance-era buildings and half-timber façades, wooden beams crisscrossing the faces of two-story houses that wear their attic spaces like little caps; narrow streets, funny little alleyways connecting them. If I ignore the people, I can almost pretend I've stepped back in time.

I buy two savory crêpes from a street vendor and eat the first one, but I don't have time to linger; the sun will soon be setting, and I need to find a place to pitch my tent. My initial impulse is to find a park, but when I do, I also find posted signs with strict regulations, including open hours and prohibitions against sleeping. I end up in a dirt parking lot tucked behind a church; another traveler, unhoused out of necessity rather than choice, tells me that as long as I'm gone by six in the morning, I most likely won't be ticketed. I give her the second crêpe as thanks and build my tent for the first time. It's not as easy as I hoped it would be, but not as hard as I feared. Then I unpackage the pepper spray and tuck it into my pocket, just in case.

I barely sleep; I keep waiting for someone to tell me to move, but no one does. In the morning, I pack up and move on. A cappuccino and a croissant, consumed on a park bench as the sun pinkens the sky. Nowhere I need to go, no one waiting for me. I could wander in any direction. By the time I finish my coffee and bread, however, I have a destination. I've decided to head toward the International Center for Cave Art. It seems as good a place as any.

I'm in no hurry, so I take my time zigzagging through the Loire Valley. I explore each town center, every museum, all the parks and waterways. One day I find a laundromat and wash nearly everything I own in one small load. Another day, when I'm too tired to wander, I tuck into a neighborhood library, reading and trying not to fall asleep (every time I nod off, a librarian "tsks" me awake). And each day I ask: Is *this* the place? Is this the day I will let my mother go?

Each time, the answer is no. Not here, not yet. Day after day after day, until I lose count of them.

This is how you build a tent. Find a piece of flat earth as hidden as you can, if you're not staying at a campground. Check for stones. Slip the tent, smooth like silk, from its nylon sheath. Spread the gray footprint tarp, then shake open the tent. The poles, collapsed and wrapped within, will clatter to the grass. These are the textures and sounds I love. Smooth, cold nylon. Orange, my favorite color, and the reason I chose this tent over the other options. The satisfying stretch of elastic as I form each pole, the shine of the silver joints as the segments snap into place.

Stretch it into shape with its pliable skeleton, two big rods and two small. When it's upright, unwind the tie of the small pouch and pound in the stakes. One, two, three, four. Stash the bags, large and small, in the tent's elasticized pocket.

Then the sleeping pad. Then the sleeping bag. Done.

The same, each time.

There is pleasure in routine, and in small places. And I'm good at being alone. When there's a designated campsite I rent a space, but when there isn't, well, it's really not that hard to disappear off the side of a road. Each evening, I construct my tent, and each morning, after taking it down, I find a bus or a train and head somewhere else.

By the end of a week, being alone in a tent is less unsettling, even sort of cozy. By the end of another, I can barely remember what it felt like to sleep in a real bed. And it's sort of silly, isn't it, to set up and take down my tent every day? What's the rush, anyway? Like I realized at the park, no one is waiting for me. The next time I find a good spot to camp, I stay for a while. Three nights? Or four? Alone like this, the function of time becomes rubbery. More like a theory than a thing I know is certain.

I lie with the cylinder of Gillian's ashes cradled in my arms. Awake, asleep, it doesn't matter—moments rise up in waves: the way she used to smile at me, before the lockdown. The flash of pride on her face when I'd show her a successful reproduction. Her contemplative expression when she stood in front of the Seurat poster.

Other memories burble up, things I'd rather not remember. I do my best to push them right back down.

Most days I stop somewhere to charge my phone—a café or a library—and every few days I find a hostel where I can pay to take a shower, a grocery store where I can refresh my supplies.

Though I see many beautiful places, nowhere seems like the right place to leave the remains. But I can't hold on to them forever, and I find I've already decided: when I get to the International Center for Cave Art, I'll choose a spot near there, as close as I can get to the art of our ancestors. I'll find a quiet stream, or a hill, or the base of a tree. Some beautiful, restful place.

The farther I travel, the more rural the countryside becomes, the smaller the villages. Out here, the façade fades—there's a France presented to travelers, I'm learning, and then there's the rest of the country, where the people make their livings in ways other than catering to tourism. It's quieter here. Fewer souvenir shops. Souvenir—really just the French word for "memory." A funny word for it. A souvenir isn't really a memory; at best, it's a symbol for one, a stand-in. Something you *buy*, not something you *make*.

But even though they're cheap and artificial, souvenirs don't fade. That *is* ironic—that the fake thing lasts, while the real thing always disappears.

More and more, I don't board a train or a bus at all; I walk the ten or fifteen miles from one village to the next, pitching my tent between them. One day, ducking into a convenience store, I spot a regional map near the register. I buy it along with the chocolate bar I came in for. I eat the chocolate on a park bench and study the map. When the chocolate is gone, I throw away the wrapper. Then I power down my phone, shove it to the bottom of my backpack.

Without it, time loosens even more. Days pass in a blur, my boots taking step after step after step along the side of a road. Eventually a car will roar past, jolting me back into the present. A driver honks at me; another throws a soda can out the window. It doesn't hit me, but sticky liquid sprays across my chest. It makes me cry, a little.

Here and there are strings of days when I don't see another person at all. I'll wake up in my tent in a thatch of rural land, and spend the day, the next day, and another in the countryside, my back against a tree, just watching. Sometimes I watch the things in front of me: the way the light changes the soft green grass from something hopeful to something desperate. The way a bird, perched on a wire, tips its head at the sound of a bird of its same kind, and flies away at the sound of another. All the layers and textures—gravel on the road, for example, and how I might gesture to its variation in a painting. What if I did a watercolor wash of grays and white, then went back over with gouache to bring in dimension? The sky one day just before a rainstorm; maybe masking fluid to preserve the pure white of the paper where the lightning cracks, and then watercolors for the rest, just layers and layers of watercolors to try to capture the luminosity, that sort of shimmer.

Sometimes I watch the things inside my head. The Seurat poster from the refrigerator door; the Painting that used to hang in our hallway. My mother, breathing. My mother, not breathing anymore.

I can pretend to not care about time, but it moves on, just the same. The days grow shorter; the nights, longer. And it's getting colder, and wetter. I have to cover my tent with the rainfly; my clothes are all musty, and nothing gets all-the-way dry.

I'm in Auriac-du-Périgord, a tiny clutch of medieval stone structures that can't house more than a few hundred people. The village's glory, the Maison Forte de Reignac, is outside of town. A cliff castle, it's up against and carved into an enormous limestone face, making use of the natural caves. I leave my backpack at reception—the receptionist makes a face—and take the self-guided tour. I wander through the period-decorated rooms, read all the plaques, look into the face of each framed portrait. All the people who may have lived here, once.

From the highest tower, a view: the Vézère Valley, thick with waxy green foliage and trees, verdant and healthy. Foothills rim the basin; a river cuts through it. Somewhere in that direction, obscured from view by all the greenery, is the International Center for Cave Art. That's where I'll go tomorrow; I've made a reservation for Friday, the first of October.

In the village I buy bread and cheese and refill my water canister. Then I walk a while, an hour or so, away from Auriac-du-Périgord and in the direction of Lascaux. When I find a little footpath off the side of the main road, I take it, wander through trees until I feel sure I'm far enough away from sight that I won't be disturbed. I slide my backpack to the ground and roll my shoulders, rub them. Then it's time to build the tent.

Like each night, when the tent is complete, I slide my pack to the far side of the sleeping bag. If I wake, lonely in the night, I can press my back against it and pretend it's a person I love. Then I take the cheese and bread and sit in the grass, lean against a tree, and watch the sun set. The Neapolitan sky, striated softly, pink and peach and golden, stretches untethered and grand. I tear a chunk of bread and take a bite of cheese, tangy and crystalized with salt. It's as much as a person can hope for.

A rustling sound, from above. Two black, shiny eyes, a twitchy gray nose, a curious, vibrating tail, hoisted like a friendly flag. I tear another, smaller piece of bread and hold it between two fingers, lifted above my head. The squirrel considers, takes a few steps down the tree, completely upside down, and stops again. My arm is getting tired, but I do my best to hold the bread aloft. At last, the squirrel finds its bravery and rushes down, wraps a little hand around my pointer finger and takes the bread between its teeth.

There's a moment when time crystalizes, my finger held in the tiny paw. When was the last time someone held my hand? There was my hand on my mother's, already cold, before they took her away. But that was me, holding hers. When was the last time someone held *mine?*

It must have been my mother. I can't recall anyone holding my hand since she died. Few people held my hand even when I was little—Big Nora did, before she died; my teachers, sometimes, and therapists, when I was little, leading me somewhere. But once I was no longer a child, it was Gillian's hand I remember, and I can't recall the last time. It's just . . . gone. It's something else I've lost, this final flesh memory. A taste—just bitter, no sweet—fills my mouth. I squeeze tight my eyes, trying to keep out the emotions that threaten to rush in.

Then the squirrel pulls away, a tiny imprint of negative space where its paw has been. It turns tail, scrambles up the tree, disappears.

7

In art, perspective comes naturally to me. Figuring out where the light source is; identifying where the vanishing point should be; manipulating the size and clarity of objects to create the illusion of depth. Perspective with people comes less naturally. I see things very clearly from my point of view . . . and honestly, I can forget that other people have their own experiences, distinct and different from mine. This is probably why, when I was younger, I never gave much thought to Gillian and Big Nora's relationship. The three of us had less than two years together. It was a hard time for me. But I've come to see how hard it was for each of them, too.

When it was the three of us, Big Nora and Gillian often disagreed about me—what to do about all the parts of me that stuck out, caused such reactions in others. Kindergarten was overwhelming; I had trouble being still when I needed to be still, being active when I needed to be active. I didn't interact with other children, and when I did, I did it incorrectly. Life was challenging for me. And so it was for them, too.

"Don't be so *hard* on her, Gillian. Can't you see she's trying?"

Big Nora and Gillian had been called to come pick me up from school after I'd bitten a classmate. I hadn't wanted to hurt him, I was just excited by whatever game we had been playing, I don't remember exactly. But I do remember how upset everyone had gotten, the way my teacher had asked me, "Why did you do that?"—and when I didn't answer, kept asking it, over and over.

Big Nora and my mother were in the living room; I was beneath the kitchen table, where I often would go when things became too much. They didn't think I was listening to them. But I always listened.

"Stop *coddling* her, Ma. She's got to learn that the world isn't going to give her space to do things like this."

"Maybe not. But *you* could. If you would give her a little more grace—"

"There's not a lot of grace in this world, Ma, and if we pretend there is, we're not doing her any favors."

"Give her *time*."

"This is your fault. She's like this because those poisons you let the doctors shoot into her—"

"Again with this, Gillian?"

"No one really knows the long-term effects! Especially with the MMR vaccine."

From under the table, I watched Big Nora reach out to Gillian; I watched Gillian turn away.

They both loved me; they just expressed that love in different ways. And maybe some of the fighting that I thought was about me was really more about *them*. Maybe they fought because Gillian resented Big Nora as much as she needed her. Maybe she'd resented her *because* of how much she'd needed her. Whatever the reasons, that time was hard. The two of them pulling in opposite directions, and me in the middle.

Then came the day of the butterfly wings and the Cakewalk. Gillian, kneeling down next to me on the asphalt.

"I have to tell you something, baby. Something terrible. Something . . . impossible."

Her toenails were painted pearlescent white.

"Something . . . something fell, from the sky. A rock. A meteorite, Little Nora. Do you know what a meteorite is? It wasn't very big, but it fell from very high, and it fell very, very fast. And it hit Big Nora. Outside of our apartment building. And . . ."

They were milky and shiny, her toenails, with rainbows inside of them.

"It killed her, Nora."

Her pinkie toenail was tiny. It was a sliver of silvery shine.

"She loved you so much. You have to remember that. How much she loved you. More than she loved me. More than anything."

One, two, three, four, five toes on her left foot. One, two, three, four, five toes on her right foot. Five plus five equals ten. Ten toes, ten toenails.

"It's an impossible thing." She choked on her tears, made an awful sound. "Absolutely impossible." She took my face in her trembling hands, damp with her tears. She tilted my chin toward her face, but she couldn't make my eyes look up, she couldn't make me see her eyes.

One, two, three, four, five, six, seven, eight, nine, ten. Ten toes on the asphalt. And around them, the painted lines and curves, bright yellow stripes and half-moons that made meaning. Yellow is a primary color. A primary color plus a primary color makes a secondary color.

"Look at me, Nora. Look at me."

That's when I started to scream.

After that day, it was a long time before I could reenter the world. I couldn't return to school; I didn't even like to leave the apartment. When Big Nora was alive, Gillian had been "no nonsense" about my behavior; she wasn't above carrying me kicking and screaming out of the house, if that was what needed to happen. But the day Big Nora died, something in Gillian shifted.

That afternoon, as soon as we got home—our apartment smelled different, already, without Big Nora—I went under the kitchen table. But instead of retreating into her room, or pulling me out from under as she had sometimes done in the past, Gillian draped a big, pink, flat bedsheet over the kitchen tabletop. Light filtered through like a membrane. She brought me bed pillows and the big pillow from the couch, too. She brought me crayons and paper, and she brought me food—bowls of fruit, a sandwich, tea. Nothing sharp or mushy.

Under the table, for days on end, I drew. First, shapes. Dots, short dark lines. Half-moons, and circles. Peaked arrow tips. Swirls. Squares. On, and on. I drew animals—dogs. Horses. Deer. I drew the face of my grandmother.

Gillian took a grievance leave from work to stay home with me. She would sit on the other side of the sheet membrane, slipping just the tips of her fingers beneath, so I'd know I wasn't alone. I didn't like the sight of her fingertips in that way. Her smooth, coral-painted nails, shell-like, which I had before so loved to rub my thumb against . . . there, under the dividing cloth, they were severed things, dead but still moving, not of my mother anymore. I would lift the sheet, bring it to the other side of her fingers, and drop it down.

"I know I haven't been as gentle with you as your grandmother was. And I'm sorry, dearheart. I swear, everything is going to change. I'm going to try harder. I'm going to be *better.* I promise."

I've read that when one's spouse dies, the surviving parent has to become *both* parents. That's what it was like with Gillian, after that. She was still *her,* of course, but she was Big Nora, too. And though she still had her moments of stress, irritation, impatience, even anger with me, Gillian kept her word. She was more patient. She was softer.

"Take all the time you need," she said. "I'll be out here waiting, when you're ready." Probably she had to prove it to me a hundred times over the course of that first week, before I trusted it—that she *would* be there. One day, I pulled back the sheet and let her crawl beneath it, with me.

Gillian didn't yell anymore. She started explaining things in a calm voice, in practical terms, in a way I could hear.

"Life isn't always an ice-cream sundae, dearheart."

That became her name for me. No reason to call me Little Nora anymore.

"The road won't move, so we have to move to the road."

"You and I are a team now, okay? And teammates don't always agree on everything, but they're always on the same side. They're always working toward the same goal."

She talked and talked and talked, and I listened. It was a terrible month. But it was a good month, too. How can both things be true?

She stayed home with me as long as she could, but eventually, she had to go back to work. We needed money, she told me. That's how we paid for the apartment, and for groceries, and for electricity and for markers and crayons and paper. I wanted those things, yes? Then she had to go back to the clinic.

I didn't want to go back to school; I knew I *couldn't* go back. And thankfully, Gillian didn't make me.

"We can't let anyone know you're here by yourself," she warned. "If anyone finds out I'm leaving you alone, they'll take you away from me." She was kneeling next to the table; on the undulating wall of my sanctuary, her shadow brushed hair from her face, a gesture that comforted me with its familiarity. "I'll leave the clinic's number, but only call if it's an emergency." I poked my head out from beneath the sheet, and let her kiss me, stroke my hair.

"I love you so much, Nora. You know that, don't you?"

I had no words, but I managed a nod, breathed her sweet pink smell.

She nodded, too. "We're going to be okay," she promised.

The first day alone, I didn't draw. I just listened to the apartment building's sounds: the tick of something electric; the hum of the refrigerator coming on, and going off, then coming on again; water flowing through pipes in the wall when the people in the apartment above flushed their toilet. The whine of hot water forced through other pipes when they used their shower. And other sounds, outside sounds. The squeal of a car pulling away fast from the curb. The clatter and bang of the trash truck lifting, emptying, and setting down the dumpster out back. Music, blasted from a car that left its windows down, paused by a red light on the street below, fading to nothing after the light turned green and it pulled away. Birds, both pigeons and songbirds, louder and more frequent than I'd ever noticed before. A long stretch of relative quiet, in the early afternoon; then the voices of children, laughing and shouting, as they made their way home when school let out. The quieter I was, the more I heard.

And it almost felt like the Painting—the one that hung in the hallway—was calling to me. After listening for a long time, I left my little cave and pulled a kitchen chair down the hall. I climbed atop it and took down the Painting, being very careful not to drop it. Back beneath the table, I cradled it in my lap, mesmerized. The Painting had something to tell me, or so it seemed; I didn't know what it was, but it comforted me, this belief. I made my eyes soft and disappeared into the Painting, I don't know for how long—hours, it must have been. I ran my finger over the ridged paint again, again, again, until, finally, the scratch-twist sound of Gillian's key in the lock.

The last night before Lascaux, alone in my tent, I am quiet. I listen, and remember.

Like the concept of breath, the concept of sleep is terrifying, if you let yourself think about it for very long. What is it, exactly, that happens? It isn't death because it doesn't last. It isn't a coma, because one can be roused from it by a sensation, like a hand on your brow, or a sound, like a bang of a truck backfiring, or a shift in light, like the blaze of a headlamp arching across the interior of your tent. Sleep is terrifying.

But for the last many months, waking has been terrifying, too.

It's the arc of light that wakes me. I'm without a body, without a place, without a time. No anchor, I both float and sink in the same moment. Then, I remember: I'm in a sleeping bag in a tent in the southern part of France, partway between Auriac-du-Périgord and

Montignac, the village closest to the Lascaux caves. I am alone in the world. Absolutely no one living knows where I am, or cares.

The roving eyeball of light glares in another sweep across me. My hand, lit up, glows white. Then the light passes, and my hand disappears again. There's a sensation of it ceasing to exist; the opposite of phantom limb syndrome, in which one feels the presence of a missing hand or foot, my hand is severed once I can't see it anymore. I grip the smooth, cool fabric of the bag I'm in; there, I feel it, I exist.

"Bonsoir?"

The voice is male. Young, but not a child or teen. A man. French. So much can be gleaned from one short word. I squeeze tight my eyes, wish to disappear. My throat is tight with fear, my heart thrums. Probably a police officer or landowner. I've been lucky all this time, camping the way I have. I guess my luck has run out.

Footsteps. The light again.

Cradled in my arms is the bamboo cylinder with my mother's ashes. When I climb out of the tent, I take it with me, even as I take nothing else. I don't know why. I'm glad I slept in my sweater and corduroys, because in the pocket of my pants is another cylinder. I've kept it there since I bought it along with the camping gear, a reassuring weight that I barely ever think about. It's smooth and cold, and I run the tip of my finger along its edge until I find the lever. I twist it.

Cyclops-like, the man stands not ten feet from the entrance to my tent. For a moment all the world is light—bright, painful, punishing. Does he know what he's doing? Does he mean to aim the light at me? My feet are bare; the ground is damp with dew.

"Hello," I say, in French. It hurts, the word. I force myself to make more, holding the larger cylinder close against my chest with one hand, keeping my finger ready on the trigger of the smaller. "I know that I'm camping without a permit. I'll be glad to pay the fine."

"Ah, American?" His head tilts and the angle of the light shifts and there's his face, marbled with shadow. "Are you alone?"

An unsettling question. I am unsettled. "What do you want?"

"Nothing, nothing. Just—some money. That's all."

And then I know—this person is not an authority, not a landowner. He's something else. Someone else. Maybe someone dangerous.

"I don't have cash. Only a card. Sorry, but I can't help you."

His headlamp nods, light dancing up and down. He takes a step closer. "Is anyone with you?"

"Don't. Please don't come any closer."

Another step. And another. He says, again—"Are you alone?"

I bring up the small canister. Even before my arm is fully raised, my finger depresses the trigger. It's a beautiful parabola: the rising arc of the spray; the falling arc of the light, as the man tucks his head. There is a point of intersection between the spray and the light, and in the light, the aerosolized particles disperse and spread.

He makes a choked sound of pain and surprise, a grunt, and then he lunges forward, knocks the canister from my hand. The air moves; when I inhale, there's a sharp deep burn, just as if I've pulled needles into my lungs. My eyes too—they shut tight against the spray, but not tight enough. They burn.

His hand strikes my forearm. The canister thuds to the ground, and then he screams and collapses to his knees.

I run. Where, it doesn't matter. Just—away.

I tuck the cylinder of my mother's ashes in the crook of my arm to secure it. The ground is uneven, and I'm barefoot. I catch my toe on something hard—a root? A rock?—I stumble, it hurts, but I manage to stay standing. The world is just shadows and shapes, not much, but enough to keep from running into a tree.

Behind me, a violent slash of light. He's managed to get up, and even if it was true that before he only wanted money, that is no longer all he wants.

There is no one in the world left to care if I live, or if I die. But the man who chases me—he cares, perhaps more than anyone else.

Except me. I'm a person, too.

What a strange thing. My entire plan consisted of bringing my mother's remains to the place she always yearned to go and seeing the art in Paris. Beyond that, I had nothing. No ticket home; no home, at all, to return to. I was ambivalent, I realize, about whether I would continue to exist. Since leaving Paris I've been traveling as if in Gehenna, both here and not here, moving, yes, but also waiting.

Now, faced with the very real possibility of a very specific death—choked out or bludgeoned by this cyclops man, if he catches me—I find I do indeed want to stay alive.

There's a sliver of moon in the sky, enough to cast faint light. As my eyes clear the poison, tears streaming down my cheeks, the shadow of a path emerges ahead. Is it the path I took from the road? No—the ground slopes downward, rather than up, but I keep going anyway; I stumble and catch myself, jump to clear a log, but when I land it's not squarely and I fall down. My head cracks against something hard and I'm spinning, and blood drips from my forehead into my right eye but there's no time for that, there's nothing to do but get up and run again.

I make it three steps before I realize my hands are empty.

I turn, drop to the dirt, feel blindly. Impossible, that I'll find it, and my heart bleeds with the loss—

There.

I grab the bamboo cylinder, turn back and run again.

He's closer now. The rustle of his feet behind me. The hot pant of his breath, angry and growing nearer. I decide more with my body than my brain—dipping behind a tree, I stand still, very still, as still as the tree, and hold my breath.

Breath. Death.

He's coming. So close I can smell him, stale sweat beneath cologne. What if this man will be the last person to touch me? What if my final human connection will be not a caress, but a violence? I press my palm against the bark of the tree. It's rough, but not cruel.

Closer. Closer. And now—he pounds past, runs deeper into the trees.

I'm so relieved I almost whimper. My legs are shaking, I can't stand any longer, but I'm afraid to move, afraid to make a sound.

Up ahead, he's slowing, stopping, silent. He's gone too far. He knows I'm here, somewhere, behind him. A cloud drifts across the moon, and darkness shrouds me. But then, like the sweep of a lighthouse beacon comes his cyclops light, and I'm bathed in it. And now he's coming for me, again.

A cry slips from me, desperate, an animal sound, and I wipe the blood from my eye and take off again, aimlessly, only away. My toenail catches on something and it pulls up and back, a shock of pain, but there's nothing to do but keep moving.

The trees grow thicker and the ground slopes steeply. I've stumbled onto a sunken lane, an old, eroded path, carving a gully into the earth. And here, above, the overgrowth reaches across the sides of the path to form a tunnel.

A holloway—that's what this is. A path trod for centuries, now a trench. Worn deep by human feet, by workhorses and carriage wheels, this is an ancient way. So much of the ancient in this part of the world. If I were to stumble on this place in daylight, I'd stop and stretch my arms across it, I would wonder whose feet, what lives, might have helped to carve it out of the earth, the way I wondered about all the people who'd inhabited the Maison Forte de Reignac.

But now is no time for wonder.

Breathe. Leave.

The path narrows and deepens and the overgrowth thickens, darkens, and I feel my way along as the holloway constricts, tightens, and my palms brush the walls, the dirt damp and soft as velvet, and I don't hear the man behind me anymore, I've escaped the light from his headlamp, and there's a pressure in my head, as if I've dived to the bottom of a pool or lifted off high in a plane, a pressure that means my body is out of its depth one way or another. My ears and my eyes and my nose and my mouth are full to bursting. Still, I push on, and on, and through, until the path begins to climb, and widen, and release, and a final velvet leaf caresses my cheek, as soft as my mother's touch, and then, there, here—I'm through, to the other side.

Weak as a newborn, I collapse to my knees. I crawl beneath a bush and pull my feet in after me.

8

Before I open my eyes, I let myself believe that it's the past. I'm home, tucked in bed, and any moment I'll hear the gurgle and steam of Gillian's coffeepot, inhale the warm fragrance.

But the air is cold and the ground is hard and I am not in my bed. I'm cramped and damp beneath a dew-wet bush. I'm no child, I have no mother. I have the bamboo canister of her ashes, but she's not her ashes, not really. I don't believe in a soul or an afterlife, so it's not that I think she's somewhere other than here. It's just—that she *isn't*, anymore, at all.

My eyes are dry and stuck shut, and when I manage to peel them open, they scrape and scratch and burn. I rub them, and my hands come away flaked with red-rust blood. I touch my temple, where I struck my head: a lump, and more dried blood. Not fresh, so that's something.

I was chased. I crawled into this bush and lost consciousness. As far as I can tell, I was not found.

Carefully, slowly, I part the spiny-tipped branches. Dirt, dark as coffee grounds. Greenery—trees and bushes and wild grass. The air is frigid, fresh, untouched. Almost glittery. I take one of Gillian's deep breaths, hold it in, release it slowly. Better.

I'm just about to get up when there's a rustle across from me. I freeze, petrified into wood. But it's just a squirrel, gray and darling, its knowing black eyes locked with mine. This could be yesterday's squirrel who shared my bread. *Was* that just yesterday? It feels like much more time must have passed than just one night—one terrible, terrifying night.

The squirrel disappears, and I crawl out. I'm shaky and scared, but alone. Still, I shouldn't go back to my tent. He could be there, waiting. Probably he's taken what he wanted and left, but I'm lucky to have escaped, mostly uninjured, and it would be stupid to go back now.

So? What next?

My feet are blackened and beat up. The nail of the pinkie toe on my left foot is angled unnaturally, dangling like a loose tooth. Gingerly, I test it, but it's no good; it's attached with just a scrap of bloodied gristle.

Better now than later. Pinching it between thumb and forefinger, I yank.

The pain blinds, the world narrows. I thud down to sitting before I pass out. After a minute, my vision widens. I don't look at the toe again. The nail is still gripped in my fingers, and I fling it away.

Okay. No shoes. No socks, even. I'll rinse my toe as soon as I find water.

Water. I don't have any, but that's okay. I've emerged from a ridge of trees and spread before me is a vast swath of untended land. It's wild out here. Over the time I've spent traveling and camping, I've been amazed over and over again by all the undeveloped land I've encountered. But there is always a town or a village—mishmashes of medieval structures and strips of modern buildings—not that far from what's entirely untouched.

No shoes. No water. I slept in corduroys and my wool sweater, a T-shirt underneath, so I'm warm enough, or I will be, once I start walking. I feel my pockets, front and back, hoping that I've shoved my debit card or my phone in one of them, even as I know that I zipped them—safely, I'd believed—in my pack, which is back in the tent. I do find a hair elastic, and though it's not as good as finding the debit card or phone, it's not nothing, as Gillian used to say. I set the cylinder at my feet and rake my hair into a ponytail, wincing as I touch the lump on my temple, and wrap the ponytail into a knot, secure it with the elastic.

Better. I'm stronger, having done this little thing. I pick up the cylinder, then turn in a slow circle, searching for the direction from which I came. For the holloway.

There. Beautiful, really, and strange. Lower than the earth around it, and with the foliage above, it's something from a fantasy story, a road for elves and orphans, magical and foreboding.

Not that way. My few possessions lie in that direction, and there was a road not far from where I camped, but I don't want to risk going back. I'll head in the opposite direction; surely it won't be long before I find a farm, or a village. Someone will help me. I can call the police. They will take me to reclaim my gear, whatever is left. I'll have to speak with the officers, I'll have to give a description and file a report. It won't be pleasant, but I can do it. It will surely be easier if my pack is still there, and my passport . . . but I won't think about that now.

Turning my back on the holloway, I walk.

It happens by degrees, the dissipation of the mist. For a while the morning air is heavy and wet. Drops of water condense and settle on the oatmeal wool of my sweater. My feet are nearly numb from cold, but that's okay, it's good, actually. Better than the alternative.

Slowly, and then all at once, the air is drier, and I'm warmer. Not warm, but warmer. I blink and suddenly the world appears, clear and bright—wild heathered landscape, alive and rustling, a great basin of it, with a ridge of hills way over there, a thick green slash at its base. I'm in the foothills, too, part of the great chain of them that circles the basin like a necklace. And then a snarl of hunger so sudden and intense that at first, I mistake it for illness. When was the last time I felt this hungry?

By midday, I'm starting to worry. I've pushed through untamed land for hours; it's unusually bad luck to have walked in a direction with no road, no country houses, for miles. I've chosen the worst possible route, and I've dug myself deep into the foothills. If I had my phone, I could find a town. Even the convenience store map would have been better than nothing, which is what I have.

My baby toe throbs. So does my head. I don't want to cry. It will do no good. But still, the tears come. I try to stop them, but it's no use, and as soon as I give in, they overcome me. I let myself sink to the ground. Something pokes me in the back of my thigh, but I let it, I don't care that it hurts. I drop my head to my hands, and I cry, and the sounds that come from me are animal-like, they frighten me, but I have no control now, I'm a kite with too much string, bobbing and diving and jerking, erratic and violent.

I could have been killed last night. Raped, maybe, and killed. The cyclops man lunging toward me and grabbing me by the neck, his two thumbs pushing in at the soft spot at the front of my throat, squeezing and shaking me like a doll. Grabbing my hair and forcing me to the ground.

I'm with my mother again, with the people who arrive in masks and gloves and white paper suits who zip her inside the silver bag, who roll her away. They ask if there's anyone they should call, and my own broken voice tells them I'm eighteen, they don't need to call anyone, I'm an adult, I don't tell them that I don't feel like an adult, nor that there's no one to call, anyway. I'm inside my pink-walled sanctuary, the membrane undulating as I draw shapes, then animals, then Big Nora's face, over and over again, the wave of her long loose hair, the arch of her eyes, the curve of her mouth, waiting for my mother to come home.

I'm wailing now, loud, and long. I'll cry forever, now that I've begun.

"Bonjour?"

A choke, a gurgle, I gasp. Adrenaline floods my system; I jump up and my open hand fists closed.

It's a man, but not the cyclops man. The cyclops man was thick, but this person is thin, underfed even, white wrists protruding from the cuffs of his coat as he holds up his hands to indicate that he means no harm. This person is also younger, maybe my age. On his back is a tall army-green pack with a bedroll, and there's something slung over his shoulder by another strap; at first, I think it's a rifle, but then I see it's three fishing poles, a strap wound around them to make a bundle.

"Hello," he says again, in French, softly, as if he's talking to a small, scared animal. "Are you all right?"

Arrange yourself.

Gillian's words—shorthand for everything I need to remember to do to not put someone off, to blend in. Shoulders down, head up. Make eye contact. I don't have to smile but at least don't scowl.

Respond when people talk to you.

I try, but nothing comes. This, I can't control. It's the same as hiccups; hiccups come, and the only thing one can do is wait until they leave. Except with my voice, it's the opposite. When it leaves, there's nothing to do but wait for its return.

Another rustle from the bushes, this time with an energy and enthusiasm that telegraphs it's made by an animal other than a human, and then here it comes—a dog, middle-sized, brownish black, barreling toward me as if we've known one another all our lives.

"Hobo," calls the young man, an English word, but the dog—Hobo—ignores him completely. He runs to me, and I loosen my fist, lower my hand so he can smell me. His cold wet nose buries in my palm. His tail wags so fiercely it swings the whole back half of his body.

Animals calm me. They always have. All animals, but especially dogs. Gillian tried to get the property management company to agree to letting us have a pet, "just a small one," she pleaded over the phone, but they never budged. So instead, as soon as I turned thirteen and was allowed to volunteer, we went together to our local shelter nearly every week. Gillian was more of a cat person but dogs were my favorite, so from four to six on Wednesdays, unless she got called away for a birth, we scrubbed out kennels and threw ragged tennis balls in the yard. This was something else the shutdown took from me; after we were all told to stay home, the shelters were closed to volunteers. The dogs must have been so lonely.

This dog goes from sniffing my hand to licking it and then climbs his front legs up my calves to take a sniff at the cylinder of my mother's remains. The young man comes over to grab the dog's collar and pull him away. He says the dog's name again, and I realize he's not saying "Hobo," he's saying "Robot," with a French accent—the word in French has the same meaning as it does in English. "Leave the lady alone."

"It's okay, I like dogs," I say in French. The words come easily, which surprises me, but the young man doesn't know that words are often lost to me, and so he makes nothing of the fact that they have returned.

"If you're sure."

I crouch and hold out a hand, and he releases the collar. Robot lunges into my arms, and his strong muscled chest, his rough warm pelt, the force of him is so solid, so reassuring, that I can soften again.

"He really likes you."

Almost all animals like me. They must know how I feel about them.

The young man kneels, too, but not so close as to make me nervous. Robot goes back and forth, nudging us with his nose and banging his fiercely wagging tail into our sides. We laugh, and it's like we know each other, just a little, because the dog likes us both. Finally, Robot settles. He thumps to his bottom and takes a few whacks at his ear with a hind leg, then lets out a deep sigh and lies all the way down, puts his chin on his paws. My hand is on his back, and I keep it there as I sink to sitting on the ground.

"Are you okay?" the young man asks again, sitting, too, but with the dog between us.

Again, I check myself—my posture, my expression, felt from the inside of my skin. *Be normal.* "I'm thirsty," I say, and he reaches into his pack and pulls out an old-fashioned metal canteen.

Briefly, I wonder if the water is drugged. You're not supposed to accept a drink from a stranger. But that's nonsensical, he didn't know he was going to find me out here. No one walks around with a canteen full of drugged water on the off chance they run into someone in the middle of nowhere. The virus floats through my mind as well, all the warnings the last year and a half about never sharing a drink, but I'm so thirsty at this point that it's a risk I'm willing to take.

The water is cool and fresh and vaguely metallic, but not in a bad way. I drink nearly half before I remember it's not mine, and who knows how long he needs it to last. I stop, wipe my chin, hand back the canteen. "I'm sorry. I didn't mean to drink so much."

"It's no problem, there's a glurb not far from here."

He doesn't say "glurb," of course. I don't know what the word he says means, but it must be a drinking fountain or a water bottle station, someplace he can refill the canteen.

"What's your name?" he asks, and I tell him. He offers me his hand. "I'm Adrien."

Reaching across the dog's back, I let Adrien take my hand in his. His palm is rough, but his grip is gentle and warm. "Very nice to meet you," he says. When he releases my hand, I let it fall to Robot's fur, relaxing into the rise and fall of his breaths. "What are you doing out here?"

"I'm lost."

"That much, I figured." He's grinning, but not like he's laughing at me, I don't think. "What happened to your shoes?"

"They're lost, too."

He reaches toward my face, and I flinch. He stops, his hand a white flag midair. Then he pulls it back to his side. "I'm sorry. It's just—the wound, there. It looks like it hurts."

He opens his pack again, searches through it. I take the opportunity to study him. His hair, longish, falls forward in dark waves, brown with glints of gold. When he looks up briefly, there's a hint of gold there, too, among the deep green of his irises. He returns to his pack to dig more deeply. There's a white line along the ridge of his left cheekbone, a scar, and I wonder how it happened, the injury that caused it. He extracts something from the bottom of the sack—a blue handkerchief—and douses it with water from the canteen before holding it out to me. His fingers are long; artistic, like mine. Gillian used to say that about my hands.

I take the handkerchief, dab it to my temple. Close my eyes at the cool relief of it.

"Your glurb," he says, indicating my foot, and then I learn the meaning of the word "ongle."

He returns to the sack and this time extracts a small, flat tin that reads ELASTOPLAST. Flipping it open, he extracts a bandage, basically a Band-Aid under a different name.

I thank him and set the cylinder aside, splash some water over my toe where the nail used to be, let it dry, apply the bandage. Protected, my toe feels immediately better.

What comes next? What should I do, or ask for?

Adrien isn't in a hurry; again, he reaches into his pack, which seems to be as magical as Mary Poppins's carpetbag, and he pulls out half a loaf of bread and something wrapped in waxed paper. Fish. Saliva fills my mouth, and Robot twitches to alert.

"Be patient," Adrien says to the dog, and he flips open a Swiss Army knife pulled from his jacket pocket, uses the tip of it to separate the fish skin, then removes the spine from the flesh in one elegant motion. Oily, pan-seared, fresh. He tears the bread and balances half of the fish on it, hands it across to me. Robot's eyes follow.

"You'll get yours," he tells the dog.

I've never eaten something so delicious. Adrien eats, too. The dog watches. When we've finished, Adrien tosses the skin—crispy, opalescent—to Robot, who catches it neatly.

I'm still holding Adrien's kerchief. I dab my mouth, the oil from my chin. "Thank you," I say, again.

He waves his hand to indicate that it's nothing, no problem. "Would you like to tell me what happened?" His voice is gentle.

Would I like to tell him? No. I would not.

"I'm grateful," I say. "I really am. But . . . I don't want to talk about what happened. If that's all right with you."

He glances at the cylinder in my arms. I'm cradling it. I hadn't noticed that I'd picked it up again. "I don't want to talk about *this*, either."

Adrien's eyebrows pull close, and I admire the arch of them. He wants to protest, but he's too polite, and so instead he raises his shoulders to indicate his reluctant acceptance and says, "Of course."

"Thank you." Then, "Listen. Do you have a phone?"

"Of course, yes. Back home." He stands. "Would you like to come with me? I wouldn't feel right about leaving you here, alone."

If he'd brought his phone, we could have checked for a signal and called the police. Adrien would have waited, I'm sure, until they arrived. As things are—no phone, and me, clueless about where we are—I have no choice but to accept his offer.

He digs into his bag once more, pulls out a pair of socks. "I'd give you my shoes, but they'd be much too large."

I'm careful as I pull the wool sock over my injured toe. It thrums like a tiny heart.

Adrien and Robot are standing, waiting politely. I get up, smooth my hair back from my forehead. I need to say something before we go. I need to make sure he understands.

"Bad things have happened to everyone these last few years," I begin. Frowning in agreement, he nods, so I continue. "I don't want to talk about any of those things. I can't. I just need to make sure you understand that before we go on."

It's his hands that show me that he does, indeed, understand. The way he laces together his long, calloused fingers, as if each hand can comfort the other, the way he wrings them, before he lets go and rubs his palms down the front of his pants, finds the crest of Robot's head, pets him gently. Adrien has had a rough time of it, too. For a moment I'm overcome with empathy—that's something people often misunderstand about me, about many autistic people; they think we are somehow emotionless, that we don't possess empathy. But the truth is that I *do* care, that I feel so deeply, that others' pain can fill me up entirely if I let it in. That was another thing Gillian tried to discourage: not to let it, if I can help it.

Still, I often can't help it. What has Adrien seen? Who has he lost? What hopes has the virus ended for him? I won't ask. The cost of privacy is privacy given, and it's one I'm glad to pay.

"I understand," he says. "Let's not talk about the past. Let's just walk, together, yes? We're two days' travel from my village, but there's another place—Montignac—that's closer. I'm glad to take you there. And we'll find you some shoes."

Montignac—that's the name of the village near the Lascaux caves. It's where I planned to get breakfast before heading to the International Center for Cave Art. I'd thought I wasn't more than a few miles away from there when I set up my tent last night. I don't know how I got myself so turned around that I've ended up this far from civilization. "There's nowhere else?"

"Lots of open country out here. I was heading to see a friend, but I can take you to Montignac first. It's no trouble."

It's a good thing I've run into this boy. "Thank you," I say.

Robot shakes himself; it's as if he's shaking off this conversation, maybe the past several years, as well, and wouldn't that be wonderful? If the shake of a dog's pelt could loosen and release all that has happened, all that we've suffered?

"Could I carry that for you? In my pack?"

The dog smiles up at Adrien with his wide, panting mouth. He trusts this boy, so I consider doing the same. But instead, I clutch the cylinder more tightly to my chest. Adrien shrugs, like it's the same to him either way, and then he hefts on his pack. Robot barks once, sharply, and the three of us head off, together.

The summer after Big Nora died, Gillian decided that we would take a trip. So she packed up the Miata and off we went, up the coast of California. At night, we slept in motels, and during the days we explored the wonders of the natural world. We walked on the wet, compacted sand of the seashore, my hand warmly safe in hers as the sea's white foam crept up and over my bare feet. We sat beneath the shade of an enormous fig tree whose roots, tall and gnarled, roamed like a mountain range beneath the great wide canopy. We stood in the thick white fog of early morning and listened to the barking of seals we couldn't see, stood and stared into the blinding white nothingness until, suddenly, magically, the fog burned away and there were the seals, on the shore and on the rocks jutting from the water—shiny-eyed, whiskered, leathery, huge.

The time from Big Nora's death until we took that trip is a blur, each day so like the one before and the one that followed that they could be interchanged without me noticing a difference. Time was a circle instead of a line. I did the same thing every day: staying alone on the days Gillian worked, hiding out in my little cave in the kitchen, drawing and reading. On the weekends we mostly stayed in, too, Gillian exhausted from all the extra hours she was working to make up for the grievance leave she'd taken. But when summer came and we took that trip, time began to fall into a line again, clear as the drive up the coast. And I began to form a string of memories, rooted along that line. One in particular endures, vividly, more than any other.

We were at the aquarium in Long Beach, our first stop. I was looking at a tall glass pillar that was filled with water and a school of little silver fish who swam as if they were one creature around and around and around in a never-ending loop. While I was watching the fish, Gillian ducked behind the pillar. Through the movement of the fish, through the clear clean water, through the curve of the glass, was Gillian. But, also, *not* Gillian. Her face through the water was wavy and loose. This could have been scary, but it wasn't. It was fascinating. That a face I knew so well—better than my own—could be distorted in this way, could become off-kilter and strange and yet, still, hers.

Maybe that was the moment I fell in love with the idea of perception, though of course it would be a while before I had the words to understand the concept. What something is, versus what something is perceived to be. Most people would say that Gillian's distorted face was simply a perception, that the real Gillian and her real face existed separate from that skewed impression. And, yes, I can understand that is objectively true, in that it is the only truth that can be objectively agreed upon. But to me, that wavy, unmoored version of my mother was not simply a perception. *That* version, in that moment, was true.

And when, a moment later, Gillian peered, smiling, from around the pillar's curve and her face was settled again . . . well, that, too, was true, wasn't it? How could one perception be more or less real than the other?

One final thing. When I looked through the curve of the glass and the school of silver fish and the wave of the water into the face of my beloved mother, the only person in my life anymore, the image was complicated by something else: the reflection of my own face, superimposed atop hers. If I looked with soft eyes, I saw my face; if I looked with hard eyes, I saw hers. If I did both at the same time—a trick I could do, but not with full intention or knowledge of how I was doing it—her face and mine fused into one.

Adrien leads us along the foothills. He's in no hurry; he goes at my pace. Robot runs forward and back, checking the trail ahead and then returning to me, nudging his nose into the backs of my knees as encouragement.

I knew the word for "river," but now I know the word for "creek," as well. I hear its burble. Robot does, too; that's when he runs ahead and doesn't come back. We find him chest-deep in the water, lapping eagerly.

"Thirsty boy," says Adrien, and the affection in his voice is clear. He peels off his shoes and socks and rolls the hems of his flannel trousers up above his knees. It's early October, but the day has warmed some, enough that he takes off his coat, too, and rolls the sleeves of his light brown shirt above his elbows. Wading in after the dog, he splashes water on his face before refilling the canteen. I find a place near the shore and wash my face. When I open my eyes, I'm struck by the same jolt as when I was a child at the aquarium, the jolt of perception. There is my face, but, also Gillian's, and—look—Big Nora's, too. Gillian's mouth is mine, and there is Big Nora's brow, the rise and slope of it. It's beautiful—painfully so—this glimpse of the women I've lost, in my own face.

I blink, stare harder, try to recapture them, but as when I was a child, once I'm trying to make the connection, to force the perception, it's gone.

I take off Adrien's socks and lay them beside me on a flat rock. I roll up the cuffs of my pants, blackened by the rich soil, and dip my feet into the creek. It's shockingly cold, and I yank them out by impulse. Then I lower them again, this time slowly, inch by inch. When they're submerged, the water rushes over them, and the pads and arches shift among the pebbly creek bed.

Adrien has taken off his shirt, thrown it to shore. He's splashing water across his chest, into his armpits now. It's such an intimate thing that I blush and look away, but the image of him remains: the nut brown of his neck, the sweet curve at the base of it, where the color shifts from tan to pale white. The pink of his nipples pursed and erect in the cold. The striation of his ribs when he lifts his arms. The concavity of his stomach; the way his trousers, though belted, hang loose on his hips. Underfed. How did he get this way? A rough bout of the virus, using up his reserves? Or maybe his family struggled financially during the pandemic, like so many others. It's possible that he's not on the road by choice. Maybe he's lost almost everything, his family too, as I have.

The sweater I was so grateful for this morning is itchy now, so I take it off. Down by the river the breeze is blocked, and I'm warm enough. The water is dappled in sun and shade, and along the shore tall reeds dip and weave and whisper. Leaning back, I close my eyes and turn my face up to the sun.

Adrien splashes back to shore, opens his pack and rustles through it. There's the clang of something metal and I open my eyes; he's dropped the bundle of rods to the ground, squats to untie them from one another. He feels me looking at him and glances up, smiling. An expression of surprise clouds his face, but he hides it so quickly that I could almost believe it wasn't there. "Would you like to fish with me?" he asks, the question almost a line of poetry in French.

I admit that I've never fished, and he offers to show me how. I should accept—I ate half of his last fish, and I owe it to him to try to replace it—but I'm so, so tired.

He reads my reluctance and is quick to say, "It's not necessary. Really. Rest, and maybe next time I'll show you how it's done." He opens a small red metal case, takes out a finely crafted orange-and-yellow lure, and ties it to the line. Then he goes to the water and casts. The current moves and takes his line with it. He lets it travel a way downriver before he flips a lock on the reel, stopping its spin. Only a few moments pass before he cranks the line back in and casts again.

The rhythm of the whir, the splash, the pause, the crank, the whir is calming. The sounds of birds in the bushes are, too, and Robot's panting as he comes and settles next to my side.

The warmth of the sun, made pink through my closed lids, the same pink as cast through the membrane of the bedsheet thrown across the table. The sensation of a breeze crossing over me, the tightening of my nipples in response to it, pleasant against the thin fabric of my T-shirt.

And then I understand what caused the shock I saw on Adrien's face. I check, and—yes—it's clear I'm not wearing a bra.

My face warms. But what a thing to be embarrassed about, the suggestion of my own body, when he's standing there in the river with no shirt on at all. And he's a Frenchman, too; aren't they used to breasts?

I could put on my sweater—maybe that would be the normal thing to do—but the sun feels so good on my arms, and the thought of the sweater feels confining now, smothering. Instead I rest my head on my sweater, turn on my side, and put a hand on Robot's flank. Together, he and I drift to sleep. Whir, splash, pause, crank. Whir, splash, pause, crank. Whir.

On that coastal trip with Gillian, the first place we went was the aquarium. After that, Pismo Beach, where we saw the seals. Then Big Sur, then Carmel-by-the-Sea, which made me think of caramels. Our last stop was Santa Cruz. Here, we stayed in a motel very close to the ocean; it wasn't fancy, but we could walk down to the beach by a steep set of stairs along one side of the building, passing through a rusting gate and out onto the sand.

It was the last morning before we'd drive back home. We woke very early and went down the staircase, Gillian carrying a bag full of towels and sunscreen, bottles of water and a wooden box. The sand—the way it had formed a paper-thin crust during the night, the way that crust cracked as I went, the way my toes sank through that hardness to the deep, cool embrace of the sand beneath—what it did was this: the crackle and buzz of worry and fear in my head, my shoulders, my heart; the particular itch on the inside of my skin that told me I wasn't safe, that the container of my body was ill-fitting and not to be trusted; the overwhelm of light, the daily sounds, scents, textures, and the new thing, too, this desperate absence where Big Nora had been, along with my newly gained knowledge about the random cruelty of the world—I don't mean to say that all of that went away, of course it didn't, but the crisp and delicate crust of sand, the crunch as my feet broke through it, the softness of the damp, cold, deep sand beneath—the surprise of it. The truth of it. The inevitability of it. I can't explain why it mattered so much to me. I can only recognize that it did.

We didn't make it much farther than the base of the stairs. I squatted down, dug my toes deep, and deeper, pushed my hands into the sand, too. Thumped to sitting, wiggled my legs into the sand, piled more sand on top.

And that morning on the beach, rather than bully or cajole me into hurrying up like she'd done before, when Big Nora had been alive—into going through the day, the world at *her* pace rather than mine—my mother flopped to sitting in the sand right beside me. She dug her toes in deep, and she paid attention to what she was doing, to how it felt; at least, it seemed to me that she did. She watched me and followed my lead, piling sand up the length of her calves, as I did mine.

The sun moved higher while we sat; other hotel guests, coming down the stairs, had to veer around us when they reached the sand, but still my mother didn't tell me what to do or hurry me along.

We sat and sifted sand through our fingers, raining it down like powdered sugar. We piled it up and dug until we reached dampness, hard-packed and satisfying to squeeze. We made a hole together, and then, as if she had read my mind, read my heart, she asked if I wanted her to bury me in it. I climbed in, sat cross-legged and still as she pushed sand in all around, crawling on her knees in a circle around me, scooping great handfuls into the hole. The press and hold of the sand all around—ahh. I could wiggle my fingers and toes—just barely. I knew that if I wanted to, I could thrash around enough to break out. But I didn't want to. The pressure of the sand was as if the beach embraced me. More than that. It defined me. It gave me edges and borders.

And when I was finally ready to pull myself out of the sand, my mother took my hand, and we walked together to the edge of the sea. With the water lapping our toes, she reached into her bag and pulled out the wooden box. "It's time for us to say goodbye to Big Nora," she told me. "Are you ready to say goodbye?"

I shook my head no, no, no, and she waited as long as it took for me to nod, finally, yes. Then she opened the box and turned it upside down, and the ashes fell dark and thick, they clouded the water, coated our feet, until the next wave came and took them all away.

The sun is setting when I wake. Adrien has pushed together a pile of kindling, leaves and dried grass, and he's just striking a match to light it. I've been dreaming of the past, and maybe what wakes me is that sound, the match against the striker. I'm glad to be woken, glad not to be dreaming anymore.

I sit up, wipe my cheeks, watch him touch the burning match to the kindling. Holding back the dark wing of his hair from his brow, Adrien leans forward, blows gently. When the first sticks begin to burn, he sits back on his heels. Then, he looks over to me, smiles.

He's fully dressed again in his shirt and coat. Nearby, he's got the fish strung from a line. Three of them—trout, I'd guess. Same as what we ate earlier cold, on bread. I hear my stomach announcing it's ready for another meal, and Adrien does, too. We both laugh.

"Where's Robot?" I ask.

"Off exploring. He'll come back when he smells the fish cooking."

I sit up, shiver, find my sweater and pull it on, then the socks. Then I pull my hair from the elastic and rake my fingers through it. It's dirty and tangled but I'm warmer this way, with it down.

Now that the fire is going, Adrien gives his attention to the fish. He's gutted them already, and I watch as he descales them, running the edge of his knife down their sides as if he's peeling carrots. He goes down to the river and returns with a skein of twine, dripping wet. He scores each fish, cutting little slits into the skin, then wraps each of them tightly in the wet twine.

"As soon as we have some coals, we'll toss them in." It's generous of him to use the plural first person. He kneels by his sack and extracts a bottle. "I don't know what I've been saving this for, but it's awfully heavy to keep carrying around. We might as well drink some, if you agree?"

It's an amber bottle with a handwritten label. There's a shadow of something inside, I can't tell what.

He opens a different tool on his knife—a corkscrew—and hands me both the bottle and the tool. "How about you open this while I get a bit more wood?" Then he wanders upstream, hands in his pockets, whistling, scanning the ground as he goes.

Before I open the bottle, I examine its label. *Calvados de Poire,* it reads, *de la Famille Forestier.* I don't know what "calvados" means, but I do know "poire" is "pear." I hold up the bottle so the liquid is made luminous by the firelight, and there's the shape again—it is, impossibly, a pear—impossible, because there's no way a pear this big could have passed through the bottle's slender neck. And yet, here it is.

I position the bottle between my knees and impale the cork with the corkscrew's sharp tip. It makes an unpleasant squeaking sound as I twist, and the sensation of the cork rubbing is also unpleasant, raising the hairs on my arms and sending a shiver up my spine. When I've gotten the screw deep into the cork, I wrap my fingers around the knife's handle and pull. It budges, but barely. Seesawing the handle, I wedge out the cork. A satisfying pop when it finally comes free.

It smells sweet with an alcoholic bite, and I peer down the neck in wonder at the miracle of the pear. I want to take a sip but don't. I wait, watching the fire and listening to it crackle.

Adrien returns first, arms full of wood, then Robot a few minutes later, grinning as he trots to us. "There you are. What have you been up to?" Adrien says to the dog, as if he expects an answer. He checks on the fire, seems satisfied. Takes the bundled fish and pushes them into the ash. "Twenty minutes," he tells me.

I lift the bottle to show him I've opened it, arrange my face into a smile.

"Ah, well done." He takes the knife, folding it closed and slipping it into his pocket. "I have just the one cup," he says, taking a thin disc of aluminum from a side pocket of his sack. It pops open into a cup, a clever design. I pass him the bottle and he pours in some of the liquid, hands me the cup. "I can drink from the bottle," he says.

"We can share the cup. I don't mind."

Too late, I remember he won't want to share a cup with me; it's not something people do anymore, since the virus. Maybe because I already drank from his canteen, he says, "That will work," and indicates that I should take the first sip.

I bring the aluminum cup to my lips. The liquid is sweet and strong and bright. Like summer.

Adrien has rolled out his bedroll near the fire and sits, gesturing an invitation. I hand him the cup, and he smells it, eyes closed, before taking a sip. "It takes me home, every time." His voice is husky—from the drink or emotion, I can't tell.

"How did they *do* that?" I point to the pear inside the bottle. "I've been trying to figure it out."

"Ah." He's lighter now, grateful for the chance to explain. "It's my family's calvados, see?" He traces the tip of his finger beneath "Forestier."

"Adrien Forestier," I say.

"That's me. The second of two sons. But the calvados has been a tradition long before I was part of the family. Many generations back."

"Okay," I say, "but how do you get the pear in the bottle?"

"The trick is not to *get* the pear into the bottle. One must have much more patience than that."

And suddenly, I see: Adrien in an orchard, a canvas tote full of empty bottles over his shoulder. He finds a hearty blossom on a limb of a pear tree, extracts a bottle from the tote, slips the bottle over the blossom.

"How long does it take for a pear to grow in the bottle?" I ask.

He laughs. "You're bright. Not that long—a season, only. The real wait comes after the fruit is grown. Alcohol is added, the bottle is corked, and then time must pass. How much time depends on how patient you can be." He hands the cup back to me. "Then, when the liquid is gone and only the pear remains, you can add more alcohol to the bottle. Recork, wait. Repeat."

The more I drink, the more I like it. Warmth goes down my throat and branches in my chest, like roots growing and spreading underground. I've never been drunk, and I probably shouldn't let myself take more than a few sips now; it's hard enough as it is to remember all the right things to do and say, all the right ways to be. And I like this, how Adrien is being with me, how I'm being with him. I don't want it to end.

Lovingly, Adrien traces his finger along the script on the bottle's label. "This is my mother's writing. She had good penmanship, no?"

Had.

"Yes. Very." I'm about to ask him to tell me what happened to his mother. Has she been taken, like mine, by the virus? But I'm the one who asked *him* not to make *me* talk about things, so instead of asking, I put the cup in his hand.

He clears his throat, sips, then hands it back, and I do too. Silence. As if sensing the shift in Adrien's mood, the dog wakes. His keen eyes watch Adrien.

The sky changes quickly now. The sun is just set, and that last purple bloom fills the sky. Almost as quickly, it's gone.

Adrien checks on the fish; Robot goes with him, sniffing as close to the fire as he can without burning his snout. I don't know by what metric Adrien determines that the fish is cooked, but something he sees must satisfy him. He has a single aluminum plate, from the same set as the cup I'm holding; he slips one of the fish onto it, cuts free the twine, and then the skin. Inside is fresh, steaming, pale meat. Robot sits at attention.

"Ladies first," Adrien admonishes as he hands me the plate and a fork—also aluminum. "You have that one. I'll eat next."

I could protest but he'd know I was being false, and anyway I'm pretty sure he'd insist. So I flake off a bite of the fish and spear it with the fork. It practically melts on my tongue. I close my eyes, taste more deeply.

"Good?"

I nod, take another bite. There's not much to say, after that. When I've finished, Adrien holds out the skin for Robot, who swallows it in one gulp. Then Adrien prepares the second fish for himself, and Robot gets that skin, too. The third fish, Adrien says, we can save for morning.

The fire is dying down. We sit cross-legged in front of the embers and pass the cup back and forth. I take the smallest sips I can. The stars are intense, so bright and so many of them, more stars than I've ever seen before. Many more than I remember from last night.

Last night. If the cyclops man had caught me, he would have killed me. Maybe he would have raped me first. Inside my head I see the arc of his headlamp across the wall of my tent, and now I'm trembling; it starts in my hands but soon it's my whole body, and I wrap my arms around myself, trying to make it stop.

"Are you cold?" Adrien asks. I don't want to tell him what happened; it won't change anything, and when I said I didn't want to talk about the past, I meant it. I don't want to talk about last night, or anything before it, and even if I did want to, I couldn't in a coherent way, or in a way that would allow me to maintain my mask of normalcy. It would undo me, to talk about the past, and I don't want Adrien to see me undone, to know that part of me. He seems to like this girl—lost, yes, but not broken. I don't want to be broken, in front of Adrien. I want to be attractive to him, the way he is, to me.

Adrien shrugs out of his coat and lays it over my shoulders, still warm from the heat of his body. It smells of the fire and the earth and of boy. It's such a normal thing to do, so classic and romantic, storybook, almost. I like it very much. It takes a little while, but my body finally calms.

Adrien leans back. He's staring up at the stars, deep in his own thoughts. I admire his shadowed profile: the straight line of his nose, a full, almost womanlike softness to his lips. He feels my stare; turns; smiles. The perfume of calvados is on his breath.

Breath, or death.

I lean in. His lips part and there's a moment, a hesitation. Then, he leans in, too. His lips are as soft and warm and sweet as I wanted them to be, and now my hands are in his hair, and his are on my face, my neck, but gentle, so gentle, an electric sweep of his thumb across the rapid pulse at the base of my throat, and my fingers tangle in his hair and I want more of him, more of *this*, right now, here. Yes.

10

At the beginning of my junior year, a boy whom I had always been aware of, but who never had been aware of me, suddenly was.

His name was Gregory. The things that I had always been aware of included: the fact that he made easy friends with everyone, so comfortable that he would even compliment a teacher on a new haircut; his obvious intellect, almost always earning among the highest marks on exams; his body, which was beautiful, but more than that, his ease in it.

In February, he invited me to go with him to Winter Formal. This was my first invitation to a school dance. I never minded not going to dances; they took place in the school gym, and I figured they were similar to sports rallies, which were mandatory affairs also held in the school gym during third period, and which I hated. The rallies were loud, echoey, exhausting explosions of chants and cheers and foot stomping, punctuated by the squeal of rubber-soled shoes against the lacquered wood floors.

Early in my high school career, my mother had encouraged me to "give it a try," to show up at a dance and just see how it went. I refused. When she said that I couldn't dismiss it until I'd experienced it myself, I'd outlined my expectations: bright lights flashing over a dimly lit arena packed with students; itchy fabrics and too-tight shoes and bodies knocking into one another, both accidentally and on purpose; speakers blasting music, most of which I wouldn't like; overly sweet beverages and dry, crumbly desserts. She admitted that I wasn't far off the mark.

But when Gregory Gershan invited me to Winter Formal, I accepted.

Gillian had always had so many feelings—frustration, and sadness, and worry, too—about how hard social stuff was for me. I know she would have loved it if I'd brought friends home after school every now and then, or if I'd been willing to do the things she remembered so fondly from her girlhood, like being on a team (she'd played volleyball) and going to sleepaway camp (she'd gone to Camp Newman, in Santa Rosa). And she took it almost personally when my teachers wanted to conference about my behavior or share their concerns about how I almost always spent my lunch hour in the library or—that long winter of eighth grade, when the library was closed for renovations—in the girls' bathroom. So when I told Gillian about Winter Formal, it was like she'd been waiting years for this moment. "We'll go dress shopping together," she said, literally *clapping* her *hands*. She was so excited that I went along with it, even though I would have much rather just ordered something online. Her selection was knee-length, with a wide neck and short capped sleeves, the entire thing covered with red sequins. I knew without trying it on that I would hate it, but I put it on anyway. It did look beautiful on me.

It fit my body the way I knew it was supposed to—in particular, my breasts, which I quite like. I have always loved breasts—my own, and others' as well. But my arms brushing against the sequins was intolerable. When I told Gillian this, she took a breath, then told me to pick one I thought I would like. I chose a dark green velvet dress that was the same cut as the red dress, but the velvet was gentle, and it warmed in a way that sequins cannot.

"You look so beautiful," she told me, and I felt it. I felt beautiful.

After we left the mall, in the car, Gillian hesitated before she put the key in the ignition. "Dearheart," she said, "I'm going to talk with you about something, and I'd like you to hear me out before you make a decision, all right?"

It was a deal we had, something we'd worked out together back in middle school, when she'd wanted me to sign up for an extracurricular activity and I patently refused. The deal was this: I didn't have to do the things Gillian wanted me to do—but I had to agree to listen and really give the idea a chance. That time in middle school, she explained that she didn't like the idea of me spending so much time alone in the apartment. When I told her that I wasn't alone, that I had my art, she clarified that she didn't like me spending so much time *without other people* in the apartment. And that it would be up to me to choose the activity. She'd support it, whatever it was, as long as I chose something that met at least two afternoons a week. I considered it and chose a still life class at the community center. The other students were mostly senior citizens, which didn't thrill Gillian, but she kept her word and supported it. And to her credit, it was something I enjoyed, and stuck with, all the way up until the pandemic.

In the car after the mall, she told me she wanted to take me to her clinic to introduce me to a midwife she worked with, Bonnie. "I just want you to know your options," she said, "and I don't want you to have to hear about them from me." There was no one at the clinic she trusted more than Bonnie, Gillian told me, and I could trust her, too.

At the clinic, Bonnie, who was very friendly and smiled after every sentence, said she was going to explain birth control methods. I told her that I had no intention of having sex anytime soon. "Better safe than sorry," Bonnie said. Her recommendation was the IUD. She could numb my cervix so I would barely feel it going in. Another option was the implant, brand name Nexplanon, a slim rod no bigger than a matchstick that would be inserted under the skin of my upper arm and would release a chemical into my body that would prevent pregnancy and wouldn't have to be replaced for up to five years. A step down from that was the shot, just as effective but for a shorter period; I'd need another shot every twelve weeks. And then, of course, the Pill—highly effective as long as I remembered to take it every day, at approximately the same time. All of these, Bonnie explained, were best if used in conjunction with condoms, both as a backup method of preventing pregnancy and as the only reliable preventor of sexually transmitted infections.

"If you have to use both anyway," I asked, "then why not just use the condom?"

"Condoms can fail, too," said Bonnie.

"And people can fail to use condoms," said my mother. In that moment, I knew my origin story.

I remember being confused that I was even being offered some of these options. Gillian had never been okay with any sort of chemicals going into my body, and she had only become more intense about such things after Big Nora died and I stopped speaking. She had joined a network of "Autism Warriors," moms who shared tips and tricks about how to parent their spectrum kids—ways to sneak unpalatable foods like spinach into brownie mixes; detox protocols for "healing" from vaccinations the kids may have already been subjected to; do-it-yourself ABA regimens to help overstimulated kids learn to control their reactions. I didn't love a lot of what came from this; there was the CAM specialist (short for "complementary and alternative medicine") who prescribed one treatment after another: detox foot pads, which were supposed to draw out toxins through the soles of my feet; a barrage of special diets, including a gluten- and casein-free regimen Gillian did along with me for nearly eighteen months until she finally broke down and we binged on pizza together (one of my happiest food memories); chelation therapy, these pills I had to take that were supposed to bind the toxins in my blood, moving them to my digestive tract so I could pass them when I went to the bathroom. The pills made me sick to my stomach.

She was always reading some study or following some expert, telling me why I couldn't have my favorite brand of ice cream anymore (it had artificial food dyes and propylene glycol), why we had to change detergents (phosphates, formaldehyde), why we had to switch out my toothbrush for a bamboo one (microplastics). She even moved my medical care from the pediatrician I'd been going to since I was a baby to a naturopath named Dr. Bob; he was willing to write a medical exemption letter so I wouldn't have to get any of the vaccines that kids are supposed to have in middle school.

But I guess the only thing worse than toxins is unplanned pregnancy, because I left the office with my arm sore from the Nexplanon implant and a long string of packaged condoms in a rainbow of colors.

Back at our apartment, Gillian asked if it would be okay if she gave me some advice. My arm still hurt, and I wasn't so sure I wanted any more advice that day. But Gillian waited patiently, and at last, I nodded.

"If you want this boy to like you, dearheart, you need to remember to pay attention to the things you show him about yourself. He doesn't need to see *everything*. Try not to do that thing with your hands, and smile when he's talking to you. Ask him questions about himself, and only talk about yourself when he asks you questions—don't get caught up in one of your rants. Okay?"

She had been telling me variations on this theme since I returned to school in the second grade. If I wanted to be invited to birthday parties, I needed to talk to the other kids on the playground. If I wanted someone to pick me for their team in PE, I needed to smile sometimes. If I wanted someone to sit next to me at lunch, I had to learn to put a lid on the things I wanted to talk about, when I felt like talking. No one wanted to hear about dog breeds or philosophy theories or paint textures ad nauseum, dearheart.

During grade school, when I did the things she suggested and obtained the desired outcome, it was as if she'd given me an incantation that made magic happen, or, by the time I was old enough to be certain magic wasn't real, like she'd taught me how to apply a formula to produce a result. If I followed the formula and did the right things in the right order at the right time, I'd get invited to a birthday party, or be picked for a team, or have company for lunch. That didn't mean the advice didn't hurt my feelings. Sometimes, it could feel as if I was supposed to pretend to be someone I wasn't. And I didn't like the way that felt.

That evening in our apartment, though, I realized that the thing Gillian wanted for me and the thing I wanted for myself were the same. We both wanted Gregory Gershan to like me. To *like me* like me. So I decided to take her advice.

He arrived just a few minutes after seven on the evening of Winter Formal. He'd asked me what color my dress would be and had chosen a necktie in a similar shade of green. He brought me a corsage—luckily, the pin-on kind, not the type one wears on an itchy band of elastic around the wrist. Gillian took our picture in the garden area outside our apartment building. Before we left, she pulled Gregory aside and whispered something to him. His eyes grew wide, and he nodded. In the car, I asked Gregory what she'd said, but he wouldn't repeat it.

The dance was exactly as awful as I had known it would be, but I wasn't sorry to be there. Gregory was friends with everyone, and he carried me along on the conversation like the ocean buoys a boat. We danced, some; I liked the slow songs, when he put his arms on my waist and I put mine around his neck, and we swayed. He smelled like chemical pine trees, and it was not unpleasant. The fast songs I didn't like, and I refused them after a little while. Gregory was a good dancer and enjoyed it, so I sat at a table while he joined the mass of bodies, bobbing up and down. I kept my hands in my lap and did my best to make my face look normal and smile "but not like a deranged person," as Gillian had instructed.

There was one moment late in the evening when it could have gone all wrong; the DJ played a song that everyone else seemed to know and love—a fast song, loud—and all around me everyone started to holler and yell and wave their arms, and the DJ cranked up the music even louder until everything began to vibrate, and whoever was in charge of the lighting made it so the lights were pulsing, too, on and off and on again, in time with the beat of the music and the thrum of the crowd and the vibration all around, and I was already full to the brim from everything—this was too much for me, far too much. I had to get out of the room. My chair fell over backward as I left the table and ran for the door.

In the hallway, I shook my hands hard, flicking my fingers, shaking off the sound, the lights, the tightness of everything. I stomped on the floor, glad I hadn't worn heels, felt the sting-slap of the linoleum on the soles of my feet. I could still hear the music, but it was muted by the auditorium's heavy door, and the hallway lighting was offensive but not painful. It would have been *not good* if Gregory had seen me like that. As nice as he was, it would have been too much for him, too weird, but luckily, by the time he came out in the hallway to find me, I'd managed to pull myself together, managed to arrange my face and my body and my hands in a way that looked normal, or normal enough, and I told him I'd just gone to the bathroom.

Better than the dance was afterward, when Gregory drove me home. He pulled to the curb in front of my apartment building and turned off the engine. Music played, but not too loudly, and he took my hand. He told me that he liked me because I was different than the other girls. I didn't gossip or care about stupid things like fashion or hair. I might have told him that he was wrong—that I wasn't categorically opposed to gossip (after all, gossip is a tool that facilitates bonding as members of an in-group trust one another with shared information), but rather that the other girls had not often chosen to share their information—or time—with me. I might have told him that I actually find fashion very interesting, and that I appreciate the art of it, but may not appear to appreciate it because when I break from my uniform of T-shirts, sweaters, jeans, and also anything other than natural fabrics, it's like I'm putting on another person's skin. For example, the dress I was wearing—I would have told him these things, but I remembered Gillian's advice and said nothing. And then he kissed me.

It was my first kiss. I liked it very much. The way our lips fit together, the feeling of someone else's tongue in my mouth. Alone in my bed late at night, I'd imagined what it would be like to be kissed, sometimes imagining the girls in my classes, sometimes, the boys, but this was nicer than I'd imagined. Even when our teeth clinked together, that was fine, too.

When he pulled away, I made a little sound and leaned in again, and Gregory laughed but in a nice way, and moved his mouth to my ear where he did something with his teeth and lips and tongue, and hot breath blowing out and then cold suddenly, as he sucked in, that felt both deeply practiced and very effective, and I wanted to do whatever it took to have that sensation again. It was worth all the rest of it—worth the dress shopping and the visit to Gillian's clinic and the Nexplanon implant and the crowded auditorium and sitting at the table and smiling until my cheeks hurt and even the loud, terrible song, toward the end. And I was grateful to Gillian, for helping me make myself seem like a person Gregory might like.

We would have done more, except for whatever Gillian had whispered to Gregory before we'd left. Because when the light flashed on in the kitchen of our apartment, he froze. Then he leaned back and cleared his throat, said he'd see me again, in class.

I suspect Gregory and I would have eventually gone further together. I would have liked to. But before we had the chance, we were all told to stay home from school. Just for two weeks, they said. To help flatten the curve.

After that, I never saw Gregory again.

The bedroll is narrow, and not as warm as the nylon sleeping bag I've lost. I wonder what possessed Adrien to choose something so bulky and inefficient, but it's unimportant when we're lying in it together, my head resting on his arm, behind me, the whole warm, electric length of him, his other arm across my waist, pulling me against him more tightly.

He sleeps, but I stare into the last red embers of the fire, thinking of Gregory. How different that was, from this. Compared to this, with Adrien, I can tell that what we did in Gregory's car was not that different from when I watched him dance: a series of moves, practiced and perfected, pleasing. Performed. This, tonight, with Adrien . . . I don't know how to define it, how to classify it. Adrien was not performing.

I like to match meaning to experience. I like to know what something is, the correct words to name things. It comforts me.

Adrien and I kissed for a long time. Nearby, full on a supper of fish skin, Robot sighed contentedly, which made us laugh. I let my hands go up under Adrien's shirt, feeling the warmth and hardness of his chest. He held me, touched my face, my neck, the line of flesh just above the V of my T-shirt. I felt his desire, I thrust myself forward to encourage his hand, wanting him to cup my breast in his palm. But instead, his hand went to the small of my back, and I had to be satisfied with the way I flattened against his chest as he pulled me close, closer, closest. It all felt so . . . normal. So nice, and so normal. Gillian would have been proud of me, how normal it all was.

Now, as Adrien sleeps alongside me, I touch my lips, remembering.

When I wake—it's very cold—Adrien is up already, repacking his sack. My cylinder is there, leaned carefully against a rock, beside the plate and cup. Glancing at me, he smiles, looks down. He seems nervous. Is it possible that he's had even less experience with girls than I've had with the two boys I've kissed? This seems unlikely, as attractive as he is, but the pandemic has made many improbable things true.

Or maybe I said or did something last night that made him sorry. Maybe I hadn't been as normal as I'd thought, maybe I hadn't managed to show him the right parts of me and tuck away the rest. Maybe I made a weird sound, maybe I kissed him wrong. And I'm just about to speak—to apologize, even though I'm not sure about what—when Adrien clears his throat. "Listen," he says. "Nora"—my name in his mouth, the way his accent shapes it, enough to make me want to be kissing him, again—"I don't want you to think that anything is expected of you—that is to say, that I would want to push anything on you . . . just because of our situation. You are in a vulnerable place, and I would hate to think—that I . . ." Here, he trails off. His mouth twists, uneasy; he's worried *he's* done something wrong, that he's pushed me to do something I didn't want to do. Actually, the reverse is true—I wanted to do much more than we did. If it had been up to me, we wouldn't have slept nearly as much.

"Please don't feel that way. I—" How can I say what I want to say, without being weird? "—I had a lovely time last night."

Adrien's hands, which have been twisting the straps of his pack as if he's trying to wring juice from them, relax. His eyebrows peak together, earnestly. He has unusually earnest eyebrows. I almost tell him this but on second thought choose not to. It might make him uncomfortable, knowing that I am making judgments about the qualities of his eyebrows.

"You're sure? I want you to know, you're safe, with me."

"I know I'm safe. A dog as good as Robot wouldn't like you if you weren't good, too."

At this, he laughs. I like the feeling of making him laugh. "Well," he says, "I've known dogs who'll go to whichever hand holds the meat, regardless of the character of the person who holds it. But, as you say, Robot is unusually glurb."

Robot, hearing his name, trots over. He nudges his snout into Adrien's hand, his way of asking if it's time for breakfast. The three of us share the last fish, Robot gorging on the skin again. It's comfortable now, tension gone.

"I could eat fish every day and never grow tired of it." I suck the last of the flavor from my fingers one by one.

"Be careful what you wish for." There's a wryness in Adrien's voice that suggests maybe he's eaten fish too many days in a row to be as fond of it as I am.

When we've finished eating, Adrien folds his bedroll and attaches it with straps to the bottom of his sack. I offer to refill the canteen, and Robot gamely accompanies me to the creek. The sky is wide and blue today, and the water, sparkly and sapphire, reflects it. A long-legged crane takes slow steps in the shallows, peering beneath the clear surface as it goes. Robot splashes after the crane, who flaps away a few feet, then resumes its dignified walk. It's chilly this morning, but Robot seems oblivious to temperature. His long pink tongue unrolls in the fresh clear water, scoops.

I've left the socks up by Adrien, and I roll up the cuffs of my corduroys. The water is bracing, clearing the remnants of last night's calvados from my brain. It's been an odd string of events, between the cyclops man and this time with Adrien and his dog, first terrifying and then kind of wonderful, disorienting, the ups and the downs are dizzying, so it's no wonder that I'm sort of spinning, no wonder that the world feels . . . different. Not quite as it should, I guess.

We'll go to the village—to Montignac. I'll find the police. They'll be able to help me recover what's left of my things, and I'll file a report. Then I'll have to get new supplies—including shoes—but my bank card is gone, and my passport . . . What a mess.

A whine, the press of a cold wet nose into my cheek. Robot, nudging me. I've been shaking my head back and forth, hard, the way I sometimes do—I hadn't noticed until his sweet snout stopped me. I glance up to the campsite; relieved that Adrien's back is to me. He didn't see me acting weird. I pet the dog's head. "Okay, buddy," I tell him. "Thank you."

Robot is right, of course—better not to spin myself out. I still have the remains, I still have a direction in which I'm heading, there are things I have not lost. One thing first, and then the next. First, water. I unscrew the canteen's cap and dip its mouth into the creek. When it's full, I drink. The water so cold it sends a shiver through me as I swallow.

At the campsite, Adrien is kicking dirt over the ashes. The fire has been out for hours, but I appreciate his caution. This time, when he offers to carry my cylinder, I accept. He lowers it into his pack with care, fastens the tie and then the strap. Then he watches mournfully as I retrieve the socks from the rock where I've left them and pull them on. "I wish I had something better to offer."

"Between the bandages, the socks, the fish, and the calvados, you've been quite generous."

He smiles, and I smile, and it feels like maybe we'll stand here smiling at each other all morning, so I ask a question just to break the spell. "You mentioned yesterday that you were heading to a friend?"

"Yes, but it's no problem. I'll drop you in the village first, and then I'll head back out. I'm bringing him some supplies."

"Your friend . . . is he very far in the wrong direction?"

"No, actually. An extra hour, hour and a half at most. If you are feeling up to it, you might be interested. He's near a cave. It's quite special. Maybe you'd like to see it?"

A cave? Could it be this simple? "What makes it special?"

"Oh, I'd hate to spoil the surprise."

What strange and fortuitous luck, that Adrien was headed to the exact place I was going. A sign, perhaps, that I am right about taking my mother's remains there. And, a little voice whispers in my head, if I go with Adrien to the caves before Montignac, we'll get to spend more time together.

"Okay," I say. "I think I would like to see it. Very much."

He offers me his hand. "All right, then."

* * *

We walk like that, hand in hand—someone else is holding my hand—for most of the morning. When the trail begins to thin and wind up into the hills, we have to separate, and my hand is emptier for having been held. That's the cost of having had something nice, isn't it?

"Tell me about the friend we're meeting." I ask mostly so that I can enjoy the sound of Adrien's voice as he answers. I don't really care about his friend.

"Ah, Jacques." Adrien's tone is warm. "It's been a long time since we've seen each other." A long branch blocks the trail; Adrien pulls it back, gestures for me to go through ahead of him. I continue up the path; when he speaks again, his voice is behind me now. "He's a funny kid. Passionate. He was so excited to return to the cave. He wasn't able to go for the past few years." Adrien's voice is easy; the hike isn't taxing him.

Like the museums in Paris—in San Diego, too—the International Center for Cave Art must have been closed during the worst of the pandemic. I'm glad it's open again now. The closer we get, the more hopeful I am that this will be the right place to leave my mother's remains, after all.

The elevation steepens, and I slow. It isn't easy to hike in socks. Robot winds behind me, pushes his nose into the back of my knee, as if he senses I'm flagging.

"Robot, leave her be."

"I don't mind," I tell him, looking over my shoulder. The tall pack on his back, the soft wave of his hair. He's a beautiful boy. My urge is always to say what I'm thinking, and I almost tell him this—that I think he's beautiful. But that would be a weird thing to say to a boy, I know Gillian wouldn't have approved, so instead, I ask him if he's had Robot since he was a puppy.

"No, actually. Robot was my cousin Marcel's dog. But Marcel had to go away, of course. He was the age of enlistment. I promised to look after Robot until he returned, but when he got home, he decided it would be best for Robot to stay with me. I have more time to spend with him, you see, and because of—because of all I'd lost. Marcel was very kind to let me keep the dog."

Adrien's voice has grown serious, and the back of my neck prickles. I don't understand all the nuances of what he's saying, or why this Marcel would have to "enlist"—if that indeed refers to military service when used intransitively, as it almost always does in English—or what for, but I do understand that we're venturing into the territory of recent history, and the losses suffered, and if Adrien starts telling me about who the virus took from him, and how, my already-tight throat will close the rest of the way and my skin will itch and I won't be able to breathe, let alone walk and talk. I swallow; my throat is swollen. Then I manage to say, "It's been terrible. But please, let's not talk about it."

Adrien is quiet, a heavy, awkward moment, and I'm afraid he is going to push forward, to insist. But at last, he says, "Of course, of course." And we go on, in silence.

11

It's midmorning when Robot's ears rise sharply and he dashes ahead, brushing past me as he goes.

"He must smell Jacques," Adrien says brightly, and it's good to hear levity in his voice again. We've barely spoken since I asked him not to tell me about what he's lost. *Who* he's lost.

A whistle—clear, loud, three quick notes, a pause, and then a fourth, longer. Adrien whistles in return, the same pattern. His face breaks open in pleasure, and he quickens his stride. "You don't mind if I pass you, yes? It's just a little way ahead." In his excitement to be reunited with his friend, he doesn't wait for my reply. If his ears could perk up like Robot's, they absolutely would.

He breaks into a jog, and then a run, even with the heavy awkwardness of his pack shifting side to side. He's around a bend, and I'm alone for a moment. Then there's laughter and two voices. One, Adrien's; the other must be Jacques's.

Something is strange—I don't see anything that looks like an "International Center for Cave Art." I recall the façade of the building from the images I'd seen on my phone; I recall, too, the main road I was to take to get to it, I had a picture in my mind of the parking lot it led to, and the cars and tourist buses that would fill it. Instead, we're at a point in the trail that barely widens, still in the middle of the French countryside, not a sign of civilization.

It seems a huge coincidence, that there might be two noteworthy caves so close to each other . . . but then, I suppose, I'm not sure how caves work, if there are areas populated with many of them spread over an expanse. Whatever the explanation, though, this cave to which we've been walking is not the one I'd been aiming for. Yet again, I'm wrong about where I thought I was. It's such a disorienting feeling, like being tossed under by a wave. I shouldn't have assumed, should have asked more questions. Sighing, I follow the sound of voices.

When I get there, the two young men are in each other's arms, each slapping the other's back, holding themselves apart to take a good look at each other, then embracing again, all the time speaking a French so rapid that I only catch scraps of words and phrases. I find myself smiling, despite my frustration at this detour, at the knowledge that Adrien has been speaking slowly and carefully for my benefit. Behind them is Jacques's camping setup, and beyond, the small rough mouth of a cave. Definitely *not* the cave I was hoping for.

Jacques turns to me and grins. His straight dark hair is cropped close at the sides with a long, raven-like wing on the top, falling forward into his eyes. Like Adrien, Jacques is also thin, but he's quite a bit shorter. There's something birdlike about him; clever and eager, he's in constant motion, and he comes over with a wide smile, taking me by the shoulders and kissing my left cheek, then my right, and then the left, again, before saying, "Poor American Cinderella has lost her slippers, and what kind of Prince Charming is our Adrien, eh, if the best he can provide for you is socks?"

"I gave her fish, too, and calvados." Adrien looks a bit insulted at the implication that he's been a poor host.

"Fish is not footwear." Jacques drops a wink before turning to a green canvas tent set up near the entrance to what must be the cave Adrien had been talking about. "Lucky for you, Nora, I have ladylike feet." He dips inside and returns with a pair of hard-soled leather boots.

"Oh, no, thanks, but I couldn't."

He waves the shoes in the air, making them dance. "I insist."

I hesitate a moment more. "I'll pay you back when I'm able to log into my account again."

He quirks an eyebrow like he has no idea what I'm talking about, and I wonder how I've bungled the French badly enough to be incomprehensible, or if maybe I've done something odd with my face or hands. Then he turns back to Adrien, and they return to their animated conversation. I move to a camp chair on the far side of the tent to try on the boots.

The chair, like the canvas tent—and like Adrien's bedroll and backpack—they could have been imported from another time, in the middle of the last century. They're in great shape—too much so to be actual relics. I wonder what it is with these boys, if it's a regional thing, as we're so far from any big cities, or if it's just a thing in their group of friends, this predilection for vintage gear. Even the boots: the leather is worn but of good quality, and each eyelet is rimmed in a thin band of metal. The soles are attached to the uppers by little nails, pounded at regular intervals all around the perimeter. The laces, too—they're round, rather than flat like the shoelaces in the boots I abandoned . . . the night before last? Is that right?

Adrien is saying something to Jacques—he mentions a brother. I am trying not to listen, but it's quiet out here, and sound carries, and even though he still speaks quickly, I catch the phrase "still in the hospital. I don't know how long."

And then Jacques says, "Glurb glurb glurb your mother," and I don't need to understand all the words to know that he's offering condolences. My eyes flash up; Adrien's shoulders are drooping, his chin wavers, tears pool in his eyes and then they are spilling, spilling down his cheeks.

The smaller boy grabs Adrien roughly and pulls him into his arms, and I untie the shoelaces, so that I can tie them again.

Jacques has a banged-up metal percolator, and when Adrien goes into his pack and retrieves a small paper bag that reveals itself to be full of ground coffee, Jacques oohs in delight and sets to work making us a pot.

"I don't know how long it's been since I last had a decent cup of coffee. Or even a *shitty* cup of coffee!" He's practically dancing as he sets the pot to boil. He finds two mugs—one ceramic, one tin—and Adrien fetches his collapsible cup from his sack. Jacques splashes some water into a bowl for Robot, who slurps it before coming to sit beside me. When the coffee is ready, we drink it in silence; the boys' reverence is palpable, and I'm grateful, too. Normally I'd take cream in my coffee, and sugar, but neither is offered, and I don't mind. It's strong and bitter, earthy and fortifying. And it's so nice just to sit here, with Adrien and his friend, and Robot nearby. It feels . . . cozy. Safe. Like a place that maybe I could relax, for a while.

When the cups are drained, Adrien says to Jacques, "I'd like to show Nora the cave. Is that okay?"

"Sure." Jacques turns the percolator nearly upside down over his mug, trying to get a few more drops. "I'll stay here and keep Robot company."

Adrien picks up a silver flashlight from where it rests outside of Jacques's tent. He tucks it into his back pocket and offers me his hand. Walking in Jacques's boots is a fantastic luxury, after the ground I've crossed over the last two days just in socks. At the cave's entrance, I stop to let my eyes adjust. This may not be the cave I was expecting, but, anyway, I'm intrigued. A pleasant scent wafts out on cool air, like clean, dry dirt.

Just a few steps in, I stop again. It *is* cooler in here than out there, remarkably so. I tell myself the shiver that tingles my spine is because of the change in temperature, nothing more.

"Don't be frightened." Still holding my hand, Adrien steps closer; I'm warmed by the heat from his body. He finds my other hand in the dark, pulls me toward him. As my eyes adjust, he becomes more than a voice and two hands holding mine: there is the curve of his face, the way his hair forms curls around his brow; there is the set of his shoulders, which, with a jolt, I know I would already recognize, anywhere; here is the warmth of his mouth, lowering toward mine.

This time, it's Adrien's hands that go beneath my sweater; wide, warm, calloused, his hands roam the expanse of my back. Fear gone, and in its place, desire. I stand on my toes, step in between his legs to get closer. He tries to move his hips away, but I go with him, and then we're at the cave's wall and he's pinned between it and me, and I curve my pelvis against the hardest part of him.

He moans, or I do, and a rush of warmth floods through me. I'm surprised by my boldness. I've often felt like a brain floating above a body, but here and now, I am my body. Is this what Gillian meant, when she used the word "*integration*"? She's gone, and I can't ask, now or ever. A sting of tears wanting to spill, but I close my eyes against the shadows, squeeze them tight, press myself against this other body. This is where I want to be. Right here, in this strange cave in the middle of the French wilderness with this boy, Adrien Forestier, the boy with the sad eyes and sweet dog, this boy here, who is kissing me, now.

There's only so much kissing you can do pressed up against the wall of a cave. I'd like to find what that limit is, but after a while, Adrien breaks away.

"Nora," he says, and the sound of my name in his mouth makes me lean in, again. At last, husky, he says, "Let me show you around a little bit, hmm? Jacques will be insulted if we don't tell him how impressed we are by his cave. And then—if you'd like—perhaps we could find you a room for the night? In Montignac?"

A room. A bathtub. A bed.

I kiss him again. His hands on my hips, Adrien gently pushes me back a step. He could have moved me easily all along, if he'd wanted to.

We arrange ourselves, me tucking in my T-shirt under my sweater, finding the hair tie in my pocket and making a ponytail, him, turning to adjust himself in his pants, raking his hands through his hair.

Then he takes my hand again. "I really do want to show you this place," he says. "It's unlike anything you've ever seen."

We've been down here long enough now that our eyes have adjusted, and we don't need the flashlight's spot to navigate. But then we take a slight turn, and all light is cut off. True black. A rustle as Adrien pulls the flashlight from his back pocket, a click as he turns it on.

The eye of light recalls to me the cyclops man. It's okay, it's okay, my brain tells itself, but only half believes it.

Adrien's pointed the flashlight now on the cave's far wall and is staring, rapt.

The circle illuminated by the flashlight has captured something—what is it? First, shapes. Dots, short dark lines stacked neatly atop one another. Peaked arrow tips. Squares. Then, an animal of some kind. Swaybacked, round bellied, it could be a horse or a cow, but from its forehead protrudes a long horn, a slash of dark pigment. A unicorn? Its flank is decorated with swirls, mostly black, one, rust-red.

They're incredible. Ancient paintings, some of the earliest that have ever been found, discovered about eighty years ago.

"Wait." I'm tumbling again. "I don't understand."

"It's incredible, yes?"

"It's impossible," I whisper.

"I thought so, too, when my cousin first brought me here. Marcel—he was the one who found this place first—he insists that Robot should get the credit. He followed the dog into a hole, a big hole, where a tree had been uprooted in a storm."

A dog, a storm, a hole—but this can't be. "I don't understand," I say again.

The flashlight plays against the wall, farther into the cave. More animals, cow-like, or oxen. Then Adrien points the flashlight up, overhead. Horses.

"Marcel went in after Robot, and that's when he saw them—these paintings. He didn't know anything about ancient art, but he knew they must be old. He came back next day and brought a few others with him, including Jacques. Eventually, of course, experts in such things learned about the discovery. They excavated the entrance, and told Marcel not to let the caves get glurb, you know, to keep them safe. Jacques took it upon himself to guard the entrance, and he camped here every night until it became unsafe to do so, but he's back, now, at his post."

Adrien moves the light across the horses, making them dance. Their hoofbeats thudding on a prairie as they run.

My throat constricts, I force out a single word: "When?"

"When did they discover it? Six years ago." His arm lowers; the light drifts, aimless, to the dirt floor. He's no longer here, with me in the cave. He's seeing something else. Something terrible. A muscle in his face tenses and jumps, frightening.

Then he turns, looks into my eyes, and says, "Just a few months after we were forced to surrender to Germany."

I don't want to ask. I have to ask. "Adrien. What year do you think it is?"

I can't see his face clearly, for the dark in the cave. I blink my eyes against it, but it does no good. There are no walls, no light. Just dark. But I can feel Adrien's hands on my arms, the soft warmth of his breath on my face as he answers: "It's 1946, of course."

12

When I was little, I believed everything Gillian believed. I mean, if a grown-up tells you a fairy is coming into your bedroom in the middle of the night to retrieve a fallen tooth and replace it with money, when you're a kid, you believe them. Why wouldn't you?

Gillian was never big on the tooth fairy, but she did have strong beliefs about living toxin-free and eating clean, so those were my beliefs, too.

Then, in seventh-grade science, we had a unit on viruses. My teacher, Ms. Callum, loved to give pretests—"We have to know what your assumptions and misbeliefs are before we can refute them," she said. I didn't love school, but I did love being right, and I was used to scoring at the top of the class on pretty much everything we did.

When Ms. Callum returned the pretests, she laid them face down on our desks the way she always did. I flipped mine over to reveal the lowest grade I'd ever received. C minus. Next to the grade: *Looks like you've got lots of room to grow here!* And a smiley face.

I raised my hand. "Ms. Callum. You scored my test wrong."

"If there's an error in the scoring, hon, you can see me after class, all right?"

I stood. "You gave me a C minus."

"I didn't *give* you a C minus, Nora. You *earned* a C minus."

The class burst into laughter. It was hot, the sound, hot and loud, and my eyes burned with it, burned with the sound and my tears.

The statements I'd marked as True: "Vaccines can cause the viruses they are intended to prevent"; "Most vaccinations are made from live viruses"; "Vaccines contain unsafe toxins"— Ms. Callum had marked all of these as false.

"You're not a good teacher."

"*Ooh*!" The class, as if one voice.

"That's enough, Nora."

In the Myth Busting section, where we were supposed to circle common misbeliefs about viruses versus bacteria, I'd only circled one "myth"—that antibiotics can treat the flu, which I knew wasn't accurate; Gillian had long told me that antibiotics were only good for treating UTIs and destroying the natural gut microbiome. But according to Ms. Callum's marks, I should have also circled three others. The quiz blurred through the scrim of unspilled tears.

"You scored my test wrong."

"Nora, I'm going to need you to sit down right now."

"I'm going to need *you* to change my grade right now." Blood pounding in my ears. Heart pounding in my chest. Paper crinkling in my hand. Everything too tight.

"All right, Nora. You can go see the principal." She scrawled a hasty note, ripped it from her pad, waved it at me. "Give this to the front office."

By middle school, I had learned that I could hold myself together all day, and then, when I was home, I could use the quiet of my room and my art as a release valve, slowly emptying the well of anxiety and tension. And lots of these kids hadn't even known me when I was younger, so they'd never seen me fall to pieces. Maybe they thought I was weird or different or nerdy, who knows what they thought before that day—but I know what they thought *after*. After I refused to leave the room until Ms. Callum changed my grade. After I started shaking my head back and forth, back and forth. After Ms. Callum called the nurse, principal's office forgotten, "Just take her somewhere to calm down." The nurse, patting my back—"Okay, hon, shh." My hand fisted around the shameful quiz. A boy's voice, I don't know whose—"Did *you* know that she's retarded?"

At home, the wrinkled quiz flattened on our kitchen table: "It's not your fault, dearheart. There are a lot of misbeliefs. Even among smart people, like Ms. Callum. The quiz doesn't ask *anything* about the chemicals that can be in vaccines or say a word about potential damages. So one-sided. I'm going to have a talk with that teacher."

All I wanted was for the bad grade to go away. All I wanted was to un-hear what the boy had said.

I took two days off school. When I returned, everyone pretended that nothing had happened. I don't know what sort of conversation Gillian had with Ms. Callum, but the upshot was that I was exempted from the rest of that unit and went to the library to do free reading.

But a seed of doubt had been planted, an uncomfortable scratching in my brain. The sense that maybe Gillian was . . . wrong. Or, if not wrong, maybe not entirely *right*. So I brought the science textbook with me to the library. There, in black-and-white: *A vaccine causes your immune system to produce antibodies to a particular virus. A vaccine is a preparation made from weakened virus particles or their empty protein coats. That is why vaccines do not make you sick.*

A few years later, when the pandemic began and everyone started to die, when the whole world was hoping together for a vaccine . . . then, I did my own research. I read dozens of articles—some explained the groundbreaking technology that was being used to create this new vaccine; some documented the incredible speed of development and global collaboration between scientists, governments, and pharmaceutical manufacturers; and others praised the unprecedented rollout of delivery. I also waded through the opinion pieces and social media posts of self-proclaimed "Granola Moms," people who sounded a lot like Gillian; they were deeply opposed to the idea of injecting toxins into their children, argued that natural immunity was the best immunity, and worried over the possible long-term effects of this new vaccine—after all, more than one of them said, look how the MMR had fueled the autism epidemic.

Horrified, I went to Gillian. I tried to explain that she'd been misinformed, or misled; I explained why vaccines are good, and safe, and that what she was hearing from her online groups wasn't only wrong, but also *dangerous*. But she wouldn't believe me. She wouldn't listen.

And she began to rotate through theories the way you can thumb through pages of a book, each more extreme than the one that preceded it:

It was no worse than the flu, not really. It was a *plan*demic, designed to crush the middle class. It was a side effect of corporate greed and the rollout of 5G technology. It was a biological weapon created by China.

It was a result of the proliferation of genetically modified crops, which allowed for the proliferation of viruses. It was bad, but not nearly as bad as the US government wanted us to believe; case numbers were inflated, and many of the worst cases being reported were "false flags," trying to distract us from other, more sinister plots.

Then, finally, a vaccine was released, along with a mandate: in order to return to work, health care workers—like Gillian—had to get it. And once the vaccine was approved for kids and teens, all students would have to get it, too, in order to go back to school. That was when Gillian tipped entirely from worry and concern into rage. It was the MMR vaccine I'd been given when I was little, she told me, that made me autistic in the first place. This virus, she decided, had been manufactured and released by Big Pharma. Their goal all along was to inoculate everyone and make huge profits while injecting us with a dangerously untested chemical brew. "The MMR 2.0," she called it, and she forbade me from getting injected.

I think she must have gotten infected at the protest outside of Rady Children's Hospital. She'd rallied dozens of her local breathwork students to attend—she'd been leading the group for nearly a year, she had students from all over. This was their first chance for an in-person meetup, and by then, they had grown quite close. She wanted me to go with her; I refused, but I watched a video about the protest online. So many faces—all angry, all unmasked. Their signs—

DEFY FASCIST LOCKDOWN

WE WILL NOT COMPLY

NO NAZI VACCINE PASSPORTS

OUR KIDS OUR CHOICE

MASK MANDATE = AMERICA'S HOLOCAUST

I DON'T COPARENT WITH THE GOVERNMENT

THEY WON'T VACCINATE ME ALIVE

VACCINES ARE POISON

VAX FREE AND THRIVING

WE WILL NOT COMPLY

The camera settled on a tight clutch of protesters. I knew before the camera found my mother that she was at the center of it. I knew because of her sign. That morning, she'd borrowed my good markers to make it. Each letter a different color, a rainbow-cheerful invitation: ASK ME ABOUT MY VACCINE-INJURED CHILD. The camera shifted to settle on Gillian's face. It filled the screen. Trembling, I closed the browser window to make her disappear.

Three days later, she was sick. Two days after that, so was I.

I don't know how I make it to the mouth of the cave.

But there I am, standing on the tongue of a giant, the rim of the cave's opening his jaw, the curved ridge above me, his palate. The hot flush of adrenaline across my chest, the sudden stink of my own panic sweat.

"Nora?"

There are things I'm good at: breaking down a problem into smaller parts and handling them, one by one. Understanding in a painting where the light source is, and how to indicate it on a canvas. Following the work of other, better artists, replicating the masters. Doing hard things. Really hard things.

In art, it comes to me almost as a gift: my ability to reproduce the work of true artists, great ones. And those same skills, Gillian told me over and over again, could be put to good use away from my sketchbook, as well. Reproducing what it was to be a normal person. *Watch, learn, imitate.*

As a child, the idea of pretending that something that wasn't happening, was, or pretending to be someone I was not, was ludicrous to me. But it was important to Gillian that I learn to pretend, and I trusted her, and over time I got better at it. It was always effortful, never easy, and I could only ever really manage it when I was calm. When I wasn't calm, when I was scared or upset—or, like now, when I'm scared *and* upset—the best I can do is limit how much I reveal. And even at that, I have often failed.

So I don't try to put on a happy face when I turn to this dangerously deluded boy, tell him that I'm leaving and that I'll appreciate if he doesn't try to talk me out of it or follow.

Still, he says, "Nora, what's wrong? Did I do something? If I did, I'm so sorry—"

But I shake my head hard, and don't hear what he says after that. When he understands that I'm serious, that I'm leaving, his voice turns clipped. This could mean that he's angry, or it could mean that he's trying not to show that he's been confused or hurt by me, or it could mean both. Or maybe all it means is that his voice turns clipped. What is meaning, anyway?

"It's not far to Montignac. You just take that path, go about three kilometers. You'll come to the Vézère—a river. The homes are split on its two banks—you'll see smoke from the stacks—and you'll want to go to the far side to find the village center. But Nora—" His voice softens, the words growing more vulnerable, and so I hold up my hand. There is a rational explanation for this cave, this place. I have no idea what it is, but there must be one. I need to get away from here—from Adrien—so I can sort things out.

"Thank you for what you've done for me." That's all I say.

Jacques is staring at me, mouth open. I should offer to return his shoes, but I don't. Robot barks once, twice—perhaps he would have made to shoot after me, because I know from the choke of his bark that Adrien has grabbed him by the scruff. At Robot's cry, I stop. I look back. Robot is panting, grinning, mouth wide. His tail wags as if this is a game, as if any second Adrien will release him and he'll run after me, or perhaps I'll run back to him. To them.

Adrien—he doesn't grin. If he had a tail, it wouldn't be wagging. His fist, grabbing fast to Robot's scruff, is white-knuckled. He looks like someone who knows what goodbye is.

You can't change people. I learned that from my mother. She tried to change me, after all. She did everything she could. She taught me how to hold my hands still at my sides and how to count to five while looking into people's eyes. She taught me how to walk flat on my feet instead of balancing on the balls of them. She taught me to put my hands in my pockets when they crept up close to my chest. She taught me to look closely—at art, at people, too—and do as they did. She taught me that people don't always say the things they mean, and that they don't always mean the things they say.

You can't change what people are, or what they believe. When someone is committed to believing something—whether it is true, or not true; whether it is about medical conspiracies or which century it is—you can't change their mind. Not on human scales of time. I tried, I really, really did. But I couldn't save my mother.

About the location of Montignac, at least, Adrien was correct. After I've followed the path for about an hour, there's the blue shimmer of a healthy river, and beyond, smoke puffing up from the village chimneys. What I should feel upon seeing those rising gray clouds, those redbrick stacks . . . I should feel relieved. Down below, in the distance, a pleasant little village, not much more than smudges of color and shadow. Down there are people. Authorities. Help. Someone who will file a report about the cyclops man. Someone who will maybe offer me a shower and a clean bed for the night, a phone so I can call my bank.

I'm alone. It was insensible to pretend otherwise, to lie with a boy by a fire or stroke the sun-warmed flank of a friendly dog.

The village is a quaint one, with old-looking structures built atop older-looking foundations, not unlike so many others I've visited. The near side of it is quiet. It's dinnertime, which might be why everyone is inside, or . . . I'm not sure when France had its last wave of the virus, if it was just recently, like it had been in the States; people here are surely still cautious, either way.

My shoes—Jacques's shoes—echo, clip clop, as I take the road toward the bridge. The sun is nearly gone and, just then, old-fashioned streetlamps flicker on with an electric buzz.

From a window above comes a woman's voice. She speaks too quickly for me to catch the words, but her tone is singsong, and then another voice—a child's—in response.

"No, Maman! I don't want to take a bath."

The mother's voice again. This time, I understand: "You must, my darling. You stink."

Their two voices, laughing. The crank of a faucet, the splash of water against porcelain.

I've stopped walking. I'm standing on the sidewalk, listening to the bathtub fill. I run my hand across my cheeks to dry them and make myself move on.

The bridge over the river is made of stone. They're amazing things, bridges. There should have to be a bridge in place in order to build a bridge. This is what I mean: the stones on either side of the bridge, on the banks of the river—those would be easy enough to place. But then come the stones that connect the spans between support columns, stones that float in arcs across wide blue swaths of water, held in place only by one another. How do they get there? Who put them there? Gravity is defied by the existence of a bridge.

A bridge is hope. That's what I've always felt. And so, in spite of the sound of water splashing into a tub, in spite of the expression on Adrien's face, I'm a bit better when I step onto the bridge. People built this bridge. People who were determined to go forward—whichever direction "forward" was for them—and so, in spite of the river, in spite of gravity, forward, they went. At the bridge's crest, I stop. Down below, the water is quiet, but it moves. Always, a river moves.

On the far bank, more of the little village rests under the pinkening sky. If this were one of Seurat's paintings rendered in a network of points, my mother would love it. (Would have loved it.) High, peaked red roofs cap sandy-colored stone structures. Cheery shutters, robin's-egg blue, frame windows. Another building: yellow bricks, a brown shingled roof. A peekaboo window way up in the attic, rounded like a sleepy eye. Down the way—a church spire, and from it, the crisp, clear ring of a bell. One, two, three, four, five, six.

The final knell takes a long time to fade, its vibrations moving through me. Six o'clock, and all's well. That is what people say in old movies. Six o'clock and all's well.

It's too much to hope to find a police station waiting for me on the other side of the bridge, but I scan the street for one, anyway. A few parked cars dot the curbs, all of them classics, but clean and in good shape. Why all the old cars?

It's 1946, of course.

It's cold. I need to go inside. Just ahead, light gleams above a green door. A restaurant, or a pub. I reach into my pocket for my mask before remembering that my pockets are empty. They'll think I'm one of *those* Americans. But there's nothing to be done except explain what's happened—the cyclops man, my things, abandoned.

Here comes a woman out of the pub. She's not wearing a mask. She turns to speak to someone behind her. Her silhouette, the bridge of her nose, the turn of her smile. A lovely woman. Her hair, neatly back in twin blond waves. A yellow scarf looped loose around her neck. A pressed brown sweater, a full skirt, woolen stockings, sensible shoes. There's a little leather handbag in the crook of her elbow. A man follows her out the door, pauses to put on a hat. He taps two cigarettes from a case pulled from the inside pocket of his coat; hands one to the lady, tucks the other between his lips; takes a lighter and offers her the flame, protecting it with one hand as he leans in. An intimate thing.

Once hers is lit, he brings the lighter to his own cigarette. Now there are two bright embers burning. Tucking away the lighter, he offers his arm; she takes it. Together, they come up the street, toward me.

"Excuse me."

"Yes?" The man pulls the cigarette from his mouth. "Can we help you?"

Up close, in the shadows of early evening, details of their dress: the sharp tilt of his hat's brim; the double breast of his coat. The fine leatherwork of his brogues. Her stockings. The length of her skirt. The sunshine wave of her scarf. The finely drawn line of her red lip.

Now, again—I'm underwater, spun, uncertain, lost.

There are questions I intended to ask, questions I practiced asking in my head on the way to the village, to make sure I got the French just right. *Where is the police station? May I borrow your phone? Can you help me?*

But instead: "What year is it?"

The woman's clean brows arch. "What *year* is it?" she repeats, and looks to her companion.

He's dubious. He jerks one side of his mouth in a grin, takes another quick pull on his cigarette. The ember glows fiercely as he breathes in, fades again. "Is this some kind of joke?"

Something in my expression must convince him that it isn't, because the grin fades. He looks to the woman again, then back to me. He drags once more on his cigarette, and his words ride out on a cloud of smoke. "It's 1946, of course."

13

The day my mother came back—the first time that I met her, at least when I was old enough to remember—was my fourth birthday. Big Nora and I were Doing Colors.

It was my favorite activity. This is how it worked: Big Nora set out four clear glass cups. They were small and sturdy and difficult to tip over, which was their best quality, after clarity. One of the glasses held water; each of the other three contained diluted food coloring in a primary color: always, from left to right, blue, red, yellow. Alphabetical. In each glass was a dropper. In front of them was a row of nine pipettes.

I would pick a color to start—usually, blue. Sometimes, yellow. Sometimes, red. Occasionally, I'd begin with clear; that's what I called the uncolored water. You can guess what happened next: pinching each dropper carefully, exactly, I'd begin to combine colors in the pipettes. Blue plus yellow equals green. Blue plus red equals purple. Yellow plus red equals orange. Those were the secondary colors.

If I mixed the primary colors with the secondary colors, other colors emerged: yellow orange; red orange; red violet; blue violet; blue green; yellow green. These were the tertiary colors.

I could also lighten the shade of any color, in a way, by adding clear to it.

The day Gillian returned, something very important happened. For the first time, I realized that I could perhaps invent new colors if I were to combine two of the tertiary colors. The thought occurred to me right before the words formed in my brain; a strange tickle, not unpleasant, went up from the base of my neck to the top of my head, making my hair electric, as if it stood on end. Until this moment, it had never crossed my mind to combine tertiary colors. On the kitchen table, there were only ever nine pipettes, plus the original four cups. That meant that there were twelve colors (plus clear). The constraints Big Nora had created for me had limited, until that moment, the vastness of color. Never mind that every day and all around me, I saw far more colors than I could create in my pipettes. Those colors did not translate to me as "Colors" in the same way as the Colors I created at the kitchen table. Nine pipettes plus three glasses equals twelve colors (plus clear). A tidy, closed system. A knowable system. A replicable system.

Doing Colors was finished when I had filled the beakers in front of me, and sometimes (when I was feeling wild), when I'd added some clear here and there, lightening things up a bit.

That day, the moment I realized there were more color combinations than I had fathomed, the world cracked open. Because if I could combine tertiary colors with other tertiary colors, and combine primary and secondary with tertiary, as well, then—given enough pipettes—I could combine those colors with one another, and so on, and so forth, and so on. This meant . . . could it mean? Yes, it did, I was sure of it:

The world is not a safe and closed and knowable system. There exists, far beyond my abilities to perceive them, an infinite number of color combinations and possibilities.

To a true artist, this would perhaps be an incredible revelation. But to me, just-turned-four-years-old Little Nora, who had yet to be diagnosed as autistic but was still very much aware of who she was, to whom limits and walls and locks meant comfort and safety, to whom nine full beakers plus three glasses of primary colors (plus clear) equaled having Done Colors to completion . . . it was not incredible. Well, in the actual definition of incredible—so extraordinary as to seem impossible—yes, it was incredible. But it was not *welcome*. I was falling, falling, falling, and there was no end to the falling, that was the worst thing of all: the colors could never cease to be combined, to be recombined, to be re-recombined; there were no limits, no walls, no locks, only a threshold, which I had crossed and, once having crossed it, I could not uncross. And only more thresholds beyond, thresholds all the way down.

I screamed. I screamed, and I swept all the cups, all the pipettes, all the droppers from the table. They crashed and shattered against the wall; the colors ran down like raindrops on a window, combining in a pool on the floor.

I was still screaming when Gillian let herself into the apartment with the key she must have taken when she left, which she'd carried with her for the previous several years, during which Big Nora didn't know where she was, or what she was doing, or who she was with, or if she might return, or when, and thus, neither did I.

She did return, just then, as Big Nora knelt beside me in the colors and the shards of glass, as she held me tight, as she formed for me limits, and walls, and locks, as I screamed and cried and railed against them—not because I didn't want her to hold me, but precisely because that was what I *did* want, and I needed to know if these walls, *her* walls, could fail me, too.

"What's the matter with her?" said the stranger in our kitchen as

Big Nora held me, rocking, amongst my ruined work of Doing Colors. That's the first thing I remember my mother saying. Maybe there were other words: "Hello," or "I'm back," or "Guess who," as she turned the key in the lock. Those five words, as I screamed and screamed.

I'm screaming again now. The woman has dropped her cigarette; the ember burns quietly. The man has gone back into the pub; through the window, I can see him with another man, this one behind a glass partition, talking on a telephone. His mouth is moving. Is he making meaning, meaning I can't understand? Or is there no meaning without understanding? Who is on the other end of the receiver, listening? Are his words making meaning to the receiver? A receiver is the part of the telephone that translates the electrical signals into sound. The receiver is also the person who receives. Is the purpose of meaning to be received? The woman reaches toward my arm but stops just before her fingers meet my— I'm dead. The cyclops man chased me, and I ran, and I tripped and fell and hit my head, but I did not get up again. Or— Maybe, not dead. No, I'm still there, lying on the ground, unconscious, and— Or maybe I'm in a hospital bed. Maybe there are needles in my veins and tubes feeding liquid into me. Machines are hooked up, too—blip, blip, blip, that's the sound machines make. I can't wake up because I've hurt my brain. It's swollen in my skull, they'll have to get a saw. Buzz, buzz, goes the saw. When they bring it to my temple it won't hurt because they'll have numbed me, or because my coma is so deep that I can't feel. Or it *will* hurt, it will feel exactly like what it is, a sharp, vibrating electric saw, cutting through my flesh and bone to open up my head, to relieve the pressure on my brain. But if it hurts, I won't be able to move. I won't be able to tell them or show them how it feels, the terror of it, because my brain believes that I'm here, in 1946, and that a blonde lady with a scarf around her neck nearly the same as my butterfly wing a yellow silk scarf with green flowering vines Big Nora's scarf on this stranger but really not because this is a dream a hallucination a thing inside my head there is no woman taking me now by the shoulders gently but firmly lowering me to sit on the curb beside a cobblestoned street she is not pressing my head down between my knees she doesn't tell me breathe just breathe shh it's going to be okay here comes the doctor he's going to help you the doctor will bring the saw and he will buzz it vibrate it against my temple *you can't let the doctors get ahold of you Nora you can't let them poison you* it will hurt and I will bleed and my skull will chip and fragment until he gets to brain and I'm up I'm screaming and kicking and biting too they can't cut me I won't let them even if there is no woman here no man in clean shining brogues no doctor with a bag with a needle and then there is a pain wait *is* there a pain is this real what is real is there a real there is a pain in my arm, and then the heartbeat *my* heartbeat slows

down

strong still

but slow

and steady

and more arms take hold

of my arms

of my head

of my legs

and the world is made of water and I float away

to nothing

14

I'm lying down, but somehow, I'm also moving. I don't know how this is possible because I can't open my eyes. This may be because I'm lying on dewy grass, face turned up to a blank, uncaring sky. This may be because I am in a coma, one either accidental or medically induced, and only my consciousness is moving, not my body at all. This may be because I'm dead and have no eyes to open.

When I find the strength to lift my eyelids—they must weigh a hundred pounds each, and who knew there were muscles, specific muscles, that a body must use to open them?—I see, briefly, that I'm in the back of an ambulance. A man in a white coat looks down at me, his face arranged in concern.

I'm struggling now, but I can't move my arms, either because they are restrained or this is a dream or both. Still, I struggle. The crunch of tires on a gravel road; the animal sound of my own garbled voice, struggling to make meaning but failing to; the soothing French of the man in the white coat: "Shh, just relax, I'm giving you something now to help you relax."

A cold influx, then, of liquid into a vein in my hand, up my arm—the path the liquid takes as it moves through my body's venous network, a network I have never seen and yet which I believe in.

And then it becomes too difficult to struggle to make meaning, to make meaning of this place and this situation, to make meaning by moving my lips and tongue and teeth. And the tiny muscles whose job it is to raise my eyelids fail, and it's dark again.

Later. Days, or hours, later? Is there "later," after death?

This time, I don't remember opening my eyes. They're just open. I'm in a room. The walls of this room are stone. A window is set into one wall, high up. Through it, light streams in.

I am in a bed. It's narrow, metal framed. The sheets are rough but clean. They are white. My hands, lying upon them, also white.

There's a bandage across the back of my right hand. That is where the needle was.

My arms are bare. I touch my body and find I'm wearing a thin garment, short sleeves and a rounded neck. This garment is not mine. This, more than the absurd walls, more than the high window, more than the rough, clean sheets, causes me to sit up.

Doing so hurts. My bones, my muscles, everything is sore. There—across the room. A door. Beside it, a straight metal chair. On it, my clothes, folded. Atop them, a yellow scarf. The lady's scarf, from Montignac. Beneath the chair are the shoes—Jacques's shoes, tucked neatly side by side. They're beautiful, paired beneath that chair—the light, the shadows—they could be the composition for a painting.

I close my eyes and am in van Gogh's *Bedroom*. Van Gogh himself felt the painting expressed repose, "à la Seurat," he said. But when I saw the painting in one of the art books Gillian and I bought at a yard sale, I didn't see repose. I saw shifting lines. I saw instability. It was a question of perspective. Maybe everything is.

Being in van Gogh's *Bedroom* helps my anxious heart return to a quieter beat. I walk myself through it, a room as familiar as my own, back at our apartment—

No, don't think of that room.

"In flat tints, but coarsely brushed in full impasto," wrote Vincent to his brother Theo, "the walls pale lilac, the floor in a broken and faded red, the chairs and the bed chrome yellow, the pillows and the sheet very pale lemon green, the bedspread blood-red, the dressing-table orange, the washbasin blue, the window green. I had wished to express utter repose with all these very different tones."

Primary colors. Secondary colors. Tertiary colors. It is restful to me, to see and name them. The narrow wooden bed is pushed into a corner. Framed portraits and a landscape hang on the walls above it. I trace the triangles of wire from which the picture frames hang. A mirror above the washbasin. A towel on a hook by the door. Two pillows on the bed, side by side. Two chairs, seats woven in rush, both empty. This is a thing I can do. I can close my eyes and enter a painting. I can leave the world I'm in, for a moment, for an hour. When I return, I'm calmer. It's always worked, and it works now.

I open my eyes. I'm once again in the plain stone room. I stand on shaky legs, I cross to the chair, I take the pile of clothes and go back to my bed. *My* bed. When did this become *my* bed? It's not my bed. It is just *a* bed. Or maybe it's *the* bed. It's *the* bed I woke up in. It's *a* bed in a room. But it's not *my* bed. I don't have a bed anymore.

My clothes are freshly washed; they're even pressed. I unfold my underwear and pull them on. It's disturbing that someone has removed them from me, handled them, handled me. But I push this away, this disturbance, and narrow myself to only the task of dressing my trembling body. The corduroys next, and I tuck the yellow scarf into a pocket before pulling off the nightgown. The air is cold on my bare flesh. I shove quickly into my T-shirt, then my oatmeal woolen sweater. It's scratchy in a way I like, a way that is knowable and known.

Adrien's face, just a flash, as I hold up his socks, but I blink it away. I return to the chair, sit, pull on the socks, careful with the little toe that has no nail—its bandage is gone—step into Jacques's shoes and lace them. Then I go to the door. The doorknob is a smooth porcelain ball. Will it turn, or will it be locked? I grasp the ball and twist. The door opens easily.

Like the room, the hallway is made of stone, the floor of roughhewn wood. It stretches long and empty in both directions. Other doors, all closed. There's no difference that I can tell other than one way goes left and the other, right. I go left, stepping softly to quiet the heels of Jacques's boots. I pass one door, and then another. As I go past a third, a voice behind it stops me.

"How are you today?" the voice asks, in French.

"I am well, thank you," comes the response. "And you?"

"Fine, fine. Nothing to complain about. Lovely weather, yes?"

"Oh, yes. Fine, fine."

It's a perfectly normal conversation, except the same voice is holding both sides of it.

At the turn of the hall, a woman, sixty-five or so, sits in a chair. A linen handkerchief holds back long gray-black hair. She wears a simple dress, gray wool, with elbow-length sleeves and a skirt that reaches to her knees. She must hear me coming—as carefully as I step, Jacques's shoes are not quiet—but she doesn't look up. Her hands are busy, crocheting a dress. She's working on the collar. The armholes are unfinished. The dress is white.

I don't want to break her concentration, even as I need to ask—*Where am I?*

A moment later, she does look up. Her eyes, traveling from the fine needlework to the planes of my face, take a moment to focus. When they do, she smiles, a wide beautiful smile. Her teeth are yellowed, lined by age and nicotine. "Hello, dear." Her hands go still, but she doesn't release the crochet hook. "You're new here. My name is Marguerite Sirvins."

I intend to respond, but it's not possible. My throat is a hallway of burrs. I choke out a sound, but it's not a word.

Marguerite Sirvins stares past me. I turn, too, but there's nothing. Her gaze comes back to me. "You should come to my wedding. My dress is almost finished. Look."

The embroidery is fine; the thread she's using is thin as filament. It's a dress of possibility. Of beginnings.

"I will be married when I turn twenty-one," she continues. Her voice is dreamy. "I've died one hundred twenty-two times. I have been crushed eleven times. I have married seven times, already. This will be my eighth."

The burrs twist. I need help, but we're alone.

"Now," she says, "I hear someone speaking to me morally in my glurb. All my bones are broken. My heart is gone. I think even my glurb is missing. They transposed it. They had to cut off a piece of my arm, and they put it back."

Again, her fingers fly busily with their work. The dress is beautiful, a piece of art. I'm so afraid, I don't know if I want to sit down or run.

"I asked for hot chocolate at breakfast," she says. Her voice is plaintive now. "I get watery soup in the morning, at noon, and at night. How can a person be healthy? The eyes pop out. The nose weeps." Her hands go still. Her chin sets defiantly. "And since I never get omelets, rabbit, or chicken, judge what kind of health I'm in."

Marguerite Sirvins doesn't notice that I'm backing away. Her eyes are down, her fingers caress the lacework. "I asked for hot chocolate at breakfast," she says again.

At the end of the hallway is an open door, double wide. I move faster now, no longer concerned about the report of Jacques's shoes on the floor, rubbing my hands down the front of my corduroys as if the woman's madness is something I could catch. Ahead—voices, but I can't make out words. Shadows and shapes, but I can't make out faces.

In the doorway, I stop. This room too is stone-walled and ancient. Its floor is newer, tiled in black-and-white linoleum squares set on the diagonal. It's a big room, too big for what it contains: about a dozen people sitting around a few scattered tables, some round, some rectangular (the tables, and the people); a Ping-Pong table that no one is using; a piano, shuttered and quiet by the far wall; a small stage behind it. Artwork on the walls. A shelf with some books and games. The men are dressed in shirts and trousers; some of the women wear skirts, others, pants. There's a man in a chair, rocking back and forth. One young woman is pregnant, maybe six or seven months along; she sits near a window with another woman, this one very thin, in a long red skirt, with a red scarf covering her hair. Both of them looking silently out. It looks like a scene from an old black-and-white film, except for the fact that it's in color.

This isn't real. That's the sensation I have, even though no one thing seems unreal. The walls are stone. The floor is wood. The tables, the chairs—they're sturdy. The people move—playing chess, darning a sock, and there, the man in the rocker, rocking.

Then I see that his chair has no rockers.

"Miss, hello. How nice it is that you are awake."

I startle at a man's voice, behind me. The accent, I can't place. Not French, nor American.

When I turn, he has his hands up, showing me his palms as if to reassure that he means no harm. He's a funny little man, short and stocky, bushy dark curls beginning to recede, thick dark brows, round tortoiseshell spectacles over bright black eyes; a personable mustache, worn with a sense of playfulness. He's ruddy—brown-red, the color of a person used to the out-of-doors. A collared shirt and corduroy blazer, both rumpled, and dark green trousers, also rumpled.

"Welcome." He keeps his hands up a moment longer before slowly lowering them and offering me one to shake. "You're safe here. I promise you that. No one will hurt you."

People promise things. That doesn't make them true.

I don't want to shake his hand, and so I cross my arms instead. He doesn't look offended. "Would you like . . . ?" Slowly, he reaches into the pocket of his blazer to extract a pack of cigarettes—rumpled. With some effort, I manage to shake my head no. When the words go, other ways of communicating are difficult, too—gestures, the ability to write.

He taps out a cigarette, puts it between his lips, mustache vibrating. From another pocket comes a lighter. A flame, an ember, a deep inhale.

"Ah." His mustache settles. "Now, shall we?" He indicates an empty table, two chairs.

The young women sitting by the window get up, the thin one offering her pregnant friend an arm. They pass us on their way to the hallway; they're too absorbed in one another to notice us, but it's clear they aren't bothered by this rumpled man's presence. So I follow him to the table.

He pulls out a chair, nods for me to sit. "Tell me: Do you know where you are?"

I don't know where I am, but I do know that not answering questions is rude, at best. I don't want to seem rude—or worse—but the burrs in my throat grow larger, and I can't even make myself shake my head.

Fortunately, he doesn't seem bothered by my lack of response. "I am François Tosquelles. I'm the doctor here, in charge." He raises his hands, palms toward the sky, as if to indicate that this embarrasses him, or perhaps that it's a thing that's out of his control. The cigarette emits a thin, acrid trail of smoke.

The woman in the hallway. The man, rocking without a rocker. The doctor.

"May I ask," he says—Dr. Tosquelles says, the doctor in charge says—"and you may simply nod or shake your head: Do you know your name?"

I want to nod, I want to answer, to appear calm. But I can't.

"Do you feel any pain?"

I'm sitting on my hands, trying to control them. I'm crossing my ankles, trying to hold my legs still. Inside I'm vibrating, I'm flying away, and I'm doing all I can to look normal, normal on the outside. But I'm not doing a good job, I know I'm not, because he's leaning forward now, his face is concerned.

"Miss, please, it's all right—" he says, but I can't hold myself still anymore, I'm rocking, back and forth, like the man, the man without the rocker.

There's an expression in English—I don't know if it translates—"off his rocker." Is this what it means? To do as the man does, to do as I am doing, moving back and forth, without a rocking chair?

A shape in the doorway: a woman in a black long-sleeved dress, knee-length. Sturdy black shoes. Stockings. A head covering. It takes me a moment to put meaning to the figure; she's a nun. "Breakfast," she calls. Most everyone pushes back their chairs and begins to file past me.

Now it is only the doctor, me, and the rocking man.

"Are you hungry?" The doctor's tone is friendly, easy.

A noise, a gurgle. It came from my throat.

"You don't care to speak, yes? It's all right. Let me tell you, you're safe here. This is the asylum at Saint-Alban."

Asylum.

Both in English and in French, the word means a safe place, a sanctuary, especially for political refugees. But it also means an institution that houses the mentally ill. Language is an imprecise thing, even when it's your mother tongue, and especially when it isn't. There is so much room for miscommunication. A word can become a wall between two people. But in this case, I'm certain that Dr. Tosquelles and I both understand "asylum" in the same way.

This is a place where those who are thought to be insane are kept. This is a place where doctors are trained to see the broken parts of people and to fix them, through one means, or another. Or, if they cannot be fixed, to imprison them, so they can't hurt others, or themselves. The thought is chilling enough to freeze me in place. I am still. I am afraid.

As if he's heard my thoughts, Dr. Tosquelles says, "When you were brought here, you expressed some . . . strong concerns. I would like to ease those concerns, if I can."

I'm watching the jerk and twitch of his mustache. His mustache fascinates me.

I do have concerns. A pressing one: How I will get out of this place, which will not happen if he believes I'm like the woman with the wedding dress, the man off his rocker. Already I'm doing the things Gillian trained me to do: I've stilled my body; I've made my expression bland; I'm looking from the doctor's mustache and up into his eyes.

And there's the *other* concern. The one regarding the troubling answer I've received to a question I've asked, not once, but twice. A question I would prefer not to ask a third time.

I take inventory of the facts, as I know them:

- Adrien Forestier believed the year is 1946.
- The couple I met in Montignac believed the same.
- The village of Montignac was staged as if the year is 1946, or thereabouts.

- Everyone here—both sane and otherwise—is dressed and comports themselves as if they, too, exist in the middle of the last century.
- I have no physical evidence of my name, date of birth, or citizenship.
- I have no money, no local contacts, no one back home to call.
- The night I was chased by the cyclops man, I fell and hit my head.

The facts lead me to four possible conclusions:

- I am dead, and this is some sort of afterlife.
- I am in a coma, and this is a dream.
- I was injured more seriously than I knew when I hit my head, suffering some sort of brain injury, and, while I am conscious, I am improperly interpreting the world around me, and an asylum is where I belong.
- The year is, in fact, 1946, and I have somehow traveled here from 2021.

There is another fact, one of which my stomach reminds me, with a grumble.

Dr. Tosquelles's mustache contracts above his lip, just for a sliver of a moment before it widens as he smiles. He stubs out his cigarette in an amber ashtray. "Ah, you *are* hungry," he says. "So we must see you fed."

15

When I was very young, I had intense food aversions. I remember this being true from my earliest memories; Big Nora understood this, and rather than try to cajole or convince me to try new things, she served foods from the short list of dishes I could stomach:

Apples. Neither green nor red. Only the crisp, sweet-tart varieties, mottled and pinkish.

Smooth things, like yogurt (only Greek) and ice cream. Nothing with chunks or lumps, like cottage cheese.

Spaghetti noodles—that shape of noodle, only—with plain red spaghetti sauce of one particular brand, the one that had no chunks of tomato.

Honey Nibs.

Every once in a while, Big Nora would suggest new things to try based on what I did eat. Corn flakes with milk. Potatoes, both French fried and hashed. Eggs, scrambled well, with salt but no pepper. Chicken, bite-sized and breaded. Her homemade matzoh ball soup with little noodles and chicken broth. Toast. Watermelon, served as a wedge. Black tea with milk and sugar. Lemonade, fresh, but from which Big Nora strained any bits of lemon pulp. Nothing mashed or smashed or lumpy.

"By the time you're seven," Big Nora told me, in a memory I have from before my mother returned, "you'll have a whole new set of taste buds from the ones you were born with. Did you know that? The things you like now will change, all on their own. Every seven years, a whole new set. I'm almost on my ninth set, myself. So there's no reason to rush you. Won't it be fun to see what those new taste buds will like?"

I climbed up on the bathroom counter to take a close look at my tongue. I stuck it out and sure enough, all over, little bumps I'd never noticed before. My taste buds.

"What happens to these taste buds, when I get new ones?"

"They'll go away. It's perfectly normal."

I knew what Big Nora meant by "go away": they would die. Part of me was going to die, before I turned seven. The funny little bumps that I hadn't even known about until I climbed the bathroom vanity to examine my tongue—they were going to die. They had barely begun to live, and already they were doomed.

I was inconsolable. Now that I knew of their existence, each bump on my tongue became my ward. I was responsible for them, I needed to keep them alive. They didn't deserve to die. That night I climbed out of bed half a dozen times to visit them in the bathroom mirror. Was it too late? Were they dying, already? How would I be able to tell, when it happened?

At last Big Nora took me to bed with her, fell asleep with the comforting weight of her arm across my body. And still I lay there, eyes wide open in the dark, staring unseeingly into the void, thinking up names—John and Sara and Kimmy and David and Minnie and Ariel. Mikey and Marvin and Grover and Sam. How many taste buds did I have? Each of them needed a name, and an interest, and a family. Each of them needed to be seen, and remembered.

As it happened, that first set of taste buds would outlive Big Nora.

How does memory work? What brings my brain from right now, sitting at this table in an asylum in southern France, a bowl of porridge in front of me, to that night of terrible fear, the night I sat shiva for the deaths of my taste buds, those named and unnamed?

The porridge has lumps.

"Are you all right?"

It's the pregnant woman—more of a girl than a woman, I can see, now that I am closer to her. No more than a year older than me, I'd guess, though it's hard to tell. She's standing across from me, one hand resting on the curve of her belly. Behind her is the other girl, holding a tray with two bowls of porridge, twin black braids reaching almost to the tray she holds.

I manage a nod.

"Can we sit here?"

I nod again.

They tuck in side by side and start to eat, neither sharing my aversion to lumpy food. All their attention goes to the task of emptying the bowls. I move the spoon in my bowl, taking feeble bites, glancing up at them in between.

"I'm Beryl," the pregnant girl tells me. "This is Penella."

They're both around my age, give or take. They look at me, expectant, but when I don't offer my name, they don't seem to mind, which is a relief.

At school, I rarely ate with others. They all had their little groups, their inside jokes, their routines. Some people were rude or mean to me, but there were many who weren't; if I'd sat at one of their tables, probably they would have made room. But it would have been so much work to try to act like them while also eating that I almost never tried.

The girl called Beryl is ravenous. When she's finished her breakfast, she looks at mine. I push the bowl to the middle of the table.

"You're not going to finish?" She's incredulous, even offended when I shake my head.

"Maybe she doesn't like glurb," says the one called Penella. There's something different about the way she holds words in her mouth, the way she shapes them. She might be mocking me.

"Doesn't like glurb," scoffs Beryl, and I can assume I've learned the word for porridge. "What would that matter?" She pulls the bowl across the table. She and Penella share my porridge, though Penella eats slowly, as if to make sure that most of it goes to Beryl.

"We saw you arrive yesterday," says Penella. "They brought you in an ambulance. You were . . . upset."

I try to remember, but I can't. They put drugs into my vein. It scares me, that there's a hole in my memory. There's the woman outside the pub. Then, later, waking in the ambulance, and then here, in a bed. The connecting tissue . . . it's gone.

"You were very upset." There's a wryness to Penella's voice. I can't tell if she's mean or not mean. Did I do something yesterday, something off-putting or deranged? Is she making fun of me? I look away, down to the table, and I catch sight of her wrist—the cuff of her left sleeve has folded back, and beneath it, along her wrist, snakes a puckered, raised pink scar.

She sees me staring, and instead of covering the scar, she slowly pushes up her cuff to display the length of it. It's ugly and new. There are older scars, too, faded light, but thick.

"I've been very upset, too," she says.

In another setting, I could think she's trying to be funny. Then she pushes up the right sleeve. Here, too, a scar; this one thin, light, a scratch compared to the first. "But I lost my nerve."

"And it's a good thing." Beryl lays a hand on Penella's arm. They look at each other, and I look at them, and I'm trespassing. "I'm glad you're okay now."

"What's 'okay'?" Penella asks, philosophically.

Now they're looking at me again, three empty bowls on the table between us. I trace a line with my eyes from one to the second to the third.

"So . . . you don't like to talk?"

Three points form a triangle.

"Maybe she's like Auguste."

A triangle is the strongest shape.

A bell rings, and most everyone pushes back their chairs, stands.

"Time for ergotherapy," Penella says. "Come on. You can walk with us."

If I refuse to go, I'll be the only person sitting here, which would be weird. If I go off on my own, that would call attention to me, too. The best thing to do—just as Gillian always said—is to try to blend in. So I follow them out of the dining room. We're in the main hallway again, with other people—patients? Doctors? Nurses? In some cases, like with the rocking man, with the nun, it's easy to tell, but others could be anyone. Only the nuns seem to wear a uniform or a badge or any sort of identifier. But no one is wearing anything modern—a T-shirt with a logo, a pair of jeans—and there's not a cell phone in sight.

Two men approach us walking in the opposite direction; one of them has a book, and they talk animatedly. "It's not enough to revolt politically, to glurb fascism," says the man with the book. "To be truly anti-fascist, one must embrace a permanent revolution of politics, society, and psychic life, all at once."

"Of course, of course, naturally," says the other man around the unlit pipe he holds between his teeth, in a tone that could either indicate agreement or patronizing consolation.

I'm reminded of the Magritte painting—a pipe, plainly, with the words *Ceci n'est pas une pipe* inscribed beneath. It's a commentary on the nature of representation, but as I think of it now, it's also a warning: nothing can be trusted. Not even my own perceptions.

Everything around me, from the furnishings to the clothes that people wear to the preponderance of indoor smokers, seems to confirm what Adrien told me in the cave, what the man in Montignac repeated: that it's 1946. If I focus too squarely on such an absurd, impossible thing, I won't be able to control my actions. I'll behave in a way that would make them correct in committing me, if that's not already what's happened.

When you don't know what to do next—Big Nora's words, from long ago—*do nothing. Take the time to take some time.*

The least likely possibility is that I've somehow traveled to a different time. Much more likely are the other theories:

- I am dead.
- I am in a coma, dreaming.
- I hit my head and am now improperly interpreting the world around me.

Death is a permanent state. If I'm dead, there's nothing I can do about it. If I'm in a coma, or if I'm awake and delusional, that may be a transient state; at any rate, I won't stay here forever. Even someone who's in a coma for thirty years leaves it eventually, one way or the other. But there's no evidence that I know of that the thoughts or actions of a person while they're in such a state have any effect on their ability to end it, and so if that's the case, all I can do is wait, anyway.

The main truth is that, whichever of these options it is, I'm terrified.

I've stopped following Penella and Beryl. They move ahead, up the hallway. When they notice I'm no longer with them, they gesture—*come on, let's go, keep up*—but when I don't join them, Penella shrugs, takes Beryl by the arm, and walks away.

All the doors look the same, and I try several before I find the room I woke up in. Once inside, I sink to the floor, back against the door. A terrible sound vibrates in my throat, a growling animal that wants out. I keep my lips clamped tight, trying to trap it inside. I crawl across the room for the pillow and hold it against my face, I don't want anyone to hear me. The world, I've long known, is a dangerous place to be hysterical and wordless; here, it could mean another injection, or worse.

Wherever I am, whatever I am, I am alone. Not lonely—I've been lonely many times—but alone. I have no one, nothing. Whether I'm asleep in 2021 or curling on the floor and shaking in 1946 or dead, I have no family left, no one who would know. And if I am alive, and yet my being so or not being so does not affect a single other thing in the universe, then how is that different from being dead? Can I be alive and yet not exist?

I crawl beneath the metal bedframe, take ragged breaths of dusty air through the feather pillow, try and try to force myself to calm. I am reminded that I am a person in a body, with my hip pressed into the hard, uneven wooden floorboards, with my face inhaling dusty air. I am a person in a body. I am a person in a body.

At least, I think I am.

Body or no body, I am thinking. Therefore, I exist. Descartes declared it. The senses can't be trusted; perception can be false or angled. It *seems* I'm inhaling dusty air through a feather pillow; it *feels* that the floor is rough and uneven. I *perceive* sounds coming from the hallway—footsteps, a muffled voice—and from my own body, my rough, ragged sobs. I *believe* I taste the salt of tears as I lick them from my lips. But what about the other things, the impossible-to-believe things? That on the other side of this door is a sanatorium for the insane in the year 1946, somewhere in the French countryside. Or further still—that I've fled from an attacker in the middle of the night, and he either caught me or he didn't, and I am out of my mind or out of my body or out of my time.

I can't know the truth of any of these things—I can be no more certain of the taste of tears than I am of my position in the universe. One does not see the yellowness of a lemon, as intrinsic as the color seems to be to its lemon-ness; a lemon doesn't actually contain yellow but rather reflects wavelengths of light that one *interprets* as yellow. A lemon—

in the sky of the painting I once loved, on the kitchen counter when Big Nora and I were preparing lemonade—isn't yellow, not in the way we think of it. This understanding could drive one further to madness, that nothing is necessarily what it seems, that nothing can be trusted.

But then—I am *thinking* about lemons, and yellowness, and the phenomenology of lemon-ness and perception, and this by itself is self-evidently trustworthy. I *am thinking*. Whether I'm mutilated and comatose in a bush somewhere, whether I'm in a hospital ward kept alive by tubes and pumps, whether I'm a consciousness loosened from its body, whether I'm a traveler through space and time—I am thinking, and therefore, I exist.

I am thinking. Therefore, I exist.

I exist. I exist. I exist.

I match the thought—real—to the sensation of my heartbeat—perceived. I match the thought—real—to the remembered experience of making lemonade with Big Nora. Pressing my nose into the lemon's rind, breathing in the tang and hope of its summer scent. The sensation of the knife's edge pressing against its thick citrus skin. The sting of juice in a hangnail. The pressure of the lemon's calyx against my palm as I grind the half-orb against the ridges of the clear glass juicer. The music of water pouring, ice cubes clinking, the long wooden spoon clacking as it stirs. The first sip, that pucker of lips, and then, way down at the bottom of the cup, the gritty sugar-syrup dredge scooped with sticky fingers. All of that, perceived. But the memory of it, the thinking—that's real.

I'm calmer. My body has loosened. I tuck the pillow under my head. Better. I take another breath, this one cooler, clearer, no dust.

One can only remain undone for so long. Or else one dies.

I'm rolling myself out from beneath the bed. I'm sitting up, then standing. I smooth my tangled hair away from my face, wish I had some way to tie it back, and then remember the lady's scarf. It's satisfying to find it where I'd tucked it earlier, in the pocket of my corduroys, and I use it to contain my hair. Another breath.

I think, therefore I exist. It's enormous, the most foundational thing, according to Descartes. The only knowable thing. And maybe it could be enough, for a mind more brilliant than mine. But for me, it's too tenuous all by itself. The scarf in my hair? I need it to exist, too. The shoes on my feet? The doorknob, hard and smooth like an egg in my palm? I have to believe that the world I'm in is real. I have to.

It's 1946, I say inside my brain, testing. And . . . it feels like it's true. Or, perhaps, it's the only thing to be believed, the only truth that holds the atoms of my world, such as it is, from scattering into entropy and emptiness. Without it, there is no meaning at all. And without that . . .

"It's 1946," I whisper, my voice thin and dry.

It's 1946. I twist the doorknob and pull open the door.

16

When just the two of us, Big Nora and I would go to the library every Friday. I was very young, so my memory has melded all those Fridays into one. We'd bring a long, rectangular basket, and she'd carry it from row to row, and we'd pull picture books from the shelves and thumb through each one to decide whether or not we wanted to bring it home with us.

Somewhere else in the library there was a young woman who did story time, sitting in the middle of a big group of children with their grown-ups—women, almost exclusively, and all of them younger than Big Nora. "Do you want to join them, Little Nora?" my grandmother would ask, but I never did.

"You have a mother, too," she would say. "She's away now, but she'll be back. And I know she loves you, very much."

I suppose that Big Nora thought that I regarded that circle of children and their mothers with something like loss. Maybe other children would, in my position. But I didn't. The word "mother"—what did it mean to me? I had Big Nora, I had the basket of books.

Still, Big Nora made a point, as I've said, of keeping pictures of Gillian around the house, of telling me that I was loved by Gillian as much as I was loved by her. It was an abstraction—the idea of Gillian's love, the idea of *Gillian*. And so it never occurred to me to wonder where she was. It really didn't matter; she wasn't *there*, and Big Nora was.

After she came home on my fourth birthday—then, I began to wonder where Gillian had been. Mostly in the context, if I'm being honest, of wishing she'd return there. Because for every grace Big Nora granted me, every way in which she made me feel safe and understood . . . Gillian was the opposite.

"What's wrong with you?"

"Why are you doing that?"

"The whole world can't stop and wait just because you're having a hard day, kiddo."

"If you don't tell people what you want, you're never going to get it."

"Hurry *up*, Nora, or I'll leave you behind."

Maybe she'd been gone to one of the places in the library books—maybe she'd been where the wild things are, or with Harold drawing purple worlds, or in the tin forest, or in the darkest dark. Maybe she'd been trapped in a tower spinning straw into gold or had been swimming with queer ocean life. And if she'd been there once . . . maybe she could go there again.

Of course, it wasn't long before Gillian was all I had left, and she actively worked to become the sort of mother I needed. I know from how she was before Big Nora died how hard she worked to change. I stopped hoping that Gillian would disappear again; I started worrying that she might.

Once, when I was eight years old, I asked Gillian where she'd been.

"I was lost for a while, dearheart. But I found my way back to you, didn't I?" And that's all she'd say about it. If I pushed, she pressed her lips into a thin, tight line and shook her head. "I'm here now," she'd say. "That's what matters."

But the question didn't go away; as I got older, I began to dream up new worlds she might have disappeared into during that absence—not fairy-tale castles or deep-sea adventures, but other places. Like, maybe she'd been kidnapped and held against her will. Or maybe she'd joined a cult. Or maybe she had a whole other family on the other side of the country. Or maybe—this occurred to me much later, after the lockdown, when Gillian began to really spin out with her theories about the virus—maybe she'd had a breakdown of some kind; maybe she'd been institutionalized. After all—to be gone most of four years, without a word of communication, only to come back without explanation . . . the older I got, the more I recognized how abnormal that had been. Too big a hole, at any rate, to plug up with those words—*I'm here now. That's what matters.*

Late one night, a month or so before Gillian died, I'd woken up to use the bathroom and found her at the kitchen table, laptop open, reading one of her subreddits. I don't know what it was—maybe the intensity of her expression, as she read—that caused me to say, "When you were gone all that time. When I was young. Were you in an institution?"

She looked up, awash in the strange white light reflected from her screen. "Is that what you think of me? You think I'm someone who belongs in the loony bin?"

Probably I didn't answer fast enough.

"Those places aren't for normal people, Nora. If you ever end up in a place like that, it's a sign that you've taken a real wrong turn, somewhere. So take another turn, as fast as you can, to get the hell out."

I go past a room full of books, a library. Several people, all men, read and smoke, some sitting at a table, others under a window, a few more in front of a cold fireplace, its hearth large enough for a person to stand in. Another man, very old, pushes a cart, returns other books to the shelves.

Another room: this one is set up like a sitting room in a family home, though the windows are not like anything one would see in an average house; they're tall, and deep, flat at the bottom and curved to a point at the top. Several couches are arranged around another large fireplace, this one banked and burning low and warm. Some books on a table, but no one is reading them. Tapestries on the walls, colorful and intricate. A few people are setting up for a game of bridge.

A woman, very thin, maybe thirty-five, sits next to a silent radio. She has her ear pressed up against its speaker, nods in agreement. When she reaches to move the dial, a tattoo—a string of numbers—on her left forearm.

Then I come upon a sewing room. I hear it before I see it, and by the time I do, the sound is so loud that I want to cover my ears. Several machines are working; they're electric and drum out stitches like gunfire. The walls are made of enormous rough blocks, stacked and mortared, and maybe the walls are the reason for the poor acoustics. This room is populated only by women. Those who aren't at the machines are doing other things: sorting through a pile of what appears to be uniforms, military perhaps, separating the shirts from the pants;

someone else is tearing long strips from unsalvageable sheets; a nun is kneeling beside a middle-aged woman, helping her thread a needle. No one else seems bothered by the noise.

In a far corner, a few women are selecting socks from a basket, assessing the damage to the toes and heels. Beryl and Penella. Beryl is standing, one hand on her belly, auburn hair falling forward as she looks down at Penella, crouched by the basket, scavenging. She comes up with a pair of stockings and a handful of woolen socks; Beryl nods, and Penella pops up to her feet. This is when they notice me and wave me in.

If I go in, I'll have to engage with them; but if I turn and leave, wouldn't that be worse? With a sigh, I join them.

Beryl asks, "Are you any good at sewing?"

I manage to shake my head.

"I don't love it, but I'm too big now to be any help in the fields, so." Maybe I look confused because she continues. "Everyone works. Dr. Tosquelles says that no one is unworthy of protection, and no one is exempt from work."

What happens if the patients *don't* work, I wonder.

"He says work is therapeutic." Penella smiles wryly. "That's what 'ergotherapy' means. But I can't stand sewing." She studies me, and despite my efforts to train my face to a mask of stillness, perhaps she sees something there, my discomfort at the racket of the machines, because she says, "I was about to leave. You want to come with me?"

I am nodding.

Penella helps Beryl get comfortable in a chair with the pile of darning, finds her a footstool. "I'll meet you at lunch," she says, and takes up two coats from a rack near the door. Then, handing one to me—"Let's go."

As soon as we're back in the hallway, the noise level drops, and I take a deep breath. But I don't have more than a second to recover from the auditory assault; without Beryl at her side, Penella moves much more quickly, and I have to take a run-step to keep up.

"You weren't with Dr. Tosquelles for very long before breakfast was called," she says. I'm surprised that she noticed, but maybe I shouldn't be; from the little I've seen, Penella already gives the impression of being a person who notices most things, who pays attention. "Probably he didn't have time to tell you much about this place. And even if he did, he's never been a patient here, so his perspective is probably different from mine. Anyway, you should know that you don't need to be scared. You will be anyway, I guess. I was, when I was first brought here nearly five years ago, but you don't need to be. You're not a prisoner. There aren't any locks or fences, or anything like that. You can leave whenever you want, but pretty much everyone chooses to stay."

Maybe I look dubious—that statement doesn't align with the little I know about asylums; in movies and books they always have locks on the doors—because Penella laughs. "It's true," she says. "And anyway, in here is better than what's out there, at least it has been for as long as I've been at Saint-Alban. They do their best, the nuns and the doctors and everyone. Of course they can't fix everything"—here, her right hand strokes the scars on her left wrist, maybe an unconscious gesture—"but they do at least try to not make things worse."

She stops, glances at me, checking to see if I'm understanding, if I'm beginning to believe her. I manage a tight nod.

She nods, too. "Everyone works, that's the main thing," she goes on, more businesslike now. "You get to choose what sort of work you do—I'll give you a quick tour, and you can decide where you want to be. There's plenty to go around, and everyone gets paid for the work they do. Where Beryl was, that's garment work—they're fixing up essentials for the asylum, and also to sell in town. In there," she says, indicating a glass-paneled door we've stopped by, "is the printing press. We have a weekly newspaper. It has articles about the state of our budget, reviews of any plays that are performed, and discussions about future plans, general news . . . things most everyone knows. But everyone reads it anyway."

I peer through the window. Inside, several young men sit around a table, two at typewriters, one with a notepad. A middle-aged man leans over a heavy metal contraption, twisting a lever, then wiping grease from his hands onto an apron front. I'm wondering who writes the articles, and I try to speak, but only a small sound makes its way out.

Maybe she understands because she says, "The club organizes it, but the press is open to everyone—patients, orderlies, whoever has something to say. Do you like to write?"

I shake my head.

We go farther up the hall, and she gestures to another door, this one without a window. "That's the room where we have group therapy, most days. Anyone can join, but it's not required. Two o'clock in the afternoon, rain or shine."

I eye the door warily. If I'm really in an asylum in 1946, there's no way I'll be opting into a situation in which I'd be expected to open up about myself to a room full of strangers and a psychiatrist. Even if I withheld the most glaring indication that I may have lost my mind—that I've traveled here from the future—I have no idea what other facets of my story might be unsafe to share. The fact that I'm Jewish, for one; the war is over, but not by much. And my autism, for another. I've read about women whose husbands had them committed just for being "hysterical," so who can guess what they might think of a neurodivergent person in a time where the diagnosis doesn't exist?

You don't need to let them see everything, Nora. It's better to keep some things private.

"Over there"—Penella gestures across the hall—"for a while, when the war was on, those rooms were our nursery, for orphans and displaced children. They've mostly found homes now. Now we use the rooms for all sorts of activities, including shoe repair. A cobbler from town comes in every other Wednesday. He'll teach anyone who's interested." She starts walking again. "Every week there's some sort of entertainment. The club organizes that, too. Sometimes they rope me into it. Clown shows, dramas, dancing. All that happens in the main room, where you met Dr. Tosquelles this morning. Over there's the photography lab." She waves at a door with blacked-out glass. "They're still working on getting that running."

She's making this place sound like a commune or something. It's not like any mental asylum I've ever heard of. And it doesn't really *look* like one, either. Where are the bars on the windows, the locks on the doors? I haven't seen a single padded room yet.

It *feels* real, the floor beneath me. It *looks* real, the hallways, the girl I'm following. But my knowledge of what an institution like this must be—especially if I'm really in 1946, as I'm trying to accept—it doesn't align. And my heart starts beating fast again, I'm bringing my hands up close to my sides. The floorboards, which felt solid moments ago, are unmoored, threatening to tilt, the walls, too.

We come to a heavy wooden door banded with dark iron hardware, and Penella pushes it open with both hands. Then we're outside, in a small courtyard, a tall stone wall, pink tinged, around us. Gillian, again—*You don't need to let them see everything, Nora.* I force my hands down and ball them in my pockets; I rock back on my heels. Countless times I've matched my behavior to Gillian's words, so often that she doesn't need to be alive for me to hear them, to comply. Across the courtyard is a wide, arched double door. *That* must be the locked door, the thing that keeps the patients in and the world out. But Penella strides across the flat hard ground of the courtyard, and pushes through that door, too, and then we're outside of the asylum.

We stand on the top step, turn our faces up to the mild white sun. The sky is crisp; it's midmorning, and it feels like fall is nearly gone. Penella stands up her collar and reties the belt on her coat. I gulp the cold fresh air, shiver, push into the coat she gave me.

"That's where I work, past the Bee." She points across a yard where a large, squared-off metal bus is parked, and beyond to a fenced-in garden. Several people are there already, working with tools to turn up the ground. "You can go back and find a place inside to work, or you can come with me."

I'm on solid ground. The air is clean and tastes of rosemary. One of the therapists Gillian found for me practiced outside, in a small garden, rich with sticky herbs and fragrant blooms. It was my favorite of the many treatments she took me to.

“I used to garden, sometimes.” The words come in a rough whisper, but they come.

Penella makes no mention of my found voice, and I am grateful. “Good,” she says with a wry smile. “Maybe you won't be completely useless.”

This is how you harvest root vegetables: Find a basket and a spade or digging fork. Rake back the mulch, then break the soil where it's crusted. Be careful with the roots as you pull free the vegetable—carrots, radishes, turnips, leeks. Repeat. Repeat. Repeat.

I don't mind repetitive work. Digging up vegetables isn't that different from drawing or painting. Each requires movements done over and over again. Each is soothing, satisfying. I focus on the sound of the spade, pushing through the soil; the moment when the vegetable, loosened, pulls free; the satisfaction of laying each in the shallow basket. If I concentrate on the vegetables, on the texture of the spade against the earth, I can let everything else go. At least for a little while, at least for now.

Once Penella has determined that I have the basics sorted, she works alongside me. She's much faster, uprooting two or three vegetables for each one that I pull. A couple of times she stops me—“No. See? Those aren't ready yet.”

The day stays cold, but I get warm from the work and push up the sleeves of the borrowed coat. Penella takes hers off entirely. A row over, two ancient nuns work in tandem; one kneels and digs, passing leek after leek to the other, who takes it and places it in her basket. Farther, in a field beyond, a pair of young men sneak looks at Penella from time to time.

I want Penella to talk with me, but, just as with Adrien—our walk in the woods feels an age ago, now—I don't want to be forced to talk about myself. A conversation is a trade. I know that. And though I've managed to make a few words, that doesn't guarantee that more will come . . . or that, if they do, they'll be the right words, in the right order, to unlock her acceptance.

Maybe Penella feels like talking, or maybe she can tell how confused and lost I am and just takes pity on me, because about an hour into our work she says, "I've been here since I was thirteen. I've seen a lot of changes."

I don't speak, just dig another turnip.

"Dr. Tosquelles had just gotten here when I arrived. He'd been detained in a camp at Septfonds, for political prisoners."

Just take in the information. My fingers grasp the handle of the spade. I angle its tip against the earth, push, and the spade pierces the surface.

"He's a communist, of course, which some people take issue with, but it makes no difference to me. My people have suffered under every regime." She turns to face me then and rises up, basket of root vegetables at her feet, spade in her hand.

I'm not a great judge of beauty. I believe that, I suppose, because I see it everywhere. In the faces of panting dogs. In blooming flowers, yes, but also in those that have been left too long in the vase, grown a fine white fur, turned the water hazy with decomposition. There's beauty in the arcs and lines of paint on a school blacktop. Beauty too in the lines of a rug, freshly vacuumed. What I mean to say is, beauty means so many things to me.

Even so, when Penella stares me right in the face, her jaw thrust forward as if she's ready to fight, her olive brow shining in the fair fall sun, beauty means something new.

"I'm a glurb, of course," she says. "Everyone hates us."

I don't know what she means.

"I'm Roma," she says, slowly, like I'm an idiot.

I nod, and her face closes as if I've confirmed her suspicions, and so I rush to add, "That doesn't matter to me."

A flash of surprise, that I've spoken again. Then her high, prideful expression returns. "Everything matters." The words are as sharp as the spade in her hand, and yet it's such a relief to hear someone say something that I totally agree with. Everything *does* matter.

"I take it back," I say. "It *does* matter to me that you're—" I pause, then land on: "one of your people. It matters very much. Just—it doesn't bother me. After all, it doesn't bother *you* that I'm—" I cut myself short. I was going to share my Jewishness, but then I remember where I am—*when* I am. And also, Gillian's refrain, that less can be more. *You don't need to let them see everything, Nora.*

Still, it's more words than I've said since I woke to find myself in this place, and Penella seems to appreciate that I've spoken; her face is stone a moment longer, and then it shifts, she's evaluating me, seeing something there, and I hold myself very still—is it something she likes, or something she doesn't like?

It's not natural for me to hold words back, when they want to come out. That's the thing about me, and language: it can be a desert or it can be a flood, rarely anything in between. But I hold myself still, hold the words in, swallow them.

"You're an interesting girl," Penella says at last.

"Interesting" is one of those words that means different things to different people. I would like clarity about what it means to Penella, in this instance. But again, though Penella's expression might be read as encouraging, as curious—I restrain myself.

There's another moment, and it seems like she's hoping I'll say more, but then—"Hmph," she says, crouches down again, and spears her spade into the earth.

We work until Penella says it's time for lunch. Sore and relieved, I put my hands to the small of my back and stretch. Penella does the same. Like mine, her hands are stained with dirt. She wipes a lock of raven hair from her forehead, tucks it beneath her scarf.

Then we take the baskets through the garden where the other workers are putting away tools and pulling off gloves, around the metal bus—the Bee—and across the hard-packed dirt, where we leave them. Penella takes the steps two at a time, eager for lunch and, equally eager, I suspect, to find Beryl, but I stop and stare at the building.

Not just a building; it's a castle. A bit run-down, maybe, but still a castle. At the top of the wide staircase, the castle's doorway arches, a cerulean passageway studded with iron stars. It brings me back to Jacques's cave, the sensation that overcame me, that I was stepping into a giant's mouth. Around this grand wooden door, thick blocks of pink-tinged stone form the archway, recalling the balustrades of the bridge I crossed in Montignac.

It's an accordion of time, of places: the cave, with Adrien; the bridge, in Montignac; this doorway, before me; the yellow painted lines on the blacktop of my childhood. The bridge I crossed, the voices of the laughing mother and child echoing in my head. My own mother, coming to me barefoot across the blacktop. Adrien, following me, shocked and hurt, to the mouth of the cave. The way I left him.

Empty-handed.

The pain in my chest, an electric shock, a punch that knocks the breath right out of me. My mother's ashes.

I turn over my empty hands as if the canister might somehow appear. Impossible, that I've left them behind. Impossible, and yet. The bamboo cylinder is lost.

17

There are lots of ways to lose people. You can lose them in an instant, the way I lost Big Nora to an object falling from the sky at terminal velocity. Or you can lose them slowly, in dribs and drabs, like water leaking from a cracked bowl. Looking back to those early days of the pandemic, there are inflection points, moments in time when I believe I could have saved my mother. But I was so glad to be given a reason to stay home that I didn't pay enough attention to what was happening to her.

No more alarm clock, blasting me awake before I was ready. No more rushing to get out of the apartment, no more riding the city bus, no more jostling through a hallway to sit in a row in a classroom and then another classroom, and then another. The other kids were upset—it was our junior year, we were finally upperclassmen, what about prom, what about parties, and on and on—but I wasn't, not about missing school, anyway. I was upset about the virus, of course. But not as upset as Gillian.

Early in the pandemic, she agreed with the cautionary measures; it made sense, at least at first, she said, for us to keep our distance. To flatten the curve. A few weeks off from school, sure. This was a reasonable request. A few months? Less reasonable. But when the vaccine mandate was issued . . . I guess if I had to choose a moment—one moment—that was the beginning of the end, it was then.

Ordering us to shoot ourselves, to shoot our *children*, full of poison—hadn't we learned *anything*, she raged, anything at all? *Demanding* that we submit to it, in order to go back to school, back to work, back into society? What sort of a country *was* this, anymore?

There were physical changes, too. Her mouth, which had often quirked as if she knew a funny secret or was about to tell a joke, beginning to reshape, as if heavy, invisible weights were attached to each corner, pulling, pulling. And a tightness developed, a twitch in the muscle of her jaw, as if she was clenching her teeth. A ridge of tendon sprang up along her neck.

No more NPR. Only one news station she would watch, angry faces with invisible weights in the corners of *their* mouths. The voices, screaming the things Gillian parroted.

And later, worse.

When Big Nora died, Gillian promised me that she'd be different. And over the years that followed, sometimes she'd say something that stung, but rarely would she say things that didn't at least feel like they were underwritten by love. Until the virus. Until Gillian's return to her subreddits, until the growing popularity of her breathwork group.

Then, she'd go on and on, explaining what she'd learned online; I'd try to listen but found the threads hard to follow, or worse. I tried to refute her, but she would only talk more loudly, more stridently, drowning me out until I retreated, resorted to nodding and saying "mm-hm" here and there. And her breathwork sessions grew from a dozen people, to a hundred, to close to a thousand. People who agreed with her breathed with her.

By the time I understood what was happening—really understood—it was too late. She got sick; we both did. I got better; she didn't. I begged her to let me call for help, but she refused.

Her last breathwork session, she was weak, she was sick—all those *people*, all those *boxes*—and she couldn't do it, couldn't function, couldn't *breathe*. She had to end the session early, log off, shut down.

The only thing I could do for Gillian was tuck the stuffed chicken she'd given me, which she'd named Feather, into bed beside her . . . and then later, when they came for my mother's body, to send Feather along, too.

And this time, when Gillian left, there was no one to watch out for me. I was alone. I was so sad. And also—angry. Angry at Gillian, for the person she'd become. Angry at all the people who'd contributed, the detox specialists and the naturopaths and the other mothers, the "Autism Warriors," the politicians and podcasters, all the fearmongers who twisted her misbeliefs into dangerous things. Angry at myself, for not being able to do enough, to *be* enough, to help her, when she needed my help.

When I'd gotten the call that her ashes were ready to be picked up, I considered leaving them there. They were just *remains*, after all—they weren't Gillian. But if I did that, I'd be saying that the person she became at the end—who believed terrible things about me, who *blamed me*, who was so full of hate that it might as well have been the thing that killed her—that that person was my mother.

Maybe if I took her ashes to a place she'd dreamed about with soft eyes, maybe then I could remember that Gillian was also the person who came back to me, the person who'd brought home the Painting that seemed to speak to me so clearly, so earnestly, if only I could decode its language. The person who may not have understood me perfectly, but at least saw my love of art, and nourished it. Scattering Gillian's remains in a place she would have loved felt to me like a choice I could make, a way to regain something I'd lost. A way to return myself to a time when I wasn't deeply, desperately, alone.

Lunch is a stew, but I manage to eat the bits of meat, the onions, some of the potatoes before passing it across to Beryl, who slurps the broth.

Inside my head is a drumbeat—*my mother, my mother, my mother.* I've lost her again, I've lost her in so many ways, and there are more important things to worry about, more pressing concerns—I've lost my place in time, it seems, or maybe my mind—but it's strange how the realization that I've lost my mother's remains makes these much bigger concerns fade into the background.

I have no idea where Adrien lives, but Jacques does. If I could somehow find my way back to the cave, maybe he'd still be there standing guard, maybe he could point me in the right direction. Or maybe Adrien will have realized he's carrying my canister, maybe he would have decided to leave it with Jacques, in case I return. Or—maybe he tossed it into the trees, as soon as I left him. I couldn't blame him if he did, after the way I acted. I'd done the thing Gillian always warned me against—I'd been deranged, bizarre. Adrien had been so kind, so good to me—oh, and that lovely dog . . . well. There's no way Adrien will want anything to do with me now. Even if I find him, and even if he still has the ashes, how could I ever expect him to want to be with me again, the way we were, together by the fire? He's probably relieved that I'm gone, regretting that he helped me in the first place. Surely he's embarrassed that we kissed, maybe even ashamed.

Beryl clears her throat, and that's when I realize I've been making a sound in mine—a sad little moan. I stop.

"So." Penella has a glass of water between her hands. She twirls it, the water sloshing this way and that but never spilling. "Do you want to tell us your name?"

I have to clear my throat before I can speak. "Nora."

"A Jewish name," says Beryl, smiling. "One of my favorites."

Warning lights flicker in my head—is it safe to talk about this, or not safe? I look more carefully at Beryl's features and realize they aren't that different from my own. "Actually, I'm 'Nora' without an *h*. The Hebrew would translate as *N-O-R-A-H*, meaning 'light.'"

"Ah. But you're Jewish, yes?"

"Well," I continue, spurred by my compulsion to tell the whole truth, whenever I can—"I don't believe in God, or anything like that, but I'm Jewish by birth—Ashkenazi."

"A Jew who doesn't believe in God?" interrupts Penella. "So, what *do* you believe in?"

What do I believe in?

Before Big Nora was killed, I would have said that I believed she would be with me all my life. Before the pandemic, I would have said that I believed Gillian was, at her core, a rational person. Before two days ago, I would have said that I believed time could only ever move in one direction.

But now . . .

"Dogs."

"Dogs?"

"Yes. Dogs."

"You believe in dogs." Penella's face is bright with humor. "What, exactly, do you believe in, about dogs?"

"Their goodness."

"You think all dogs are good?"

"Y-es. But sometimes people make them do bad things."

"Bah." Penella dismisses me with a wave of her spoon. "That's the same thing the Germans and the Vichy will say, now that the war is finished. That they weren't all bad. Just that they were made to do the bad things. One way or the other—whether they wanted to be bad or whether they were forced to be—the result is the same, isn't it?"

There's not much I can say to that. So I don't say anything at all.

"Anyway," Beryl tells Penella, "it's not a requirement to believe." Then, to me—"Spelled like yours, your name can mean two things."

"Yes."

Here we are, three young women at a table, having a nice conversation about the spelling and meaning of my name. And at the same time, my mother's remains are somewhere, out there. "Terrible, or magnificent."

"Well," says Beryl, "we're so glad you're speaking, Nora." She reaches across the table to squeeze my hand.

There's more work in the afternoon, this time in the kitchen. My job is to dry the dishes, says the chapped-face nun, who gives me a dish towel and tells me to call her Sister Martine. A slow, round man named Henri is washing them. He is thorough and careful and taps the scrubbing brush against the side of the sink three times between each dish. I don't mind that he's slow; standing in the kitchen drying dishes is as good a place as any for me right now. And I'm glad that he doesn't speak to me.

As I take each dish and rub it dry, stack it on the industrial metal countertop, I try not to perseverate on the layers of impossibility that fold one upon the next like the fine lamination of a croissant. Where I am, when I am, who I am . . . where my mother's ashes might be and how I might be able to get them back . . . it's too much to bear all at once. I'll slip away if I open that aperture. I have to keep a tight focus on the work right here in front of me—this dish, wet and warm. I can dry it with the unbleached linen towel. There. Done. Added to the stack. This is a thing, a thing I can do, and I can do it well.

I can focus on facts that I know, and the dishes I am drying, and that's all. So. Facts. What do I know about 1946?

When was the invasion of Normandy? 1944? "The beginning of the end of World War Two," that's what Ms. Cacey said last year, from a box on my computer screen. Allied troops landed on France's northern shore and, despite heavy losses, secured the beach. Behind Ms. Cacey's head was a bookshelf. Several of the books on the shelf were romance novels. They pressed onward across France, liberating Paris, expelling Germans as they went. I liked that Ms. Cacey read romance novels. She must need a distraction, from everything. A huge loss for the Germans in its own right, the Allies' victory in France also tied up the Nazi troops, preventing them from moving to the Eastern Front to fight off the Soviets, who switched teams throughout the war, turncoats, side to side. A baby cried, sharp and loud. Ms. Cacey apologized and said she'd be right back, jumped up from her chair and turned off her camera. But she didn't mute herself. Mute, unmute, mute, a strange thing to be able to choose to do. Losing France led to losing Russia which led to Hitler shooting himself in the head and Nazi Germany surrendering in the spring of 1945, March or April, I don't remember which. Ms. Cacey, angry: "I *told* you not to leave him in the high chair, he gets scared when he's alone. It's not that hard to take care of *one baby*, Steven!" Mothers and babies, too close, too close. Try to not think about them.

Not that long ago, to be Jewish in France, believing or otherwise, would have been a dangerous thing. But Beryl doesn't seem to feel unsafe, so that's a concern I can set aside, at least while I'm within the confines of the asylum. As for the other part of me, the part Gillian taught me to disguise . . . that part, I've been right to keep hidden, as much as I can. The twentieth century was even less kind to women than the twenty-first; "hysterical," that's one thing they called women, tying emotionality to the possession of a uterus. "Melancholic," attributed to women who were grief-stricken or depressed. "Neurotic," women who were anxious, unsettled, noncompliant. "Mad"—that diagnosis could get a woman committed. "Nag." "Extremist." "Witch." So many labels. So many ways to weaponize language. Gillian wasn't right about everything, but she was right about this.

I add the plate I've been drying to the stack. The last one.

"Henri," says Sister Martine, pushing in through the back door, a basket of carrots on her hip, "if you keep washing that pan, you're going to scrub the metal right off it."

He laughs and nods but keeps scrubbing.

"You can go on out," she tells me, hefting the basket onto the worn wooden chopping block behind me. "That pot is the last, and he could be another hour with it."

I fold the washcloth and set it on the counter, then untie the strings of the apron she gave me. It goes on a nail beside a wall calendar.

I glance at Sister Martine, my heart pounding like I'm doing something wrong. She's turned away, not paying any attention to me.

The calendar hangs by a nail, folds open to show a fall landscape on the top, with the year "1946" in script. On the bottom half is the month—October.

"Sister Martine?"

"Hmm?"

"Could you tell me—what's the date, today? I can't remember."

"It's the sixth, child. Sunday."

I trace my finger along the calendar. Two nights have passed, I think, since Adrien found me—the first spent with him; the second here, in a stupor. I can't do the math in my head, but it seems that the calendar is telling me I've come roughly seventy-five years back in time.

I turn my attention away from the calendar and toward the basket of carrots. The carrots smell earthy, I tell myself, like clean dirt, and sweet. Not a pink smell of sugar like cotton candy; a yellow smell, bright and crisp, with a bit of spice at the back of my tongue. It calms me, to name these sensations, and right now, I need to be calm.

Seeing me staring at the carrots, the nun picks one, breaks off its green and passes it across her apron to knock off some of the dirt before handing it to me. "Go on, then," she says, kindly, and so I do.

The dining room is empty. Another fireplace at the far end, clean swept and bare. No ashes, there. It makes sense, I guess, that there are so many fireplaces; this place must be hundreds of years old. It's been updated in some ways, like the glass panes added to the windows, the huge gas stove and oversized metal sink in the kitchen, electricity, plumbing. But these things are layered atop the older truth of the place. Like everything is.

Through the dining room and back into the hallway. Far away is the tinkling of the piano, being played by someone who doesn't know what they're doing. Most people don't pay me any attention at all. This group of men talks animatedly, waving their hands expansively, in argument or agreement, I can't tell.

There is Marguerite Sirvins, still working on her wedding gown. An irreverent thought: What does she plan to wear on her wedding night?

Then I'm through the door and across the courtyard and pushing open the heavier arched blue door, and back on the wide stone steps. No one has stopped me. No one has asked me a single question. My clenched fist grips the carrot, damp with nervous perspiration. I pass it to my other hand and wipe my sweaty palm on my corduroys.

Maybe the thing to do is just . . . leave. Start walking, and don't stop. The cave is out there somewhere. Gillian's ashes, too. If I did manage to find Adrien, I'd have to try to apologize for the way I acted, if he would even be willing to listen. But that's a worry for later. I go down the steps and pause at the bottom, tensed for someone to yell at me, but no one does. No fences or walls close off the asylum from the outside world. Between the lack of uniforms or doctors' coats and the strangely missing fences and all the unlocked doors, it seems Penella was telling me the truth. It appears I'm entirely free to leave.

This thought should be a relief. But instead, the immensity of choices overwhelms. How do I even go about finding the cave? In Montignac, I was sedated, loaded into an ambulance, driven who knows how far to this place . . . and which direction did we even come from? I'm Little Nora again, Doing Colors at the kitchen table and realizing that there are more possible variations than could be contained by all the pipettes in the world. Here around me, there's north, south, east, and west, of course. Then, between these four corners, there's every possible degree of variation, and if I want to get precise about it, every fraction of every degree in between. And then, if I even *do* manage to find the cave, to find the ashes . . . what then?

When I was eleven, my teacher Mr. Millikan introduced us to Zeno's dichotomy paradox: For a person to walk any distance from point A to point B, he must first walk half that distance. This is a logical necessity. But, before he can walk that half distance, he must necessarily traverse half *that* half distance. And half that half. And so on, and so on, ad infinitum. There is no end to the halving that can be done, no end to the requirements you must satisfy before reaching your end goal, and so it's impossible to ever move from A to B. And yet—we do that impossible thing all the time. How can this be? What if the only reason we are able to perform the impossible is because we are unaware of its impossibility? And thus, made aware, are we unable to travel any distance at all? Are we doomed to remain wherever we stand, unmoving, unchanging, forever?

The problem so haunted me that I couldn't sleep. I was so distraught, so inconsolable, that Gillian gave me one of her "special gummies." Deeply stoned, finally able to relax, I slept. Now, I see that Zeno's paradox is the matching bookend of my personal Doing Colors paradox. And if one can never begin, *and* one can also never end . . . well.

Once again, I must contemplate whether I'm really here, at all. Maybe I'm a muted box on someone's screen. Or ashes in a tube. Or a person composed entirely of dots, posed in the shade of a tree. Is there any marked difference between any of these possibilities? If the person we are is determined by all the things that came before us—the choices others made for us, like whether or not to vaccinate us for various diseases, like whether to raise us or abandon us, like whether to take us to temple or not, like whether or not to emigrate to the States . . . then the choices we will make are predetermined, and we bear no responsibility at all for those choices, and maybe for our actions. And then, of course, are all the decisions that were made on *those people's* behalf, the ancestors and the lovers and the oppressors and the strangers, all. If the world and all the actions within it are causally determined, then what was the path of determination that led Steven to leave the baby unattended in his high chair? Was Ms. Cacey *always* going to forget to mute herself when she left the screen to tend to the baby and chastise Steven? Before she was ever born or even conceived, when she was an egg inside a fetus inside her grandmother's body, was it determined already that one day she would stand up from her desk while teaching a remote lesson on the end of World War II and, in her haste to answer her baby's cry, forget to mute herself, even though she remembered to turn off her camera? Was some part of her predetermined to make the choice to go invisible, but not unheard?

Was Ms. Cacey a good teacher or a bad one? A good mother, or a bad one? A good wife, or a bad one? A good person? Or a bad one? (*Was* Ms. Cacey, or *will* Ms. Cacey *be*? If it's 1946, how long will it be until Ms. Cacey's grandmother is pregnant with her mother, with the egg that will become one half of Ms. Cacey's genetic story nested inside, like those dolls with one containing the other, and the other inside that?)

My mother is ashes in a container in a boy's knapsack, lost to me somewhere in the French countryside in the year 1946. I don't know where he is, and even if I did, I wouldn't be able to reach him before first reaching half the distance, and half the distance of that, and—

My legs begin to tremble, and I sit on the bottom stair.

There's the clang of a heavy metal panel slamming shut. I'm not alone. Footsteps, then the grumble and whine of an engine, struggling to turn over. It's Dr. Tosquelles, thirty yards away, behind the Bee's steering wheel. He releases the key; silence. Moments pass, and then he tries again. The sick whine of an engine that wants to start but can't.

"Shit." His voice travels out the bus's open window. Grumbling, he gets out and opens the engine panel again. More grumbling sounds as he knocks the butt of his screwdriver against something inside. *Clang, clang clang!* Engine panel closed again; back around to the bus door; hefting himself into the driver's seat; palms together in a quick prayer, mustache twitching as he whispers; then the key shoves into the ignition. I'm holding my breath along with Dr. Tosquelles in the moment before he cranks the key.

Another sick whine. Another failed attempt. "Shit, shit." He turns, and appears to notice me, finally. "Do you happen to know anything about diesel engine repair?" he calls.

I shake my head.

"Bah." He hops down, closes the bus door. "A machine should not be smarter than man. It's not the natural order of things."

What would Dr. Tosquelles say about my cell phone? A brief, ridiculous moment of humor that belongs only to me, imagining this odd little man with his funny little mustache finding himself as out of sorts in my time as I find myself in his.

"What's funny? I could use a smile."

"Nothing. Just . . . remembering something."

Like Penella, Dr. Tosquelles doesn't comment on my returned voice. Instead, he says, "A memory is not nothing," and scratches the top of his balding head with a sharp end of the screwdriver before tucking it into the back pocket of his trousers. He's left a line of grease across his scalp. I point to his head; he takes a handkerchief from a pocket, scrubs it across his scalp, and, seeing the grease smeared on the cloth, laughs deeply. When he asks my name once again, I tell him, and he holds out his hand to shake. This time, I do.

Then he sits beside me, sighing as he settles and turns his face up to the sun. "Soon it will be very cold." He closes his eyes. "It doesn't get as cold where I'm from."

Why is he talking to me so casually, as if we're friends rather than doctor and patient? "Where are you from?" I find myself asking.

"Catalonia." His eyes are still closed, and his mustache twitches, as if in pleasure from the warmth of the sun. I only vaguely know what Catalonia is. It's an area in Spain, close to the French border, and I know that, historically, there was political turmoil there—the area wanting independence from the rest of Spain. I don't know what year all that happened, I wasn't paying close enough attention, or maybe Ms. Cacey didn't go into it.

"I had to leave six years ago," he continues, sitting straighter, opening his eyes. His hands are folded loosely across his knees; he looks not at me but at the bus, as if part of his mind is occupied with the engine problem. Six years ago, I was twelve.

"Why?"

"The short answer—fascism. The longer—I was part of the resistance and had to run like a criminal when Franco took power. I'm a psychiatrist by profession, not a soldier, so my time at the front during the war against Franco was better spent taking care of the combatants—the soldiers and officers—than shooting a gun. Then, when I found myself interred in a camp in France . . ." He shrugs, as if to say that one cannot control such things. "Again, I set up practice. It's one of the places where I conducted very good psychiatry, in this concentration camp, in the mud. Then, the doctor who was running this place, Saint-Alban—a good man, Dr. Paul Balvet is his name, he's moved on from here, since then—Balvet heard of the work I was doing and in January of '40 he wrote, recruiting me to help. There was a huge amount to do, you see, not just therapeutically, but also practically. We had to prepare the asylum for the war; we expanded the rudimentary gardens, collaborated with the villagers to plant and harvest and store up reserves, side by side with the patients. Everyone worked. Everyone had a hand in what we did, what we made. A place like this is for the patients, but others sheltered here too, during the fighting—many Jewish families; persecuted artists and intellectuals; rebel fighters, too. And here, we kept one another safe through the war. We turned no one away." He stops, sighs. "Did you know that in asylums such as this, here in France alone, tens of thousands of patients died during the war? Not from fighting. Just from living. Starvation. Exposure to the elements.

At Saint-Alban, not one patient died for these reasons."

"That's . . . good."

"Good!" Dr. Tosquelles laughs, slaps my knee. "Yes. Very!"

"And . . . now that the war is over . . . people just . . . stay?"

"They're free to leave, of course. This is not a prison. It's something different, here, that we've built. That we continue to build."

"What—is it, exactly?"

"This is a place of healing. Here, we are working—together, mind you. All of us, together—to attempt to heal alienation. To be mentally ill, yes, that is alienating. And also—to live in a capitalist society. That, too, alienates. Separates. Sickens. Here, at Saint-Alban, we are all equal. Patients, doctors, guests—" He nods to indicate that I fall into this last category, a relief, I suppose, given the options. "Nobody is undeserving of protection. And no one is exempt from the work of liberation. After all, Nora, all of us—each and every one of us—everyone needs to be healed, yes? After what we have endured? After what this world has become? The only cure is to heal not just the patients, but the world. And now, with the war won, fascism defeated . . . perhaps there is a chance."

Alienated. Separated. Sickened.

For the last few minutes, sitting in the sun with this man and listening to his story, I've been able to forget all the rest of it, but now it all comes back, a kaleidoscope of all the ugliest moments:

My mother is lying in her bed. Her skin is gray; her breath is shallow. Her chest rattles. From the television she refuses to turn off come the angry voices of her new gods. They're always screaming at us. I'm sick, too, but not nearly as sick as she is.

"Mom. Please." She's always been Gillian to me. But toward the end, I don't know why, she becomes Mom. "Let me call the hospital. They have medicines they can give you. They can help. Please."

"No doctors." She fights to get the words out. "Just a cold."

"It's not a cold. You know it's not. Mom, why won't you let them help you?"

I couldn't heal my mother, then. No one could. Now, this man believes he can heal the world, that the world can be healed. And it's not nihilism that I don't believe him. I know where we end up, after all. No matter how far we try to travel, we cannot move even half that distance.

I brought Gillian's remains to France with a childish hope that the act of spreading them could erase the person she became at the end, could recall to me the person she was before—but could that have even been possible? My mother left, my mother returned, my mother left again, and died. Or, seen another way: no matter how far she traveled, maybe she never really moved at all.

My body is heavy with inertia, exhaustion. I'm not ready to give up on finding Gillian's remains, but whatever energy I had is gone. Slowly, heavily, I pull myself to my feet. "I think I'll go back in."

"Nora."

I turn back; Dr. Tosquelles smiles. "Don't forget this," he says, and he hands me—so ridiculous, absolutely absurd—the carrot.

18

When it's time to sleep, I find that I've been moved into a large dormitory filled with rows of beds, twenty altogether.

When it was just me and Big Nora, though I had a room and a bed of my own, I never slept in it. I kept my stuffed animals piled on the mattress, and sometimes we would string a blanket over the light fixture to make a fort. But I slept with Big Nora. When Gillian returned, she moved into my room. A year later, when Big Nora died, Gillian took her room. Then the little room was mine again, and there I spent every night, alone. (I was not a girl who was invited to sleepovers.)

Now, as I stand awkwardly among the rows of beds, listening to the chatter of women—some conversations sensical, others less so—watching some slipping out of skirts and sweaters, pulling on nightshirts and nightgowns, pinning up their hair in curlers, spreading cold cream across their cheeks, and others being helped out of their day clothes and into their night things by nurses and other residents, I dearly miss my little room.

Sister Martine comes into the dormitory with a bundle in her arms. She scans the women, finds me. "For you." She holds out the bundle. It's a pink flannel nightshirt; a washcloth and towel; a toothbrush.

"Showers for women are Tuesdays and Fridays." When I look at her blank-faced, she reminds me, kindly, "This is Sunday." Then an elderly woman calls for help with changing her sheets, and I'm alone, again—as alone as one can be in a room full of other people, which, I've learned many times in my life, is really quite alone.

"Most everyone changes in front of each other, but some women are private." It's Penella, in a long white shift. Her headscarf is gone and she's unbraiding her hair. Loose, it reaches almost to her waist. There's a lock of white near the front, over her left temple, growing out of a scar. "If you want to change in peace, there's a curtain over there."

She nods to the corner, where there's a folding screen.

"Okay. Thank you."

I turn to go to the screen, but she touches my elbow gently. "Beryl wanted me to tell you that she found a bed for you. Near the window, over by her and me."

I scan the room and there's Beryl, her stomach even larger than before in an unconstraining nightgown. She lifts her bare arm in a wave, which I return.

After I change, I go over to them. Beryl's turned back the thin woolen coverlet and sheet of the third bed from the window. She pats its one flat pillow. It's a meager bed, but it smells fresh; seeing it, I'm hit by an ocean of fatigue. There's a box beneath my bed; I tuck my clothes inside it, set the shoes beside it.

Rustling and some laughter as the other women get into their beds. Someone switches off the lights, and then there's whispering for a while. I lie on my back with the blanket and sheet pulled to my chin. The blanket is tucked tight under the end of the mattress, pinning my feet in a way that I like. In the bed next to me, second from the window, is Beryl; in the bed against the wall, under the window, is Penella.

I'd told myself that when I was alone, I'd sort through everything the best I could, try to make a plan. I'm remembering what Penella said—*In here is better than what's out there, at least it has been for as long as I've been at Saint-Alban.* With a shiver—what is out there? In 1946, war is over, but barely. I have no idea how dangerous the thing I'm planning to do might be. It was one thing to travel the French countryside in 2021 with access to money and camping gear and pepper spray and a phone that could connect me to any information I might need, and quite another to roam penniless, alone, without resources or even the vaguest idea of how to get to where I plan to go . . . an autistic Jew on a continent still broken from a war with an antisemitic eugenicist dictator who almost took over the world. How can I make a plan without understanding what I might encounter?

With this question comes a wave of despair so overwhelming that maybe it knocks me out, because the next moment I'm aware, it's hours later.

The room is filled with sounds of women deep in sleep. The tall window frames a wedge of yellow moon. I blink into the darkness, waiting for my eyes to adjust. But before they can, there's another sound, perhaps the sound that woke me.

A moan. Pleasure, and then a little laugh, a gentle "shh," the rustle of sheets and blankets being pulled higher.

Beryl must have gotten up to use the toilet; her bed is empty. But in the bed beneath the window—Penella's bed—is a shape too large to be a single body. She's snuck someone in. I lie perfectly still. I wonder who he is. One of the boys from the garden, maybe? Earlier, in the garden, I saw two of them watching her stretch.

The blanket moves, and moves again, the humped shape beneath it rising up like a Halloween ghost. Another sound, another moan of pleasure. I close my eyes to give privacy to Penella and her ghost, but I can't keep her sounds from entering my ears.

I'm a girl again—eight, nine, ten. On the other side of the wall is Gillian's room, Gillian's bed. Noises that mean she isn't alone. By morning, her visitor is almost always gone. On these mornings, Gillian is soft and dreamy and pliant; she doesn't seem to be as bothered by anything I'm doing or saying. But then, for a short span of months when I'm just shy of eleven; a third person at our kitchen table. A wedge of chest hair—black—peeks from the neck of the robe he wears—Gillian's, flowered. On these mornings, Gillian puts on lipstick before breakfast; adds chocolate chips to the pancake batter; turns on music, even when I tell her not to. His name is Larson. I hate him. He smells like cigarette smoke and makes slurping sounds when he drinks his coffee. And he's always touching my things—moving around my supplies on the table to make room for his newspaper; closing my art book without marking the page it was open to; using my best pencil to fill in his crossword puzzle—bringing it to his lips, opening his mouth, moistening its tip with his tongue.

I knew Gillian was happy when he was there. I knew she liked him. But the thing with the pencil was too much. It was intolerable. My reaction was intense enough—and loud enough—to bring our neighbor Mrs. Kwon to our door. "Everything okay in there?" she called.

"Just fine!" Gillian called back, but her face was not fine. It was Picasso's *Weeping Woman*, sharp lines and unnatural colors, distorted and unfamiliar.

It had been years since I'd been beneath the table, but I went there, then, closing my eyes and covering my ears, rocking and crying, scaring myself with my sounds.

A conversation—a fight—between Gillian and Larson. Movement around the table. A coffee cup, breaking as it hit the sink. A little later, a slammed door.

The music stopped. Gillian's presence, as she sat in one of the kitchen chairs. Her cotton candy smell. Her hand, heavy and familiar, on my head. We were alone, again.

I stopped crying. I opened my eyes.

Her lips, still red with lipstick, were a hard line. "He was one good thing, Nora. And now he's gone."

But Gillian isn't here, in this room with Penella and her pleasure sounds. I'm here, and I can go somewhere else, too, somewhere other than back to my childhood, back to Gillian—I can take myself to the fire with Adrien, Robot sleeping safe nearby, and I've pushed Adrien back onto the bedroll, and my hands are warmed by his skin. My mouth is full of his honey tongue, and I'm learning how to make him make that sweet sound. A sharp peak of pleasure shudders through me. The French call it la petite mort, "the little death," and if this is what death is, okay, okay. All right.

I'm still, and the bed by the window has fallen silent. Will Penella's guest go, now that they've finished? I peep open my eyes, wondering who he is.

But no one climbs from Penella's bed. And that's when I notice that the bed between hers and mine—Beryl's—is still empty.

When I wake again, it's morning, and Beryl is in her own bed, next to mine. She's asleep on her side, facing me. Her hair—dark auburn curls, half as long as Penella's, but still longer than mine—tossed across her pillow. She smiles in sleep, and I know why.

The air is chilly, and I'm in no hurry to get up. Once up, I'll have to try to figure out where the caves are, and how I might get to them. It's a herculean task, overwhelming.

Beyond Beryl's bed, Penella's is empty. She made it before she left; the covers are drawn up tight, her nightgown folded on the pillow. Slowly, the room around me shifts and wakes: a yawn, the springs of the mattresses screeching as women sit up, bare feet padding across the worn wood floor. At last, Beryl wakes. If she's startled to see me lying in the next bed and watching her, she doesn't show it. She rubs her eyes, smiles more broadly, and tells me good morning.

When she sits up, it's slowly. She rotates around the sphere of her belly, scooting back and to the side before swinging her legs around and over the edge of the bed. Yawns and stretches her arms overhead. Soft patches of downy reddish hair under her arms. Her beauty is entirely different from Penella's. Penella is a storm—thunderclouds of hair, the lightning strike of her glare, the rumble, like thunder, that brews constantly right beneath her skin. Alive, electric. Beryl isn't a storm. She's a body of water. A river, a creek? The sea? Maybe it's because she's pregnant and I tend toward the literal, but she's a place that's both itself and also more: rich with life, deeper and more complicated than one can know from the shore.

"Did you sleep well?" Beryl asks.

I nod.

"Are you hungry for breakfast?"

I am.

"Well," she says, rocking to standing, "come on, then."

At the breakfast table, I'm silent. That's not unusual, but it's the reason that is different. I know something about Penella and Beryl, something they don't know that I know, and this feels like a lie. I see it, the thing that I know, in the way they attend to each other. Penella carries the tray with both their bowls together, the rims kissing. Beryl spreads a napkin between the bowls and lays two spoons upon it, side by side. The spoons are two bodies in a bed, the roundness of one slipping neatly, tightly, into the concavity of its mate.

"Nora, are you all right? Your face is going red!"

My gaze snaps up from the spoons. Beryl looks concerned, but Penella eyes me differently—knowingly, perhaps—and my face flames hotter.

As we're finishing our breakfast—I manage to eat half my porridge today, before passing it to Beryl—Dr. Tosquelles, who's seated at another table, stands, and taps his spoon against the side of his ceramic coffee cup. The conversations fade to a hum, and then silence, as most everyone turns toward him.

Seated next to him, a woman—the size of a large child but full-grown—raises and drops her arms, again and again. As her arms go up, they move the fabric of her skirt; as they drop, they strike the edge of her chair. Swish-*thump*, swish, *thump*, beating like a metronome.

"Friends." Dr. Tosquelles touches his mustache with a napkin, pat, pat. "Today I'll be heading up a contingency of foragers. Who would like to join? We'll be looking for the last of the chanterelles and oyster mushrooms. Sister Martine promises to make us quiche for supper." He sips loudly from his cup. Here and there, hands go up.

I'm tempted to raise mine; this is exactly what I need—a guided trip beyond the asylum's grounds. If I went, I could ask the others what they might know about the cave, maybe begin to get a sense of where we are in relation to it. But I'd also be out in the world, among strangers, I could be overwhelmed like I was yesterday in the yard—

"Nora," says Beryl, reaching across the table to touch my hand, "tell Penella to go. She should!"

Her hand is about the size and shape of mine. But her nails are lovely; mine are bitten to the quick, and my nailbeds are ragged from picking. I curl my fingers, ashamed. "You should go," I say.

Beryl pats my hand once, twice, and then pulls away. The absence of touch is enough to bring tears to my eyes. "Good," she says, as if that's settled. "And you too, Nora. You go, too. Mushroom quiche. My favorite!"

Dr. Tosquelles tells us to meet out front in half an hour and heads off briskly after draining his cup and setting it in the bin of dishes to be washed. Beryl says she can't stand another day of needlework, so she plans to go see if Jojo Chassang might need help setting up for movie night.

"You have movie nights?"

"Of course," says Beryl, grinning. "We're very civilized here."

We say goodbye and then Penella says, "Come on. I've got to make one stop before we go." She crosses the dining room and pushes through the swinging door into the kitchen. There's Henri, back at his station at the sink, elbow-deep in suds and whistling discordantly as he scrubs. Penella is filling a bowl with gruel scraped from the bottom of the large, dented pot, still sitting on the stovetop.

There's another door I didn't notice yesterday, between two floor-to-ceiling sets of cabinets. It's painted the same gray blue, chipped and smudged around the handle with greasy fingermarks.

Knocking matter-of-factly as she turns the handle, Penella pushes open the door and steps through. "Auguste," she calls, "you missed breakfast again."

I stand in the doorway and just—stare.

The room is either a destruction zone or a genius's workshop, or, more likely, both. Across from me is the only untouched surface—a large, curved window that marks the northeast corner of the castle, looking out over the kitchen garden where Penella and I worked yesterday. Diagonal muntins divide the beveled panes into stacked diamonds, each catching light and throwing it in a kaleidoscope of rainbows across the room. Shelves line all the walls—some narrow and tall, others deep and wide. Most of them are full, or at least half-full, of a collection of the strangest sculptures I have ever seen. They are too many, too varied, too bizarre for me to take in all at once, and so I blur my vision and let my eyes wash across them, taking them in in pieces—a flash of bright red, a sharp carved block, a stone, a shell, a spiked shard of glass. Piles of what looks at first to be trash, everywhere—scraps of wood and metal and glass, a jar of buttons full to overflowing, another of loose screws and bent and rusted nails, a third stuffed with feathers. Rolls and rolls of twine. Flattened pieces of tin and brass, stacked in a precarious tower.

The table in the middle is the nexus of all the creation. It's a workbench, large and worn, and at it sits a man, maybe twenty-five or thirty, in a green peaked felt cap; he hasn't stirred from his work since we entered his room. *His* room. That's clearly what this is. Because the creations around him, the disarrangement of the table, the stacks of tools, even the dance of rainbows twinkling across everything—the space *is* this person. Auguste.

Penella manages to find a porridge-bowl-sized gap on the table. After she's delivered the food, she puts a hand on Auguste's shoulder and peers at his work. There's a gentleness about her—the hand on his shoulder, her softened expression—that I've only seen before when she's with Beryl. She strikes me as the sort of person who doesn't make friends easily, but those she makes, she keeps.

Auguste is whittling an odd-shaped chunk of wood that's beginning to take on the features of an animal's face—maybe a pig or a boar, given the size and shape of the snout. "Ah, a self-portrait, I see," Penella says, grinning.

Auguste doesn't answer in words or even glance at us, but he raises and drops the shoulder her hand rests on, a sort of friendly rebuff.

Penella laughs, pats his shoulder. "Don't forget to eat, all right? And there will be quiche, later." With a raise of her chin, she indicates she's ready to leave. I haven't moved from the doorway, and I'm sorry to go. Just as with the boy at the Museum of the Counterfeit, I recognize Auguste. Well—I recognize myself *in* Auguste. And even though I've never been in this room before, I recognize it, too. It's his version of my corner in the kitchen. My sanctuary, for so many years. The drop cloth beneath my easel. The stack of canvases, leaned against the wall. The color studies taped up all around the window. The art books—there, in a stack; this one, splayed open on the table. Homesickness, sharp as a stomach cramp.

Auguste is an artist, we share that . . . but not only that. I see how he holds his right shoulder, high and tight. I see the tilt of his head. I see how close in he leans to his work, the clench-unclench-clench of his jaw.

Auguste is autistic, I'm almost certain. I don't know how they name his difference in this time, in this asylum. Is he a guest? A patient? Can one be both here?

There's a second whittling knife on the workbench, near Auguste's elbow, and the ache in my heart spreads down my arm, to my hand. I haven't made anything since before Gillian died. I haven't even wanted to.

But Penella is waiting, and this is my best chance to begin to get a grasp on where I am and where I need to go, so I back out of the doorway. Penella follows and closes the door, and then we're in the kitchen again and it's as if it's disappeared, all of it—the man in the green felt cap, the sculptures, the diamonds of glass, and the rainbows, too. But it hasn't disappeared. Even though I can't see it anymore, it's still there.

19

It's a fine day for foraging. Well—I've never foraged, so I don't know, but I suppose I say that because it's a good day for *anything*, really. The sky is slate but dry, the air is frigid but still. About ten of us head for the line of trees that smudges the horizon. We cross through the asylum's garden, which is larger than I thought, and then a field of wheat that rustles around us, whispering secrets. I run my hand along the tall golden stalks, the sticky bulbous heads.

On the far side of the wheat field we emerge onto a paved road, a thin strip of black that curves and disappears to the left, continues straight to the horizon on the right. Is this the road that brought me to the asylum from Montignac? I glance left, right, left again, but the road is completely foreign to me. The group heads left, and I go with them—toward or away from Montignac and the caves, I have no idea.

Dr. Tosquelles falls in the middle of the pack, chatting easily with this person and then that one. In his corduroy trousers and flannel coat, a pack on his back that holds some of our lunch provisions, he could be anyone. Penella pulls naturally to the front, maybe because she's a born leader, maybe because she doesn't want to set her pace to anyone else's, or maybe just because she doesn't feel like talking, which I can certainly understand. The decisiveness of her stride tells me this isn't her first trip to the forest.

A wide wicker basket swings from the crook of my arm. It's empty now, but others have said that if we're lucky, it will be brimming with mushrooms by the time we head back late this afternoon. I tried to make my face enthusiastic even though I can't stand mushrooms. It's the texture: spongy; and the truth of them: fungal. But I don't say this. Almost everyone in our foraging party is underweight. Even if no one here has died of starvation, as Dr. Tosquelles told me yesterday, some of them look like it had been a real possibility.

A while later, we turn off the paved road and onto a dirt footpath, winding toward a thatch of trees. As we walk, I ask a few of the others if they've heard about a cave somewhere in the region, an ancient cave discovered six years ago by a boy named Marcel and his dog, Robot. One woman, who's carrying a porcelain baby doll, acts as if she doesn't hear me—or maybe she truly doesn't, I can't tell—and two others shake their heads. A fourth person, extremely tall and thin, as willowy as the stalks of grain, nods enthusiastically—"Yes," he says, "the cave!"

He speaks so fast that my brain can't keep up, and I tell him three times, "Slowly, please, speak more slowly." Finally he does, but what he's telling me still doesn't make sense until I realize that he's not talking about *my* cave, at all.

"All their lives," the man is saying, "from childhood, the people are chained. By their ankles and necks, chained! So that they have no choice but to look, to stare, at one cave wall. That's all they know! That one wall. They cannot see one another; they cannot even see themselves. What a way to live a life, no? And behind the prisoners, a fire burns. And between them and the fire, men go back and forth, back and forth carrying objects, you see, just as puppet showmen have screens in front of them at which they work their puppets. But the prisoners don't know those shadows of men and their objects cast on the cave's wall are not the truth, do they? How could they know?" He stops, takes me by the shoulders. His expression is so alive, so intense, that I gasp. "How could they know," he says again, shaking his head. "They think it's the true world, but it's just an illusion."

"Not that cave," I try to interrupt, push away his hands—he's telling me Plato's allegory of the cave—but he barrels on and on about the shadows, the puppet show, the rare few who manage to escape the cave and see the true reality beyond. When I first read about the allegory of the cave, it seemed a brilliant philosophical musing; now, here, from this man, it strikes me as unbalanced rambling. A chilling thought, how close these two extremes may sometimes sit. When he bends to tie his shoe, I speed up, leaving him behind.

The smudge of trees has begun to individuate when Dr. Tosquelles falls into step beside me. "You're settling in?"

"I suppose." I shift the basket to my other arm. It isn't heavy, but it's awkward.

"Would you like me to carry that?"

I shake my head.

He digs into his coat's inside pocket for a pack of cigarettes and lighter.

"Aren't you worried about starting a fire?"

He lights the cigarette before answering. "It rains here so much this time of year that the grasses are wet on the inside."

We walk on, Dr. Tosquelles taking an occasional pull on his cigarette. I wonder if *he* may be familiar with the caves. He's not from here, but he does seem like a person who knows things. I'm on the verge of asking when a man—"Paul Éluard, a visiting poet, just arrived," is how Dr. Tosquelles introduces him—steps up on his other side, and the two of them begin an earnest discussion. I'm not trying to eavesdrop, but neither of them is a quiet man, and soon I've learned that Paul Éluard's wife has very recently died. Her name was Nusch. He cries freely as we walk, wiping the tears from his cheeks without shame or embarrassment, as if they're a fact of nature, the way one might wipe raindrops from a windowpane.

Their names—Paul and Nusch Éluard. I've read of them somewhere. In an art book. Yes—the Picasso book Gillian and I found at an estate sale. It included sketches of this man, Paul. And of Nusch. This man next to Dr. Tosquelles was—*is*—Picasso's best friend. And his wife, Nusch, she was Picasso's lover, their affair encouraged—"Perhaps orchestrated," the book had claimed—by Paul, himself. Because he loved them both so much.

Now that I know who he is, I can't stop looking at him. I remember in particular two sketches of him, side by side: one a profile, the other, straight-on. The profile had been cubist, clean lines in pen and ink, no shadows; an inverted triangle indicating the neck, horizontal lines for shoulders; a hatchwork of intersecting lines to create the planes of his face—the cheekbone; the temple; the brow. Only a few curves—a rosebud curl on the apple of his cheek; two shell-shaped curlicues within the greater C of his ear. These curves—the soft places among the network of straight lines . . . so loving. As if one was a place to drop a kiss, the other, a safe repository for confidences, whispered.

The other portrait, in which the poet faces the viewer, meets our gaze—more vulnerability, there. Not cubist, but realistic, plain. Pencil, shadowed and smudged. Hooded eyes; a small, closed, gentle mouth. Hair, receding and soft. A bare throat; beneath, a tangle of hard scratched lines, I didn't know what to make of that.

I'm sneaking glances now at Paul Éluard, on the far side of Dr. Tosquelles. He's in profile, as we walk, and yes, his nose—straight, strong, represented truly in Picasso's cubist rendering. And the curve of his ear, as his head tips down, as he listens—the shell shape of it. True. There's also a smudged-pencil quality to him, as in the other portrait: the shadow under his eye, dark from grief; lids heavy, almost purple. The two sketches layer over the face in front of me, double with the remembered images from the art book.

"Time is overflowing," says Paul Éluard, and Dr. Tosquelles nods sympathetically, throws an arm around his shoulders. My whole body vibrates with the magic of it, being beside this portrait made real, and the knowledge that right now—in the fall of 1946—Picasso himself is alive, and somewhere, not far away.

I slow my pace until they pull ahead.

Time is overflowing.

After we turn off the road, I give up looking for signposts or anything familiar. If we're anywhere close to where I'm trying to go, I can't tell. As we approach the tree line, I let go of trying to orient myself and take in the beauty of where we've come.

The forest is cool and full of shadows. We walk deeper in, and everyone goes quiet, together. The air is damp and still, fragrant from the trees. The ground here is soft; there, a fallen tree, its bark pulpy and yielding. Farther in, fluorescent moss creeps up trunks, feathery grasses strain for sunlight.

When we reach a clearing, Dr. Tosquelles swings the pack from his back, opens it, and extracts a bag full of small knives—some that fold; others, part of a multi-tool, like Adrien's Swiss Army knife; and a few short, dull table knives, probably borrowed from the kitchen. He hands them around. Then he goes over the basics: Never pull the mushrooms by their heads, as they're delicate. Always leave the base, so they can regenerate. Pay attention to the cap—avoid anything that's bright red or has white spots. Also avoid mushrooms with scaly or slimy caps (though who would want to eat such a thing anyway, I can't imagine). And pay attention, too, to the foot—the mushroom's stem. If it's ringed, that's a danger sign. If it changes color when it's cut, turning red or blue, drop it on the ground rather than into our baskets. And don't eat anything until either he or Penella has had a chance to examine it.

I listen carefully, but when we're set loose, I don't turn my attention immediately to mushroom hunting. I'm trying to remember what sorts of trees Adrien, Robot, and I passed on our way to the caves. I close my eyes to focus and see Adrien, tall pack on his back, turning his head to smile at me. My chest is tight with loneliness. I swipe my eyes and swallow, push down the hard hot lump. Even though we've come several miles, I need to move, to walk away from this feeling. Ahead is a slope, and I climb it.

A quick glance behind—some people are searching, others rest. No one seems to notice or care that I'm heading off on my own.

Dr. Tosquelles is sitting on a fallen log beside the very tall man, who's having some sort of a fit, or maybe a breakdown; he's crying and talking, rocking back and forth, and Dr. Tosquelles, lit cigarette dangling from his lip, is nodding in rhythm with the tall man's movement. Then his arm goes across the shoulders of the tall man, who turns to him, buries his face in his neck, dissolves in tears.

I look away. Too much, too much—the pain, the caregiving, too.

The vista gives me no new information. There's a creek, yes, that winds from the floor of the valley out into the fields beyond, and a paved road, different than the one we walked this morning, I'm almost certain, a flat black line, far to the . . . north? Wedges of trees; a patchwork of fences. Curves and lines, light and shadows. This place—this time, too—so foreign to me, in every way. Searching the horizon is no help.

My throat has softened, though, and I can breathe again. Down the hill, the tall man has recovered; he's red around the eyes and nose but he's laughing about something—miraculous, isn't it, that one can laugh just moments after such despair? The middle-aged woman has strapped her baby doll to her chest in a makeshift sling to free her hands for foraging, and a man in his mid-forties with cystic acne is busy touching everything twice, first with his left hand, then with his right.

"Hey." I gasp. It's Penella, eyeing me. "Your basket's empty." Hers is a cornucopia of fungus. "Haven't you found anything yet?"

Guilty, I scan the ground, spy a thatch of broad white caps sprouting along a rotted-out log. I point to them. "How about those?"

Penella goes over to the log, crouches down, cuts one of the mushrooms. "Yes," she says. "Fine." I crouch too and we work side by side, slicing stem after stem, the white meat severing smoothly. When they're all harvested, I stand and search for more of the same kind.

"I'm going to look down by the creek," Penella says. I nod but don't look up, and she catches me by the sleeve. "That's my way of inviting you along."

It's not a great way, in my opinion—much better would have simply been to say, "Do you want to come with me?" But I've never been great at inference. I've always thought that if someone wants to say something, they should just say it, and if they don't want to say it, they just . . . shouldn't. Nevertheless, I follow Penella down a slow slope toward the sound of moving water. There are so many ways to be misunderstood and to misunderstand. I hate that people don't just say what they mean, in the simplest language possible. Instead we're taught to encode, to bury meaning in suggestion and implication. It turns every conversation into a guessing game, and it exhausts me.

The bank of the creek is a wonderful place to mushroom hunt. Penella nods yes to the first three I find, and a hard no to the next several. Then she points me to a log, partially rotted. "There," she says, and I lower myself to the log, go to work.

She puts her basket on a rock, gathers her long skirt up above her knees, squats, opens her knife, and beheads mushroom after mushroom, her blade slipping through white stems, stopping against the pad of her thumb.

Near her the creek burbles merrily, and together she, the creek, and the fecund beauty of the forest form a scene of such . . . *importance,* that's the word, that I'm pinned perfectly still by it. Suddenly, from where she kneels, Penella sharp as her blade—"Don't look at me like that."

Embarrassed, I look away. "Like what?"

"Like you're worshiping me or something."

"I'm not worshiping you."

Penella cuts the last of the clutch of mushrooms and stands. She takes the basket and walks slowly along the bank, eyes trailed on the ground. When she spies another cluster she grabs her skirt again, hefts it above her knees, kneels, cuts. "Good. You shouldn't."

"It's just—you're beautiful." The words are thick, hard to say, and yet, they insist.

"Sure. I know." She doesn't look up from her work, but her dark brows pull together, displeased. "Beauty is stupid," she says at last, the blade in one hand, a newly severed mushroom in another. "It's a weapon women think they wield until someone turns it against them." She puts the mushroom in her basket, returns to work. If I listen very carefully, I can hear the slip of her blade through the stems. Her sleeves are pushed up; some of her scars are bright pink, fresh, but others are whitened, almost exactly the shade of the mushroom's flesh.

I don't agree with Penella—that beauty is stupid—but I know that she's right, about it being a weapon that can cut both ways. I'm not beautiful. That's all right with me; I don't spend much time looking in the mirror, so it's better that there's beauty outside of me that I can see and appreciate, rather than in my own face, which is almost always invisible to me. My mother felt differently. She often mentioned that a different hairstyle might better suit my features, or that I could put more effort into what I wore—that clothes are about more than comfort, things like that. And then, there was our battle over whether or not I should get braces.

When I was a freshman, Gillian asked our dentist for a referral to an orthodontist. Not because my bite was off; for aesthetic reasons. "It never hurts to have a pretty smile, and it often helps," Gillian said.

The thought of little metal things glued to my teeth for months on end, strung together by a wire that would be ratcheted tighter and tighter, forcing my teeth to shift—unbearable. I couldn't even stand to wear a shirt with an itchy seam. Even before we'd crossed the parking lot, I told Gillian I wasn't going.

"There's nothing wrong with being pretty, dearheart," she said, unlocking the car. "Why make it *harder* for people to like you?"

Maybe I should have just done it. After all, how different would it be to shift my teeth from learning to shove my hands into my pockets, or remembering to ask more questions and "give fewer lectures"? But I couldn't have something in my mouth like that—I could barely manage the half-hour dental cleaning twice a year. And for what? So that my left incisor would line up more perfectly? To close the small gap between my two front teeth?

I wouldn't do it, I told her. If she forced me to, I'd bite the orthodontist's hand. I'd snip the wires. I absolutely *would not* submit to braces.

I could tell I'd won. Her body sort of . . . deflated. She shook her head. And then she said, "What is crooked will not be able to be straightened, and what is missing will not be able to be counted."

I could tell from the way she said it that she was quoting something, but I didn't know then that it was from the Torah. Unlike Gillian, who'd had a Bat Mitzvah, I had no formal Jewish education. Still, even before I looked it up, I knew what she meant.

And I knew that she wasn't talking about my teeth.

"You look troubled." Penella appraises me.

I admit I am.

"Well?" says Penella. "Want to tell me?"

I do. I do want to tell her. I don't know where to start, or how. But I do know that I am so, so tired of being alone. Maybe Penella is someone who could be a friend—a true friend.

All my life, friendship has been a difficulty. When I was in elementary and middle school, Gillian used to say, "I just don't get it. Don't you *want* to make friends?"

I didn't answer, because the answer was so obvious as to not be worth saying aloud: Yes, I wanted friends. The problem was that "friends" didn't want me. And after enough failed attempts, my desire for them faded, too. Or, more precisely—my desire to make the attempts faded.

"Make" is an interesting word. It can mean two things: to create, or to coerce. Neither of these tactics results in a friend. One can make a painting, or a sculpture, or a mess. One can coerce a person, through threats or promises, to sit beside you at the lunch table. I'd done both of these things. Neither resulted in friendship.

Still, I could try again, now. Here. With Penella. After all the things I've gone through, everything I've endured, *this* feels terrifying. Why is that? The answer is, of course, because I want it so badly.

"I lost someone," I say at last. And, of course, the phrasing pleases me—even when I'm troubled, I find solace in language.

"You're smiling."

I flatten my lips. It would be too complicated to explain. "Not about the person I lost."

"So?" she asks. "Who did you lose?"

"My mother."

"Ah." Penella stabs her blade into the earth. "I'm sorry to hear that. A girl needs her mother."

"Did you . . . lose your mother, too?"

"I lost my whole family."

"I'm very sorry." When she looks up, we have a moment—a hopeful one, it seems to me. A flash of recognition, of sameness. It makes me hungry for more. "Were you close? You and your mother?"

"What do you mean, close?"

"Did you . . . well, did the two of you get along?"

She raises an eyebrow. "What do you know about the Roma?"

I have to admit, not much.

"For the Roma," Penella says, "family is the most important thing. *Family* is home. Not country, not structure—family. Understand?"

"Yes," I say.

"So there you go. Yes, I was close with my mother. Family was her home. Her *children* were her home, her greatest treasure, her every delight."

I'm trying to imagine what this might have felt like. At first, I can't—I don't think I was Gillian's home, or treasure, or delight; I think I was her burden. Then I remember those brief years with Big Nora, and I understand.

"Do you want to tell me what happened to your mother?" Penella asks.

I clear my throat. "Well, she got sick. She needed help. And . . . it feels like it was my fault. Like I was supposed to save her, and I failed."

"It's been a terrible time," Penella says. "So much loss. It's tragic, that your mother is gone." She's looking past me now. I have the feeling that she's talking about my mother but thinking about hers. When she speaks again, she confirms it: "My mother was an exceptional woman. It's very painful, as I think you understand, to talk about her."

I nod.

"Ours was a traditional family. Nine of us. My mother, my father, Father's mother, two uncles who were not yet married, me—the oldest—and my three younger siblings, including the baby, Luca. Mother had just birthed him, at the end. But I'll get to that. First—my mother. As I said, our family was traditional. Proud. And very close. If I told a secret or something embarrassing to my younger sister at breakfast, my uncle Ion would be teasing me about it before lunch. But my mother was different. If I told her something—something precious, something important—she never teased. She took me seriously. She . . . *saw* me, I suppose is the clearest way to say it. She saw things about me that I didn't see—or want to see—myself. Especially as I got older." Penella clears her throat, wipes the back of her hand against her nose. "You know what the Vichy government did to us, of course?"

I shake my head.

"Where have *you* been?" she asks, but I'm not meant to answer. "The French never liked us, never claimed us as their own, which, fine. The wars they fought—those were *their* wars, not ours. When my parents were young, it was live-and-let-live, for the most part . . . but that changed with the war. Suddenly the government made it illegal to be a 'nomad,' as they call it. Can you believe it? It's like telling the hawk that it's breaking the law when it flies." Her gaze goes to the sky; mine follows. "We were made to carry identity cards and have them stamped whenever we came to a new place, and then it got worse—much worse."

She looks down, across the water. When she turns back, her voice is softer. "Many families were herded up, caged . . . not like cattle. Cattle have value. Cattle are fed and kept warm, protected from disease." She pauses. "But my family was not caged." She's quiet. Then she swipes tears from her cheeks, roughly.

I want to comfort Penella, but I don't know how. What would be welcome, and what would be an intrusion? Do I hug her, hold her hand? When I'm upset, sometimes I need to be left entirely alone; the smallest touch on my shoulder can send me over the edge. But other times I need pressure, either given in a tight embrace or manufactured through a wrapped blanket, wedging myself into a corner. What does Penella need?

Before I can decide and offer, her face has returned to the determined, high expression that seems to be its set point. "Even before the war, the French never saw my people as their equal. But to the Vichy, we were vermin. And to kill vermin, if that's what people are to you, it's not so hard, I suppose. And once my family was gone . . . it became difficult, you understand. They all died—even my mother, even baby Luca—and I lived. How can I explain that?"

"And that's why . . ." I gesture to her wrists.

"It's the last thing my mother would have wanted." She looks down at the long white scars, runs the tip of her knife up and down, a caress. "This, my mother would have been ashamed of." She takes the knife away from her flesh, stabs it in the earth again. "Mothers aren't supposed to have a favorite child, but everyone knew I was hers. To begin with, I looked the most like her. My mother used to say that my face was like a mirror into her past. I loved that. Because she was beautiful, yes? That's something every girl wants to be, before she knows better. And also she liked that I had a temper, because she did, too. My father was the peacekeeper; my mother was never afraid to wage war. Especially for her children, and most especially for me. If she felt I wasn't getting what I deserved—even in a trade among my siblings, even from my father—she'd be right there, defending me. But then, before she died—before they all died—she and I had a . . . not a rupture. That's too strong a word. Just—she began to see in me something that was *not* a mirror of herself. Not a reflection of what she hoped for my future." She's looking up, now, just sort of staring at the trees, but if I had to guess I'd say she isn't really seeing them, at all. Finally, she blinks, clears her throat. "In any case, they are dead. And I am not. And I know my mother would want me to live, to live enough for all of them. So I am trying."

I want to know what the "not rupture" had been about. Am I allowed to ask? Is that weird? Or is she maybe hoping I will? At last, I say, "I'm glad you have Beryl. That you and she have each other. At least you're not alone."

Penella narrows her eyes. "That we have each other?"

I nod.

"You saw us, didn't you? Beryl and me, in bed together."

"I wasn't trying to spy," I say. "You're in love, the two of you, aren't you?"

She's quiet for the briefest of moments. "We're in love." She says it like she's testing the words, or me. "It's unnatural, yes?" She lifts her chin.

"People used to think so," I begin, and then stop. Even in 2021, it's not as if homosexuality is universally accepted. It's true that gay marriage became legal in the States in 2013, but it's also true that our previous president did everything he could to make things more dangerous for people who are queer, and to make things safer for those who want to strip away their rights. Things aren't simple, anywhere, anytime. Homosexuality has been cyclically accepted and rejected by many societies, at many different times. Some of my favorite painters were involved in queer relationships, even if that's not a word they'd have used.

I know what I want: to be Penella's friend. For her to like me. For her to be someone I can talk with about the things that matter to me, to her, too. I want to give her what she wants, if I can figure out what it is, and I want her to know that I think love of any kind is beautiful, lucky. I'm trying to get the words right, in the right order, to figure out what to say, but also what not to say, to choose the right words and the right tone and the right expression, but it's taking too long, and I'm leaving Penella to guess what I think, to make assumptions.

"For my people, something like what I have with Beryl would not be accepted. It would be considered . . . unclean. Forbidden."

If Penella's mother had lived, if she'd seen her daughter loving another woman . . . would she have thought Penella was "broken"? Or would she have gone to war for her? And by the same measure, if her mother had lived, would Penella have ever allowed herself to love a woman? Or would she have sacrificed that part of herself, to spare her?

My relationship with Gillian was all one way, me forcing her to make sacrifices, over and over again. All the way back to when she returned on my fourth birthday to find me—difficult, needy—and then to be left alone with me when Big Nora died . . . my consistent failure to be who she wanted me to be, who she *needed* me to be. Then, with the man, Larson. *He was one good thing, Nora. And now he's gone.* Did she mean that Larson was *a* good thing, one good thing among many? Or did she mean he was *the* one good thing—the only good thing in her life? Then at the end, she disappeared herself down a rabbit hole of conspiracy theories and bad science, refusing to protect herself against disease, refusing treatment once she'd been infected . . . because of me.

I don't think it wouldn't have been like that, with Penella and her mother. She said her mother was *proud* of her. If her family had lived, she and her mother would have found a way, together. I can tell by the way she talks about her mother's love—how deep it was, and how earned. "You feel guilty because you're happy with Beryl, and you couldn't be with her, if your family was alive," I begin. "But—"

In an instant, Penella folds closed her knife, stands. Her face closes as surely as the blade. I've said the wrong thing. I've said a terrible thing.

"I didn't mean that you're *glad*," I begin, but she's taken her basket and walked away.

On the way back to the asylum, Penella keeps to herself again, skirt swishing around her ankles as she strides in front of us all, alone. I trudge along, the basket of mushrooms heavy in the crook of my arm, a wave of desperation, of truth:

What is crooked will not be able to be straightened, and what is missing will not be able to be counted.

Bile burns my throat.

Stupid. Stupid. Stupid.

And the ashes, too—what was I even thinking? That if I found the right place to spread them, I'd be able to let go of this mess, this burden? This knowledge of what my mother surely felt, even if she wouldn't admit it: that I was a problem to be fixed, not a person to be loved?

What is crooked will not be able to be straightened, and what is missing will not be able to be counted.

We're at the wheat field now. On the far side is the asylum. Suddenly, I'm cold. The wheat rustles, loud; I've been so deep in thought that I didn't notice the shift in weather. The wind is up, the sky is menacing with thunderheads. Lightning flashes, a shock of silver in the sky. A low, long rumble. And then the sky cracks open.

20

Sister Martine is waiting for us when we come through the kitchen door. "Soaked like soup, the bunch of you," she says, handing us towels. "Leave your shoes by the door, don't bring mud across my clean floor."

It's a festive atmosphere, everyone huddled around the hot oven, steam rising from their sweaters, clinking mugs of cider. I want nothing to do with it.

"We still have time for group conversation, my friends," calls Dr. Tosquelles, tapping a finger on the face of his watch. "Open to all!" I know he's talking to me—I'm probably the only one here who hasn't been to group therapy yet—but I won't look at him.

One by one the mugs are drained, set in the sink, and the kitchen clears out. Then it's just me and Sister Martine, who's emptied the baskets of mushrooms across her worktable and is sorting them.

"Are there dry clothes anywhere?" I ask.

She looks up from the mushrooms. "Wet all the way through, eh? There's a cabinet in the sewing room with odds and ends. You can leave your things in the laundry. We'll see they make their way back to you sooner or later."

I nod, turn to go.

"Everything all right, dear?"

I pretend not to hear, push through the swinging door.

The sewing room is empty, which is a relief. In the cabinet, lots of skirts and dresses, some workwear—coveralls, overalls—a few military uniforms, blue, and one pair of dark green flannel trousers. I choose the trousers, find a blouse—dove gray, very soft, gathered at the shoulders and the cuffs. It's missing a button, but at the bottom. There's a bin of undergarments—I ignore the girdles and the bras and fish out a pair of silky underwear. In the darning basket are two socks that nearly match; I'll just have to wait for my boots to dry, but when a crack of lightning floods the room, followed by the low report of thunder, I know I won't need shoes for a while, anyway. I change out of my wet clothes; the pants fit fine but the blouse is thin, so I go back to the cabinet and rummage for another layer. There's a cardigan and a pullover; I decide on the cardigan, but when I reach for it, my hand brushes something rabbit-soft. I pull it out of the cabinet and hold it up. It's a vest; white, but not purely so; the slightest tinge of yellow, too, a reminder that this is the pelt of a creature, a real being that once was alive.

In normal times, I would never wear a fur. They're the result of a cruel industry, and a senseless one, at least from a practical stance; other fabrics and fibers are just as warming. And whoever made it fashion to wear another's skin atop one's own? But the vest reminds me of the sweater I once had, the one I loved so much that I wore it for school pictures two years in a row.

I take both things—the cardigan and the fur vest. The vest is weighted and calming, luxuriously warm.

The door to the room where they hold group therapy is closed now, and there are voices behind it; I rush past. In the main room, people are setting up rows of chairs, most likely in preparation for the movie Beryl mentioned; I hurry past this door, too. Here comes Beryl, smiling and waving, but I'm not interested in company, what I want is to find some small and quiet place, a place to tuck inside, a place to disappear.

It should be simple to get lost in a castle. But I open half a dozen doors and find people behind each—reading, playing cards, a man clipping his toenails over a trash bin. At last I climb two flights of stone staircases and then a rickety wooden one into a long, skinny attic; at one end is a stack of boxes and cartons, a few wooden chests, a dress form. At the other, under a window, is an old four-poster bed, covered with dusty sheets. I don't care about the dust; I climb beneath the top sheet, pull it up and over my head. I'm on my side curled into a ball. My hair, flattened beneath my cheek, is damp and smells like rain. My feet are dry and warm. My fingers are interlaced. My knees are stacked, the right atop the left. I'll stay here. I'll stay right here.

It's a long, sleepless night. The rain pounds and then patters and then whispers against the roof. The sky grows darker, goes black, and begins to lighten again.

Over and over, I replay the conversation with Penella, take right turns instead of wrong.

"There's nothing unnatural about love," I tell her.

"I'm sorry your family is dead, and I'm sorry you've had to hide who you are."

"You deserve love."

I'm alone, talking only to myself.

I'm the last living person in my family. I've been orphaned, in every way. I've lived through a worldwide outbreak of a disease that has killed nearly five million people—my mother among them. I've given up my home and all of my possessions. I've traveled across the globe with a canister of my mother's ashes. I've survived an attack by a stranger in a forest in rural southern France. I've traveled through time to 1946. I've lost the ashes. I've found myself here, in an asylum for the insane.

Each of these truths, unbelievable—unacceptable—on their own. But I'd rather accept all of them than this last truth: in spite of all the ways I contorted myself, all the ways I tried to be the person Gillian wanted, *needed* me to be . . . I was never going to be that person. And if I wasn't worthy of my mother's love, how can I be worthy of anyone else's?

Isn't it terrible that morning always comes?

Time keeps moving, you can't slow it or stop it, not even if you find yourself displaced. It's a machine, a ticking slow-rolling steamroller, and it's relentless and crushing and unavoidable.

Well. There's one way to step out of its path.

The choice is—has always been—breath, or death.

I blink up at the triangular window; it's little and high, tucked against the roofline that peaks, just there. For a small window, it lets in a lot of light. The storm has passed; it's a bright fresh day. Dust motes wander and spin.

No one has disturbed me, up here. I wonder if they think I've run off, or if anyone even notices I'm missing. It almost makes me cry, wondering. I could stay right here. I consider it—what it would be like, to sink into stillness. After all, I've already disappeared from my life, such as it was a week ago. It wouldn't make a difference—to anyone—if I never got up again. Finding my mother's lost remains, scattering them somewhere, when it's not going to change anything about how she felt about me, or how she died . . . that's not a reason to get out of bed. It's an exercise in futility. Maybe everything is.

I don't want to move . . . but my bladder doesn't care what I want. I put it off as long as I can, but eventually I have to throw back the sheet and get out of bed.

Luckily, I have the restroom to myself—it's very early, still. I'll go to the kitchen, find some water and some bread, and then go back up to the attic. I know I can't hide forever, but I can't bear to see anyone, not yet.

When I turn the corner toward the dining room, Marguerite Sirvins is in her chair in the hallway, working on her dress. She looks up. "You should come to my wedding. I'm inviting you. My dress is almost finished. Look."

I don't want to talk; not to her, or anyone.

"I've died one hundred twenty-two times. I have been crushed eleven times. I have married seven times, already. This will be my eighth."

It doesn't matter if I speak or stay silent; her side of the script remains unbroken. "Now I hear someone speaking to me morally in my glurb. All my bones are broken. My heart is gone. I think even my glurb is missing. They transposed it. They had to cut off a piece of my arm, and they put it back."

I'd like to help her, but if I were to say something, I'd probably only make things worse. I turn and go toward the kitchen. Behind me, plaintively: "I asked for hot chocolate at breakfast. I get watery soup in the morning, at noon, and at night. How can a person be healthy? The eyes pop out. The nose weeps." As I go through the dining room: "And since I never get omelets, rabbit, or chicken, judge what kind of health I'm in."

On the far side of the dining room, my hand on the swinging door, I stop. The encounter with Marguerite Sirvins has overwhelmed me. I'm brimful, the way I can become, filled this time not with the pounding beat and flashing lights of a high school dance, but the despair of a single woman lost inside herself.

Those places aren't for normal people, Nora. If you ever end up in a place like that, it's a sign that you've taken a real wrong turn, somewhere. So take another turn, as fast as you can, to get the hell out.

After a long moment, I push through to the kitchen and hope to find it empty. But Sister Martine is already here—does she ever leave?

I haven't brushed my hair or washed my face, and I know what I must look like, but Sister Martine either doesn't notice or pretends not to. Instead, she compliments my new clothes and asks if I'll take a bowl of porridge in for Auguste. He's not in his workshop yet, but he should be arriving any moment.

I don't say anything, but I pick up the bowl.

It's only the second time I'm in this room, and I feel like I'm trespassing without Auguste. I should probably just set down the bowl and leave, but I can't resist looking at his creations. So many sculptures filling the shelves, and tucked in among them, scraps of material, little cans of nails and broken glass, not a wasted inch, anywhere. Here is a general upon a horse; the general's trunk and the horse's body are carved out of a single piece of wood. The general's arms are attached to his body so they can swing, as if he had shoulder joints; his tall red hat is adorned with tiny links of a metal chain; a red button secured by a length of red twine hangs around his neck; his cuffs are ribboned in red. He sits his mount in a relaxed swagger. The horse is saddled and bridled in bits of leather cleverly knotted and tied. There's not a detail overlooked; each sculpture is complex, each a whole world in a single object.

A fish with human teeth and legs and a flounce of feathers, both real and carved; a fish-wolf-boar creature, with fangs and a length of chain hanging from its snout; an armored fish-hippo, again with real teeth—children's? An animal's?—each tooth fastened to the wood with tiny, rusted metal hooks, and a marble eye rimmed with a round of red leather.

So many of his carvings are animal-people amalgams. Their features are radically different from one another . . . but look—the horse man is bridled; the bird man has bandaged arms. Parts of these creatures are free; parts of them are hobbled. Their faces, though rough-cut, are provocatively ambiguous. Flat mouths. Eyes wide open. The expressions could mean one thing, and also its opposite. Horror, or ecstasy? Fear, or fascination? Impossible to say. I love them.

Other things, too: delicately carved houses, with disturbing proportions: the doors too small, windows too large, roof shingles somehow menacing. Several incredibly intricate boats, or ships, I suppose—made of wood and metal and leather and fabric and twine, painted and stained, works of such staggering delicacy but yet, somehow . . . brutal.

Again, in his houses and boats: freedom and constraint. Right alongside each other. Auguste may not talk much, or at all, but he clearly speaks in his work.

I didn't come in here intending to feel better. I didn't even intend to come in. But that's the thing about art: it insists. I set down the porridge and find Auguste standing in the open door, watching me, his green felt hat tipped earnestly forward.

"I brought you breakfast. I've been looking at your work."

At first, he makes no indication that he's heard me. Then he shrugs as if to say that it makes no difference one way or the other, crosses to his workbench, and sits on his stool. So I turn back to his figures. One in particular fascinates me.

The bird man. He's beaked, but a smudged line of red gives the suggestion of lips, downturned. His arms, connected to his body by nails, are articulated, able to swing back and forth. But they're wrapped in yellowed bandages, as if he's come through some terrific battle, injured but alive, and transformed in some awful, animal way. Scraps of leather around each ankle seem to imply that he's been hobbled, but he wears what looks like a military medal on his chest, which seems to imply honor. Zipper teeth around his neck and head. And, perched on each shoulder of the bird man: a bird.

The line that my mother quoted me about the crooked and the missing—it's part of a chapter that also contains a much more famous verse: *The thing that has been, it is what will be; and what has been done is what will be done: and there is nothing new under the sun.*

All the colors that can possibly be combined have already been combined. All the stories that can ever be told have been told already. All losses have been suffered; all victories have been won.

But Auguste's bird man? It seems singular, to me.

"I really like your work," I tell Auguste. I hardly notice how natural it is for me to speak here, about this. "I like how nothing in it is easy. Like, here"—I point to the bird man's bandages—"these could be sleeves of a shirt, you could have cut the fabric the way you did for the pants, sort of rectangularly? But instead, you've wrapped the arms. Like he's been injured. And he's a bird, obviously, because of the beak. Except he has arms. So it makes me wonder about what happened to his wings. Because you could have given him wings—here, coming out of his back—but you didn't. And so what I think is that he *had* wings, once, but now they're arms. And that's got to be painful. Unnatural. For a bird to have arms. It feels like the wings were cut off. And then the arms were added, later. That's why they're nailed in like this, rather than part of his body. And that's why you gave him the bandages."

I don't look to Auguste for confirmation; that's not how art works, that's not how I want it to work. I don't need him to affirm my interpretation. Auguste made the bird man, and now it exists.

I'm calmer now. Talking about art, thinking about it, is the same as it's always been; it's a place for me to pour myself. A container that always has room for me.

Auguste hasn't touched his porridge. He's hunched around his work, carving pinprick holes along the edge of the wooden animal-beast in front of him, a sort of part deer, part turtle. There's a second stool, tucked beneath the table.

"Is it all right if I stay?"

He stops working, his delicate, calloused fingers frozen midair. Then he shrugs again. So I sit, watch closely. The pinprick holes aren't uniform: some are deep, others barely scratches. Sometimes he rotates the tool, rubbing it inside the hole to enlarge it, other times he pokes straight in and then pulls out, leaving a neat prick. Eventually, though, the network of holes reveals itself to be taking the shape of a reptilian leg, the latticework of holes finely rendered, uneven, impressionistic scales. It reminds me of *A Sunday on La Grande Jatte*, how, when you pull back a little, the sum of the work is greater than its parts.

Remembering Seurat brings me again to Gillian, to the sum of the parts of her and me. *Don't do that with your mouth, dearheart. Don't do that with your hands, dearheart. Not everyone with a dog wants you to stop and pet it, Nora. Try not to get caught up in one of your rants. He was one good thing. What is crooked will not be able to be straightened*—I'm stepping back now, further, and further—and the image that's forming isn't what I believed it to be. It's not a mother who loved me in spite of everything. Instead, with distance, and time, and contrast, I see a gueule cassée—a broken face. My own. Not lovable. Not loved.

I don't cry very often. I hate the way my sinuses get so stuffed up, I hate not being able to breathe through my nose, I hate the feeling that I'll never stop crying, once I've begun. I hate the way other people look at me when I cry. Sometimes the expressions are pitying; other times, they're annoyed or embarrassed on my behalf. I hate that crying is a thing that happens to my body without my consent.

But I'm crying now. My elbows on Auguste's worktable, my head in my hands. It takes a long time before it stops. When it finally does, I sit up, wipe my face, sniff.

Auguste is beside me, still working. He's rocking, a small motion, back and forth with his upper body while his hands work steadily.

I almost apologize for crying. If I were with my mother, or at school, or with almost anyone, really, I would. But I can tell Auguste isn't bothered. Not because he doesn't care that I was crying; just that it doesn't *bother* him, that I was. Those aren't the same things—not caring and not being bothered—but they can look the same, if you don't pay close enough attention.

Suddenly, he stops. Reaching into a basket beside him, he withdraws a hunk of wood and sets it on the table near my hands. Then he pushes over a tool—a carving implement with a spoon-like blade—and returns to his work.

I pick up the block. "I haven't made anything in a really long time," I tell him. "And what I used to do was paint."

Auguste doesn't say, *I'm sure whatever you make will be wonderful* or any of the other platitudes most people would offer. He doesn't say anything at all, which is good, because how would he know what I would make, or if it would be wonderful? Those are things people say to make other people feel better. But they can't *know*.

At first, I'm frozen with the block of wood in my hands. But I've never carved anything; maybe carving doesn't need to feel fraught, the way that painting does. And Gillian isn't here, to see it. Closing my eyes, I run my fingertips along the ridges of the wood, wondering what sort of shape might be hidden inside. An image flashes in my mind. So I open my eyes, shrug out of my vest, and pick up the carving tool.

Beside me, Auguste works, too, the tip of his tall cap folded forward, his energy folded forward along with it. On the far side of the door, voices and the clatter of dishes as breakfast is served; later, by the time I've roughed in four legs, a head and a tail, more voices, more clattering, water running as dishes are scrubbed clean. I hope no one will come in, and no one does. I turn the block this way and the other, I blow away curlicues of carved wood, I rub my thumb along the indentations as I discover the shape inside. It's rudimentary and childish, but that's all right.

When I'm finished, hours have passed. I don't know how I know I'm finished; that's the way it is with art, sometimes. The hum settles, and then you're done. It's not very good, barely recognizable as what it is, but anyway, it doesn't matter. Done is done. And it's something I've made, separate from anyone else. If I hadn't made it, this figure wouldn't exist. Flawed as it is, it's an original, the first I've made in many years.

I place it in front of Auguste, who looks up from his work for the first time. He lays down his tool, picks up the dog. He turns it over and over, rubs the same spot I love the most about it—the sweet divot between its rough-hewn ears.

"I made it after a dog I met, called Robot."

He nods vigorously, holds it against his chest.

"You can keep it."

He nods again, pats it. He's still holding it when I leave.

21

The rest of the day, I avoid everyone. I hurry past the group therapy room; I wander in the garden; I ignore Beryl when she waves to me at dinner, try not to look at Penella beside her, take my plate up to the attic. Then it's morning again, and I return to the workshop. This time with two bowls of porridge.

Auguste is working on one of his ships, one I would have thought for sure was finished. He's taken it down from the shelf and is affixing a small carved soldier into its hull. Half a dozen others are lined up like cigars on his worktable, not identical but of a kind. He has an expression on his face—a sort of smile, like he's holding a secret.

It makes me nervous. "I'm back."

Instead of shrugging, he jerks his head—*Over there,* he's telling me, *by the window.*

I set down the bowls of porridge and go to the corner with the good light. An easel, positioned on an angle. A well-used wooden palette. A hip-high bench with a half-dozen brushes, each a different size. A banged-up metal box beside them. I flip the latch; handfuls of small silver tubes, each tagged with a swatch of color. A few canvases lean against the wall.

Words escape me again; fortunately, with Auguste, I don't need them. Clutching a handful of paint tubes, I look over my shoulder. Auguste is grinning now, and with the light like this his eyes are a curious brown gold that reminds me of something. Maybe I'd figure out what except that he reaches out and touches my rough-hewn dog, gives it an affectionate pat on the head.

I spend the whole day in Auguste's workshop, but I don't paint. I putter—organizing things, lining up brushes and finding some rags and sorting through the paint tubes, discarding those that are too old and stiff to be used anymore, taking stock of what's left. I pull over the second stool and sit on it, then stand right back up again.

It's such a nice thing Auguste has done for me, and I don't want to disappoint him. But I don't know if I can paint anymore. I don't know if I want to.

That night, Beryl finds me in the attic. I know it's her even before she appears, from the heavy, slow steps she takes up the stairs. "It's freezing up here." She stops at the top of the staircase to catch her breath, both of her hands on her lower back. "Do you mind if I join you?"

I'm in bed, a quilt I've taken from downstairs around my shoulders. I scoot over to make room.

"Blanket," she says, and I pass her some. Now we're shoulder to shoulder, leaning against the bedstand, both tucked in. "That's better."

I still haven't said anything.

"Hey," says Beryl, leaning into me, "do you want to tell me what happened between you and Penella?"

I shake my head.

"That makes two of you, then," she says, as if to herself. "Two mules' heads."

My stomach turns. Why hasn't Penella told Beryl what happened in the forest, what I said? Probably because it was such a terrible thing to say, she can't even bear to repeat it.

"Do you like it up here? Even though it's cold enough to crack a stone?"

I shrug.

She sighs. Pats my knee. "All right," she says, and she groans as she rolls to standing. "Suit yourself."

But before she leaves, one hand on the banister, she adds—"It's not all or nothing, you know. There are many places in between."

Every time I think about Penella—the way she folded her knife and walked away—every time I recall what I said, my stomach churns with bile. Once, when I'm passing through the dining hall with my plate, she gets up from beside Beryl and starts to cross toward me; I practically run to avoid her. How can I be so *wrong*, all the time? Why do I keep failing people I want to help?

The only place the sick feeling abates is with Auguste. Art is—and has always been—a way to quiet the voices. So even though I was hesitant to do so, I begin to experiment with the oil paints. For the last few years, I worked primarily in acrylics, which dry much faster; with the oils, there's a whole new set of rules and constraints and variables to learn. I work on color studies—quick sketch-like paintings on burlap and plain brown paper, just exploring how the oils interact.

For a while, that's enough to take up all the space in my brain, to push away everything else. Gillian and her ashes. Penella, too. She and I pass like strangers when we see each other in the hallway or the bathroom—but eventually the color studies aren't enough to wash away the disquiet, and the choice becomes to either start a painting or deal with reality.

I choose the smallest canvas, about the size of a desktop screen. It needs primer, which I apply in thin coats with my widest brush, reapplying after each layer dries, over a span of several days. Auguste is pleased I've finally taken up a canvas, I can tell; he takes quick glances at me, and the corner of his mouth quirks in a smile.

"I'm glad *you're* happy about this," I tell him. "Maybe you could give me an idea about what to paint."

He answers with a jerk of his shoulders; *Not my problem,* he's saying, but in a funny way.

The canvas is ready, but still, I'm not. I don't have anything to copy—probably I could skulk around the asylum and find something, but that would involve talking to people. I don't want to paint something pretty, or nice, or pleasant. I don't really want to paint anything at all. What I want is to disappear.

A tingle in my brain, in the very back of my head. A memory. I close my eyes, I reach for it. I arrive. I'm not yet six years old, in my pink-sheeted cave; the Painting is cradled in my lap. I'm nearly eleven; Gillian and her boyfriend are in the kitchen, so I'm in the hallway, avoiding them, reaching to trace the arcs and lines, running my fingertips along the curious thickness of the golden wheat. I'm eighteen, alone in the emptied kitchen, my backpack by the door; I'm looking at the Painting for the very last time.

It was a place I could always go—into the Painting—when I needed to disappear. What if I tried to reproduce it? Could I do such a thing? It would be a challenge to replicate anything from memory, let alone something so complex. I don't know if it's even possible, if I can even remember the Painting clearly enough to try.

I remember the proportions. The main elements, too, of course: in the foreground was a bedroom, its angles reminiscent of Picasso's. In the midground, a field, golden. A river. And the sky, of course. The placement of the discordant objects feels fuzzier . . . where exactly was the lemon sun? And the egg? And what shapes were shimmering in the field?

I return the canvas to the stack—"Be patient with me, Auguste," I say when he quirks with annoyance—and reach for charcoals and paper. My fingers vibrate with nerves. But I soften my eyes the way I used to do, allowing myself to be both here, and not here. And I let my hand guide my brain instead of the other way around.

The field comes first, and easily, I sketch it in with a few wide strokes. Then the bend of water, a squiggle that suggests movement. Trees, too, in the distance.

I stop. The perspective is off. I set the paper aside, pick up another, start again.

Light and shadow move across the room, time melts like Dalí's clocks until a fistful of days are gone and I sit back and set down the charcoal. A pile of discarded sketches layer like moments beneath the table, and in front of me—all there, roughed in.

The next hurdle is to try to re-create the colors—golds, rusts, browns. I create a palette that's close. It's pleasing, and pretty, but it doesn't *feel* right. Is it the tint that's off? The saturation? I mix colors and mix them again, set sheet after sheet of fresh color studies beneath the window—the field, the trees, the sky with its lemon sun—step close in and farther back, look at them through a curtain of shadow, in the brightest light of midday. The colors are better but still, the *feeling*—it's not there, not yet. I try again, again. It's not right, it's not right, it's not right . . . and then I glance up from my work through the glass to find Beryl and Penella, arms linked, collars up against the wind, heads tilted toward one another. A glint of orange among the gold light filtering through the trees; a glint of gold among the copper strands of Beryl's curls. Penella's crimson scarf dancing in the wind.

More red. A drop of it, in each color of my palette. Yes.

I have the shapes; I have the colors. I could paint now. I could lose myself in the work. I could disappear. It would be numbing and wonderful, to take myself away from the way it feels to be here.

I look out the window again; Beryl and Penella aren't there anymore. It's empty outside.

Still, I don't reach for the canvas. What's stopping me? And then I know—I don't want to escape. I don't want to disappear. I don't want to be numb. I want to *feel*. Just—not like this.

22

It's nearly three o'clock. From the group therapy room, a loud burst of laughter. I stand before the closed door. Murmurs of voices, sounds without shapes.

"Is there still time for me to share?" It's the poet's voice.

"Of course, of course." Dr. Tosquelles.

Then, a long pause. So long I wonder if he's changed his mind. "My Nusch," he says at last. Another long silence. Then: "I have never met someone as *alive* as she. And yet, somehow, she is dead. How can such a thing be? And the rest of us—shadows, compared to her, mere *shadows*—but here we are."

What if Paul Éluard is speaking not metaphorically, but literally? What if we *are* all shadows, each and every one of us? Are we the shadows in the cave? Are we real, outside of another's perception of us? Do I exist, outside of my mother? Outside of who she believed me to be? *Can* I?

"Here we are," echoes Dr. Tosquelles's disembodied voice, as if in response to my thought.

"My Nusch," says Paul Éluard, again. And that's all.

"All right, my friends. Until tomorrow."

And now, other sounds: a chair being pushed back, the crinkle of paper. Footsteps, coming to the door. I straighten, step back.

The door opens. "Nora," says Dr. Tosquelles. His mustache twitches. "How nice to see you." He steps into the hallway to allow others to filter past: the poet, a woman with her knitting; the rocking man, who's not rocking now. "What can I do for you?" I look past Dr. Tosquelles, into the room; yes, there's Penella, helping Beryl to her feet.

"I was looking for them," I say, gesturing.

"By all means." Dr. Tosquelles extends his arm, inviting me inside. "The room is yours," he says, and closes the door behind him.

The heat is cranked up, a long row of radiators under the windows steaming. Beryl is standing beside a cushioned armchair. Penella watches me come across the room, her expression unreadable.

"Nora," says Beryl, and smiles.

A flash across Penella's face, a shift in her weight.

"Hello," I say. Then, to Penella, "I wondered if maybe . . . we could talk? There's something I need to explain."

"What a good idea," says Beryl, putting her hand on Penella's arm. "I'll leave the two of you alone."

"Don't go," I tell her. "Stay. Please."

"All right." Beryl takes the armchair, and Penella sits on a footstool beside it. I pull another chair close to them, but as soon as I sit, I get nervous, and I don't know where to start. "You wanted to say something to Penella?" Beryl prompts.

I clear my throat. Turn to Penella. "I want to tell you that I'm sorry. That I was wrong to say what I said. Sometimes I can't even speak at all, and maybe that's better, because when I do speak, I don't always say things the right way."

Penella's lips are pale. At last, she says, "You weren't wrong. What upset me—was hearing you speak truth." Beryl's hand touches her shoulder. "I would do anything—give *anything*—to bring back my family. I'd give my own life. But what you said was also true. And I hate it. It makes me ashamed." She looks down to the tangle of her hands, the scars on her wrists. "How can we accept good things when they're born out of tragedy?"

Beryl's hand leaves Penella's shoulder, goes to her own hard, round stomach. Penella doesn't notice; she's lost inside her pain.

Is each of us lost inside a private realm of suffering? Is *that* what it means to be a person? A flash of terrible knowledge: this is what Gillian believed—if not always, at least at the end.

I shake my head. "What I wanted to say—what I would have said next, if you hadn't left—is that it sounds like what you and your mother had was really special. Like she really *saw* you. And loved you. And if she'd lived . . . if your family had lived . . . the two of you would have found a path, together. I really think you would have."

Don't do that with your mouth, Nora. Don't do that with your hands, Nora. Make your face look normal and smile, but not like a deranged person, Nora. Paint like that *artist, Nora. Be like* that *girl, Nora.*

"I want to tell you about my mother. If you both want to hear?" They nod, and wait until I'm ready. "Where I'm from, doctors give children a series of vaccines. To keep them from getting sick from a variety of things. Do you . . . have those here? Vaccines?"

Beryl laughs, but kindly. "Of course," she says. "They were harder to get during the war, but yes."

"That's what I thought. I just wanted to be sure." I stop again, to consider what I want to say next, and what words I want to use to say it. "When I was very young—just a few months after I was born—my mother went away. I don't remember her leaving, of course. She left me with my grandmother, who took good care of me. She didn't return until my fourth birthday."

Penella and Beryl listen closely. I can feel them, listening.

"I don't remember much from the time she was gone. I remember the things I liked—certain foods, and some activities. I liked to feel the textures of things, and to think about their colors, and shapes. I liked to find patterns, too. I liked to close one eye and see the world like this—and then close the other and feel the way it snaps a little, the way it moves. I liked the feeling of my grandmother's skin on the back of her hands. I liked that our apartment was quiet, and calm. I liked when I met a dog at the park. I didn't like other things—the feeling of constricting clothes, for one thing, I remember this shirt I had? It had a collar that buttoned to the top. And I remember feeling like it was choking me, pressing on my throat and I couldn't breathe, and I remember how upset I got—scared and panicked, we were shopping when it happened, and everyone around us was watching as I tried to get the buttons undone but couldn't, a whole display of paper-wrapped cookies spilled everywhere when I knocked into it, but my grandmother didn't yell at me. She helped me take the shirt off—right then in the middle of the store—she helped me take it off and then we left, left our groceries and the cookies and everything, and the first trash can we saw, she threw the shirt right in. 'Good riddance to bad rubbish,' she said—probably I'm translating that wrong, I don't know, but I know how I *felt* about it—I felt *elated*, to be free of the shirt. For it to be in the trash. I felt understood."

"I would have liked to have met your grandmother," says Beryl.

"She would have liked that, too." I stop, remember. "Then, my mother returned. She wasn't home for very long—a few days, maybe a week—when she told my grandmother that she'd—" The words are burrs, I can't say them. I'm moving, rocking myself in the way that can calm me, and my mouth opens and closes without sound. Beryl and Penella wait. They're patient. I try again. "'You ruined my girl.' That's what she said. My mother—she believed that the vaccines my grandmother had allowed the doctor to give me had broken something inside of me. That they made me—the way I was. The way I am. Ruined. That's what she said I was. Ruined."

"Oh," says Beryl. "Nora."

"I've spent a lot of time—" My throat is tight; the words squeeze out in a whisper. I take a breath, try again. "I've spent a lot of time feeling sorry—really sorry—that I couldn't make myself into the person she wanted me to be. She wanted me to be more like other people, or at least to *act* like them. She told me not to move my body in ways that felt natural to me, ways that felt good. To not talk about the things that were important to me. To not talk too *much* or too *little* or too loudly. To look and behave in ways that made *other* people comfortable. Everything she said to me—everything she taught me—was about hiding my broken parts and making myself seem more like other people. 'Normal' people. And I tried. I really, really tried. But I couldn't do it. And when my mother died—with her very last breath—she blamed me."

I see my mother in my head. I hear the rasp of her labored breath; I smell the staleness of the room. I hear my own voice, pleading—"*Please,* Mom, why won't you let them help you?"

And her response—the way she struggled to sit up; the way her face contorted with rage and fear. "Because they'll poison me, just like they poisoned you!" Then, falling back into her pillows—that was when she noticed Feather, the toy chicken, which I'd tucked in bed beside her—her face went blank, her voice dropped to a whisper, spent—"It was you."

The last words she spoke, pinning the blame squarely on my failings.

I'm shaking my head, back and forth, back and forth, so hard it's as if my brain is hitting one side of my skull, then the other. Sounds come from my throat and fluids come from my nose and eyes and I'm doing the things my mother hated, I'm moaning and I'm rocking, I'm squeezing shut my eyes.

A weight, warm and firm across my shoulders. A scent—rosemary. Penella's. When she touches me, I stiffen. I can't believe that she really wants to hold me. *This* me—this mess that's pouring out of me. But she doesn't let go, she pulls me in tighter, actually. And then, I give in. I let myself go soft in her arms. I'm crying, and she's rocking me, and now she's crying, too, and I *feel* it, her pain, the pressure of it, trying to come into me. I push back, resisting, the way I always have—it overwhelms me, others' pain, it terrifies me. I'm pushing it away, sealing myself apart from it, turning in, and in, and in, the way I always have. But then, I'm not sure why, I don't know if it's defeat or acceptance or something else, but I realize that maybe I don't *want* to resist it anymore. Maybe what I want is to soften. To open. To let it in, to let all of it in, even if it hurts—even if it overwhelms—Penella's pain, and Beryl's too, and Auguste's; Paul Éluard's, and Marguerite Sirvins's; and beyond that, beyond them, the unnamed suffering of those before and those after, and, of course, my very own. It's a wave, a tide, an ocean of pain—it's terrifying to open to it, to accept it all . . . and then—

Oh, the relief, to let it fill me—my heart and my stomach, my mouth, my ears and my eyes, I let it in, all of it. It bursts me open.

A moment. An eternity. Both. And then, the wave recedes. I'm taking short gasping breaths, I'm out of the ocean, resting on the shore. It's right behind me, the ocean of pain, maybe it always will be—but I'm not in it now, and I'm not alone.

Before she lets me go, Penella squeezes me even more tightly, lowers her lips to the top of my head and says, her words warm in my hair, "Your mother sounds like a real cunt."

I don't know why this is so funny to me. So wonderfully, terribly funny. But it is, and then I'm laughing, laughing, truly mad with laughter, and she laughs, too, her white teeth flashing, the pink of her tongue in her open mouth so *real*, so *alive*, and I love her. I love her so.

23

Life is comprised of a series of stories. Humans make sense of the world by telling each other—and themselves—these stories.

This is how the world began.

This is where we came from.

This is who we are.

This is why it matters.

History. Religion. Philosophy. Science. Anthropology.

This is right, and this is wrong.

This is who's in charge, and this is why.

This is what happens if we do good things. This is what happens if we don't.

This is what love is.

We believe the stories. We accept them. And then we operate from those set points.

But sometimes we learn something new. Something that forces us to reevaluate the set points we've been operating from. And then the story changes.

At the beginning of *A Brief History of Time,* Stephen Hawking writes that the philosopher Bertrand Russell once gave a public lecture about astronomy after which a woman in the audience asserted that it was rubbish—our planet doesn't orbit the sun, she said. It rests on the back of a giant tortoise. Russell asked: If this is so, then what is the tortoise standing on? She replied that it was turtles, all the way down.

When I read this, the first thing that struck me is that tortoises and turtles are different creatures. Tortoises, which are land animals, have domed shells, whereas turtles, who are water creatures, have flatter shells—arguably, a better platform for holding a world. So, which did she mean? The turtles would float, wouldn't they, and constantly shift? If so, perhaps the tortoise stack would make the better choice, after all. To me, this was the most interesting part of the anecdote. That the woman in the audience used the animals—tortoises and turtles—interchangeably, and no one corrected her.

And thinking about stacks of tortoises or turtles reminded me of a story Big Nora had read me, over and over—it delighted me so—*Yertle the Turtle*, about a despot turtle (he was supposed to represent Hitler, I'm remembering now) who forced all the pond's turtles to build a turtle-stack as his throne, only to ultimately be tumbled by a rebellious belch from the bottom turtle, Mack. At the very end of the story, my favorite lines—*And the turtles of course . . . all the turtles are free/As turtles and, maybe, all creatures should be.*

All my life, since Big Nora died and Gillian became my sole caregiver, I'd truly believed that my mother was helping me make sense of a complicated and complex world, that it was necessary for me to learn the rules she taught me, rules as clear as the lines on the blacktop at school. Here: safe. There: not safe. Do this, act this way: safe. Do that, be that way: not safe.

I believed that she taught me these things to protect me. To keep me safe. To help me. But at home—in my art, and with my mother—there, I had believed, I was free. Here: free. There: not free.

But what if instead, this was what my life was: not free; not free; not free not free notfree notfree notfree notfreenotfreenotfreenotfree notfreenotfreenotfreenotfreenotfreenotfreenotfreenotf

The doctors. The therapists. The special diets, the vitamins, the tonics. The *advice,* the *rules*—Not like *that,* Nora. Put down your *hands,* dearheart. Try to smile, but not like a deranged person. I don't know, couldn't you paint something that makes more *sense?* Look, try something like this. Make something *pretty,* dearheart. If you want people to *like you,* Nora, you're going to have to . . . On and on and on.

notfreenotfreenotfreenotfreenotfreenotfreenotfreenotfreenotfree notfreenotfreenotfreenotfreenotfr

Tortoises—or turtles—all the way down.

The thing is, I don't think Gillian was a cunt.

But when Penella said what she said—*Ta mère a l'air d'être une vraie salope*—I felt something I did not expect, something I never expected to feel, about my mother. I felt . . . *relief.*

I hadn't said anything but the truth of what my mother and I were. I hadn't hidden any part of myself. What Penella said doesn't change the ways that I still feel, on some level, broken.

But it does make me wonder if maybe I wasn't the only one who was.

And it felt wonderful—*wonderful!*—to laugh about it. I've never laughed at Gillian before. It never even occurred to me to. But come on. Some of her beliefs *were* laughable . . . or, they would have been, if they hadn't been so dangerous.

That's the sobering thought. How dangerous her beliefs were. Fatally so.

Also, this: if Gillian wasn't "a cunt" (or a bitch or a slut, which *salope* can also mean), but if the things she said and did were not my fault—something I'm trying to believe—then, what? What was the story of my life, and hers?

Those places aren't for normal people, Nora. If you ever end up in a place like that, it's a sign that you've taken a real wrong turn, somewhere. So take another turn, as fast as you can, to get the hell out.

If someone had asked me a month ago if I would voluntarily stay in a "place like that," the answer would have been no. And yet, here I stay, day after day, developing a routine: breakfast with Beryl and Penella, followed by chores—on my favorite days, gathering eggs from the chicken coop, on my least favorite, cleaning the bathrooms. Late mornings are for art, an hour at least before lunch and sometimes straight through it.

My work is going well. Not perfectly—it's hard, frustrating work, truly an absurd thing to do, to try to replicate something I can only see in memory—but it's oddly satisfying. A special kind of puzzle only I can solve. And it feels . . . different than anything else I've ever done. More true, even though it's a reproduction. I think this is because I'm not using the work to disappear. I'm using it to feel more present than I've ever been.

Afternoons when the weather is fair I go outside, either with Auguste, who likes to ramble and collect bits of things to incorporate in his sculptures even though his workshop is already full to overflowing, or with Penella and Beryl, equally slow due to Beryl's growing pregnancy.

At two o'clock, Beryl or Penella—sometimes both—disappear into group therapy. Later, dinner, during which Penella and Beryl quietly exchange with me the parts of the meals I can't stomach for the parts of the meals I can; followed by evening activities—movie nights, a screen pulled down over the small low stage in the main gathering room; sing-alongs; reading the paper on the days it's published; chess and checkers and cards. Occasionally, I attend these things; more often, I skip the activities and retreat to my attic room. There, wrapped tightly in my quilt, I cocoon in bed. I empty the fullness of my day by being alone.

Sometimes there's a patient who has a fit, screaming or thrashing about. There are some epileptics, given to seizures, too. When there's a problem, those who can, help; the rest of us stay out of the way, helping by not making things worse. Sometimes, Penella disappears, and Beryl worries, and when Penella returns, purple crescents under her eyes, Beryl fusses, and I give them space to be alone together.

Sometimes I wake in the middle of the night to stare at the violet sky through the high triangular window. I wonder if it looks different, this same slip of sky, in my own time. I wonder where Adrien is—in a bed in a room, looking out a window? Or on his bedroll beside a dying fire? Has he kept Gillian's ashes, or left them behind?

At the beginning of our life together, when I was just a baby, my mother ran away from me. In the middle of our lives, she taught me how to put on a mask and said I should never take it off. And at the end of our shared life, she blamed me for what happened, even as it was her decision not to accept help, her need to have someone to blame for who I was that brought her to that decision. The last words she spoke—"It was you." She couldn't catch another breath after that.

And without breath, death.

That's our story. And if it's not because I was broken, as she believed, and not because she was a cunt, as Penella believes—then, why?

"I don't know if you ever really loved me," I whisper to my mother in the dark. It scares me, the truth of it. But it's not just fear that I feel. Right there, beside it—relief.

"The main thing," Penella says, "is not to judge me by what you're about to see. Promise."

"Sure," I agree, even though I have no idea what she means. "Of course."

I've had another good day, a string of them, at work alongside Auguste. Dinner was plain—chicken and vegetables and bread, all separate, all palatable. Now, after evening chores, I find that I don't feel the need to be alone. I'm not over-full; I have room tonight, for more. So, alongside most everyone else, I file into the multipurpose room. Rows of chairs have been unfolded with an aisle down the middle, just like a real theater. At the front of the room is a pull-down screen, and at the rear is the projector. Beryl is there, helping a man to load a reel of film onto it. Jojo Chassang.

He's a funny little man; shorter than Beryl by half a foot at least, he can't weigh more than a hundred pounds. He's neatly dressed in a pair of slim pants—women's pants, I think, because of the placement of the pockets—a black-and-white-striped shirt, collarless with long sleeves, and a black silk kerchief tied around his slim neck. His head is bowed seriously to his work, and Beryl's dexterous fingers are helping string the film into place.

Out of habit, I break them each into the series of shapes I'd use to convey them. They're a study in contrasts: Beryl, so close to the end of her pregnancy now, Rubenesque and Titian, a series of orbs and curves; Jojo, slim and androgynous, all sharp lines and angles—a pointed chin, a squared-off shoulder, a flat chest and triangle waist, even sharp-toed black patent leather shoes.

When everyone is seated, Dr. Tosquelles, who's seated in the front row next to the poet, stands and turns. He waves to get the group's attention; when he has it, he bows, puts a hand over his heart, and speaks.

"Here at Saint-Alban, we are more than doctors and patients, yes? Often, I ask myself of this place, 'Who is healing who?' Because we are living proof, are we not, of the hypothesis: if we can create a space, opened from within and from outside, if you can assemble a group of people—doctors, nurses, nuns, artists, poets, philosophers, patients, and, within each of these categories, some mentally ill and some not—and if we can be given the tools we need to say out loud, or in art, or in action, *who we are* and how we have been shaped by history—by what we have lived through, yes, but also what we have endured, and who we have lost, the little dramas of family as well as the broad saga of country and polities and war . . . well, then, we can—*all* of us, eventually—feel better." He looks around, dark hair a wild cloud of curls and tangles rising in a puff from his head, eager dark eyes two gleaming points behind the lenses of his round spectacles, catching me with them.

He brings his hand to his mustache, runs his fingers along one side from root to tip. That mustache, so absurd—why grow and groom and care for such an unnecessary thing, when he's been through the things he must have endured, when he runs a place such as this, with people under his charge who have tried to kill themselves before and who may, at any given moment, do so again?

The mustache, it seems to me, is the opposite of a mask. Its purpose isn't to disguise; it's to reveal. What is he revealing, by growing it and grooming it? I tilt my head. It's a vulnerability, this vanity. I admire it.

Dr. Tosquelles claps briskly, twice. "All right. Roll the film, Jojo!"

The rest of us applaud as someone turns off the lights. The room goes dark and then a switch on the projector is flicked with a loud click, and a circle of bright white light shines on the screen, and the audience hoots and hollers in anticipation.

Under the applause is the hum of the projector working, and layered in, too, are the collective sounds of a body of people gathered together: the squeak of a shoe against the floor; someone clearing their throat; another body blowing its nose; a few people whispering, causing someone to laugh over a joke I'll never know. Normally, this sort of situation would make my skin feel itchy on the inside—so many people, so many sounds. But I notice that I *don't* feel that way.

The film begins to rotate with a high, soft *tick tick tick*, and everyone falls silent. The picture starts. A stage, with the curtain pulled closed—it's black-and-white, of course; though I know color film has been invented, I imagine it's much too expensive for most films, and certainly an amateur one—and there's the sound of someone playing the piano. The acoustics are tinny and weak, but it's clear enough to recognize that the pianist is playing a simple set of scales, rising and falling in repetitive waves. And then the curtain is pulled, the stage revealed.

A mime centerstage, alone. A white-painted face; a black beret; a black shirt, long-sleeved, and a long dark skirt. With a start, I realize it's Penella. I never would have guessed that she'd be willing to take part in something like this. Beside me, she stiffens with embarrassment.

The mime is in a box; she's feeling the invisible walls. They don't bother her; her expression stays placid, even as she explores her confines. Certain of her limitations, she lowers to the floor, sits cross-legged, content.

Then others begin to take the stage, coming in from both wings. They're not dressed as mimes, but they're wearing an assortment of unusual costumes. A woman and a man, each dressed for ballet; inexpertly, she spins, and inexpertly, he guides her. Several people crawl on hands and knees, wearing rudimentary animal costumes: here, a dog pants his tongue and wags his rear end, from which a tail loosely hangs; there, a lady in a unitard sits prettily and cleans herself by licking her paw, passing it across her face.

Three men dressed as children in caps and short pants run onstage and begin a game of jacks, laughing and slapping each other's backs when someone makes an especially good catch, racing across the stage to retrieve the ball when it bounces away.

Children and dancers and dogs and cats. And in the middle of all the chaos of their movement, Penella the mime, sitting very still in her invisible box, watching.

The audience laughs as one of the boys turns cartwheels and crashes into the dog, who bares his teeth and threatens to bite.

Another group comes on stage. But there's nothing loose or vibrant about these actors; they walk slowly, in lockstep, a march. A half-dozen of them, men and women together, dressed in identical pajama-like suits, vertically striped dark and light.

The audience's laughter cuts off. We're all uncomfortable now, or at least I am. The antics onstage intensify, the ballet dancers switching from measured if imperfect ballet into a tightly choreographed swing dance; the group of boys growing rowdier and rowdier, breaking into a play-fight that involves trying to knock the caps off of one another's heads; the dog catching sight of the cat and beginning to stalk her, the cat arching her back and hissing savagely.

The prisoners in the camp uniforms continue their march diagonally across the stage, and at the center, the mime grows agitated. She bangs on the walls of her cage; her mouth opens in a silent scream; she pulls the beret from her head and tears at her hair; she yanks at the neck of her shirt; the white cake makeup runs now, with her tears.

What does it mean? I don't know. Then, one by one, each of the prisoners stops, lies down, closes their eyes, and folds their hands across their chest. Dead. Dead. Dead. Now all six of them are on the floor, the stage strewn with their corpses. Still, life beats on; the dog catches the cat and begins to rut on top of her. The boys' play descends into a brawl; the dancers, more in love with every swing, every dip, every lift, an ecstasy made discordant and awful to watch in the midst of all the rest.

My mother would hate this.

The thought comes—from where, I'm not sure. But it's true. Gillian would hate this. It's bizarre. It's rough and uncomfortable and amateurish. She would have no idea what to *do* with it. She would be embarrassed, sitting here.

Suddenly the mime stops banging the walls. She's remembered something. Reaching into an invisible pocket, she withdraws an invisible key. She fits it in an invisible lock, rattles it—will it work? Yes, the invisible handle turns, and she pushes open the invisible door. No one onstage notices her, the living or the dead. On quiet feet, each step carefully articulated, heel to toe, she walks.

Will she stop the rutting dog, pull him from the cowering cat beneath him? Will she break up the fight between the boys? Will she stop to honor the dead, to pray over their bodies? Or will she follow the dancers, either to disrupt or join them?

No. She does none of these things. Instead, as she crosses the stage, the camera moves. All this time it's been still, so still that I forgot there was a camera at all. Now, it follows her to the edge of the stage and down the stairs. Her hair parts in curtains around her ruined face. The neck of her shirt is a ragged wound. As she steps offstage, the bright crisp lighting falls to shadows, casting her face in darkness. There, at the base of the stairs, is the piano. Playing it, eyes glued to the sheet music, is Dr. Tosquelles.

The mime moves to stand beside him. The camera, behind her, looks over both their shoulders, closes in on the sheet music, the name of the song he's playing. "A Life Absurd but Beautiful."

And then the reel goes black, the music ends, the film is over.

Around me, the audience breaks into thunderous applause. They stamp their feet; someone whistles high and sharp. Dr. Tosquelles stands again, turns, bows, gestures to his fellow actors to get up, too, to come to the front to be recognized, waves to the back of the room for Jojo Chassang. The lady who played the cat and the man who was the dog come to the front hand in hand; the gang of boys laughs and pushes one another jovially as they line up, side by side. The corpses wave their hands solemnly; the dancing couple two-steps their way to the front.

With a sigh, Penella stands and goes to join her fellow thespians.

Penella's performance—no, not a performance; a revealing, a revelation. The mime was trapped, at first complacent, then, later, out of her mind with rage and sorrow. And then she found something—a key—in her own pocket. Such rawness. Such . . . vulnerability.

Is this an essential human experience, the thing Penella has enacted? Are there ways in which each of us is isolated, closed off, trapped? And must it be so hard—so incredibly hard—to recognize the box, to choose to leave it?

Free. Or not free.

Penella's mime freed herself. And then what? She had to walk through the terrible, frightening world. Any of the things that happened to the others—the cat, the children, the dancers—could have happened to her. It's a dangerous world. Often ugly and cruel. But what are our choices, really? We can leave the box and take our chances. Or we can draw the box closer, and smaller, and tighter, until it becomes . . . well. Not a box.

A bamboo cylinder.

All around me the audience rises, and I do, too. I clap my hands until they sting.

24

Those soldiers from the First World War—the ones with broken faces and special masks—some of them wore the masks all the time. Not just out in the world, but at home. Some of them were even buried in their masks. They left them on even when they were doing the most intimate things—eating, using the toilet, making love. Some of their children never, their whole lives, never saw their fathers without them.

I don't know how I feel about that. The artists who made the masks did a wonderful thing for those soldiers, of course. They did the best they could for them. If the masks made the soldiers feel better, if they helped them reclaim something they'd lost, then I'm glad they had them. But . . . what's the line between choosing to wear a mask, and feeling compelled to? It makes me really sad, that so many of those men couldn't ever take theirs off.

I'm with Beryl in the sewing room, helping her sort through sheets. Which can be repaired, and which should be cut into squares, then hemmed, to become napkins?

The machines are an assault. I don't know how Beryl can stand it, how she can sit here looking . . . *beatific*, when to me it's like a tiny sharp hammer banging on the inside of my skull. But everyone else seems fine, not just Beryl; I'm the only one with a problem. If I'm the only one *with* a problem, does that mean that *I'm* the problem?

"Beryl."

"Mm-hm?"

"Can we do this somewhere else? The noise—I hate it."

Beryl looks up. Her brows are knitted, too, and maybe she'll be annoyed, maybe she'll tell me to get over it—"Of course, sure. How about the library?" She drops the sheet into the basket, stands. "Hey! Why are you crying?"

I take the basket. "Nothing. No reason. Just—thank you."

She strokes my arm; her gaze is an embarrassment of riches.

We finish our task in the library, watching the rain come down in sheets. There's a fire in the fireplace. A man is dealing out a hand of cards. Someone is playing the piano.

After dinner, I'm in the kitchen with Henri. A teacup in my hands. He's humming as he scrubs a white oblong serving dish. Not a song; one note, held for a very long time, as long as he can make it in one breath, then another note, almost the same as the first but not quite, as long as he can stretch it.

It's the sort of thing that, if I did it, Gillian would have stopped me. If Gillian were here, she'd pull her eyebrows together in the way that made the dent between them, she'd shake her head.

Gillian is not here. But I am. I close my eyes. When Henri ends his breath-hum and takes a new breath to begin the next, I do, too.

Hmmmmmm. I've started with my lungs stretched full, the sound that comes from me is loud and true. It vibrates in my chest, the sound. It feels *good*. Maybe this is what it feels like for a cat to purr, this satisfaction of sound.

At the bottom of my breath, I open my eyes, find Henri watching me. I smile, and he does, too. We take another breath. I finish drying the teacup. *Hmmmmmm.*

The next day, Beryl and I are in the chicken coop, gathering eggs. There are a dozen hens at Saint-Alban. In the daytime they're allowed in the kitchen garden where they find grubs, eat snails, and aerate the ground as they scratch and peck. In the evenings, Sister Martine shoos the stragglers into the coop and latches it shut. There are a variety of breeds—Houdans and Marans and some Bresse Gauloise. Most of them lay brown eggs; some lay white. My favorite chicken is a Charolais, a large, shy girl with the prettiest red comb and bright yellow legs. Plump and with pure white plumage, she looks just like Feather. It's silly to miss a toy, but I do.

I reach under the Charolais, find a warm, hard egg.

Just as I'm retrieving it, Beryl gasps, a hand low on her belly.

"What's the matter?"

"Nothing," she says. "Just—give me your hand." I put the egg in the basket, and she presses my palm to her body. Beneath my hand, the world of her stomach is taut and warm. Her palm, pressing on the back of my hand, warm, too. Then—a sharp jab, a kick. "Did you feel that?"

My throat is thick. I nod. Yes. I felt it. I feel it.

"Are you scared?" I ask.

"Yes."

That afternoon, in the hallway, Marguerite Sirvins is working on her wedding dress.

"Hello," I say, but she doesn't look up. "I brought you something."

Her needle stops.

"It's hot chocolate." I've also brought a little stool, and I set it beside her, the mug atop it.

She looks at the mug, then up at me. "You should come to my wedding. My dress is almost finished. Look."

"It's beautiful."

She looks at the mug again. "I asked for hot chocolate at breakfast."

"I made some for you. I'll make you another cup tomorrow."

She looks at the mug. At the floor. At me. At the dress, in her lap. "I get watery soup in the morning, at noon, and at night. How can a person be healthy? The eyes pop out. The nose weeps." She makes another stitch.

Later, when I go by again, the cup is empty.

The task that once felt impossible—reproducing a complex painting from memory—is nearly complete. I've done good work with the foreground—the angle of the closed door, the shape of the bed, the shoes and their shadow, tucked beneath a chair. I spent a long time on the wall around the wheat field, a dark braid of browns and blacks. I've washed vast swaths of the canvas with silvery light; there's the ring of trees, all the shades of green I can remember. I've hung a lemon in the sky. The water was tricky, trying to recall just where the creek was dappled, where it lay in shadow, but I'm pleased with it.

The abstract shapes will be next, the other objects, too.

I've learned so much, working on this painting. The process has made me a better artist. I had to become one, to meet the challenge.

Maybe when it's finished, if it were displayed next to the original in the Museum of the Counterfeit, it wouldn't fool anyone. I'll never know; the original is lost to me. But the *feeling* I have when I look at what I'm making—the sense of wonder, the whisper of a secret hope—the feeling is the same as it was, before. And that's something.

Behind me, Auguste is working again on his ship sculpture. Every time I think he must be finished he devises some new way to embellish it. Today he's using bits of twine to string tiny buckets he's carved to the masts. I like working like this, side by side.

Today, I'm trying to figure out how the artist formed the raised ridges. It wasn't just thickened paint . . . there was a graininess, too. As a child, I touched the wheat heads and abstract shapes dozens of times, maybe hundreds, reading them with my fingertips. Now, with my thumb, I caress the pad of my pointer finger, recalling the texture. Maybe if I mixed something into the paint. Could I make it adhere and build up texture, without cracking? There's a plant in the corner of the room . . . would soil work? I scoop some into a little dish, add some yellow and red, a bit of linseed oil. A fresh sheet of paper to experiment—what if I use the tip of a palette knife instead of a brush—

But the soil just turns the paint to mud. I ball up the paper, throw it toward the trash bin near the window, miss. After I've retrieved the paper and thrown it in the bin, I take a moment to look outside, then focus on the window itself. The diamonds of glass between the lead muntins are beveled, such pleasing sharp angles. Through the beveled edges, the world outside is a little warped, like seeing the world through water. Through the flat glass: normal. A hair over, through the bevel: wavy, dreamlike. If I stand just so, if I close one eye to see the world through the flat glass, then close the other and open the first to see the world through bevel: Here. Not here. Here.

The tiniest shift of perception—the distance from one side of your nose to the other—and things change so much. Here. Not here. Safe. Not safe. A good mother? Or a bad one?

Love? Or hate?

I look again, through both eyes. The two fields combine, and depth returns.

All three images are true. What the left eye sees, what the right eye sees, and what they see, together. The truth of the combined image does not invalidate what my left eye sees alone, or my right. Multiple angles; multiple truths. This is uncomfortable for me—my brain prefers the clarity of a singular answer.

But I can't deny the truth of this complexity. It's right here, before my eyes.

There's a sound in the doorway behind me. The tap-tap-tap of claws on hard floor. I've only half turned when Auguste jumps up, moving so quickly his stool tips and falls. I catch it before it hits the ground, but Auguste couldn't care less. He's flying around the table and dropping to his knees, wrapping the dog in his arms and making happy, snuffling sounds. The dog answers in kind. He's thumping his tail against the ground and his gray-black snout nudges into Auguste's armpit.

"Robot?" I say.

Shoving his nose farther, the dog's head pops out from beneath Auguste's arm. His ears go up and he barks once, happily. Wriggling through Auguste's embrace, Robot knocks him to sitting. Auguste laughs and Robot runs to me. I go to the ground, and he climbs into my arms, licking my face in quick, sloppy kisses, whining, and wagging his tail so fiercely that his whole back half whips side to side. Auguste, still laughing, crawls over to join us, and Robot is in an ecstasy of hellos.

Adrien. I look to the door, and as if I've called him into existence—there he is.

The light from the kitchen renders him a tall dark shadow, but I recognize the shape of him as if I've known him all my life. The set of his shoulders. The wire of his limbs. The way he lifts his chin when he realizes it's me.

He's found me. I don't know how. Did he go to Montignac, did he meet the woman with the yellow scarf, did she tell him about the way I acted, the ambulance that took me away? However he did it, he's here. We're looking at each other across the workshop, there's an expression on his face I can't parse—he doesn't look relieved to see me, or glad . . . and after the way I left him, why would he have tried to find me, at all?

I'm frozen, unsure whether or how to close the distance between us, when Auguste turns, too, and sees him in the doorway.

Nimble in a way I didn't know he could be, he leaps to his feet, arms flung wide, and calls—"Brother!"

It's Auguste who goes to Adrien, Auguste for whom Adrien opens his arms. Robot barks and jumps in a happy circle around the two of them. Brothers.

There's so much I need to say that I can't say anything at all. I don't want to look at Adrien, I don't want him to look at me, to have to figure out what to do with his face, what to say. I put my hand on his arm, step around them, and slip away.

"Did *you* know Auguste had a brother?" Beryl asks Penella, who nods.

We're at dinner; I keep looking up, wondering if I'll see Adrien, but he doesn't come in. He and Auguste must be eating alone together, or maybe they're off on a walk.

"I was here when Auguste was first brought in," says Penella, "a few years ago. He's quite a bit older than his brother—I believe he was ten when Adrien was born. That was the first time he ran away, Sister Martine told me all about it. She said that he was detained for riding a train without a ticket, and the police brought him home. After that, he left whenever he got the chance, always to board a train. He was returned again and again, sometimes after being gone for weeks at a time. It was hard on the whole family, especially when their mother was suddenly widowed."

"Poor lady. What happened to her husband?" Beryl has finished her soup, brings the bowl to her mouth for the last sip.

"Sister Martine didn't say, exactly. Something sudden. His heart, maybe. Or a stroke. He was in the field. Adrien was with him. He was eight years old or so."

I close my eyes. Young Adrien, still a child, but starting to stretch toward adolescence. He's wearing a brown-and-gold sweater vest and dark corduroy trousers, neat little work boots. He's with his father in an orchard. Adrien is on a ladder near a tree; his father hands him up a bottle. The trees are full of blossoms. Adrien takes the bottle; he fits the mouth of it over a branch, and now the blossom is inside. He reaches down for a scrap of fabric to tie the bottle to the branch, and his father reaches up, the white muslin strip waving like a friendly flag. But the wind takes the fabric; up it goes, and away, like a kite snipped from its string, as Adrien's father falls to the ground amongst his trees, as Adrien watches.

"A few years after that, Auguste caused a train to derail."

"My God. How?"

"He didn't mean to do it. He put rocks—small rocks, pebbles—on the tracks, in a tunnel. When his mother brought him here, she was inconsolable. He wasn't trying to hurt anyone, she insisted. He'd never want to hurt a soul. He just loved trains, that's all. And he thought the train would crush the rocks. He wanted to see what that would look like."

Auguste, having piled his pebbles on the track, crouching on the far side of the tunnel, waiting for the train to emerge so he can retrieve the flattened stones. Instead, the awful sound of a train—so beloved to him—screeching and crashing and smashing as it flies from the tracks, colliding with the inside of the tunnel.

Now I'm with my mother. We're on our trip up the coast, on a wooden boardwalk by the sea. We're standing in front of a machine. It has a window at the front; there are gears inside. Gillian gives me a penny and two quarters and shows me where to put them, in three divots in a slot, and she pushes the slot into the machine. Then she places my hand on the wooden handle, covers it with her own, and together we crank. The gears turn, the penny moves, and a moment later a flat oval of copper drops into a pan at the bottom of the machine. SANTA CRUZ CALIFORNIA, it reads. Gillian traces her finger across the words as she reads them. The profile portrait of the man is gone; now there's a beach chair, water, a leaping dolphin, a sailboat, the sun. The circular penny has become this thin oval thing. "It's the same penny," Gillian tells me. "Exactly the same, and totally different."

Exactly the same, and totally different.

"The court decided he wasn't responsible for his actions, but that he needed to be cared for and watched so he couldn't do any more damage, that's how he ended up at Saint-Alban. The first year he was here, he ran away four times. And this was the middle of the worst of the fighting—it wasn't safe for him to be taking off like that. Each time he left, everyone worried we'd never see him again. Twice, the local villagers brought him back. Once, he was gone for nearly a month, and we all pretty much figured he must be dead. He came back on his own that time, skinny like a corpse. The fourth time, Dr. Tosquelles took off after him himself, and when they returned, Dr. Tosquelles gave him a room of his own to make art. He hasn't run away since. I suppose that's how he's traveled. With his work."

Winged creatures. Elaborate ships. Auguste Forestier's work, which had seemed so bizarre, so absurd, through this lens makes its own sort of beautiful meaning.

"What about their mother?" Beryl asks.

"She died," I say.

Neither of them is surprised. A dead mother is something so many of us share.

I have a dead mother, too. This memory of her, of Santa Cruz, and the penny—I'd forgotten it. Either that, or it never happened, and I've just created it. Have I found meaning? Or have I made it? No matter which, there at the table in the dining room of Saint-Alban, I taste the salt air of Santa Cruz. I feel Gillian's hand on my head. I close my eyes to hold on to it, the way I once held that flattened penny (*did* I?), but when it fades, I let it go.

After dinner, I take up my space by the sink, working through the stack of plates and cups and platters that need drying, wondering about

Adrien, and hoping. Henri is at my side, scrubbing away at his favorite pot. Sister Martine sits at the far end of the kitchen, planning out the week's meals.

Then the kitchen door pushes open, and it's Adrien, his knapsack over a shoulder. His eyes meet mine, and I feel myself smiling, even as my stomach twists. I'm setting down the dish towel, running my hands down the front of my apron, and he's looking at me. He is about to speak.

That's when Sister Martine looks up from her notepad. "Adrien Forestier, dear boy!" She sets down her pencil and crosses the kitchen, her skirt swishing as she goes. She opens her arms, and he steps into them. She kisses his cheeks—one, the other, the first again. "Such a blessing you've returned."

I pick up the dish towel, train my eyes to the dishes, and listen. Sister Martine tells him how sorry she is about his mother. Then they hug again. When they break apart, Sister Martine pats him twice on the arm, as if to say that's settled. In a businesslike voice—"I know you just arrived, but Dr. Tosquelles is hoping you'll be willing to make a trip for him tomorrow. There's a part he needs for the Bee, in Bordeaux. Shouldn't take more than a few days."

He agrees, she slices a piece of pie, insists he sits and eats. They know each other well. How many trips has Adrien made here? Jacques, at the cave, asking about Adrien's brother. Adrien's response—"Still in the hospital. I don't know how long."

When the final plates are dry, the last pieces of silverware polished, the counters wiped, the sink drained, Sister Martine says, "Okay, okay, off with you so I can have my whiskey in peace." Adrien takes up his knapsack from where he's hung it by the door, and Sister Martine waves us out of the kitchen with a dishcloth.

It's quiet in the hallway.

"Would you like to take a walk?" I ask, just as he says, "Are you very tired?"

He laughs and says, "Yes," and I say, "No," and all that settled, we go to the main door and to the courtyard, and then through the arched blue doors.

"I owe you an apology," I tell him as we stand beneath the arch. "And an explanation. Will you let me try?"

I can't bring myself to look straight at him, but I see in my periphery the way he holds his chin—stiff, high—and the moment when it softens, when he nods.

The garden is cast in a moonlit glow. Beyond it is a vineyard, bare branches slung over wires. I don't know if I'm leading or following, or if we're just wandering together. On the far side of the vineyard, beyond the curve of a hill, is an old wooden rotunda, open on the sides but roofed. I've never been this far before. Inside, a U-shaped bench is built along three sides. Beneath the bench is a basket full of pillows and blankets, slightly damp from the mist. When we pull them out and shake them, I smell rosemary.

Together we spread the blankets on the rotunda's floor and lean the pillows against the base of the bench. We kick off our shoes and sit side by side beneath the top blanket, looking out of the rotunda into a sky full of stars. Near our feet, Robot circles once, twice, three times, and then settles with a groan. Next to me, on my left, heat radiates from Adrien's body. My toes reach for the warmth of Robot's pelt.

After Big Nora died, when I'd moved out from under the table and back into my room, I found that if I wrapped myself in a blanket and then wedged my body between the mattress and the wall, I could sleep without dreams. This was a great relief; since her death, my sleep had been haunted. Not by specific images, but rather by movement; when I closed my eyes, I felt unmoored, as if the edges of my body had gone fuzzy and dim, as if I might break into tiny pieces and dissipate into mist, or dust. Wrapped and wedged, my body felt contained, held together, safe.

Over time as I got older, I found other ways to create that sense of containment. Searching for patterns and shapes in the world was one such way. Here is a rectangular window, broken into one two three four five six square panes, two per row. Here is a license plate with only odd numbers. Here is a clock that reads 12:12.

Here is a boy by my side, a dog at my feet. This is another way to find my edges. With someone.

Adrien is leaning back on his hands. My hand is close to his, and I move it even closer, hoping. When our hands touch, Adrien is still for a moment, and I don't dare breathe. Then he covers my fingers with his, leans his arm against mine, and we are holding one another up. In my chest, a flower unfurls.

"The first thing I want to say is that I'm sorry."

"Oh?" He's cautious. I don't blame him.

"I got scared at the cave, and I ran off."

"Nora," he says, "whatever I did, whatever I said—"

I shake my head, hard. "You didn't do anything wrong."

"You're sure? I want you to tell me if I did. I've gone over it again and again. Trying to understand what happened."

Poor Adrien—he's been carrying this weight, all this time, believing that he did something to make me run off. Terrible. I can feel it now, from his perspective.

"You didn't say—or do—anything wrong. I'll explain. Just—I'm sorry. I am very sorry."

He lets out a breath. "Okay," he says. "Whatever it was, okay."

"To explain why I ran, I need to tell you other things, first. Some of them are . . ." I reach for how to explain it. Finally, I ask, "If I tell you something unbelievable, do you think you can believe me?"

He's quiet for a long time. I've almost given up on an answer when he speaks. "I was nine years old when my father died. Auguste is older than I, but you see that he has his limitations."

This is true—Auguste does have limitations. I share some of them, though not all. Some of Auguste's limitations have caused him to become a patient rather than a guest at Saint-Alban; some have contributed to who he is as an artist, to creating fantastical creatures and astonishing works crafted from an artistic vocabulary that neither Adrien nor I have access to. Also—Adrien is Auguste's brother, and as such, *he* has limitations, as well, limitations around the way he perceives Auguste, the language rules within which he understands him. I, on the other hand, am Auguste's friend. Auguste and I have our own language rules, our own understandings.

All these thoughts swirl together—along with such tender feelings, hope, love—in the moment's breath Adrien takes before he continues.

"So it was up to my mother and me to take care of things when the war began. I was too young to fight, just twelve years old, and anyway

Germany took us so quickly that for us it was over almost before it started. Over but not ended, if you can understand." A pause. Then, "Do you remember how when we met, you said that we had all been through terrible things?"

I nod. "I remember."

"What I'm trying to say is that I've already been forced to accept the unacceptable. To believe the unbelievable. Could these things truly have happened to my family? My father, my brother, my mother? They couldn't have. And yet, they did." He looks like he's going to tell me more—but then he shakes his head. I understand. He's said all he can, for now. Robot whines, wags his tail, bumps his nose into Adrien's chest. Adrien lets go of my hand to embrace the dog. He kisses Robot's head, smooths his fur, tells him what a good boy he is, and they grow calm, together. It's so interesting—how taking care of another can calm you, yourself.

When Robot knows his job is done, he circles back at our feet, rests his chin on his paws, sighs. I tell Adrien how very sorry I am. That I'll be ready to listen to more, if he ever wants to share it. Then, it's my turn.

"From shortly before my sixth birthday until I was nearly eight years old, I did not speak. For over two years, not a single word."

This is the first thing I tell Adrien. The first thing I want him to know about me. Then the rest of it. How my mother left when I was very young—how I used to believe that it didn't matter, that I had Big Nora, and I loved her. That I didn't think it had hurt me, Gillian's leaving. What happened when she returned, about how *angry* she was—with who I was, with who I am—how she worked, first, to make me want to be someone else; then, after Big Nora died, to teach me to *pass* as someone else. I tell him the things I hid from him—things I've never put into words before. I don't use the word "autism," not because I'm ashamed of it but because I don't think it will translate to this time. But I tell him that's what I was doing when we first met—wearing a mask, is what I say—and that I'm trying not to, anymore, but it's hard, really hard, because after all this time I'm not sure what's the mask and what is me. I tell him that people can be hard for me, and perspective taking, and reciprocity. That I get overwhelmed by sensation, exhausted by the work of decoding, that I often don't know how to name what I feel, let alone what other people might be feeling. I start to rock as I'm telling him all of this; I stop myself—*too weird*, comes Gillian's voice—but when the motion stops, so do my words, and if I'm going to give Adrien the whole truth, this is part of it, too, so I let my body move again.

I tell him about my mother's death and how I came to France to honor her and spread her remains. Here, he starts to speak, but I shake my head, hold up a hand, I have to say it all at once, now that I've begun. "I don't expect you to still have the container, you couldn't have known what it was, please don't feel bad if you've discarded it somewhere along the way, it's my fault if they're lost, not yours."

I tell him about waking up *here*, at Saint-Alban, about meeting Beryl and Penella and Auguste—his brother!—about how they are my friends. The first real friends, I tell him, of my entire life.

And then I tell him what else I've awoken to, in this place I was never meant to be: a new perspective of the story of my mother and myself.

It's the longest I've ever spoken. It takes a long time, long enough for Robot to wake, stir, tire of the sound of my voice. He gets up and shakes, trots down the rotunda's steps and off in the direction of the main building, hunting for a late-night snack, or Auguste, or both. When I'm finally done, I'm glad for the darkness.

Adrien is quiet for a long time, long enough that I feel a flash of fear: Will he leave, too? Am I—all of me, what I've showed him—too much, too strange, too difficult? But he doesn't leave. He puts an arm—warm—around my waist. "What a shame," he says. "What a loss, for your mother. That she couldn't see you. Thank you for showing yourself to me."

I turn to him, take his face in both my hands, and touch my forehead to his. We stay like that, animals, breathing in and out together. He must feel it, too, the thing that's between us, because his voice is husky when he asks if I'm okay, if I want to be here, if he can kiss me, and again my words fail so I nod and nod. I tilt back my head, his lips are just above mine, so close I could touch them with the tip of my tongue, but Adrien hesitates, goes still. A sound comes from my throat; I don't mean to make it; I didn't know I could make such a sound; but he responds. His hand comes up to the base of my neck. His fingers tangle in my hair, pulling me closer, and his sweet gentle mouth slants down, and then it doesn't matter anymore what is his and what is mine. We're tangled together, our edges blur. More, more of this, more.

It's too cold to sleep outside, and yet, we do—eventually.

I've never seen a real naked man before. Of course, I understood the basic constructs—most men, though not all, have a penis, testicles, a flat chest, thicker body hair. I saw illustrations in health class textbooks, both in the eighth grade and again sophomore year. More beautiful renditions in art books, and statues at the museum. It wouldn't have been hard to find photos or even videos if I'd wanted to. I suppose I wasn't all that curious. Women's bodies have always held far more interest for me. Breasts. The dip of the waist. The roundness of hips. Curves. I have always loved the shape of an arc. Mostly, these were the shapes I drew, the shapes that drew me to them. But in the rotunda, my mouth full of Adrien's tongue, my hands full of Adrien's hair, my entire body became suddenly, ravenously, curious about lines.

It feels so . . . *good*, to desire. It feels good to want, again. My head rests on Adrien's naked chest, my hand warm against the fur of his thigh. Dreaming, perhaps, Adrien half speaks; his hand on my hip grips tightly, then relaxes. I smile into his chest. Has the feeling of me made its way into his unconscious? Am I in his dream now? What am I doing in there? If I do things here, will they be replicated, there? Curious, I move my hand from his thigh to between his legs. He wakes in stages—first, growing thick and hard in my palm, and then his hand on my hip tightening, massaging my flesh, and then kissing my head, he asks, voice husky—"Again?"

Later, much later, I sleep.

Dawn is damp and bone-chillingly cold, mist settled heavy as a cat. But in our nest of blankets, we've made a pocket of warmth for one another. I'm curled away from Adrien, and his body wraps around mine. The warmth and softness of him, the solidness, too . . . I push into him, and he pulls closer.

Eventually, reluctantly, we begin to arrange ourselves for the day. The sun's not up yet, the valley's basin is filled with milky mist. I fold the blankets, Adrien turns to take something from his bag. "I thought I'd lost the capacity for hope," he says, "after these past few years. And I had no reason to think I'd meet you again, but—keeping this for you, hoping to return it—felt . . . good. Really good, to have something to hope for again." The bamboo cylinder, smooth and hard and cold. Here it is, just as I left it. Adrien has kept it safe.

He shoulders his bag, and I carry the cylinder—what does it mean, my relief at its return? This complicated feeling, such a tangle of gladness and sorrow, yes, both are true, both—and we go together past the silent Bee, toward the wide blue door, across the courtyard, and into the asylum's main hall. The whole place is heavy and quiet with sleep. I'm awkward now, aware of all my parts again, my hands and my feet and my nose and my hair and my teeth. I'm not sure what to say; what *does* one say after a night like the one we've shared? The two things that leap to mind—"Goodbye" and "Thank you"—neither seems right.

Maybe Adrien senses my discomfort, because he speaks first. "I'll let you go again," he says. "But this time, just for a couple of days while I run the doctor's errand, yes?" A slow, shy grin.

I promise, yes. We kiss, the warmth of his mouth familiar in a way I like. He turns to leave; I stay and watch. The swirl of curls at the nape of his neck. The rod of his spine; the pleasing ratio of shoulders to hips. Arcs and lines that are so beautiful to me. When he turns a corner, I shake my head a little and head to the women's dormitory; maybe Beryl and Penella are awake, I want to tell them about my night.

Most of the beds are full of sleeping women—it's early, still—but Beryl is up, sitting on the edge of her bed, and Penella is beside her. For half a second I'm filled with anticipated pleasure, imagining their reaction when I share where I spent my night, and with whom—but then I register Beryl's posture. Head forward, back hunched, hair damp with sweat as if she's been working hard, for hours. When Penella looks up, her face lights with relief. "There you are," she says. "We called for the midwife hours ago; go see if she's arrived yet."

I don't move. She turns to Beryl, her voice softer—"Can you get up? Come on, let's go to the infirmary."

"I'm not infirm," Beryl says, and when I hear the smile in her voice, some of my tension drains. Still, she lets Penella help her to her feet.

Penella, to me—"You're still here?"

Rebuked, I tuck the cylinder beneath Beryl's bed and go quick as I can to the kitchen, hoping to find Sister Martine, and, with luck, the midwife. But as I push through the swinging door, I smell the bitter tang of a burning cigarette. It's Dr. Tosquelles, leaning against the sink, smoking; Paul Éluard is here, too, head shoved into the pantry. He emerges with the remains of last night's pie and a look of triumph. They're still in rumpled clothes from the day before; they've been up all night, talking.

"Nora!" says Dr. Tosquelles. "Everything all right?"

"Penella sent me to see if the midwife has arrived."

He pushes off from the sink and drops his cigarette into a cup of tea on the countertop. It extinguishes with a hiss. "Let's find out."

I follow him through the asylum, toward the main door.

It's pink, outside, the day breaking with gorgeous hope. I follow

Dr. Tosquelles across the courtyard, and we've almost reached the cerulean door when it pulls outward, opens, and a woman steps through.

A pain in my chest, a shock like touching wire to water. There she is—my mother.

25

When my mother returned, the day of my fourth birthday, I didn't know who she was. How could I?

Big Nora had shown me pictures. They were displayed in many places in our small apartment: next to the couch; on the breakfast bar in the kitchen; one, in a frame on the table next to my bed. That one was my favorite, but not because of the photograph. It was the frame I loved. Pink plastic that shone when the table lamp was lit. When I rubbed my thumb across it, the texture was perfectly smooth, slick, cool.

"What's the matter with her?" My mother's first words.

The conversation that followed between her and Big Nora is missing. There's a blank spot in my memory between that one question—"What's the matter with her?"—and the time later, after my Colors had been cleaned up and I must have taken a bath, when we sat around the round kitchen table, each with a cup of tea.

whatsthematterwithherwhatsthematterwithherwhatsthematter

Big Nora had the tall yellow teacup. The other woman—"I'm your mother"—had the short pink mug. I had my favorite teacup. It was wide at the bottom, which made it hard to tip. It had a handle on each side, which I liked as I used both of my hands equally well. It was orange with a pink star painted on one side, between the two handles, and a yellow moon painted on the other.

"It's going to take some time for her to adjust," Big Nora said.

"I know that, of course it will," said the woman who was my mother. "It'll be an adjustment for all of us."

When Big Nora asked where she'd been, my mother wouldn't say. "The past is past. I'm here now, and we can all make a fresh start."

"It's been almost four years," said Big Nora.

"I can count, Ma. I know how long it's been."

"One, two, three, four, five, six, seven, eight, nine, ten, eleven, twelve, thirteen, fourteen—"

"What's she doing?"

"Counting."

"—fifteen, sixteen, seventeen—"

"I can see that, but why?"

"—eighteen, nineteen, twenty. Twenty-one—"

"She likes to count. It helps her feel calm."

My mother's hand on my arm. "Nora, honey, there's no reason for you to be nervous."

"Change makes her nervous."

"I'm not change. I'm her mother."

"Don't be ridiculous, Gillian."

"Don't call me ridiculous, Ma."

"Then don't *be* ridiculous, Gillian."

"Why's she rocking like that? Nora. Nora! Look at me, Nora."

"Give her time, hon. She just needs time."

Big Nora is the moon. Gillian is the star.

I counted and counted, rotating my teacup this way, that way, this way, a pendulum swing.

"Why is she rocking like that? What's the matter with her?"

A hand on my arm. "Nora."

My eyes are closed again. My hands are tight across my body. The hand on my arm squeezes. Again, Dr. Tosquelles's voice—"Nora."

I take a shaking breath. Again, I open my eyes.

She's still there. She's still *here*.

Her face is young, but her expression is familiar—mouth turned down, forehead waved with lines. Arms crossed, her energy pulled away, disturbed, or afraid. I force my hands to my sides, shove them in my pockets.

Dr. Tosquelles asks again, "Are you all right?" Another nod, and though he looks unconvinced, Dr. Tosquelles accepts it, turns to Gillian. "You're the midwife, yes?"

Gillian pushes her hair back from her face, the bright golden waves of a true blonde—a young woman's hair. She can't be much older than I am, maybe twenty-one or twenty-two. She's dressed in a sweater, a simple skirt, woolen stockings. Over the bend in her elbow, a carpetbag. These are the possessions of someone who's from this time. Or someone who's been here long enough to possess such things.

"I'm her apprentice," she says, her French slow and childlike, her accent awkward. "The midwife is . . ." She stops, searching her words, switches to English. ". . . stuck at another birth, where there's been a complication. She sent me."

It takes me a moment to access my words, but when I do, I translate for Dr. Tosquelles; Gillian's face lights in delight, and I can't help but feel the familiar jolt, having pleased my mother. "You speak English. Oh, thank God!"

Now Dr. Tosquelles is speaking.

"So she's *not* the midwife, just the apprentice?" I nod. "That should be all right, the two of us can work together, I've twice been called on in emergencies, though of course glurb is not my specialty—" He's talking much too fast; I can tell that Gillian can't keep up, and when Dr. Tosquelles notices, he nudges me to translate. When I've finished, he nods. "You," he says to Gillian, slower, in French. "What is your name?"

"Gillian." To hear her name, from her mouth—it takes all my control to keep myself from rocking again. She extends her hand; they shake. Then he gestures her to follow, and I do, too.

It's impossible. That Gillian is here, that *she's* the midwife's apprentice. Impossible.

And yet.

In the infirmary, Beryl is sitting on the edge of a bed, her chin tucked to her chest, hands cradling her belly. Penella stands beside her, a hand on her back. They both look up when we enter, relief plain on their faces. But when Dr. Tosquelles explains that the midwife couldn't come, and that he'll be assisting Gillian, her apprentice, Beryl's expression flashes from relief to something else. Dr. Tosquelles is crossing to the sink to wash his hands, he doesn't see her face, her hand clutching her belly, the way she practically dissolves.

"No," she says, struggling to her feet. "You can't be here. You can't stay."

"Are you sure?" Penella asks Beryl, her voice a private whisper. "Even him?"

Eyes screwed tight, tears seeping, Beryl nods.

Penella straightens and turns to Dr. Tosquelles, who's drying his freshly washed hands. "No men are to touch Beryl in such a way."

"Ah," says Dr. Tosquelles, and he sets down the hand towel. "Are you sure?"

A shuddered cry from Beryl.

"I see. All right. This woman, then—Gillian—she'll be in charge."

At the sound of her name, Gillian smiles at Beryl. I don't know how much she's understood of the exchange, but she can see that Beryl is upset, she wants to reassure her. "I'm here to help until the midwife can come," she says. Well—what she actually says is "I am here for to help the midwife is later," but I know what she means, and the others do, too.

To Penella and me, Dr. Tosquelles says, "The two of you will do as Gillian asks, yes?"

We nod.

He is slow to leave. When he reaches the door, he stops. "If there is a problem, you call. I will come right away." Then—reluctantly—he leaves.

Penella helps Beryl into bed. "You've done this before?" she asks Gillian.

Gillian is at the sink, washing her hands. In English, she says, "I've been an apprentice for about six months, and I've attended and assisted at many births. I know what to do. But the truth is, if the midwife doesn't arrive in time, this will be my first solo delivery."

Penella and Beryl look to me, and I translate.

"Okay," Beryl says, and she leans back, propped against a stack of pillows.

"Let's take a look." The pitch of her voice is higher than the Gillian I last knew, but the tone is familiar. I've heard it many times—when she was woken in the night by a call from one of her clients, when she was trying to reason with me. Calm, in control. "When I was pregnant," she continues, "I was so scared. And my birth was—well, it wasn't what I'd expected, to say the least. But then, they rarely are. I promise, I'll take care of you. You're going to be fine."

I'm reluctant to translate this; Gillian can't *know* that Beryl will be fine. But Beryl looks at me with such worry that I do my best. "She knows that births can be difficult," I tell Beryl. "She says she's going to take good care of you."

Beryl's face softens into relief. She nods, puts her feet up on the bed, and opens her legs.

"Take a deep breath," Gillian says.

She tends to Beryl with such gentle care. I know this Gillian, and I also know the Gillian whose patience has run out, who is not careful, not gentle. Is each of us a single person, the way Seurat's *A Sunday on La Grand Jatte* is one painting? Or is each of us a series of selves, a million points or more, each its own creature? Left eye. Right eye. Both eyes open. All three, true.

"You've got some time, still." Gillian pulls away, goes to the sink to wash again. My mother. And—just down the hall in the dormitory, tucked beneath Beryl's bed—her remains.

There's a knock at the door; it's Sister Martine, who asks if we need another set of hands. When Gillian says we're doing fine, she looks relieved. "I've always been a bit squeamish about these things," she says with a vague gesture, "but I'll make sure that lunch is waiting for you, later."

Time passes in the way it can when something important is happening. When Gillian was very ill, I sat by her side for hours and hours, but it could have just been moments. At the beach after Big Nora's death—then, too, time stretched and shrank. And when I paint, not always or even often, but every now and then, time disappears. No—it doesn't disappear. It breathes. If time normally progresses ahead, even and straight like a train, in these moments, it breathes. In and out. In and out, again. Time folds and folds, and space does, too, like the paper-thin layers in a croissant, like a gathered sheet, like the whorls in a shell found by the sea.

Dawn becomes day, a pinkish wash lights everything. The infirmary is warm, maybe from the heat coming off Beryl's body as she exerts herself, and when it gets too hot, I go to the window and lay my hand against the cold glass. We're on the far side of the asylum. Out there is the rotunda. Beyond is a field of wheat. As the sun moves higher, the field goes from dark to golden green. It's defined by a low wooden wall that grows lavender with light. On the far side of the wall is a white farmhouse, trees, gentle hills. A web of lines—some curved, others straight—indicate the boundaries of various parcels. Here, wheat field. There, orchard. Here, tamed land. There, wild.

There's a series of paintings that van Gogh produced, the landscape he viewed through the barred window of his cell at Saint-Paul Hospital. I saw them in one of the museums in Paris. A field of wheat and the lines of wall that enclosed it. In those paintings was a white farmhouse and distant mountains. The boundaries of his cell's barred windows gave him a frame. It wasn't this hospital; it wasn't this window, this field. But it could have been.

Behind me, Gillian is helping Beryl shift from one side to her other. A side-lying birth is better than giving birth flat on your back. I know this because Gillian told (will tell) me. It was a Saturday morning, we were in the Miata, she'd been out until the middle of the night at a birth, but still, she'd woken early to take me to an estate sale that listed "art books" in its description. "If you give birth on your back, it compresses the vena cava, which reduces blood flow to the baby. On your side, the baby has a straighter shot down the birth canal. There'll be less tearing, too." She was aglow with it, then, the thrill of birth.

Beryl's nightgown is bunched at her waist and the flanks of her buttocks are revealed to me, white as the moon. She's become a creature, a birthing beast. She's here, but she's also far away, turned inward.

"Come hold her leg." An order. This tone I know, too. Penella is by Beryl's head, stroking sweat-damp hair from her temple. I go around to the other side of the bed, take the weight of Beryl's top leg in both my hands. Beryl stiffens, the orb of her belly tightens and shifts as a contraction ripples across her. Another contraction right atop it, and then a third, they move like waves across the ocean of her body, and now Beryl leans into Penella's arms, and Gillian reaches between her legs, and I hold her leg, bent and heavy as a log.

"Here's the head," says Gillian. I translate and Beryl groans and tosses her head like a horse. "That's it, again, again," says Gillian, and with each contraction Beryl works to birth her child, and Penella and I support her. Another push, and then one more. Then—damp dark hair, a mottled forehead, a slick squished face. Bluish. A cord around the baby's neck.

"Stop," says Gillian, calm but firm. "Don't push."

Beryl says something but the words are far away. There's a pulse in my ears, a pressure in my chest. I don't know what to do—but Gillian does. She's hooking a finger beneath the cord, it's not easy, the cord is tight, but she manages, and I know it will be okay, it's going to be fine. Then she tugs, and I know just as surely that the cord won't come free. Not in time. Both are true. Breath, and death.

My mother's hand is on the cord. It's too tight—and then it isn't. I don't know if it's something she does, or if it's something that just happens, but the cord loosens, and Gillian pulls it up, over the baby's head.

"Okay," she says, and Beryl groans and bears down and the baby slips into Gillian's hands. A girl, still as a doll.

Gillian rubs her chest, her fragile breastbone. "Breathe," she whispers, breathing herself, blowing onto the baby's face—*breath, or death*—and then, at last, a sharp inhalation, four limbs splaying. A wail, a loud bright cry, a protest or a welcome. Both. She's covered in a mix of waxy white goo and bright red blood; her skin is bluish purple and pink; her cry is brave and loud.

"Oh!" says Beryl. Penella helps her sit up; with shaking fingers, Beryl unfastens the buttons of her nightdress, reaches for her baby, gasps when she's placed in her arms. The umbilical cord still binds them; it protrudes from the baby's dilatated navel, stretched round and open, not a closing like we call it—a button—but an opening, a portal that connects. It stretches, pulsing, across Beryl's stomach and between her legs, disappearing up inside of her. Once, a cord just like this one, made of flesh and blood, connected me to my mother. We were one, before we were two. We were joined, before we were severed.

The baby cries and roots and searches by instinct for the nipple; it's dark and large and studded with golden liquid. She finds it and latches tight. Her mother gasps in pain and delight. Penella's color returns; her face is bathed in light.

"One more job to do, to deliver the placenta," Gillian says. It's as if I'm seeing her through that column of water at the aquarium—here is the most capable version of her, and the version she will become, and the version that will unbecome. True, true, all true.

She puts a hand on Beryl's belly. "This will be uncomfortable," she warns, and pushes. I translate and flinch in sympathetic pain, and so does Penella. It's not long before the placenta emerges, large and meaty, beautiful gore. Gillian has told me about the placenta, but I've never seen one before—*It's the most amazing thing, dearheart. The only organ a person grows and then discards. And it's not just the mother's cells that grow it, the embryo's cells contribute, too. Amazing.*

"Okay," says Gillian. "You're done." This needs no translation. She clamps the cord, cuts it. It's a death, this severing. An end of something. A necessary end—for the baby to live, it must be cut free—but still, an end. I squeeze shut my eyes against the sting of tears.

At last Beryl is cleaned and tucked into fresh sheets, and the baby is wiped and swaddled and returned to her mother's arms. Then Gillian asks, "Does she have a name?"

Beryl's gaze doesn't stir from the baby's face, but she shakes her head. "Not yet."

It's a time before she's ready to let us hold the baby—first Penella, then me. I'm nervous at first; I've never held a baby before; but as soon as she's in my arms, this tiny newborn animal, I'm enraptured. Look—here are the tiny feet that kicked my hand.

Then Gillian, who strokes the baby's cheek. With the baby in her arms, Gillian grows wistful and soft. Her expression is not one I recognize. This baby didn't do anything to earn that expression—it's just given.

Did Gillian look at me like that, when I was placed into her arms for the first time? Or the last time she held me, before she walked away?

So many questions I thought I'd never have answered. But now—well.

26

After the birth, Sister Martine and Dr. Tosquelles come to admire the baby; then Gillian shoos us all out, tells us the mother and baby need their rest. Everyone obeys except Penella, whose expression seems to dare anyone to try to make her leave.

In the hallway, Sister Martine says to Gillian and me, "You'll want to clean up and rest, I'm sure. But lunch will be waiting, whenever you're ready."

I translate, and Gillian nods. "Thank you," she says, in French. Then, in English, "Between the birth I was assisting at, and this one, I haven't had a meal or a wink of sleep in over twenty-four hours."

After I translate, Dr. Tosquelles says, "We'll get you sorted and fed," and gestures for her to follow. I can't tear myself away; Gillian is like a magnetic force, pulling me along. And since I'm the only person who can translate, neither of them seems to think it's strange I'm still here.

As we go up the hallway, Gillian peers into doorways—the library, the sewing room, the metalworking shop, all of which are humming with activity. It's after we pass Marguerite Sirvins in the hallway that she asks, "What sort of a place is this?"

"Well," says Dr. Tosquelles—even now, escorting Gillian to a room where she can rest, he can't help but expound on his theory that it's not people who are ill, it's the world, and that in order to heal us, we must heal the world. He's marching up the hallway, he's gesticulating with his hands, mustache twitching as he speaks, and Gillian, I can tell, has completely lost the thread.

"So this is a—" She's searching for the words, she can't find them, so instead she taps her finger on her temple, a blunt but effective means of asking what I know she must be thinking: a mental institution.

We've reached the room I first woke to, when I arrived at Saint-Alban. Dr. Tosquelles stops in front of the door. And, with a playful grin—"Spiders in the ceiling, every one of us." Leaving me to translate, he bows and departs.

She's uncomfortable now, I can tell. "You don't need to worry," I say—I don't want her to change her mind about staying. "It's perfectly safe here."

She looks up and down the hallway, wary. "So . . . are *you* a patient? You don't seem like one," she rushes to add.

Those places aren't for normal people, Nora. If you ever end up in a place like that, it's a sign that you've taken a real wrong turn, somewhere. So take another turn, as fast as you can, to get the hell out.

"I'm more of a guest." I clear my throat. "My mother was my last living relative. After she died, I came here—to France. I wanted to try to honor her, by spreading her remains in a place she wanted to come."

"I'm so sorry you lost your mother," my mother says to me.

"She was . . . very sick."

"Then maybe it's for the best."

I am looking in the face of my dead mother. "Maybe."

"Well," she says, turning to the door.

"How long have *you* been in France?" The words come out loud—too loud, I can tell by the way she flinches. But probably she thinks she owes me something after what I've shared about my mother—*That's how conversations work, dearheart*—because she turns back, says, "It's been a little less than a year that I've been . . . here."

In the slight hesitation between words, I hear what she doesn't say: that "here" is not just a place, but a time.

A little less than a year—is that how long it's been since she left me and Big Nora? If so—maybe she never meant to be gone so long. She'd gotten a passport, so she must have intended to leave the country. I was probably an overwhelmingly hard baby. She boarded a plane, same as I did. Did she land in Paris, too? Maybe she needed to get a way for a little while and planned to return home before I was old enough to remember her absence, but somehow she ended up in the same thatch of overgrown land where I camped that last night; maybe she stumbled or ran through the holloway that could have brought *me* here, to this time. And maybe for the next three years, she'll be stuck here, in the 1940s, not able—but wanting?—to get home.

She starts to open the door—I can't let her disappear. "In all the confusion, I never introduced myself." I stick out my hand. "My name's Nora."

"Oh, funny," she says. "That's my daughter's name." She reaches out, and her hand touches mine. Our fingers wrap around each other's palms. Her hand is warm, and soft, and *alive*. "Are you okay?" she asks.

I blink back tears. "It's just—mothers and daughters, I guess."

"Mothers and daughters are complicated," she says. Then, as if she's worried she's said something wrong, "I don't mean you and your mother. Maybe everything was simple, for the two of you."

I shake my head.

She laughs, sadly. "Not for me and my mother, either."

"Your mother?"

"She's who I left my daughter with—my mother. Also named Nora. We call her Big Nora; the baby, Little Nora."

"That's . . . cute."

"Adorable." There's a wryness to her tone; I don't know why, and I don't know how to respond.

I need to say something, though, to keep her here, talking. "How old is she? Little Nora?"

"Now, she'd be . . . almost four years old."

I was an infant when Gillian left. This means two things. First: if Gillian has only been "here" for a year, then it stands to reason that she was gone but still in our time for the better part of three years. Which means that for most of the time that she was gone, Gillian *wanted* to be gone. I still don't know where she was—traipsing around Europe? Chasing after an old boyfriend—maybe whoever my father was? "Barely more than a sperm donor" is all she'd ever said about him. Was she looking for someone else—an old friend, a lost love, herself? Or was she only running, running away, running away from me?

And the second thing it means (or could mean, though I don't want to think any harder about time travel, such as it is, than I have to): very soon, she'll be going home.

"Do you miss her?"

Her eyes narrow in a way I recognize; I'm testing her patience. She takes a breath in through her nose, purses her lips to release it, raises her shoulders and rolls them back. "Of course I miss her."

"Then why are you still here?"

It's the sort of question that I think is perfectly reasonable but that others would consider rude—even ruder than my last—and if I'd asked such a question back home, I would've gotten a lecture about boundaries, and she would have made me apologize. But here, I'm not her daughter; she's not my mother. We're two young women about the same age, speaking a shared language in a foreign land.

And maybe that's why her expression changes. "Honestly? I'm not sure."

I hold my tongue between my teeth, give her every chance to say more.

She sighs, rubs her face. "I mentioned before about my daughter's birth?"

"Yes."

"Have you heard the term 'C-section'?"

If I'm a young American woman in 1946, would I know what this is? "I'm . . . not sure."

"It's a medical procedure. A surgery. When a woman is pregnant, and the doctors feel like something isn't going well—if vaginal birth is going to be dangerous for the mother or the baby, or if there's an emergency of some kind—they give the woman anesthesia and then cut open her abdomen to take out the baby that way."

"Oh," I say.

"Are you sure you want to hear all this?"

"Yes. I'm sure."

She sighs, rubs her face. "I didn't mean to get pregnant," she tells me. "I wasn't married, I wasn't planning on becoming a mother, not anytime soon, anyway. But then once I *was* pregnant, I was at least looking forward to giving birth."

"You *were?*"

She laughs. "I know that sounds weird. But it's always amazed me—women's incredible life-giving force, the sacred feminine."

If I were Gillian's teenage daughter in 2021 rather than her contemporary in 1946, I would remind her that though most birth-givers are cisgender women, not all of them are. But this is information I keep to myself now. "It's not weird."

Maybe she believes I'm telling the truth, because she continues. "The thing is . . . that's not the birth I had. I wanted to give birth at home. That was my plan. But I lived with my mother—housing is expensive, where I'm from—and she got scared that my labor wasn't progressing fast enough. So she called an ambulance, and the next thing I knew, I wasn't a birthing mother anymore. I was a *patient*. And doctors . . . well, doctors are just people with knives." Gillian looks up at the hallway light—it's a trick she taught me (will teach me)—to stop from crying. "And the baby was . . . *born*, I guess, but it was more like she was pulled out of me, and then I was in so much pain, for so long—a C-section is major abdominal surgery, they take out all your *organs* and put them on a *table*—that nursing was hard, Nora never got the latch right, she was fussy and particular from the start, and my mother was just better at it, anyway—at swaddling her, and giving her the bottle, and . . . everything. Honestly, it just felt like I was in the way." In spite of herself, the tears come. "I don't know why I'm telling you all this. I'm overtired. And I'm being ungrateful—I should be glad my mom was there. That she was able to do the things I couldn't. But they didn't need me there. So I left."

"I didn't know any of this."

She sniffs. "Why would you?"

"I wouldn't." I'm rocking up onto the balls of my feet, then flattening them, rocking up again. "It sounds like maybe you were depressed. That happens sometimes. After a person gives birth. Maybe you needed to talk to someone." I don't know if postpartum depression is a syndrome that was named in this time.

She shakes her head, hard. "You go to one of those doctors, they just want to slap a label on you and pump you full of drugs." She swipes tears from her cheeks as if she's angry at them. This Gillian, at any rate, I know. "Anyway, since being here, apprenticing with the midwife . . . it's been healing for me. To help other mothers have the birth that was stolen from me, to find—" She shakes her head, cuts herself off. "That's selfish of me, right? What kind of a mother leaves her kid?"

I open my mouth, but no words come.

"I don't know why I'm telling you all of this," she says again. "I'm going to take a nap."

"Gillian—"

She's opened the door. Stepped through. Closed it.

I'm in the hallway, alone. I'm taking short little breaths. I want to rattle the doorknob, I want to insist she speak with me. But instead, I turn and go down the hallway, past room after room where people are working—setting the press for the paper, running the sewing machines, tooling leather and refitting soles on shoes. Out the main door; the sky is brilliant blue, the air is ice cold. Across the courtyard and through the larger door, the tall wide arch. The world beyond.

I shake my hands, flicking away tension through my fingers, again, again, again. I'm alone. I sit on the top step; cold seeps through the stone.

It's better out here. I was overwhelmed, in the hallway with Gillian. Too much to take in, too much to process. My heart is still pounding; I wait until it calms.

I need to organize myself. I need to organize my thoughts.

My mother had a traumatic birth. It left her feeling isolated, inadequate, unnecessary. And probably with untreated postpartum depression. She abandoned me, yes . . . but not because I was broken. Because *she* was. I am so sorry for her. So deeply, terribly sorry.

And also: I know where the story goes. Gillian will go home. She will bring this brokenness with her. When I'm not yet six, Big Nora will be standing in exactly the wrong place, and she will die. For the next twelve years, Gillian will parent me in the way she decides I ought to be parented, and I will feel broken too. She will become lost in conspiracy theories and medical quackery, succumb to a preventable disease, and die. She will tell me it is my fault. I will believe her.

So much heartbreak, so much loss.

More, I know, than I could ever have broken. More, I know, than I could ever fix.

In books and movies about time travelers, there's always a *reason* for what's happened. Something in the past is wrong, and it needs to be righted. Or something in the present is wrong, and a trip to the past is necessitated. There's a prophecy that needs to be fulfilled or union that needs to be saved or a disaster that needs to be averted. There's the chance to make a fortune, or witness a historic event, or salvage your parents' marriage.

Maybe there is a reason, a greater *meaning*, for what's happened. Maybe everything has happened precisely as it had to, to bring me to this moment. Now. Here.

But then, all of that is fiction. The universe, we know, is almost certainly not shaped like that. If there is anything I could do that could change anything, then it would have been changed in the life I've already lived. No matter what I say, Big Nora will die on Halloween when I'm almost six years old, struck by a meteorite that falls from the sky. My mother will become who she becomes. I will become who I become.

But then, how did I get here at all? Where is "here"? Am I even in my universe anymore, my reality? The universe I know, as far as I know, isn't shaped in a way that would allow for a holloway-shaped wormhole to form in southern France, nor for one shoeless girl to traverse it. If I am in a different universe, is it possible that in this one, I might be able to stop Big Nora from being struck? And if she were to live . . . what then? It's impossible to know who Gillian would have been if she had never suffered that loss. Who I would have been. Gillian could have been a different mother. She could have lived a different life. She could have . . . gotten the vaccine that could save her life.

A splintered timeline, infinite realities. Endless Big Noras, Little Noras, Gillians. Some of them better off. Others, far worse.

I'm four years old, Doing Colors, unlocking the truth of infinity.

I'm here on the steps of Saint-Alban, overwhelmed again—still—by the terror of it.

The poet is sitting by the fire.

I'm not looking for him—I'm not looking for anyone—but he is who I find.

He's smoking, of course, he almost always is. There's a book in his lap but he's not reading, his eyes are on the flames. The chair across from him is open. I sit.

He stubs out his cigarette in the ashtray beside him. "Nora," he says. "Hello."

"Hello, Mr. Éluard."

He shakes out another cigarette, offers me one.

"No. Thank you."

When the cigarette is lit, he throws the match into the firebox. Its tiny flame is consumed by larger ones.

"I want to ask you something."

He inhales deeply; the cigarette's ember glows. "So. Ask."

"What would you do if—somehow—you were to see your wife again?"

He laughs. "I would make love to her, of course."

"Well—but—what if she didn't recognize you? If she didn't know who you were?"

"Ah! Then we could fall in love, afresh, all over again." His face turns wistful, imagining.

I try again. "But if you wouldn't get to keep her. If she wouldn't stay."

"So—I have a moment with my Nusch. But she doesn't know who

I am, or what we are to one another. Yes?"

"Yes. And there's a chance that if you say the right thing, you might make the life you once shared . . . better. Or, if you say the wrong thing, that you could destroy everything you had."

He thinks a moment, smoking. "Quite the puzzle box you're designing." He taps his cigarette against the side of the ashtray. "Do you know what it is—surrealism?"

"Yes," I say. "Surrealism is a movement—artistic, philosophical, cultural. It began in Paris, after World War . . . after the Great War. Its aim is to channel the unconscious and to free oneself from the confines and entrapments of the logical and rational."

His brows shoot up, his forehead waves into wrinkles. "Exactly so. Quite the surprise, you are. All right. So. Everywhere, all the time, Nora, we are entrapped. Like a sticky spider's web—the censorship of the mind. Religion. The conventions of society. Traditional marriage. Bourgeois values. Capitalism, that alienating machine. And rationalism, yes? Its obsession with *classifications*, with *answers*. All of it—dehumanizing. Limiting. What about the unconscious, Nora? What about dreams? What about the fantastical? And *desire*?"

He stubs out his cigarette half-smoked, runs both his hands through his hair, disappears into the flames. It's a long time before he comes back, but I wait.

At last, he returns to me. His eyes are clear. "So," he says. "My Nusch returns, but she brings nothing from our past, and with no promise of anything ahead. If I tamper, who can say what the result will be. All we have is this—this one moment." His mouth quirks in a wry smile. "The answer stays the same. I would love."

27

The poet would love.

Not a helpful insight, though, for me.

Sister Martine is in the kitchen, already working on dinner. "Are you hungry for lunch?" When I shake my head, she says, "Well, then, will you help me with the potatoes? The pot is heavy."

We each take a dish towel, wrap the handles, go together across the kitchen to the sink where she's set a large metal strainer. Steam wafts up as we dump in the potatoes.

"And can you smash them? I'll add the butter." She picks up the strainer, tips the potatoes back into the pot, hands me the masher.

Mashed potatoes are not a food I can stomach. Making them isn't as bad as eating them, but it's not much better.

"And then later," she asks, "will you collect the eggs?"

I nod. That, at least, is my favorite chore.

She cuts slabs of butter, drops them into the potatoes. "The midwife is resting?"

"She's just the apprentice."

"Maybe after today, she's due for a promotion," says Sister Martine. "The apprentice, then. Resting?"

"Yes."

"You're sure you're not hungry? You must be, you missed breakfast."

"I'm not hungry yet." The butter melts and disappears.

"So," she says, "Auguste's brother . . . a handsome young man, hmm?"

My face grows hot; I hope the steam disguises it.

"He left midmorning to run the doctor's errand. And he asked me to give you a message." She brings the jug of milk, pours in a stream of it. "He says to wait for him," she whispers, and bumps her hip into mine.

Now I'm *really* embarrassed. I just shake my head and stir. Sister Martine laughs. She wipes her hands on her apron front and unties it. "There are sandwiches in the larder, when you're hungry. And don't forget about the eggs."

I find a lid for the potato pot and take the masher to the sink to rinse it. There, on the drainboard, is the little dog I carved. I don't know how it ended up here. Setting the masher in the sink, I pick up the carving. Rub my thumb across the sweet divot between its ears. My shoulders soften, just a bit. I do love dogs. So much so that when Penella asked—not that long ago—what I believed in and I grasped for an answer that felt true, "dogs" was what I arrived at. And I do believe in dogs—more than I could ever believe in destiny, or karma, or God. I don't believe that things are meant to be. I don't believe that good things happen to good people, or that what goes around also comes around, or that no crime goes unpunished.

Look at history. In the Second World War, over six million Jews were murdered; a quarter million disabled people were "euthanized" under the T4 program, and Dr. Tosquelles told me that tens of thousands more were starved to death, here in France alone. Also queer people, Romani people, intellectuals, and some huge number of civilians, all dead. Did *they* get what was coming to them? Of course not; the very suggestion is obscene.

And in my time, seventy-five years from now? By the fall of 2021, when I landed (will land) in France, five million confirmed deaths, from one novel disease . . . and that was just the *reported* number, it will certainly rise, with time. How about those people? Did *they* have it coming to them? Even those who, like Gillian, refused vaccination, refused medical intervention . . . did they deserve to die? Did their punishment fit the crime?

What I'm trying to say is: I do not think the universe is built in such a way that the scales of justice always balance. The children in Michigan did not deserve the water they had no choice but to drink. The man in Minneapolis didn't deserve to be restrained by a knee to his neck until he perished. The wicked aren't always punished; the good are not always rewarded. So it's unreasonable, this—hope—that I could do something *now, here* . . . to change something then, there.

And yet.

It feels as though there must be something I could do to change . . . *something.* Without ruining everything. I'm thinking of the penny I smashed in Santa Cruz, the pebbles Auguste laid on the tracks in the tunnel; what degree of change is enough to matter, and what degree is precipitous of disaster?

If, say, I could somehow convince Gillian to prevent Big Nora from standing exactly where she will be standing, the Halloween before my sixth birthday . . . would it even work? Or would the meteorite strike her somewhere else? I'm considering telling Gillian this, and maybe I will . . . but I remember Big Nora's death, which means it happened (happens). Does that mean that I'll be (have already been) unsuccessful?

How about something smaller? Maybe I can't save my grandmother's life, but might there be something—anything, one single thing—that could change how my mother was, for my sake, and for hers, too? I really can't do *that*? Is there anything I could possibly say that could change something in my mother? Something that would matter?

"Hi."

I gasp, and the carving drops to the floor.

"Sorry. I didn't mean to startle you." The words are English, and I turn to see Gillian, pushing through the swinging door. "The sister mentioned something about lunch?"

I bend down to retrieve the carving, set it on the butcher block. "In the larder," I manage to say. "I'll get it."

The larder is dim and quiet. I take a moment to compose myself before finding the sandwiches—two of them, plated and covered with cloth napkins. When I emerge, Gillian is by the butcher block, the carved dog in her hand.

"Cute," she says, and sets it down.

We pull two stools to the carving block. The sandwiches are roast beef and cheese with thin slices of onion, which I pull out.

"Mmm," says Gillian. "The food is so *good* here."

I know what she means—in 1946. "Better than at home?"

She nods, takes another bite. "Much better. The food here is all—"

She stops, but I know what she was going to say. *Real.* I've heard it hundreds of times: the food that was (will be) available isn't *real* food. It's processed, preserved, pumped full of chemicals. "—fresh," she finishes.

If there is a divine providence—which I don't believe—it sent us to this moment, here. We're in a kitchen, aren't we? And the kitchen is where Gillian and I always communicated the best. At our table, over art. Does it mean something that we're at a kitchen table here, now, or does it *not* mean something—because this "table" is really just a butcher block, or because fate is a fantasy?

"Would you like a glass of water?" I ask.

"Yes, thanks."

I take two glasses from the drainboard, fill them at the sink. When I hand her one, she drinks deeply. I know her so well that I'm nearly certain I know her current thought. *Drinking water, right out of the faucet.*

"I wanted to thank you," I tell her, "for taking such good care of my friend."

"Oh, it was my pleasure."

"I never would have guessed that this was the first birth you attended by yourself. You were wonderful. Really."

She smiles. "Thank you for saying that."

"Well, it's the truth."

"I'm lucky to have found something so meaningful. Not everyone is so lucky." Here is where my mother finds meaning. She takes another bite. "You know," she says—chews, swallows—"I've been thinking about what I said to you earlier. About my mom. I might have given you the impression that I don't like her very much. And that's not true. After all, I named my daughter after her, didn't I?"

"You did."

"I'm lucky she was there for me. And Little Nora. It wasn't the way I intended things to go—to leave them like that. I was hopeful, when I was pregnant. And then after . . . well, I just don't think I'm meant to be a mother."

Again, I try—"Don't you think maybe someone could help you . . . if you're depressed, or something like that?"

"It's not *depression* to see things the way they are, is it? And anyway, there are bigger problems—much bigger—than mine. The place I came from. . . . *Where* are you from, again?"

"Oklahoma."

"Ah," she says. "Yes. Well, I'm from California—as far west as you can go. And things there . . . well, in some ways, they aren't all that different from here. Here, there—the world is a terrible place. It never changes, not really. Look at everything we have—machines and technology, medicines and surgeries, all of them supposedly to prolong our lives, make things better . . . and still, we kill ourselves. We kill each other. We make the world worse, more hurtful, more hateful. Wars, and illnesses. It's terrifying. What sort of a world is this, to bring a child into? What was I even thinking?"

She's talking about the time she left—2004. What's disturbing is how simple it is, for her to talk to someone who thinks she's talking about 1946, in the same words. Here, the Second World War just ended, and the world is still fighting through a tuberculosis epidemic; I was born the year the United States invaded Iraq, and the world was dealing with the SARS outbreak. Even more disturbing is what she doesn't know—that during the era from which I traveled here, the early

2020s, there will be a US president who will say of a conflict between American Nazis and protestors that there were "very fine people on both sides" and will attempt a coup after losing his second election; there will be one of the deadliest pandemics the earth has ever seen; and that she will die.

Still, we are in a kitchen. We are here. I have to try. "It's true the world has many problems. It always has, and it probably always will. But . . . well, do you know the Seurat painting, *A Sunday on La Grand Jatte?*"

"It's my favorite."

"Okay," I say. "You know how it's made? With all the points of color? To see the whole picture, you have to step back a little, to take it all in."

She nods.

"That's one way to see it. But also, you can step in close. Really close. And look carefully at just one part of the picture. Like the lady with the parasol, and the little girl. Up close like that, focusing just there, you see things you couldn't, from far away. You see the texture, and the way the points are arranged, color by color. And it's beautiful that way, too. Maybe even more beautiful, to some people."

"Okay," she says. She thinks I'm being strange. But I'm not her daughter now, as far as she knows, and so I press on.

"Well, maybe life is like that. Enormous. Overwhelming. But also, if you step in closer, and closer, if you choose just one little area to focus on, just, say, one little girl, you can find meaning there, too. If you can love her . . . I mean, if you can treat her very gently, if you can try to see who she is, if you can understand the specific group of points that comprise her, if you can understand that that person, just as she is, is part of that larger painting . . . maybe that can matter more than what the rest of the world looks like. Maybe that can be a way to change it."

I feel like I've pulled open my chest and handed Gillian my heart. *See me,* beats my heart.

She's quiet. She finishes her sandwich, wipes her mouth, folds her napkin. Drinks the last of her water. I'm holding my breath, while I wait. Then—

"That's a really nice thought. But it's not the way the world actually works. The world is terrifying, and dangerous, and cruel. Little girls? They get broken. The best thing people can do—the only thing—is be stronger. To believe anything else is naïve, at best."

I have accepted that my mother was angry. Cynical. Misled. I've discovered that she was most likely also depressed. But now I see something else—something I didn't recognize before. I think that maybe, more than anything, she's afraid.

Fear can't be reasoned with. That's why I couldn't say anything to save her before. It's why I can't say anything to save her now.

My cheeks are damp. I dry them with my napkin.

I can't sit here any longer. "I need to get the eggs for Sister Martine."

The coop is past the kitchen garden, around the side of the castle. Half a dozen hens meander outside the structure, scratching and pecking the soil. A skinny rooster perches on the peak of the coop, shaking out his feathers and occasionally making himself known. There's a metal basket by the door; I take it with me. It's mulchy inside, smells like cedar or pine because of the wood chips spread on the ground. Along the back wall is a row of nesting boxes. The nearest box is empty except for a speckled brown egg, which I settle in the basket.

The next box has a hen inside. Her feathers are warm and soft and the bed of hay is prickly. I feel around until I touch the smooth hard warmth of a shell. "Sorry," I tell the hen as I take her egg. "Thank you."

Twice in my life, I've given up eating meat. The first time was when Gillian gave me the stuffed toy, Feather. Until then, it had never occurred to me that "a chicken" and "chicken" were the same thing. I don't know how I'd slotted the feathered creature and the food product into two buckets, but that's what my brain had done: "a chicken" was the creature: feathered, soft, an egg layer; "chicken" was the meat: breaded, broiled, used to make broth. Chicken was one of the only foods I would eat, at the time. When I found out the truth of things—that "a chicken" and "chicken" belong in one category, not two . . . well.

"Dearheart," Gillian said, "I had no idea you didn't know what you were eating. I never lied to you! It's right there in the name—*chicken*!"

But it felt like a lie to me. I could *hear* the difference between "a chicken" and "chicken"; therefore, she *must* be expressing that difference through tone. The idea that she could say one thing and I could hear another. I couldn't fathom it. What I received was what she put out. To believe otherwise would be like saying that someone throws a sock at you, but you catch a tomato.

Though I remember when I stopped eating "chicken," I don't remember when I started again. My second observance of vegetarianism occurred when I learned that some cultures of people consume animals that most Americans protect as pets, and that most Americans eat an animal that one *billion* people in India consider sacred. I was in the seventh grade. A girl named Trinity made a boy named Yúzé cry by calling him a "dog eater" over and over again, shouting it on the playground and then later whispering it to him in class. Mr. Robinson sent her to the principal's office and lectured us for twenty minutes on cultural mores around food—this is when I learned about the cows—but the damage was done. Yúzé's parents enrolled him in a private school across town.

That time, I remained a vegetarian for two years, until I was a freshman. Then, suspecting that animal *products* might be nearly as bad as animal *meat,* I started researching the harm done to dairy cows—babies taken from their mothers, repeated impregnation, restrictive confinement, forced overproduction of milk—and egg-laying chickens—males "sexed" at birth and then killed, either suffocated or ground up in "large industrial macerators," the surviving females housed in industrial barns, farmers manipulating their light and feed—first keeping them in near-dark, then switching to twenty-hour days of bright lights to trigger an overproduction of eggs—not to mention how they'd been bred over centuries to lay eggs big enough to routinely cause prolapsed cloacas and egg binding . . . well. I could arrive at no ethical conclusion other than veganism.

Of course, my research led me down a further rabbit hole. Almonds, for one—the amount of water and pesticides used to support the average California almond enterprise are criminal. The pesticides kill bees (epically bad not only for the bees, but also for the environment at large), and they make their way into the groundwater, poisoning the limited amount of water all animals (including humans) have access to.

And that's just almonds. Chocolate, coffee, berries . . . chase most threads far enough, and they lead somewhere terrible. Exploitive labor practices. Environmental ruin. Then there's the consideration of the forced labor used to mine the cobalt that fueled the battery of the very implement on which I was doing my research. Layer upon layer upon layer of complicity, of suffering, of pain. All the way to the core.

When the pandemic began, what I ate or didn't eat seemed like a less pressing concern than the world's events, my mother's unraveling. I ate what was served and didn't complain about it.

Now, here, not only do I eat "chicken," but I eat *these* chickens. That's something I never imagined I could do—admire an animal one day, have it for dinner the next.

A favorite philosophical query, from childhood: Which came first: the chicken, or the egg? The answer, of course: it depends.

From a causal chain perspective, there's the problem of infinite regress: if every cause requires prior cause, then the chain stretches backward, for infinity. Aristotle solved this with the concept of an Unmoved Mover: "an immortal, unchanging being, ultimately responsible for all wholeness and orderliness in the sensible world." No offense to Aristotle, but I find this solution to be deeply unsatisfying.

Then, there's the teleological interpretation: something only *is* based on its purpose. Things exist because of their use. Therefore, the chicken must be first, as without it, there would be no chicken to lay the egg. Plato agreed; the chicken is the ideal Form, the egg just material that creates it. Chicken first.

On the other hand, ask a process philosopher: *Process, not product,* she'd say, *therefore, egg first.*

Chicken first? Egg first? Chicken? Egg? Everything I remember will happen; otherwise, how could I remember it? It's impossible to change anything, and equally impossible that I could arrive—or be brought—to this place, this moment, that I could meet my mother just as I'm realizing how a few alterations in how she saw me might have changed things, for both of us . . . only to discover that there's no way I can change anything at all.

It's quiet in here, soft with shadows. A good place for resignation.

A rectangle of light floods the coop as the door opens; it wedges away to nothing as it closes again.

It's her.

"Hi," she says.

"Hello."

She picks her way toward me through the hay. "Listen. I'm heading back to the village. But before I leave, I want to apologize. I shouldn't have called you naïve."

"You didn't."

"Well. I implied it."

"That's true."

"Anyway, I'm sorry. It's just . . . it's not easy to talk about the past."

An apology from Gillian is a rare thing. "You didn't ask for my opinion," I offer.

"That's true," she says, but with a smile. The Charolais leaps down from her box, brushes against Gillian's leg. She draws back, shivers. "They're so creepy, don't you think?"

"What are?"

"Chickens."

"That's not—" I stop myself. Gillian *likes* chickens . . . doesn't she?

I always believed she did. Do I know anything anymore, anything at all? The question returns: Chicken? Or egg?

The surrealists often feature eggs in their work. To them, what's important is its symbology, what the egg represents—mystery and potential, metamorphosis and life.

"Since when have you been afraid of chickens?"

"I don't know . . . all my life, I guess."

But what about Feather? Why would Gillian have chosen a stuffed *chicken,* if she's always been afraid of them? She even chose the name.

Wait.

It hits me, a wave of understanding.

I can't change anything. I can't save Big Nora, or Gillian, or even Little Nora, from what we all will suffer.

But that doesn't mean that nothing I can do right now matters.

"I've been thinking more about my daughter. About why I'm still—here. And the truth is—" Now, Gillian's voice breaks, a terrible confession of a secret shame. "—the way your friend Beryl looked at her baby? I've never felt that way. I don't know that I ever will."

How do you get the pear in the bottle?

"Maybe it's true you haven't felt that way yet." My voice is soft but clear. "But I think that you will."

"How could you know that? How could you know anything about me, at all?"

Because—I think but do not say—though you might not be a natural mother—or even a *good* mother, in many ways—I understand now that it was love you felt for me. Or, will feel. Your love will be imperfect. Murky. Even damaging. But still, for better and worse—it's love.

The trick is not to get the pear into the bottle. One must have much more patience than that.

The Charolais struts close, pecking near my feet; I set down the basket and pick her up, hold her close. Her heart is beating so very fast. I stroke her small, feathered body.

My other favorite artists—the abstract expressionists. To them, arriving at an answer is never the point. Questions and answers exist on a ticking timeline; but when one is present—in a moment, in a painting—time collapses. There is no "before" or "after," no "if," or "then." There is just this moment. This gesture. This murky, ambiguous mark.

I take a step closer to Gillian. We're just the same height. With a flash of memory—or premonition—I see the day that she'll look into my face and know who I am. *This* me. Her last words—*It was you*—I thought that she was blaming me. But I was wrong. She wasn't blaming; she was remembering.

What do I want her to remember, at the end?

I stroke the hen's warm, feathered back. "Will you let me do something for you?"

Her eyebrows pull together, her body tenses.

"Here." I hold out the chicken, my hands pinning her wings. Gillian balks, but I wait. Trembling, she takes the hen. "Hold her tight to your chest—yes, like that—and one hand across her wings—there."

Gillian is nervous, I can hear her breaths, fast and shallow, but she does what I tell her to do. The Charolais fusses for a moment, then settles.

"Oh," says Gillian. "This isn't so bad." Her right hand restrains the chicken's wings; her left smooths the feathers on her back.

A moment ago, my mother was afraid of chickens. I never knew that, before. Because the Gillian who goes home won't be. She will choose a stuffed chicken for Little Nora, a gift for her first day back to school. Little Nora will carry that stuffed creature with her everywhere, for years. She will feel a little safer. A little more secure. A little more loved. Because of this. Because of me. And when her mother is taken for cremation, Nora will send Feather, too. So Gillian won't have to go alone.

I can't change the things that made me feel so broken. But I can help create the things that will teach me that, just maybe, I wasn't.

"When you go home," I tell Gillian, "it won't be any better than how you left it. But you can be a good mother."

"How could you possibly know that?"

"I don't think my mother thought she would be a good parent, either. And sometimes, she wasn't. She got a lot of things really wrong. But other times—important times—I know that she tried. And trying matters."

"What if I go back, and I make things worse?"

You will. "You won't."

My mother will go home. She'll blame Big Nora for making me the way I am, she'll be *afraid* of the way I am. She'll yell and blame and punish and shame; then, when Big Nora is dead, she'll soften . . . but only on the outside. She will be angry, withholding, and sometimes cruel. Her fear will underwrite everything. I will contort myself into a Gillian-shaped box. She will give me what she can. It will be incomplete, and flawed, and never enough. She will take at least as much as she gives. And yet—because of me, right now, here, in this moment—she won't be afraid of chickens anymore.

I can't change my mother into someone who will care for Little Nora the way that Little Nora needs, or deserves. But still, Little Nora will grow—I will grow, have grown, am growing—into a person who isn't led by fear. A person who stays soft, stays curious. A person who cares *why* and *how* my mother became who she became . . . and unbecame. A person who wants to honor her mother, even if many things she did weren't deserving of being honored. A person who will survive many times, many things, to arrive *here* . . . in a position to send souvenirs of hope to a little girl who needs them.

Gillian is both here, and not here. She strokes the chicken's downy back. "She's so soft." Her voice is full of wonder. "Do you know what would be the cutest name for a chicken? Feather. Wouldn't that be sweet?"

"Yes," I agree. "Perfect."

What about the unconscious, Nora? What about dreams? What about the fantastical? And desire?

Yes, I say. Yes.

28

All my life, even before I slipped backward through time, I felt unmoored. But since my fourth birthday, there was a place I could go that felt knowable, and known. I could take a chair from the kitchen and pull it down the hallway; I could climb atop it; and I could peer into a world that felt painted just for me.

Look, the Painting whispered. *Do you see? A bedroom, safe and snug. A bed; a chair; a window. Shoes just your size, for when you're ready to go outside. Walk through the field, listen to the wheat's golden whisper. Look up; see the shimmer in the sky? The sun is a lemon, and it loves you. The dog is smiling, and he loves you, too. This is the way the world can be. You are safe. You are loved. You are safe.*

The Painting taught me what I loved: Lines, curved and straight. Finding meaning, and making it. Unconventional perspectives. Unexpected beauty, and beauty in unexpected places. Color. And texture. And light.

And as I got older, it offered me hope. Because my mother had seen something of value in the Painting, something beautiful in its strangeness. We'd seen the same thing in it, even if at different times. And if we saw the Painting the same way, once . . . there was a chance that we could be aligned, again.

I needed that hope, even if it was false. As Gillian changed—growing angrier, more fearful, more hurtful, too—the Painting told me to hold on. Until the end came, and there was no more hope to hold. My mother left me, and I had to leave the Painting.

I came to France, alone and adrift. I wandered farther and further, both. I was attacked; I stumbled backward through time; I found myself in an asylum. Again, and again, and again, I had to choose: Give in? Or go on?

Each time, I went on. And on. And on.

And now, here I am.

It's easy to finish the Painting, now that I know what it needs.

Not soil. Not sand. In Auguste's room, I unscrew the top of the bamboo cylinder, which Adrien has kept safe, which he has returned to me.

My mother dug with me in the sand. She told me I was broken. How can both be true? And yet, they are.

I can't change the future, or the past. I can't save anyone. But I can take what I have, and transform it into art. Paint, linseed oil. And some of my mother's ashes. With the fine edge of a knife, I spread the mixture onto the heads of wheat. Ashes in the sky, and the water, and the earth.

I don't have to wait for the final layer of paint to dry to know that this time, the thickened ridges I've built will be just right. A field of wheat, bordered by a cord of hair. Shoes, beneath a chair. A wedding dress, an egg, a ring of trees, a mushroom. A lemon sun, the grinning mouth of a dog. Orbs and arcs, lines and angles. Light, shadows. A curve of water, flowing. I know this Painting. It's no reproduction; it's my very own.

* * *

We're sitting on the steps of the courtyard. The baby has a touch of jaundice and the sunlight will do her good, even though it's cold. She's been suckling, and now she releases the nipple with a milky, contented sigh. On the far side of the courtyard, the cerulean door is swung outward, framing a bit of road, a bit of ground, a bit of sky. Out there, Dr. Tosquelles is switching out the Bee's hubcaps, an exercise in futility, it seems to me, as the thing still won't run. If all goes as it should, Adrien will return tomorrow evening with the engine part he went to Bordeaux to retrieve.

From behind us comes Penella, damp hair loose and a comb in her hand. Beryl passes the baby to me as Penella settles on the step lower than us, between Beryl's legs, and Beryl works the tangles from her hair. Penella tilts back her head, face to the sun, enjoying the scratch of the wide-tooth comb against her scalp, the gentle pull through her hair. The baby is a solid warm force in my arms. She doesn't have a name yet; Beryl says she's still thinking about it, names are important and the baby's just two days old, so what's the hurry? Auguste is circumnavigating the yard, eyes on the ground, searching for treasure. He sees it everywhere, treasure, the way I see beauty. This is something else we share.

Clanging sounds as Dr. Tosquelles works on the hubcaps. In my arms, the baby mewls and stretches. Beryl finishes combing Penella's hair. She's running her fingers through it now, with such beautiful intimacy. I can't tell whether I wish I were Beryl, or Penella, or myself with someone touching *my* hair like that, or if I want to have my hands in someone else's hair—Adrien's. I want it all.

These women on the steps. This baby. Dr. Tosquelles with his banged-up silver bus; Auguste taking yet another turn around the yard. When he passes beneath the large olive tree on the far side of the yard, he's framed for a moment by a silver-green bough.

This is a painting, too.

It's the first of December, one week before my birthday. I'm not nervous or worried; I know she'll come soon—today or tomorrow, the day after at the very latest. She has a journey ahead of her, and only seven days to make it. The sky is mottled pink with cotton candy clouds. And—look. Here she comes now, carpetbag over her arm. I stand, smile, wave.

She steps off the road and up the path, and I go out to meet her. "Nora!" she says.

"You're leaving."

"I haven't stopped thinking, since we were in the coop. About my mother, and my daughter."

"You're going home."

"Well, I'm going to try."

"Will you come in for a minute? I want to show you something."

"It's not another chicken, is it?" She laughs, and I do, too. It's strange; I like her, this Gillian. Maybe, in a different timeline, a different world, we could be friends.

We stop on the stairs so Gillian can greet the baby and her mothers, and I wait for a bit while they chat. Then we go inside, to the kitchen and through it. I push through the paneled door into Auguste's workroom; press the light switch.

Across the room is the Painting. We stand in front of it. We regard it together.

"Did you paint this?"

I nod.

"It's . . ." She reaches out, stops just before touching the raised wheat heads, then runs the tip of one finger across them. Shivers. "It's bizarre. I've never seen anything like it."

For most of my life, I would have traded nearly anything for my mother's admiration and approval. But not now. I don't need Gillian to like the Painting. I just need her to take it home with her.

The paint is dry, or dry enough. It's an easy thing, to pull out the staples holding it to the frame, to roll the canvas and wrap it in thick brown paper, to tie it with a cord of twine. When I cut the twine, I feel it at my very core.

I hold it out. "It's a gift," I tell her. "For your daughter."

She hesitates, unsure, but I'm not worried; I know she'll take it. I know from my own memory that Gillian won't tell Little Nora the Painting is a gift, that it's *hers*, to do with as she sees fit. But Little Nora will wonder over it; study it. She will see something in the Painting that she doesn't have words for, but that she loves, just the same. She will disappear into it again, again, again, it will be a home, a refuge, a blueprint for a future when her present hurts too much.

My mother takes the Painting and slips it into her bag.

"You know," I tell Gillian, "there's a cave around here, somewhere not too far. I think you'd really like it."

"A cave?"

I nod. "With ancient art. There's a boy—Jacques—guarding it. If you make it there, on your way home, will you tell him that I send my thanks for his shoes?"

We're outside the castle now. We're crossing the courtyard. Gillian is pushing open the wide cerulean door.

"I wish we'd had more time," I say.

"What for? We don't even know each other."

In many ways, this is true. It will always be true. But even so, right now—(whatever "now" is)—I am more interested in a moment than a story. More invested in one dot than the larger picture, whatever that picture may be.

I reach out, hoping. And though she does so uncertainly, she does the same. I'm careful the way I'd be with an animal (*We're not* animals, *Nora*. Oh, but we are, we are). Slowly, carefully, I press my cheek against hers. Warm, and soft. Young, and so very alive. She trembles like she'll pull away but then she doesn't. I don't know what to say. There are no words for this.

So instead of speaking, I breathe. In for four, hold for four, release for four, stay empty for four. I begin again, one, two, three, four—and this time, she breathes with me. Four, and four, and four, and four. Up, across, down, across.

This is a truth: my mother loved me. But love isn't a straight line. My mother loved me, and she believed me to be broken. Sometimes—like when she let me (will let me) hide beneath the pink membrane in the kitchen, like when she sat (will sit) on the beach and covered me in sand, and covered herself, too, to see what it was that I liked about it—she just loved me, plain and simple. *All* of me. Other times, like when she left me as a baby, when she screamed (will scream) at Big Nora—*You ruined my girl,* when she told me that what was crooked (me) can never be straightened—her love will pull away like the ocean at low tide.

I can't repair my mother. Not this version, or any other. I never could. We're very different people, with very different languages, and very different ways of seeing the world. Often, communication failed us—has failed us, will fail us again. But on the steps of Saint-Alban, we do box breaths together. It's a small thing, this moment. But it's also everything. Breath, or death.

It feels like a long time before I let her go, but what do I know about time. Even after I release her, there's a moment—maybe an eternity—when she stays still, her cheek against mine. Maybe she's reluctant to leave.

But she does leave.

She will always leave.

She always left.

For whatever reason—whatever string of reasons—the story of my mother and me will end in heartbreak, tragedy, despair. Still, regardless—*The answer stays the same. I would love.*

I'm alone in the arch of the doorway, trying not to blink. I don't want to miss a moment of these last moments that she and I are in the world together. She grows smaller, and smaller, and smaller, until I can't tell what is her, and what's the road. And then she disappears.

29

It's springtime now.

A few months ago, not long after the baby was born, we had a naming ceremony. Everyone who wanted to join was invited, and though Beryl said no gifts were necessary, I think everyone was glad to have something to celebrate.

Auguste presented the baby with his biggest sculpture, the bird man, setting it solemnly beside her bassinet. Dr. Tosquelles gave her a stack of books; Sister Martine brought a honey cake ("The baby won't even know what's happening, but her mother deserves a sweet treat"); others gave her flowers, and a handmade doll, and a beautiful dress fashioned from lace doilies—this, from Marguerite Sirvins, who had set aside her own wedding dress just long enough to make it. Paul Éluard recited a poem: *There is certainly another world, but it is in this one.* Warm as a bug in her bassinet, the baby cooed.

We ate and we drank and we danced as Dr. Tosquelles played song after song on the old piano until the baby started to get fussy and Beryl told us it was time to get on with things. Then Dr. Tosquelles rose from the piano bench and shut the lid. Turning to us, in his most ceremonial voice: "How shall this baby be called?"

And Beryl answered: "Her name will be Leonora. The name my mother had."

"Leonora, you are beloved!" said Dr. Tosquelles, and everyone cheered.

Penella loosened the red silk from her hair, kissed the baby's face, and tied the scarf around her right arm.

I'd considered many options for a gift—painting her something or bringing her a found treasure from outdoors—but settled on giving her the softest thing I owned. The yellow scarf. Like Penella, I kissed the baby's face. Then I tied it to her left arm. Leonora's.

The Bee is finally up and running thanks to Adrien, who, it turns out, knows a bit about diesel engine repair.

When he returned from Bordeaux, I took him by the hand and led him up the stairs, all the way to the attic, showed him the nook with the dusty bed. I felt shy, but I hadn't needed to. We washed the sheets and made it fresh, and now if I wake in the night, I can press my back against him, a person I love.

Dr. Tosquelles is pleased as a peach and anxious to put the Bee to use, so the first fine day, those of us who want to go load up the bus with blankets and a folding metal table and a dozen folding chairs. Baskets of bread and cheese and leftover macaroni salad. A few bottles of cider.

Robot yelps and wags his tail, darts back and forth between us as we go from the castle to the bus and back again. It's before eight in the morning when we pile in: Dr. Tosquelles behind the wheel and Robot jumping in straightaway. Adrien is on his heels, Auguste beside him, a canvas sack slung across his chest and the tip of his felt hat leaning forward as his eyes sweep the drive, the bus's metal steps, the aisle. He takes a window seat and Adrien slides in beside him. I'm across from them. Nearby are Beryl and Penella and the baby—everyone calls her Little Nora now.

The poet is aboard—he's leaving next week, returning to Paris, but he's here today, and that's all that matters, he says. Sister Martine is also on the bus, coming along to mind a few of the patients who need more constant care. Robot runs up and down the aisle, checking on all of us. When we're settled Dr. Tosquelles calls, "Pray for the Bee, my friends!" We share a held breath as he cranks the key, as the engine grumbles. When it roars to life, we cheer, a cacophony of unkempt celebration. Robot barks, punctuating our cheers, and then we're off, the motley bunch of us, bumping down the hard-packed dirt path. Little Nora laughs and squeals, waving her fat little arms until we turn onto the thin, paved road, and then the Bee flies smoothly.

It's beautiful country. Heathered and wild, speckled with farmhouses, horses, cattle. A flash of a creek's gray-blue water; a squiggle of smoke rising from a stone chimney; a sudden shift and lift from a wall of brush as we startle a flock of pigeons nesting there and they take off in silver-winged flight.

After a while, satisfied that all's well, Robot jumps up onto my bench. He circles tightly and thumps down, rests his chin on my knee, sighs. My hand is on his scruff. Soft, warm, such a luxury. What a thing, to be trusted by an animal like this. I let my forehead rest on the cool clear glass of the window.

I wake when the road grows rough again. Dr. Tosquelles has turned us off the main way and onto a smaller lane. Adrien flashes me a smile as he makes his way to the front of the bus, holding on to the seatbacks as he goes. He and Dr. Tosquelles confer about the route. "It'll come up suddenly," Adrien says. "Go slow, or you could miss it." Then, there it is, a slice of gray-brown dirt among the trees, the sky wide and bright above. In spite of Adrien's warning, Dr. Tosquelles has still been maneuvering the Bee at quite a clip, and so, as he cranks the wheel, he cries out, "Hold on to your hats!"

Those with hats, do; the rest of us grab the seatbacks in front of us as the Bee wobbles and turns, indignant. I keep a hand on Robot's back, wrapping my arm around his chest to keep him from slipping off the seat. When the bus straightens, Dr. Tosquelles calls over his shoulder, "So sorry! My mistake!" and we grumble our complaints good-naturedly.

The lake, when it appears, is a violet gem. You'd think Adrien had created it himself, the way everyone heaps praise on him. He accepts it gamely, giving a mock bow as he returns to his seat beside Auguste. Dr. Tosquelles finds a flat spot in the grass, and Robot is the first of us off the bus. He bounds down the steps and runs straight for the water; with a leap and a splash, he's in, and away he swims.

"That's the last we'll see of him for a while," says Adrien, watching fondly as the dog paddles away, only his sleek dark head above the surface.

It's a perfect afternoon. Though clouds gather and threaten, it doesn't rain, and then the wind plows through and blows them all away. The lunch we've brought is ample, and the fishermen—and Penella—have good luck. Paul Éluard reads to us from his notebook—*I have passed the doors of coldness, the doors of my bitterness, to come and kiss your lips*—and Auguste finds three old cans, a broken brooch, and an abandoned bird's nest, all of which he packs carefully into his canvas sack.

My friends and I follow a finger of creek up through a tangle of greenery to an open space with a shade tree, where we rest. From time to time, a squirrel peers down at us. Beryl is leaning back on her elbows, watching Penella talk to the baby. None of us understand the language Penella speaks with her, but Penella says she's considering teaching me. Auguste whittles a stick; Adrien lays on his back, his head in my lap, staring up at the fresh green leaves as they quiver in the springtime air. I rake my fingers through his hair.

Each one of us—except Little Nora—has suffered. All of us have lost people we loved.

It took time for my friends to share their full stories with me, their losses, but they did. Beryl, whispering through choked sobs over the head of her sleeping baby, whose mouth was a milky rosebud on her mother's nipple. Penella, striding angrily through the fallow wheat field as I rushed to keep up, her voice a broken roar. Adrien in our bed, words muffled against my chest, dampened with his tears. Auguste, by opening a drawer and pulling out a sculpture he had hidden there—a twisted train, with broken wings. Terrible stories. Each one almost too terrible to believe. But of course, I believed them. I believed them all.

The day is closing. Far away, the Bee's horn sounds. I give Beryl the baby—Little Nora has a fistful of my hair, Beryl and I laugh and untangle it together; Adrien packs our things; Penella offers a hand to Auguste, who takes it.

It's time to go. I pick up the quilt to shake away the leaves, but I'm dizzy and lightheaded; maybe I stood up too fast. My heart pounds and the world sparkles like I might faint. I rest my hand against the rough bark of a tree. I close my eyes. There's a whooshing sound, loud like the ocean, but it's inside my head. I'm spinning, or the world is spinning around me.

Right now, my mother is dying. Right now, Little Nora is realizing that color is infinite, uncontainable. Right now, I'm stepping off a trail. Seurat is at his easel. A baby is being born, a meteorite falls from the sky. I'm being held by a boy. Someone is painting on the wall of a cave, and someone else is discovering it. Auguste is piling pebbles on a train track. My mother's face is loose and wavy through water. Adrien is tying a bottle around a white pear blossom, his father is steadying the ladder and smiling.

Little Nora is gazing at a Painting—a field of wheat, bordered by a cord of hair. She's wondering why the artist included a bed, a wedding dress, a ring of trees, a lemon sun, a mushroom, the grinning mouth of a dog. She leans in—here, the paint looks thicker. What did the artist do? She reaches out a curious finger, runs it down the raised tactile ridge. Does she feel something now? Does she remember me?

The spinning slows, slows, stops.

I'm going to open my eyes. I know what I'll see when I do.

There it is, its opening a perfect circle. An invitation: *Would you like to go back?* the holloway asks. *I could take you there.*

I *should* go. Shouldn't I? And yet—

If there's one thing I've learned, it's that people can disappear at any time, in so many ways. Nothing is certain. And here . . . here is Beryl, and Penella, and Adrien, and Auguste. Here is Little Nora.

Humans are herd animals, Nora. We aren't meant to be alone.

My mother was wrong about many things. But about this—I believe that she was right. If you're lucky enough to find people who love you, people you can love in return . . . does it really matter where they are? Or when?

Maybe time, like love, isn't a straight line. Maybe it's a curve and an arc and a spiral, too. Maybe it's a cord wrapped around the neck of a half-birthed child. Maybe time is a cave, so deep there seems no end. Maybe it's a constellation, each moment a sharp bright point, revealing its meaning only if one can step back, back, back again—or in, closer and closer, and closer, still. Maybe time is a breath, held and released.

A sound behind me, a rustle. I don't have to turn to know it's Robot, come to find me. Wide mouthed, smiling. He barks. A clean, crisp note. Perfectly clear in its meaning.

"Okay, Robot. Okay." My hand is on his head. I stroke the velvet softness of his ear. And the two of us turn and go, together, into our future.

Author's Note

My work on *Holloway* began in early 2021, when the whole world was trying to find its feet again after the unsettling, terrifying events of the COVID-19 crisis and, closer to home, the politically driven misinformation campaigns and lies that undermined so many people's trust in medical experts and caused them to question their very reality.

At the same time that was happening, I was uncovering a new understanding of myself. Through a lengthy assessment with a clinical psychologist, I affirmed what I'd long intuited: the intrinsic neuroatypicality of my brain, and the fact that I am autistic. This felt like a homecoming.

And at the same time *that* was happening, I had been nearing the end of the process of writing my first historical novel, *The Blood Years,* based on my grandmother's childhood and teen years as a Jew during the Second World War, and while that was a long and complicated process in itself, I felt instinctually that there was something about that time period that I still had yet to explore.

As a writer, I'm often guided more by intuition than I am by a hard-and-fast plan. I'm not sure how I can explain why it was clear to me that these three strands belonged in one braid; in fact, I didn't worry too much about putting into words the "why" of how they made sense even to myself. My core belief is that everything is connected in a multitude of ways that we can't always see, the way mushrooms connect forests through tiny mycelial threads; and these were the mushrooms, trees, and flowers in the forest of my mind—the things that interested, fascinated, troubled, and compelled me at that moment in time. I trusted that the story would unfold in such a way as to reveal its thematic meaning as I wrote.

What I didn't yet understand (and what I learned over and over again, over the following four years) was that this is not a storytelling path that leads to quick results. The work on this book felt, at times, very little like storytelling at all—it felt, truly, like story*listening*. And the more I listened, the more I heard.

"Listening" took many forms. Some of it felt like following a voice that led me through the tangled connections of my own mind and learning how to put into words the way it feels to be the person I am. Lots of it was about researching things I love, like art and philosophy and history and literature. And much of it was about exploring less pleasant, murkier topics, digging into the complexities of how and why people have become radicalized in the past, and again, in recent times.

How did everyday Germans tolerate or even justify Hitler's rise to power, and accept, embrace, or ignore the atrocities committed in his name? How, in my country, had so many of my fellow citizens become radicalized, hateful, even violent, and brought that hate and violence out into spaces of social interaction and political discourse? Were these people necessarily *evil*, the people who participated in or sat by as their Jewish neighbors, intellectuals, queer people, Roma, and disabled people were rounded up and taken away? How about the people who, in the 1980s and '90s, became addicted to talk radio hosts who embraced baseless conspiracy theories, targeted racial minorities, vilified undocumented immigrants as an "invasive species," condemned the LGBTQ community (saying, during the AIDS epidemic, that "gays deserve their fate"), and scorned women and feminists by popularizing slurs like "Feminazi"?

And then, the waves of radicalization that followed, enabled by a media landscape that allowed for the weaponization of fear, doubt, and anger by people who stood to benefit from it. A far-right radio host and conspiracy theorist who claimed that the Sandy Hook Elementary School shooting of twenty children and six adults was a hoax staged by the government and used "crisis actors" to push for gun control. A former doctor whose paper falsely linking the MMR vaccine to autism led to panic and distrust of accepted vaccine therapies and decades of suffering by the autism community, despite the paper being widely discredited and the doctor's medical license being revoked. A political commentator and right-wing pundit who pushed the "Great Replacement" theory, antisemitic and anti-immigrant rhetoric that claims a cabal of "elites" (a word historically coded as a reference to Jewish people) were orchestrating a flood of non-white immigrants to the United States to strip power from white people, leading to a rash of white supremacist violence, including the 2017 "Unite the Right" rally and shootings at synagogues, mosques, and other houses of worship. That same commentator also cast doubt on the veracity of the violence incited by the American president on January 6, 2020, and pushed COVID-19 skepticism and anti-vaccine rhetoric. A longtime anti-vaccine activist who elevated and merged anti-MMR rhetoric with COVID-19 vaccine skepticism. And President Donald Trump, who leveraged conspiracy theories to gain and keep power (and return to it in 2024) through the "birther" movement, which falsely claimed that President Barack Obama was not born in the United States. By working to undermine people's faith in our democratic institutions and promoting the idea of a "deep state" of "elites" who were working against him, he gave a platform to QAnon, a movement that is formed on the baseless belief that Trump is secretly battling a "cabal" (the word derived from the Hebrew word "kabbalah," referring to a Jewish mystical tradition and reframed to mean a small, powerful group working to establish dominance and control) of satanic, cannibalistic pedophiles.

Overwhelming! Exhausting! And while it seems impossible that people would be willing to believe such hateful, ignorant drivel . . . they have. Just as they have before. As Opa, one of the characters in my novel *The Blood Years,* often said, "Everything is cyclical."

And yet, something else that has remained true, throughout each and every cycle, every autocratic, hateful leader's reign, every fear-based othering of a minority group, is the persistence of reason, dignity, and justice. Always, there are people who protect and defend those who are scapegoated and endangered. This was true in the 1940s, the early 2020s, and today.

My research for this novel led me to discover what would become *Holloway*'s main setting: the asylum at Saint-Alban-sur-Limagnole, which is a real place. Those who chose to work and live at Saint-Alban-sur-Limagnole during the 1940s believed in protecting and nurturing human connection, as well as the steadfast importance of art.

It can be tempting to think that art is inessential—that it's something "extra" and "fun" that we can do when more serious work has been laid to rest. But art—along with philosophy and caretaking—is not peripheral. It is essential work. Art is a mirror; it is a messenger; it is an end in itself. From the marks of the earliest cave painters, through the first impressions a child makes on a page, all the way to the works we hang on the walls of our most revered institutions, artmaking is an innate trait of the human animal. In the best of times—and the worst—we make art. Many of the characters in this book are based on the doctors, patients, and guests who called the asylum home during the 1940s and beyond; interested readers will find that Dr. François Tosquelles, the poet Paul Éluard, and the artists Marguerite Sirvins, Auguste Forestier, and Jojo Chassang all resided there.

Given my proclivity to see connections between disparate parts of our universe, I was not surprised when I learned that the asylum of Saint-Alban-sur-Limagnole is located not all that far from the Lascaux caves—another real place, which was indeed discovered in the autumn of 1940 by a dog named Robot and his human companion, Marcel Ravidat—whose museum nearby houses reproductions of its ancient artwork you can visit today (as Nora tried to do).

Isn't life amazing? And terrifying? And beautiful? And rage-inducing? And deeply strange, too?

Like Nora, I know how important human connection can be. *Holloway* is the result of the insightful care and hard work of many generous people: dear friends Martha Brockenbrough, Brandy Colbert, Nina LaCour, Justin Minkel, Erin O'Shea, and Eliot Schrefer, who read and discussed many drafts of the story; Eric Zahler, for his help with French translations; the caretakers of Saint-Alban-sur-Limagnole, who allowed me the privilege of touring the castle and its grounds; artists, writers, and researchers whose work on this time period and place informed my own; the Clarion team, including the brilliant and steadfast Jordan Brown, who truly understands this book and my brain; and Paige Pagan, Erin Clarke, Corina Lupp, Jenna Stempel-Lobel, Jessica Berg, Macey Fairchild, Christina MacDonald, Mary Magrisso, Andy Ball, Shannon Cox, Elise Damasco, Mimi Rankin, Patty Rosati, Lindsey Treibel, Page Edmunds, and Rich Thomas. I'm grateful also to Sara Crowe and Rubin Pfeffer, both champions of my career, and Sarah Jarrett, who is responsible for *Holloway*'s beautiful cover art. And a special thanks to my love, Keith Arnold—Honeyman—who designed and led me on the most amazing research trip through France, planning out every detail and delighting in my delight. I'm pretty good with words, but those that could capture how much I love you maybe don't exist.

Dearest reader, I hope that *Holloway* will inspire you to look around—at your history, your curiosities, and your very self—with fresh eyes and a sense of wonder. How terrifying it is to have to fight for survival at a time when the survival of so many of us is under threat; and yet, how lucky we are, to have the examples of those who came before us to give us hope and encouragement that we, too, can carry on in this imperfect, art-filled, terrifying, desperate, beautiful world.

As my Paul Éluard asks: "What about the unconscious, Nora? What about dreams? What about the fantastical? And *desire*?"

Yes, I say. Yes.

The author, photographed before the front of the asylum at Saint-Alban-sur-Limagnole